ONE NIGHT SHIFT

TAMED BY HER ARMY DOC'S TOUCH

BY
LUCY RYDER

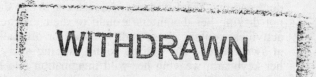

MILLS BOON

Amy Andrews has always loved writing, and still can't quite believe that she gets to do it for a living. Creating wonderful heroines and gorgeous heroes and telling their stories is an amazing way to pass the day. Sometimes they don't always act as she'd like them to—but then neither do her kids, so she's kind of used to it. Amy lives in the very beautiful Samford Valley, with her husband and aforementioned children, along with six brown chooks and two black dogs. She loves to hear from her readers. Drop her a line at www.amyandrews.com.au

After trying out everything from acting in musicals, singing opera, travelling and writing for a business newspaper, **Lucy Ryder** finally settled down to have a family and teach at a local community college, where she currently teaches English and Communication. However, she insists that writing is her first love and time spent on it is more pleasure than work.

She currently lives in South Africa, with her crazy dogs and two beautiful teenage daughters. When she's not driving her daughters around to their afternoon activities, cooking those endless meals or officiating at swim meets, she can be found tapping away at her keyboard, weaving her wild imagination into hot romantic scenes.

IT HAPPENED
ONE NIGHT SHIFT

BY
AMY ANDREWS

Published in Great Britain 2015
by Mills & Boon, an imprint of Harlequin (UK) Limited,
Eton House, 18-24 Paradise Road, Richmond, Surrey, TW9 1SR

© 2015 Amy Andrews

ISBN: 978-0-263-24682-7

Harlequin (UK) Limited's policy is to use papers that are natural,
renewable and recyclable products and made from wood grown in
sustainable forests. The logging and manufacturing processes conform
to the legal environmental regulations of the country of origin.

Printed and bound in Spain
by CPI, Barcelona

Dear Reader

This is the first book I've written where my hero is a nurse. I've been toying with doing it for a long time, but I didn't really have a scenario in my head until recently. Then I saw ex-military triage nurse Gareth in my mind's eye and knew I had my hero.

He's tough and strong and self-reliant, but after thirty doctor/paramedic heroes I thought I'd meet resistance from my editor over Gareth being a nurse and Billie, the heroine, being a doctor. Not the case, however. I was given free rein to bring their story to life and I'm so grateful—because Gareth is just the hero that Billie needs: supportive when required, but challenging her to be the person she *is*…not the person others want her to be. And Billie is just the woman Gareth needs—dragging him back into the world of the living. Helping him live, laugh and love again. Showing him that there is another life for him.

Both of them have pasts that make going ahead with the future complicated. Both of them are facing demons. But that is the beauty and power of love. And for Gareth and Billie falling hard is inevitable.

I hope you enjoy their journey.

Love

Amy

Dedication

I dedicate this book to all my lovely nursing friends
from the former Royal Children's Hospital.
Twenty-one years is a long time to be in any
one place and I have enjoyed every moment—
even the harrowing ones. I will miss you all.

Recent titles by Amy Andrews:

200 HARLEY STREET: THE TORTURED HERO
GOLD COAST ANGELS: HOW TO RESIST TEMPTATION
ONE NIGHT SHE WOULD NEVER FORGET
SYDNEY HARBOUR HOSPITAL: EVIE'S BOMBSHELL
HOW TO MEND A BROKEN HEART
SYDNEY HARBOUR HOSPITAL: LUCA'S BAD GIRL
WAKING UP WITH DR OFF-LIMITS
JUST ONE LAST NIGHT…
RESCUED BY THE DREAMY DOC
VALENTINO'S PREGNANCY BOMBSHELL
ALESSANDRO AND THE CHEERY NANNY

**These books are also available in eBook format
from www.millsandboon.co.uk**

CHAPTER ONE

GARETH STAPLETON DROPPED his head from side to side, stretching out his traps as he kept his eyes on the road.

He was getting too old for this crap.

It had been a long, crazy shift in the emergency room and he needed a beer, a shower and his bed.

Saturday nights in a busy Brisbane ER were chaotic at the best of times but the full moon had added an extra shot of the bizarre to the mix. From now on he was consulting astrological charts when requesting his roster.

He yawned and looked at the dash clock—almost midnight—and was grateful for his shift ending when it had. The waiting room had still been full as he'd clocked off and he didn't envy the night shift having to deal with it all.

Suddenly, the car in front of him—a taxi—swerved slightly into the opposite lane and Gareth's pulse spiked.

What the hell?

Despite only going at the speed limit, he eased back on the accelerator as the taxi corrected itself. Gareth peered into the back windscreen of the car, trying to see what the guy was doing. What was distracting him? Was he texting? Or talking on the phone?

He couldn't tell *what* the driver was doing but at least the taxi appeared to be empty of passengers.

Gareth eased back some more. He may only be driving a twenty-year-old rust box but he had no desire to be collateral damage due to this clown's inattention. Luckily they were on a long, straight section of road linking two outer suburbs so there were no houses, no cars parked on either side, just trees and bushland.

The taxi wobbled all over the lane again and Gareth's stomach tightened as a set of oncoming headlights suddenly winked in the distance. His fingers gripped the steering-wheel a little firmer as a sense of foreboding settled over him.

Gareth's sense of foreboding had served him well over the years—particularly in the Middle East—and it wasn't going to be disappointed tonight.

He watched in horror as the taxi swerved suddenly again into the path of the oncoming car. Gareth hit his horn but it was futile, the crash playing out in front of him in slow motion.

The driver of the other car slammed on the brakes, swerving to avoid what Gareth could have sworn was certain collision. He waited for the crash and the sound of crunching metal but, thankfully, it never came. The taxi narrowly missed the other car, careening off the road and smashing into a tree.

But now the oncoming car was in his lane and Gareth had to apply his brakes to prevent them crashing. Luckily the other driver had the good sense to swerve back into his own lane and they both came to a halt almost level with each other on their own sides of the road.

Gareth, his heart pistoning like a jackhammer, automatically reached for his glove box and pulled out a bunch of gloves from a box he always kept there. He ripped his seat belt off and pushed open his door.

'Are you okay, mate?' he asked as he leapt out, his fingers already reaching for the mobile phone in his pocket as he mentally triaged the scene.

He wrenched open the door of the other car, noticing

absently it was a sleek-looking two-seater, to find a pair of huge brown eyes, heavily kohled and fringed with sooty eyelashes, blinking back at him. A scarlet mouth formed a surprised-looking O.

A woman.

'I'm…I'm fine.' She nodded, looking dazed.

Gareth wasn't entirely sure. She appeared uninjured but she looked like she might be in shock. 'Can you move? How's your neck?' he asked.

She nodded again, undoing her seat belt. 'It's fine. I'm fine.' She swung her legs out of the car.

'Don't move,' he ordered. 'Stay there.' The last thing he needed was a casualty wandering around the scene. 'I'm Gareth, what's your name?'

'Billie.'

Gareth acknowledged the unusual name on a superficial level only. 'I'm going to check out the taxi driver. You stay here, okay, Billie?'

She blinked up at him and nodded. 'Okay.'

Satisfied he'd secured her co-operation, Gareth, already dialling triple zero, headed for the smashed-up taxi.

It took a minute for Billie to come out of the fog of the moment and get her bearings. She'd told Gareth—at least that was what she thought he'd said his name was—she was okay. Everything had happened so fast. But a quick mental check of her body confirmed it.

She was shaking like a leaf but she wasn't injured.

And she was a doctor. She shouldn't be sitting in her car like an invalid—she should be helping.

What on earth had caused the taxi to veer right into her path? Was the driver drunk? Or was it something medical? A hypo? A seizure?

She reached across to her glove box and pulled out a pair of gloves from the box she always kept there, her heart beating furiously, mentally preparing herself for potential gore. Being squeamish was not something that boded well for a doctor but it was something she'd never been able to conquer.

She'd learned to control it—just.

She exited her car, yanking the boot lever on the way out, rounding the vehicle and pulling out a briefcase that contained a well-stocked first-aid kit. Then she took a deep breath and in her ridiculous heels and three-quarter-length cocktail dress she made her way over to the crashed car and Gareth.

Gareth looked up from his ministrations as Billie approached. 'I thought I'd told you to stay put,' he said, whipping off his fleecy hoody, not even feeling the cool air. His only priority was getting the driver, who wasn't breathing and had no pulse, out of the car.

'I'm fine. And I'm a doctor so I figured I could help.'

Gareth was momentarily thrown by the information but he didn't have time to question her credentials. She was already wearing a pair of hospital-issue gloves that *he* hadn't given her, so she was at least prepared.

And the driver's lips were turning from dusky to blue.

He needed oxygen and a defib. Neither of which they had.

All the driver had was them, until the ambulance got there.

'I'm an ER nurse,' Gareth said, rolling his hoody into a tube shape then carefully wrapping it around the man's neck, fashioning a crude soft collar to give him some C-spine protection when they pulled him out.

'Ambulance is ten minutes away. He's in cardiac arrest. Thankfully he's not trapped. Help me get him out and we'll start CPR. I'll grab his top half,' Gareth said.

Aided by the light from the full moon blasting down on them, they had the driver lying on the dew-damp grass in less than thirty seconds. 'You maintain the airway,' Gareth said, falling back on protocols ingrained in him during twenty years in the field. 'I'll start compressions.'

Billie nodded, swallowing hard as the metallic smell from the blood running down the driver's face from a deep laceration on his forehead assaulted her senses. It had already congealed in places and her belly turned at the sight, threatening to eject the three-course meal she'd indulged in earlier.

She turned away briskly, sucking air slowly into her lungs. In through her nose, out through her mouth, concentrating on the cold damp ground already seeping through the gauzy fabric of her dress to her knees rather than the blood. She was about to start her ER rotation—she had to get used to this.

She opened the briefcase and pulled out her pocket mask.

Gareth kicked up an eyebrow as she positioned herself, a knee either side of the guy's head, and held the mask efficiently in place over the driver's mouth and nose.

'Very handy,' he said, noting her perfect jaw grasp and hand placement. 'Don't suppose you have a defib in there by any chance?'

Billie gave a half-laugh. 'Sadly, no.' Because they both knew that's what this man needed.

She leaned down to blow several times into the mouthpiece. Her artfully curled hair fell forward and she quickly pushed them behind her ears as the mask threatened to slip. The mix of sweat and blood on the driver's face worked against her and Billie had to fight back a gag as the smell invaded her nostrils.

If she just shut her eyes and concentrated on the flow of air, the rhythm of her delivery, mentally counted the breaths, she might just get through this without disgracing herself.

'What do you reckon, heart attack?' Gareth asked after he'd checked for a pulse two minutes in.

Billie, concentrating deeply, opened her eyes at the sudden intrusion. Rivulets of dried blood stared back at her and she quickly shut them again. 'Probably,' she said between breaths. 'Something caused him to veer off the road like that and he feels pretty clammy. Only he looks young, though. Fit too.'

Gareth agreed, his arms already feeling the effort of prolonged compressions. The man didn't look much older than himself. ''Bout forty, I reckon.'

Billie nodded. 'Too young to die.'

He grunted and Billie wondered if he was thinking the same thing she was. The taxi driver probably *was* going to die. The statistics for out-of-hospital cardiac arrests were grim. Even for young, fit people. This man needed so much more than they could give him here on the roadside.

They fell silent again as they continued to give a complete stranger, who had nearly wiped both of them out tonight, a chance at life.

'Come on, mate,' Gareth said, as he checked the pulse for the third time and went back to compressions. 'Cut us some slack here.'

A minute later, the silence was pierced by the first low wails of a siren. 'Yes,' Gareth muttered. 'Hold on, mate. The cavalry's nearly here.'

In another minute two ambulances—one with an intensive care paramedic—pulled up, followed closely by a police car. A minute after that a fire engine joined the fray. Reinforcements surrounded them, artificial light suddenly flooding the scene, Billie and Gareth continued their CPR as Gareth gave an impressive rapid-fire handover.

'Keep managing the airway,' the female intensive care paramedic instructed Billie, after Gareth had informed her of their medical credentials. She handed Billie a proper resus set—complete with peep valve and oxygen supply. 'You okay to intubate?'

Billie nodded. She could. As a second-year resident she'd done it before but not a lot. And then there was the blood.

She took another deep, steadying breath.

Gareth continued compressions as one of the advanced care paramedics slapped on some defib pads and the other tried to establish IV access.

In the background several firemen dealt with the car, some set up a road block with the police while others directed a newly arrived tow truck to one side.

The automatic defibrillator warned everyone to move away from the patient as it advised a shock.

'Stand clear,' the paramedic called, and everyone dropped what they were doing and moved well back.

A series of shocks was delivered, to no avail, and everyone resumed their positions. IV access was gained and emergency drugs were delivered. Billie successfully intubated as Gareth continued with cardiac massage. Two minutes later the defibrillator recommended another shock and everyone moved away again.

The driver's chest arched. 'We've got a rhythm,' the paramedic announced.

Gareth reached over and felt for the carotid. 'Yep,' he agreed. 'I have a pulse.'

'Okay, let's get him loaded and go.'

Billie reached for the bag to resume respiratory support on the still unconscious patient but the intensive care paramedic crouched beside Billie said, 'Would you like me to take over?'

Billie looked at her, startled. She'd been concentrating so hard on not losing her stomach contents she'd shut everything out other than the whoosh of her own breath. But the airway was secure and they had a pulse. She could easily hand over to a professional who had way more experience dealing with these situations.

Not to mention the fact that now the emergency was

under control her hands were shaking, her teeth were chattering and she was shivering with the cold.

And her knees were killing her.

She looked down at her gloves. They were streaked with blood and another wave of nausea welled inside her.

Billie handed the bag over and then suddenly warm hands were lifting her up onto her shaking legs, supporting her as her numb knees threatened to buckle. A blanket was thrown around her shoulders and she huddled into its warmth as she was shepherded in the direction of her car.

'Are you okay?'

Billie glanced towards the deep voice, surprised to find herself looking at Gareth. He was tall and broad and looked warm and inviting and she felt so cold. She had the strangest urge to walk into his arms.

'I'm fine,' she said, gripping the blanket tighter around her shoulders, looking down at where her gloved hands held the edges of the blanket together.

Dried blood stared back at her. The nausea she'd been valiantly trying to keep at bay hit her in a rush.

And right there, dressed to the nines in front of Gareth and a dozen emergency personnel, she bent over and threw up her fancy, two-hundred-dollar, three-course meal on the side of the road.

CHAPTER TWO

BILLIE WAS THANKFUL as she talked to the police a few minutes later she'd never have to see anyone here ever again. She doubted if any of these seasoned veterans blinked an eye at someone barfing at the scene of an accident and they'd all been very understanding but she was *the doctor,* for crying out loud.

People looked to her to be the calm, in-control one. To take bloodied accident victims in her stride. She was *supposed* to be able to hold herself together.

Not throw up at the sight of blood and gore.

Billie wondered anew how she was going to cope in the emergency room for the next six months. For the rest of her life, for that matter, given that emergency medicine was her chosen career path.

Mostly because it was high-flying enough to assuage parental and family expectations without being surgical. The Ashworth-Keyes of the world were *all* surgeons. Choosing a non-surgical specialty was *not* an option.

Unless it carried the same kind of kudos. As emergency medicine, apparently, did.

And at least this way Billie knew she'd still be able to treat the things that interested her most. Raw and messy were not her cup of tea but infections and diseases, the run-of-the-mill medical problems that were seen in GP practices across the country every day were.

But Ashworth-Keyes' were *not* GPs.

And Billie was carrying a double load of expectation.

She glanced across at Gareth, who was looking relaxed and assured amidst a tableau of clashing lights. The milky phosphorescence of the moon, the glow of fluorescent safety striping on multiple uniforms and the garish strobing of red, blue and amber. He didn't seem to be affected by any of it, his deep, steady voice carrying towards her on the cool night air as he relayed the details of the accident to a police officer.

Billie cringed as she recalled how he'd held her hair back and rubbed between her shoulders blades as she'd hurled up everything in her stomach. Then had sourced some water for her to rinse her mouth out and offered her a mint.

It seemed like he'd done it before. But, then, she supposed, an ER nurse probably *had* done it a thousand times.

Still…why did she have to go and disgrace herself in front of possibly the most good-looking man she'd seen in a very long time?

She'd noticed it subliminally while they'd been performing CPR but she'd had too much else going on, what with holding someone's life in the balance and trying not to vomit, to give her thoughts free rein.

But she didn't now.

And she let them run wild as she too answered a policeman's questions.

Billie supposed a lot of her friends wouldn't classify Gareth as good looking purely because of his age. The grey whiskers putting some salt into the sexy growth of stubble at his jaw and the small lines around his eyes that crinkled a little as he smiled told her he had to be in his late thirties, early forties.

But, then, she'd always preferred older men.

She found maturity sexy. She liked the way, by and large, older men were content in their skins and didn't feel the need to hem a woman in to validate themselves. The easy way they spoke and the way they carried their bodies and wore their experience on their faces and were comfortable with that. She liked the way so many of them didn't seem like they had anything to prove.

She liked how Gareth embodied that. Even standing in the middle of an accident scene he looked at ease.

Gareth laughed at something the policeman said and she watched as he raked a piece of hair back that had flopped forward. She liked his hair. It was wavy and a little long at the back, brushing his collar, and he wore it swept back where it fell in neat rippled rows.

She'd noticed, as they'd tried to save the driver's life, it was dark with some streaks of grey, like his whiskers.

And she liked that too.

His arm dropped back down by his side and her gaze drifted to his biceps. She'd noticed those biceps as well while they'd been working on their man. How could she not have? Every time she'd opened her eyes there they'd been, contracting and releasing with each downward compression.

Firm and taut. Barely covered—*barely constrained*—by his T-shirt.

Billie shivered. She wasn't sure if it was from the power of his biceps alone or the fact he was wandering around on a winter's night with just a T-shirt covering his chest.

Why hadn't someone given him a blanket?

Although, to be fair, he did look a lot more appropriately dressed for a roadside emergency than she did. His jeans looked snug and warm, encasing long, lean legs, and he *had* been wearing a fleecy hoody.

It sure beat a nine-hundred-dollar dress and a pair of strappy designer shoes.

He looked up then, pointing in the direction she'd been driving, and their gazes met. He nodded at her briefly, before returning his attention to the police officer, and she found herself nodding back.

Yep, Billie acknowledged—Gareth was one helluva good-looking man. In fact, he ticked all her boxes. And if she was up for a fling or available for dating in the hectic morass of a resident's life then he'd be exactly her type. But there was absolutely no hope for them now.

The man had held her hair back while she'd vomited.

She cringed again. If she ever saw him again it would be too soon.

Gareth was acutely aware of Billie's gaze as he answered the police officer's questions. It seemed to beam through the cold air like an invisible laser, hot and direct, hitting him fair in the chest, diffusing heat and awareness to every millimetre of his body.

It made her hard to ignore.

Of course, the fact she was sparkling like one of those movie vampires also made her hard to ignore.

The gauzy skirt of her black dress shimmered with hundreds of what looked like crystal beads. Who knew, maybe they were diamonds? The dress certainly didn't look cheap. But they caught the multitude of lights strobing across the scene, refracting them like individual disco balls.

As if the dress and the petite figure beneath needed to draw any more attention to itself. Every man here, from the fireman to the paramedics, the police to the tow-truck driver, was sure as hell taking a moment to appreciate it.

Their attention irritated him. And the fact that it did irritated him even more. She was a stranger and they were at an accident scene, for crying out loud!

But it didn't stop him from going over to her when the police officer was done. He told himself it was to check she was feeling okay now but the dress was weirdly mesmerising and he would have gone to her even if she'd not conveniently vomited twenty minutes ago.

She had her back to him but, as if she'd sensed him

approaching, she turned as he neared. Her loose reddish-brown hair flowed silkily around her shoulders, her hair curling in long ringlets around her face. Huge gold hoop earrings he'd noticed earlier as she'd administered the kiss of life swung in her lobes, giving her a little bit of gypsy.

He smiled as he drew closer. She seemed to hesitate for a moment then reciprocated, her scarlet lipstick having worn off from her earlier ministrations.

'You sure know how to dress for a little unscheduled roadside assistance,' he said, as he drew to a halt in front of her.

Billie blinked, surprised by his opening line for a moment, and then she looked down at herself and laughed. 'Oh, yes, sorry,' she said, although she had absolutely no idea why she was apologising for her attire. 'I've just come from a gala reception.'

This close his biceps were even more impressive and Billie had to grip the blanket hard to stop from reaching her hands out and running her palms over them. She wondered if they'd feel as firm and warm as they looked.

'Aren't you cold?' she asked, engaging her mouth before her brain as she dragged her gaze back to his face.

He did a smile-shrug combo and Billie's stomach did a little flip-flop combo in response. 'I'm fine,' he dismissed.

Billie grimaced. Where had she heard that already tonight? 'I really am very sorry about earlier.'

'Yeah.' He grinned. His whole face crinkled and Billie lost her breath as his sexiness increased tenfold. 'You've already said so. Three times.'

She blushed. 'I know but...I think I may have splashed your shoes.'

Gareth looked down at his shoes. 'They've seen far worse, trust me.'

'Not exactly the impression I like to give people I've just met.'

Gareth shrugged. She needn't have been worried about her impression on him—he doubted he was going to forget her in a long time, and it had nothing to do with his shoes and everything to do with how good she looked in those gold hoops and sparkly dress.

And if he'd been up for some flirting and some let's-see-where-this-goes fun he might just have assured her out loud. He might just have suggested they try for a second impression. But *hooking up* really wasn't his thing.

Hooking up at an accident scene even less so.

'We haven't exactly met properly, have we? I mean, not formally.' He held out his hand. 'I'm Gareth Stapleton. Very pleased to make your acquaintance—despite the circumstances.'

Billie slipped her hand into his and even though she'd expected to feel something, the rush of warmth up her arm took her by surprise. She shook his hand absently, staring at their clasped fingers, pleased for the blanket around her torso as the warmth rushed all the way to her nipples, prickling them to attention.

Gareth smiled as Billie's gaze snagged on their joined hands. Not that he could blame her. If she felt the connection as strongly as he did then they were both in trouble.

Just as well they wouldn't be seeing each other again after tonight. Resisting her in this situation was sensible and right. But if there was repeated exposure? That could wear a man down.

Sensible and right could be easily eroded.

'And you're Billie?' he prompted, withdrawing his hand. 'Billie…?'

Billie dragged her gaze away from their broken grip, up his broad chest and deliciously whiskery neck and onto his face, his spare cheekbones glowing alternately red and blue from the lights behind him.

What were they talking about? Oh, yes, formal introductions. 'Ashworth-Keyes,' she said automatically. 'Although if you want *formal* formal then it's *Willamina* Ashworth-Keyes.'

Gareth quirked an eyebrow as a little itch started at the back of his brain. 'Your first name is *Willamina*?'

Billie rolled her eyes. 'Yes,' she said, placing her hand on her hip. 'What about it?'

Gareth held up his hands in surrender. 'Nothing. Just kind of sounds like somebody's…spinster great-aunt.'

Billie frowned, unfortunately agreeing. Which was why she'd carried over her childhood pet name into adulthood.

'Not that there's anything *remotely* spinsterish or great-auntish about you,' he hastened to add. The last thing he wanted to do was insult her. The *very* last thing. 'Or,' he added as her frowned deepened, 'that there's anything wrong with that anyway.'

This woman made him tongue-tied.

How long had it been since he'd felt this gauche? Like some horny fifteen-year-old who couldn't even speak to the cool, pretty girl because he had a hard-on the size of a house.

Not that he had a hard-on. Not right now anyway. Or probably ever again if this excruciatingly awkward scene replayed in his head as often as he figured it would.

Billie's breath caught at Gareth's sudden lack of finesse. It made her feel as if she wasn't the only one thrown by this rather bizarre thing that had flared between them.

And she'd liked his emphasis on *remotely*.

She laughed to ease the strange tension that had spiked between them. 'Only my parents call me Willamina,' she said. 'And generally only if I'm in trouble.'

'And are you often in trouble?'

Gareth realised the words might have come across as flirty, so he kept his face serious.

Billie felt absurdly like laughing at such a preposterous

notion. Her? In trouble? 'No. Not me. *Never me*.' That had been her sister's job. 'No, I'm the peacekeeper in the family.'

Gareth frowned at the sudden gloom in her eyes. The conversation had swung from light to awkward to serious. It seemed she wasn't too keen on the mantle of family good girl and suddenly a seductive voice was whispering they could find some trouble together.

Thankfully the little itch at the back of his brain finally came into sharp focus, obliterating the voice completely.

'Wait…' He narrowed his eyes. 'Ashworth-Keyes? As in Charles and Alisha Ashworth-Keyes, eminent cardio-thoracic surgeons?'

Billie nodded. *Sprung*. 'The very same.'

'Your parents?' She nodded and he whistled. Everyone who was anyone in the medical profession in Brisbane knew of the Ashworth-Keyes surgical dynasty. 'That's some pedigree you've got going on there.'

'Yes. Lucky me,' she said derisively.

'You…don't get on?'

Billie sighed. 'No, it's not that. I'm just…not really like them, you know?'

He quirked an eyebrow. 'How so?'

'Well, I'm no surgeon, that's for sure. I'm a little too squeamish for that.'

Gareth surprised himself by laughing at the understatement but he couldn't help himself. 'Really?' he asked, looking down at his shoes. 'You hide it well.'

Billie shot him a cross look but soon joined him in his laughter.

'And?' he asked. 'What else?'

What else? Being a surgeon was all that mattered in the Ashworth-Keyes household. 'It's…complicated.'

Gareth nodded. Fair enough. Complicated he understood. It really wasn't any of his business anyway. 'So what field is the next Ashworth-Keyes going to specialise in? Clearly something…anything that doesn't involve the letting of blood? Dermatology? Radiology? Maybe…pathology?'

Billie shook her head. 'Emergency medicine,' she said. Even saying it depressed the hell out of her.

Gareth blinked. 'Really?' Surely Billie understood the squeamish factor could get pretty high in an ER?

'Yep,' she confirmed, sounding about as enthusiastic as he usually did just prior to starting a night shift. 'I'm starting my six-month emergency rotation at St Luke's ER next week in fact.'

Gareth held his breath. 'St Luke's?'

'Yes.

Crap. 'Ah.'

She frowned at him in that way he'd already grown way too fond of. 'What?'

'That's where I work.'

'You…work at St Luke's?'

He nodded. 'In the ER.'

'So we'll be…working together,' she murmured.

'Yup.'

And he hoped like hell she didn't look as good in a pair of scrubs as she did in a black sparkly dress or *sensible* and *right* were going to be toast.

CHAPTER THREE

BILLIE'S FIRST DAY at St Luke's wasn't as bad as she'd thought. Gareth wasn't there and she was able to slip into the groove of the department during daytime hours when there were a lot of senior staff around to have her back and take on the more raw and challenging cases.

She was content to take the nuisance admissions that everybody grumbled about. The patients that should be at their GPs' but had decided to save their hip pockets and clutter up the public waiting room instead.

Billie really didn't mind. It was satisfying work and she took to it like a duck to water. Her previous six months had been her medical rotation and she'd thrived there as well, treating a variety of cases from the humdrum to the interesting.

It was Thursday she wasn't looking forward to. Thursday was the start of three night shifts and from nine until eight the next morning there were just three residents—her and two others—and a registrar, dealing with whatever came through the doors.

Actually, Thursday night probably wasn't going to be so bad. It was Friday and Saturday night that had her really worried. The city bars would be open and the thought of having to deal with the product of too much booze and testosterone wasn't a welcome one.

There would be blood.

Of that she was sure.

Nine o'clock Thursday night rocked around quicker than Billie liked and she walked into St Luke's ER with a sense of foreboding.

Her hands shook as she changed into a set of scrubs in the female change room. '*St. Luke's ER*' was embroidered on the pocket in case Billie needed any further reminders that she was exactly where she didn't want to be. Jen, the other resident who had also started her rotation on the same day, chatted away excitedly and Billie let her run on, nodding and making appropriate one-word comments in the right places.

At least it was a distraction.

Thankfully, though, by the time the night team had taken handover at the central work station from the day team, Billie was feeling a little more relaxed.

Things were reasonably quiet. The resus bays were empty and only a handful of patients were in varying stages of being assessed, most of them with medical complaints that didn't involve any level of gore.

Billie knew she could handle that with one hand tied behind her back. In fact, she was looking forward to it.

A nurse cruised by and Helen, the registrar, introduced the three new residents. 'Who's on the night shift, Chrissy, do you know?'

'Gareth,' she said.

Billie's pulse leapt at his name. Helen smiled. 'Excellent.'

Chrissy rolled her eyes. 'Yeah, yeah,' she joked. 'Everyone loves Gareth.'

Helen laughed. 'He's highly experienced,' she said, feigning affront.

'Sure,' Chrissy teased. 'And those blue eyes have nothing at all to do with it.'

'Blue eyes? I hadn't noticed.' Helen shrugged nonchalantly.

'Who's Gareth?' Barry, the other new resident, asked as Chrissy left to attend to a buzzer.

'Brilliant nurse. Ex-military. Used to be in charge around here. Not sure why he was demoted…think there was some kind of incident. But, anyway, he's very experienced.'

'Ex-military?' Billie's voice sounded an octave or two higher than she would have liked but no one seemed to notice. No wonder Gareth had taken charge of the scene so expertly on Saturday night.

'Apparently,' Helen said. 'Served in MASH units all over. The Middle East most recently, I think. Exceptionally cool and efficient in an emergency.'

Billie nodded. She knew all about that coolness and efficiency.

'Also…' Helen smiled '…kind of easy on the eyes.'

She nodded again. Oh, yes. Billie definitely knew how easy he was on the eyes.

'Right,' Helen said. 'Let's get to it. Let's see if we can't whittle these patients down and have us a quiet night.'

A quiet night sounded just fine to Billie as she picked up a chart and tried not to think about seeing Gareth again in less than two hours.

Gareth came upon Billie just after midnight. He'd known, since he'd checked out the residents' roster, they'd be working together for these next three nights.

And had thought about little else since.

She had her stethoscope in her ears and was listening to the chest of an elderly woman in cubicle three when he peeled the curtain back. She didn't hear him and he stood by the curtain opening, waiting for her to finish, more than content to observe and wait patiently.

She looked *very* different tonight from the last time he'd seen her. Her hair was swept back in a no-nonsense ponytail. The long curling spirals were not falling artfully around her face as they had on Saturday night but were ruthlessly hauled back into the ponytail, giving her hair a sleek, smooth finish. Her earlobes were unadorned, her face free of make-up.

And...*yup*. He'd known it. Even from a side view she rocked a pair of scrubs.

'Well, you've certainly got a rattle on there, Mrs Gordon,' Billie said, as she pulled the stethoscope out of her ears and slung it around her neck.

'Oh, yes, dear,' the elderly patient agreed. Billie was concerned about her flushed face and poor skin turgor. 'I do feel quite poorly.'

'I don't doubt it,' Billie clucked. 'Your X-ray is quite impressive. I think we need to get you admitted and pop in a drip. We can get you rehydrated and give you some antibiotics for that lung infection.'

'Oh, I don't want you to trouble yourself,' Mrs Gordon said.

Billie smiled at her patient. The seventy-three-year-old, whose granddaughter had insisted was usually the life of the party, looked quite frail. She slipped her hand on top of the older, wrinkled one and gave it a squeeze. It felt hot and dry too.

'It's no trouble Mrs Gordon. That's what I'm here for.'

Mrs Gordon smiled back, patting Billie's hand. 'Well, that's lovely of you,' she murmured. 'But I think that young man wants to talk to you, my dear.'

Billie looked over her shoulder to find Gareth standing in a break in the curtain. He did that smile-shrug combo again and her belly flip-flopped once more. 'Hi,' she said.

'Hey,' Gareth murmured, noticing absently the cute sprinkle of freckles across the bridge of her nose and the clear gloss on her lips. Her mouth wasn't the lush scarlet temptation it had been on the weekend but its honeyed glaze drew his eyes anyway.

'Thought I'd pop in and see how you were getting on.'

'Oh…I'm fine…good…thank you.' She sounded breathy and disjointed and mentally pulled herself together. 'Just going to place an IV here and get Mrs Gordon…' she looked down at her patient and smiled '…admitted.'

Gareth nodded. She looked cool and confident in her scrubs, a far cry from the woman who'd admitted to being squeamish after losing her dinner in front of him on Saturday night. He had to give her marks for bravado.

'Do you want me to insert it?'

Billie frowned, perplexed for a moment before realising what he meant. He thought she'd baulk at inserting a cannula? Resident bread and butter?

God, just how flaky had she come across at the accident?

Another thought crossed her mind. He hadn't told anyone in the department about what had happened the other night, had he? About how she'd reacted afterwards?

He wouldn't have, surely?

She looked across at him and Helen was right, his blue scrubs set off the blue of his eyes to absolute perfection. The temptation to get lost in them was startlingly strong but she needed him to realise they weren't on the roadside any more. This was her job and she *could* do it.

She'd been dealing with her *delicate constitution,* as her father had so disparagingly called it, for a lot of years. Yes, it presented its challenges in this environment but she didn't need him to hold her hand.

'Do you think we could talk?' she asked him, before turning and patting her patient's hand. 'I'll be right back, Mrs Gordon. I just need to get some equipment.'

Gareth figured he'd overstepped the mark as he followed the business like swing of her ponytail. But he *had* seen her visibly pale at the sight of the blood running down the taxi driver's face on Saturday night. Had held her hair back while she'd vomited then listened to her squeamishness confession.

Was it wrong to feel protective of her? To want to alleviate the potential for more incidents when he was free and more than capable of doing the procedure himself?

Her back was ramrod straight and her stride brisk as she yanked open the staffroom door. He followed her inside and Billie turned on him as soon as the door shut behind them.

'What are you doing?' she asked.

Gareth quirked an eyebrow at her. 'Trying to help? I wasn't sure if putting in IVs made you feel faint or nauseated and…' he shrugged '…I was free.'

She shoved her hands on her hips and Gareth noticed for the first time how short she was in her sensible work flats. He seemed to have a good foot on her. Just how high *had* those heels been the other night?

'Would you have offered to do anyone else's?' she demanded.

Gareth folded his arms. 'If I knew it made them squeamish, of course,' he said.

'Putting in an IV *does not* make me squeamish,' she snapped.

'Well, excuse me for trying to be nice,' he snapped back. 'You looked like you had a major issue with blood on Saturday night.'

Billie blinked at his testy comeback. She looked down at her hands. They were clenched hard at her sides and the unreasonable urge to pummel them against his chest beat like insects wings inside her head.

She shook her head. What was she doing? She was acting like a shrew. She took a deep breath and slowly unclenched her hands.

'I can put in an IV,' she sighed. 'I can draw blood, watch it flow into a tube, no problems. It's not *blood* that makes me squeamish, it's blood pouring out where it shouldn't be. It's the gore. The messy rawness. The missing bits and the… jagged edges. The…gaping wounds. That's what I find hard to handle. That's when it gets to me.'

Gareth nodded, pleased for the clarification. The ER was going to be a rough rotation for her. He took a couple of paces towards her, stopping an arm's length away.

'There's a lot of messy rawness here,' he said gently.

'I know,' Billie said. *Boy, did she know.* 'But that's the way it is and I don't want you protecting me from all of it, Gareth. I'm training to be an emergency physician. I'm just going to have to get used to it.'

She watched as his brow crinkled and the lines around his eyes followed suit. 'Why?' he asked. 'Surely this isn't the right speciality for you?'

Billie gave a half snort, half laugh. That *was* the million-dollar question. But despite feeling remarkably at ease with him, there were some things she wasn't prepared to admit to *anybody*.

'Well, yes…and there's a very long, very complicated answer to that question, which I do not have time to tell you right now.' *Or ever.* 'Not with Mrs Gordon waiting.'

Gareth nodded. He knew when he was being fobbed off but, given that she barely knew him, she certainly didn't owe him any explanations. And probably the less involved he was in her stuff the better.

He was a forty-year-old man who didn't need any more *complicated* in his life.

No matter what package it came wrapped in.

He'd had enough of it to last a lifetime.

'Okay, then,' he said, turning to go. 'Just yell if I can help you with anything.'

He had his hand on the doorknob when her tentative enquiry stopped him dead in his tracks.

'You didn't…you haven't told anyone about the other

night, about what I...?' He caught her nervous swallow as he faced her. 'About how I reacted? Please...don't...'

Gareth regarded her seriously. If she'd known him better he would have given her a *what-do-you-think?* look. But she didn't, he reminded himself. It just *felt* like they'd known each other longer because of the connection they'd made less than a week ago.

It was hard to think of her as a stranger even though the reality was they barely knew each other.

He shook his head. 'I don't tell tales out of school, Billie,' he said.

He didn't kiss and tell either.

The sudden unwarranted thought slapped him in the face, resulting in temporary brain malfunction.

What the hell?

Pull it together, man. Totally inappropriate. Totally not cool.

But the truth was, as he busied himself with opening the door and getting as far away from her as possible, he'd thought about kissing Billie *a lot* these last few days.

And it had been a very long time since he'd *wanted* to kiss anyone.

CHAPTER FOUR

FIVE HOURS LATER, Gareth knew he was going to have to put Billie's I-don't-want-you-protecting-me convictions to the test. He had a head laceration that needed suturing and everyone else was busy. He could leave it until Barry was free but, with the Royal Brisbane going on diversion, a lot of their cases were coming to St Luke's and things had suddenly gone a little crazy.

They needed the bed asap.

If he'd still been in the army he would have just done the stupid thing himself. But civilian nursing placed certain restrictions on his practice.

Earlier Billie had demanded to know if he'd have given another doctor the kid-glove treatment he'd afforded her over the IV and had insisted that he not do the same to her.

Would he given any other doctor a pass on the head lac?

No. He would not.

Gareth took a deep breath and twitched the curtains to cubicle eight open. Billie looked up from the patient she was talking to. 'I need a head lac sutured in cubicle two,' he said, his tone brisk and businesslike. 'You just about done here?'

She looked startled at his announcement but he admired her quick affirmative response. 'Five minutes?' she said, only the bob of her throat betraying her nervousness.

He nodded. 'I'll set up.'

But then Brett, the triage admin officer, distracted

him with a charting issue and it was ten minutes before
he headed back to the drunk teenager with the banged-up
forehead. He noticed Billie disappearing behind the curtain and cursed under his breath, hurrying to catch her up.

He hadn't cleaned the wound yet and the patient looked
pretty gruesome.

When he joined her behind the curtain seconds later, Billie was staring down at the matted mess of clotted blood and
hair that he'd left covered temporarily with a green surgical
towel. 'I'm sorry,' he apologised. 'I haven't had a chance
to clean it up yet.'

She dragged her eyes away from the messy laceration
and looked at him, her freckles suddenly emphasised by her
pallor, her nostrils flaring as she sucked in air. 'I'll be…
right back,' she said.

She brushed past him on her way out and Gareth shut
his eyes briefly. *Great.* He glanced at the sleeping patient,
snoring drunkenly and oblivious to the turmoil his stupid
split head had just caused.

Gareth followed her, taking a guess that she'd headed for
the staffroom again. The door was shut when he reached
it. He turned the handle but it was locked. 'Billie,' he said,
keeping his voice low, 'it's me, open up.'

The lock turned and the door opened a crack and Gareth
slipped into the room. She was just on the other side and
her back pushed the door shut again as she leaned against it.

Billie looked up at him, the swimmy sensation in her
head and the nausea clearing. 'I'm fine,' she dismissed, taking deep, even steady breaths.

'I'm sorry. I had every intention of cleaning it up…so it
looked better.'

Billie nodded. 'It's okay. I'm fine,' she repeated. 'I just
need a moment.'

Gareth nodded as he watched her suck air in and out

through pursed lips. She lifted her hand to smooth her hair and he couldn't help but notice how alarmingly it shook.

She didn't look okay to him.

'You look kind of freaked out,' he said. 'Do you need a paper bag to blow into? Are your fingers tingly?'

She glared at him. 'I'm not having a panic attack. I just wasn't expecting…that. I'm better if I'm mentally prepared. But I'll be fine.' She turned those big brown eyes on him. 'Just give me a moment, okay?'

'Okay.'

She nodded again and he noticed tears swim in her eyes. Clearly she was disappointed in herself, in not being able to master her affliction.

Gareth shoved a hand through his hair, feeling helpless as she struggled for control. 'Try not to think about it like it is,' he said. 'Next time you go out there it'll be all cleaned up. No blood. No gore.'

She nodded. 'Okay.'

But her wide eyes told him she was still picturing it. 'You're still thinking about it,' he said.

'I'm not,' she denied, chewing on her bottom lip.

Gareth took a step closer to her, wanting to reach for her but clenching his hands at his sides. 'Yes, you are.'

She gnawed on her lip some more and he noticed she'd chewed all her gloss off.

'Look. I'm trying, okay?' she said, placing her palm flat against his chest. 'Just back off for a moment.'

Her hand felt warm against his chest and he waited for her to push against him but her fingers curled into the fabric of his scrub top instead and Gareth felt a jolt much further south. As if she'd put her hand down his scrubs bottoms.

Oh, hell. Just hell.

Now he was thinking very bad things. Very bad ways to calm her down, to take her mind off it.

For crying out loud, she was a freaked-out second-year

resident who needed to get back to the lac and get the stupid thing sutured so he could free up a bed. Gareth had dealt with a lot of freaked-out people in his life—the wounded, the addled, the grieving.

He was good with the freaked out.

But not like this. Not the way he was thinking.

Hell.

And that's exactly where he was going—*do not pass 'Go', do not collect any money*—because all he could think about now was her mouth.

Kissing it. Giving her a way to *really* forget what was beyond the door.

It was wildly inappropriate.

They were *at work,* for crying out loud. But her husky 'Gareth?' reflected the confusion and turmoil stirring unrest inside him.

The look changed on her face as her gaze fixed on his mouth. Her fingers in his shirt seemed to pull him nearer and those freckles were so damn irresistible.

'Oh, screw it,' he muttered, caution falling away like confetti around him as he stepped forward, crowding her back against the door, his body aligning with hers, his palms sliding onto her cheeks as he dropped his head.

Billie whimpered as Gareth's lips made contact with hers. She couldn't have stopped it had her life depended on it. Her pulse fluttered madly at the base of her throat and at her temples. Everything was forgotten in those lingering moments as his mouth opened and his tongue brushed along her bottom lip.

Back and forth. Back and forth. Again and again.

Maddening. Hypnotic. Perfect.

The kiss sucking away her breath and her thoughts and her sense. Transporting her to a place where only he and his lips and his heat existed. The press of his thighs against hers was heady, her breasts ached to be touched and her belly twisted hard, tensing in anticipation.

She didn't think she'd *ever* been kissed like this. And she never wanted it to stop.

She slid her hands onto his waist, anchoring them against his hips bones, feeling the broad bony crests in her palms, using them to pull him in closer, revel in the power of his thighs hard against her, fitting their bodies together more intimately.

A groan escaped his mouth, deep and tortured, as if it was torn from his throat and then Gareth pulled away, breathing hard as he placed his forehead against hers, staying close, keeping their intimate connection, not saying anything, just catching his breath as she caught hers.

'You okay now?' he asked after a moment, looking down into her face.

Billie blinked as she struggled to recall what had happened before the kiss. To recall if there had been anything at all—*ever*—in her life before this kiss.

He groaned again, his thumb stroking over her bottom lip, and it sounded as needy and hungry as the desire burning in her belly. 'We can't…do this here,' he muttered. 'We have to get back.'

She nodded. She knew. On some level she knew that. But her head was still spinning from the kiss—it was hard to think about anything else. And if that had been his plan, she couldn't fault it.

But it was hardly a good long-term strategy.

He took a step back, clearing his throat. 'You all right to do the lac now?' he asked.

The laceration. Right. That's what had happened before the kiss. She tried to picture it but her brain was still stuck back in the delicious quagmire of the kiss.

'Give me five minutes and then come to the cubicle. I promise it'll be a different sight altogether.'

Billie nodded. 'Okay.' She shifted off the door so he could open it.

And then he was gone and she was alone in the staff-room, her back against the door, pressing her fingers to her tingling mouth.

Billie took a few minutes to review the chart of her head lac patient. His blood alcohol was way over the limit. He'd gone through a glass window. The X-ray report was clear— no fractures, no retained glass—but she pulled it up on the computer to satisfy herself nonetheless.

The laceration wasn't deep but it was too large for glue.

Ten minutes later she pulled back the curtains of the cubicle. Gareth faltered for a moment as he looked at her and she didn't have to be a mind-reader to know what he was thinking.

The way his eyes dipped to her mouth said it all.

'All ready,' he said briskly, as he indicated the suture kit laid out and the dramatically changed wound. The blood was gone, leaving an uneven laceration, its edges stark white. It followed the still-sleeping patient's hairline before cutting across his forehead.

Billie swallowed as she took in the extent of it. It wasn't going to be some quick five-stitch job.

'Size six gloves?'

She nodded as she dragged her gaze back to Gareth, thankful for his brisk professionalism.

'Go and scrub,' he said. 'I'll open a pair up.'

Billie stepped outside the curtain and performed a basic scrub at the nearby basin. When she was done she waited for the water to finish dripping off her elbows before entering the cubicle again. She reached for the surgical towel already laid out and dried her hands and arms then slipped into her gloves, hyper-aware of Gareth watching her.

She took a deep breath as she arranged the instruments

on her tray to her liking and applied the needle to the syringe filled with local anaesthetic.

She could do this.

She glanced at Gareth as she turned to her sleeping patient. His strategy had worked—she wasn't thinking about the gruesome chore ahead, all she could think about was the kiss.

'Good grief,' she said, screwing up her nose as a blast of alcoholic fumes wafted her way. 'Think I should have put a mask on.'

'Aromatic, isn't he?'

'It's Martin, right?' she enquired of Gareth as if they'd been professional acquaintances for twenty years. As if he hadn't just kissed her and rocked her world.

Gareth nodded. 'Although he prefers M-Dog apparently.'

Billie blinked. 'I'm not going to call him M-Dog.'

Gareth laughed. 'I don't blame you.'

'Martin,' Billie said, raising her voice slightly as she addressed the sleeping patient.

Gareth shook his head. 'You don't have much experience with drunk teenage boys, do you? You need to be louder. You don't hear much in that state.'

She quirked an eyebrow. 'You talking from experience?'

He grimaced. 'Unfortunately, yes.'

Billie returned her attention to the patient. 'Martin!' she called, louder, firmer. But still nothing.

'Allow me,' said Gareth. He gave the teenager's shoulders a brisk hard shake and barked, 'Wake up, M-Dog.'

The teenager started, as did Billie, the demand cutting right through her. It was commanding, brooking no argument.

And *very* sexy.

Had he learned that in the military?

'Hmm? What?' the boy asked, trying to co-ordinate himself to sit up and failing.

Billie bit down on her cheek to stop from laughing. 'I'm Dr Keyes,' she said as Martin glanced at her through bloodshot eyes. 'I'm going to put some stitches in that nasty gash in your head.'

'Is there going to be a scar?' he asked, his eyes already closing again. 'Me mum'll kill me.'

Billie figured that M-Dog should have thought about that before he'd gone out drinking to excess. But, then, her sister Jessica had never been big on responsible drinking either. She guessed that was part and parcel of being a teenager.

For some, anyway.

'Martin, stay with me,' Billie said, her voice at the right pitch and command for M-Dog to force his bleary eyes open once again. 'I'm going to have to put a lot of local anaesthetic in your wound to numb it up. It's going to sting like the blazes.'

He gave her a goofy grin. 'Not feelin' nuthin' at the moment.'

Billie did laugh this time. 'Just as well,' she said, but the teenager was already drifting off. 'Okay,' she muttered, taking a deep breath and picking up the syringe. She glanced at Gareth. 'Here we go.'

Gareth nodded. She looked so much better now. She had pink in her cheeks, her freckles were less obvious and she'd lost that wide-eyed, freaked-out expression.

Billie's hand trembled as she picked up some gauze and started at the proximal end of the wound, poking the fine needle into the jagged edge and slowly injecting. M-dog twitched a bit and screwed up his face and Billie's heart leapt, her hand stilling as she waited for him to jerk and try and sit up. But he did nothing like that, his face settling quickly back into the passive droop of the truly drunk.

Clearly he *was* feeling no pain.

Gareth nodded at her encouragingly and Billie got back to work, methodically injecting lignocaine along the entire length of the wound, with barely a twitch from M-Dog. By the time she'd fully injected down to the distal end, the local had had enough time to start working at the beginning so she got to work.

Her stomach turned at the pull and tug of flesh, at the dull thread of silk through skin, and she peeked at Gareth.

'Talk to me,' she said, as he snipped the thread for her on her first neat suture.

He glanced at her, his gaze dropping to her mouth, and the memory of the kiss returned full throttle. 'What do you want me to talk about?'

Not that, Billie thought, returning her attention to the job at hand. *Anything but that.* The military. The *incident* that had caused his demotion, which Helen had hinted at earlier. But neither of those seemed appropriate either. Not that appropriateness hadn't already been breached tonight. But they needed to steer clear of the personal.

They'd already got *way* too personal.

'Tell me about the patients out there.'

And so he did, his deep steady voice accompanying her needlework as they wove and snipped as a team.

CHAPTER FIVE

THE REST OF the night and the two following were better than Billie could have hoped. The gore was kept to a minimum and she managed to get through them without any more near nervous breakdowns.

Or requiring any more resuscitative kissing.

Not that she wasn't aware of Gareth looking out for her. Which should probably have been annoying but which she couldn't help thinking was really sweet. *And* kind of hot.

She knew the last thing he needed was having a squeamish doctor to juggle as he ran the night shift with military-like efficiency—overseeing the nursing side as well as liaising with the medical side to ensure that the ER ran like a well-oiled machine. But he seemed to take it in his stride as just another consideration to manage.

He was clearly known and well respected by both nurses and doctors alike, he was faultlessly discreet, he knew everybody from the cleaning staff to the ward nurses, he knew where everything was and just about every answer to every procedure and protocol question any of them had.

By the time she'd knocked off on Sunday morning she was well and truly dazzled.

St Luke's was lucky to have Gareth Stapleton.

Which begged the question—why wasn't he *running* the department as he apparently used to? What had happened to cause his demotion? What was *the incident* Helen had made reference to? Annabel Pearce, the NUM, was good too, but from what Billie could see, Gareth ran rings around her.

Billie yawned as she entered the lift, pushing the button for the top floor. Her mind drifted, as it had done a little too often the last couple of days, to the kiss. She shut her tired eyes and revelled in the skip in her pulse and the heaviness in her belly as she relived every sexy nuance.

Not only could Gareth run a busy city emergency department but he could kiss like no other man she knew.

And Billie had been kissed some before.

She'd had two long-term relationships and a few shorter ones, not to mention the odd fling or two, including a rather risqué one with a lecturer, in the eight years since she'd first lost her virginity at university. She liked sex, had never felt unsatisfied by any of her partners and wasn't afraid to ask for what she wanted.

Essentially she'd been with men who knew what they were doing. Who certainly knew how to kiss.

But Gareth Stapleton had just cleared the slate.

She wet her lips in some kind of subconscious memory and grimaced at their dryness. Between winter and the hospital air-con they felt perpetually dry. She pulled her lip gloss out of her bag and applied a layer, feeling the immediate relief.

The lift dinged and she pushed wearily off the wall and headed to the fire exit for the last two flights of steps to the rooftop car park. She jumped as a figure loomed in her peripheral vision from the stairs below, her pulse leaping crazily for a second before she realised it was Gareth.

And then her pulse took off for an entirely different reason. 'You took the stairs?' she said in disbelief. '*All* eight floors?'

Of course he had. Super-nurse, freaked-out-doctor whisperer, kisser extraordinaire. What wasn't the man capable of?

'Of course.' He grinned. 'It's about the only exercise I get these days.'

Billie shook her head as they continued up the last two flights, which was torture enough for her tired body. By the time they'd reached the top and Gareth was opening the door, her thighs were grumbling at her and she was breathing a little harder.

Of course, that could just have been Gareth's presence.

Was it her overactive imagination or had his 'After you' been low and husky and a little too close to her ear?

She stepped out onto the roof, her brain a quagmire of confusion, thankful for the bracing winter air cooling her overheated imagination. She zipped up her hoody and hunched into it.

Gareth was hyper-aware of Billie's arms brushing against his as they walked across the car park to their vehicles. 'You on days off now?' he asked.

She nodded. 'Three. How about you?'

'Me too.' Which meant they'd be back on together on Wednesday. An itch shot up Gareth's spine.

Fabulous.

Three days didn't seem long enough to cleanse himself of the memory of the kiss and he really needed to do that because Billie, he'd discovered, was fast becoming the only thing he thought about.

And that wasn't conducive to his work. Or his life.

The last woman he remembered having such an instantaneous attraction to wasn't around any more, and it had taken a long time to get over that. In fact, he wasn't entirely sure he'd managed it yet. He grimaced just thinking about the black hole of the last five years.

Billie was in the ER for six months and the next few years of her life would be hectic, with a virtual roller-coaster of rotations and exams and killer shifts sucking up every spare moment of her time. She didn't have time to devote to a relationship, let alone one with a forty-year-old widower.

They were in different places in their life journeys.

They reached their cars, parked three spaces from each other, and he almost breathed a loud sigh of relief.

'Well…' he said, staring out at the Brisbane city skyline, 'I guess I'll be seeing you on Wednesday.'

She looked like she was about to say something but thought better of it, nodding instead, as she jingled her keys in her hand. 'Sure,' she murmured. 'Sleep well.'

Gareth nodded, knowing there was not a chance in hell of that happening. 'Bye.'

And he turned to walk to his vehicle, sucking in the bracing air and refusing to look back lest he suggest something *crazy* like her coming to his place and sleeping off her night shift there.

In his bed.

Naked.

Get in the car, man. *Get in the car and drive away.*

He opened the door, buckled up and started the engine. It took a while for his car to warm up and the windscreen to de-mist and he sat there trying not to think about Billie, or her sparkly dress, or her cute freckles.

Or that damned *ill-advised* kiss.

A minute later he was set to go and he reversed quickly, eager to make his escape. Except when he passed her car, it was still there and she was out of it, standing at the front with the bonnet open, looking at the engine.

He groaned out loud. No, no, no! *So close.* He sighed, reversing again and manoeuvring his car back into his car space. He disembarked with trepidation, knowing he shouldn't but knowing he couldn't not offer to help her.

'Problem?' he asked, as he strode towards her.

Billie looked at him with eyes that felt like they'd been

marinating in formaldehyde all night. If possible he looked even better than before. 'It won't start,' she grumbled.

'Is it just cold?'

'No. I think the battery's flat.'

'Want me to give it a try?'

'Knock yourself out,' she invited.

Gareth slid into the plush leather passenger seat and turned the key. A faint couple of drunken whirrs could be heard and that was it. He placed his head on the steering-wheel. Yep. Dead as a doornail.

'Did you leave your lights on?' he asked, as he climbed out.

She shook her head. She'd taken her hair out of her pony-tail and it swished around her face, the tips brushing against the velour lettering decorating the front of her hoody. Her nose was pink from the cold.

'The car automatically turns them off anyway.'

Of course it did. It wasn't some twenty-year-old dinosaur. A pity, because if it had been he could have offered her a jump start. But with the newer vehicles being almost totally computerised, he knew that wasn't advisable.

'Do you have roadside assistance?'

'No. I know, I know...' Billie said, as he frowned at her. She rubbed her hands together, pleased for the warmth of her jeans and fleecy top in her unexpected foray into the cold. 'It expired a few months back and I keep meaning to renew it but...'

His whiskers looked even shaggier after three nights and his disapproving blue eyes seemed to leap out at her across the distance. 'You're a woman driving *alone* places, you should have roadside assistance.'

Billie supposed she should be affronted by his assumption that she was some helpless woman but, as with everything else, she found his concern for her well-being completely irresistible.

He sighed. 'I'll drive down to the nearest battery place and get you one,' he said.

Billie blinked as his irresistibility cranked up another notch. Was he crazy? 'It's *Sunday*, Gareth. Nothing's going to be open till at least ten and I don't know about you but I'm too tired to wait that long.' She shut her bonnet. 'I'll get a taxi home and deal with the battery this afternoon after I've had a sleep.'

Gareth knew he was caught then. He couldn't let her get a taxi home. Not when he could easily drop her. Unless she lived way out of his way. 'I'll give you a lift,' he said. 'Where do you live?'

He hoped it was somewhere *really* far away.

Billie would have been deaf not to hear the reluctance in his voice. And she was too tired to decipher what it meant. Tired enough to be pissed off. 'You don't have to do that, Gareth,' she said testily, fishing around in her bag for her mobile phone. 'I'm perfectly capable of ringing and paying for a taxi. I could even walk.'

She watched a muscle clench in his jaw. 'Don't be stupid,' he dismissed. 'You've worked all night and I'm here with a perfectly functioning car. It makes sense. Now... Where. Do. You. Live?'

She glared at him. 'Only a really *stupid* man would call a tired woman stupid.'

Gareth shut his eyes and raked a hand through his hair, muttering, 'Bloody hell.' He glanced at her then. 'I apologise, okay? Just tell me where you live already.'

'Paddo.'

Paddington. *Of course she did.* Trendy, yuppie suburb as befitted her sparkly dress and expensive car. 'Perfect. You're on my way home.' He was house-sitting in the outer suburbs but she lived in his general direction.

She folded her arms. He could tell she was deciding

between being churlish and grateful. 'If you're sure you don't mind?'

Gareth shook his head. 'Of course not,' he said, indicating that she should make her way to his car. 'As long as you don't mind slumming it?'

Billie shot him a disparaging look. 'I'm sure I'll manage.'

Gareth nodded as she passed in front of him. The question was, would he?

CHAPTER SIX

THEY DROVE IN silence for a while as Gareth navigated out of the hospital grounds and onto the quiet Sunday morning roads. He noticed she tucked her hands between her denim-clad thighs as he pulled up at the first red traffic light.

'Are you cold?' he asked, cranking the heat up a little more.

'Not too bad,' she murmured.

Gareth supposed the seats in her car were heated and this was probably a real step down for her. And maybe when he'd been younger, before life had dealt him a tonne of stuff to deal with, he might have felt the divide between them acutely.

But he'd since lived a life that had confirmed that possessions meant very little—from the pockmarked earth of the war-torn Middle East to the beige walls of an oncology unit—he'd learned very quickly that *stuff* didn't matter.

And frankly he was too tired and too tempted by her to care for her comfort.

Her scent filled the car. He suddenly realised that she'd been wearing the same perfume last Saturday night but he had been too focused on the accident to realise. Something sweet. Maybe fruity? Banana? With a hint of vanilla and something…sharper.

Great—she smelled like a banana daiquiri.

And now it was in his car. And probably destined to be so for days, taunting him with the memory.

She shifted and in his peripheral vision he could see two narrow stretches of denim hugging her thighs, her hands still jammed between them.

'So,' Gareth said out of complete desperation, trying to *not* think about her thighs and how good they might feel wrapped around him, 'you called yourself Dr Keyes...the other night. With M-Dog.'

Yep. Complete desperation. Why else would he even be remotely stupid enough to bring up *that* night when they were trapped in a tiny, warm cab together, only a small gap and a gearstick separating them, the kiss lying large between them?

But Billie didn't seem to notice the tension as she shrugged and looked out the window. 'It's easier sometimes to just shorten it. Ashworth-Keyes is a bit of a mouthful at times and, frankly, it can also sound a bit prissy. I tend to use it more strategically.'

'So drunk teenagers who go by the name of M-Dog don't warrant the star treatment?'

Billie turned and frowned at him, surprisingly stung by his subtle criticism. 'No,' she said waspishly. 'Some people respond better to a double-barrelled name. There are some patients, I've found, who are innately...snobbish, I guess. They like the idea of a doctor with a posh name. Guys called M-Dog tend to see it as a challenge to their working-class roots...or something,' she dismissed with a flick of her hand. 'And frankly...' she sought his gaze as they pulled up at another red light and waited till he looked at her '...I was a little too...confounded by our kiss to speak in long words. I'm surprised I managed to remember my name at all.'

Billie held his gaze. If he was going to call her on something, he'd better get it right or be prepared to be called on it himself. She might be helplessly squeamish, she might not be able to stand up to her family and be caught up in the sticky web of their expectations but she'd been taught how to hold her own by experts.

There was nothing more cutting than a put-down from a surgeon who thought the sun shone out of his behind.

'Yes,' he said after a moment or two, his throat bobbing as he broke eye contact and put the car into gear. 'That was…confounding.'

Billie almost laughed at the understatement. But at least he wasn't denying it. They'd studiously avoided any mention of the kiss since it had happened, but it *was* there between them and she knew he felt it as acutely as she did.

She'd spent the last couple of days telling herself that it hadn't meant anything. That it didn't *count*. That Gareth had used it only as a strategy to snap her out of her situation.

But it had still felt very real.

They accomplished the rest of the trip in silence, apart from her brief directions, and Gareth pulled up outside her place in under ten minutes.

'Thank you,' she said, unbuckling.

Gareth nodded. 'No problems,' he murmured, as he let the car idle.

He waited for her to reach for the door handle but she didn't. 'No. I mean for everything,' she said. 'For just now but also for the other night. For what you did. For how you helped…calm the situation. For the kiss.'

Gareth swallowed hard as Billie once again mentioned the one thing he was trying hard not to think about. She'd been right when she'd said it was confounding and he wished she'd just leave it alone so he could put it away in his mental too-hard-to-deal-with basket.

'Don't,' he said. 'Don't thank me for that.' Confounding or not, it hadn't been proper. 'What happened…it pretty much constitutes sexual harassment.'

Her snort was loud in the confined space between them, the world outside the warm bubble of the car forgotten.

'That's rubbish, Gareth,' she said. 'Kissing me at work is only sexual harassment if I didn't want or encourage it, if it was unwelcome, and while I appreciate you trying to give me a pass on my behaviour, you can be damned sure I wanted you to kiss me, very *very* much. We're not *just* two people who met at work, we're not *just* colleagues, and you know it. We're both adults here so let's not pretend there hasn't been a thing between us since the accident.'

Gareth looked at Billie, her brown eyes glowing at him fiercely, her chest rising and falling, stretching the fabric of her hoody in very interesting ways across her chest. He found it hard to reconcile this woman with the one who had been a pale wreck over a head lac or vomiting at the scene of an accident.

He nodded. 'Of course. You're right. I apologise.'

The *thing* pulsed between them and God knew he wanted her now.

He looked away, inspecting her house through the windscreen for a few moments, the heater pumping warm air into the already heated atmosphere. It was one of those old-fashioned worker cottages that had been bought for a song twenty years ago, renovated and sold for a goodly sum.

'Do you want to come in? For a coffee.'

Gareth shut his eyes against the temptation, feeling older and more tired than he had in a long time. 'Billie,' he murmured, a warning in his voice.

Billie looked at his profile. 'Don't trust yourself, Gareth?' she taunted.

He looked at her, her lip gloss smeared enticingly, a small smile playing on her mouth, a knowing look in her eyes, and his tiredness suddenly evaporated.

He didn't trust himself remotely.

'Billie… This isn't going to happen.'

She looked at him for long moments. 'Why not?'

The enquiry could have come across sounding petulant. If she'd pouted. If she'd injected any kind of whine into her voice. But she didn't. She just looked at him with that slight smile on her mouth and asked the very sensible, very reasonable question.

They wanted each other. They were both single and of age.

Why not indeed?

Gareth sighed. 'You're, what, Billie? Twenty-seven?'

She shook her head. 'Twenty-six.'

Gareth groaned. Dear God, It was worse than he'd thought. 'I'm forty years old,' he said. 'I think you need to play with boys your own age.'

'You think I'm too young for you?'

He nodded. 'Yes.' *Way* too young. 'And…'

'And?' She skewered him with her gaze. 'You think I'm too forthright, don't you?'

'No! I don't care about that. I like forthright women.' His wife, a complete stranger at the time *and* stone-cold sober, had come right up to him in a bar and kissed the life out of him in front of everyone.

'Well, then?'

'Billie…' he sighed. 'I'm at a different stage of my life than you are. You've got many years ahead of you, with a lot of hard work and dedication to get where you're going. You don't have the time to devote to serious relationships and I'm—'

'It's *coffee*, Gareth,' she interrupted.

Gareth shook his head at her, his gaze drifting to her mouth, the gloss beckoning, then back to her earnest brown eyes. 'It's not just coffee and you know it.'

She shrugged then slid her hand onto his leg. 'Would that be such a bad thing?'

A hot jolt streaked up Gareth's thigh and he was instantly

hard. His hand quickly clamped down on hers as it moved closer to ground zero. 'Give me a break here, Billie. I'm trying to do the right thing.'

'How very *noble* of you,' she murmured glancing at her hand held firmly in place by his before returning her attention to him. 'Look…I understand that you think I need kid gloves after the other night but I really don't need you looking out for me in *this* department. I think this *is* the right thing.'

Gareth's sense of self-preservation told him otherwise. There wasn't one part of him that believed their *coffee* session would be the end of it. And, despite her confidence right now, he'd met enough doctors in this stage of their careers to know how many relationships didn't make it.

His wife's death had left Gareth very wary. It had taken a huge chunk out of him. One that had never grown back. He had no intention of lining up for another pound of flesh. And something told him Billie could do exactly that.

So she wanted a fling? Not going to happen. Not when they worked together.

'I'm not into recreational sex.'

'*Really?*'

She smiled then, her voice clearly disbelieving. She tried to move her hand further north but he held tight for a few moments before finally giving away to her insistence. Gareth watched her palm move closer to his crotch, torn between stopping her again and grabbing her hand and putting it where his groin screamed for attention.

She halted just short of his happy zone and he tore his gaze away from her neat fingernails so very, very close to his zipper.

'I think you must be the only man in the world who doesn't see the value in a little harmless physical release,' she said.

Gareth absently noticed that the windscreen was fogging up on the inside and tuned in to the roughness of her voice and the heaviness of his own breathing as the pads of her fingers brushed awfully close to nirvana. He knew if he didn't stop this now, he wouldn't.

And with his normal self-control lulled due to lack of sleep, he was just weary enough to succumb.

'*I think* you're tired,' he said, turning his face to look at her. 'We're both tired. *I think* people can make bad decisions when they're tired.'

She slid her hand home and Gareth shut his eyes, biting back a groan as pleasure undulated through the fibres deep inside his belly and thighs.

'I'm awake now,' she murmured, her voice husky in the charged atmosphere. 'And I gotta say…' she paused to give his erection a squeeze '…you don't feel that tired to me.'

God.

She was trying to kill him.

Gareth gave a half-laugh. 'Trust me,' he said, his eyes opening as he gathered his last scrap of self-control and removed her hand from his hard-on, '*that* is a really unreliable measure of tiredness. Of anything, for that matter.'

Billie's stomach plummeted, and not in a good way, as she placed her hand back between her thighs. She'd felt so sure that she'd be able to persuade Gareth to stay and she squirmed a little in the seat to ease the ache that had started to build between her legs in delicious anticipation.

'I'm sorry, Billie.'

She tossed her head and looked out the window. 'It's fine,' she said.

Billie supposed she should feel embarrassed or mortified. And perhaps if she'd been more mentally alert she might have been. Hell, if she'd been more mentally alert she probably wouldn't have propositioned him at all.

Or been so damned persistent.

No doubt the mortification was yet to come but for now she just felt disappointed.

'I just…don't want you to do something that you might regret tomorrow,' he continued. 'This kind of step needs to be taken when all your faculties are intact and I don't want to be on your dumb-things-I-did list, Billie. We have to work together for the next six months and I've been around long enough to see how awkward that can be in the workplace.'

Billie nodded. Just her luck to develop a thing for the first man she'd ever met who didn't think with his penis.

She turned to look at him. 'You have one of those?'

He frowned and his eyes crinkled and he looked all sexy and sleepy and perplexed and she wanted to drag him into her house, into her bed *so freaking bad* even if it was just to snuggle and sleep. 'One of what?' he asked.

'A dumb-things-I-did list.'

His frowned cleared and then he laughed. 'Oh, hell, yeah.'

His laughter was deep and rich and warm, a perfect serenade in their intimate cocoon, so nearly tangible Billie felt as if she could pick it up and wrap it around her like a cloak. Interesting lines buried amidst all that stubble bracketed his mouth and she squeezed her thighs together tight, trapping her hands there.

Hands that wanted to touch him.

Billie didn't have that kind of list, although she suddenly wished she did. Even if it meant he was at the top. Although no doubt there were plenty who would think living out her sister's dreams to keep her parents happy was a really dumb thing to do.

The unhappy thought pierced the intimacy and Billie stirred. She didn't want it in here with them. She unbuckled her seat belt. 'Thanks for the lift.'

Billie reached for the handle and pulled; the door opened a crack and cold air seeped in as she half turned her body, preparing to exit. But Gareth's hand reached across the interior, wrapping gently around her upper arm.

'You understand it's not about *not* wanting you, right?'

Billie's heart almost stopped in her chest. She looked over her shoulder at him. He looked bleak and tired and *torn*.

'I know,' she murmured, and then, without thinking about it, she leaned across the short distance between them and kissed him quick and hard.

For a brief few seconds she felt him yield. Whiskers spiked her mouth and scraped her chin and she tasted the spice of his groan.

And then she pulled away—pulled away before she did something crazy like straddle him—and exited the car without looking back.

CHAPTER SEVEN

WORKING WITH GARETH on Wednesday wasn't as excruciating as Billie had thought it was going to be. She *had* suffered a degree of remorse over her behaviour and *had* been prone to episodes of acute embarrassment during her days off whenever she remembered how persistent she'd been, but he'd soon put her at ease with his brisk professionalism.

It helped that he didn't come on until the afternoon so she was already in the groove when she first fronted him. And then, of course, he was focused and businesslike as always and by teatime she'd almost forgotten that she'd groped him in his car and more or less invited him into her bed but been knocked back.

She didn't regret it, as he had predicted. She doubted she would have regretted it if he'd taken her up on her offer either.

But she was mindful of how it must look to him. How *she* must look. What he thought of her she had no idea. She'd known him for less than two weeks and in that time she'd swung wildly from being a vomiting, hyperventilating wreck to a penis-squeezing vamp.

That made her cringe.

He seemed so sophisticated, so *together,* compared to her.

Why it should be a concern she didn't want to think about. He was right—she had a tough few years ahead of her career-wise and being in a relationship had not been part of her plans.

Her parents and all the extended members of the Ashworth-Keyes surgical dynasty had said the same thing. Specialising was hard on your social life and not a lot of relationships survived. Career first, personal life later.

So, yeah, Gareth's words of wisdom had resonated with her the other morning.

But still… He made her want things. And specialising wasn't one of them.

Gareth's mobile rang as he sat at the table in the staffroom. He was pleased for the reprieve. Billie was sitting opposite him and he swore she was just wearing that lip gloss now to drive him crazy. Thankfully Kate and Lindy, two of the junior nurses on the afternoon shift, were having their break as well and the three women were engaged in a conversation about television vampires.

Amber's picture flashed on the screen and he smiled as he slid the bar across to answer. 'Hey, sweetheart,' he said as he answered the phone. Billie glanced at him, a little frown drawing her brows together, and he got up and wandered over to the sink, his back to the table. 'Everything okay?'

Apparently not. His stepdaughter was crying so hard he could barely make out her garbled reply. A hot spike of concern lanced him. 'Amber?' he said, trying to keep his voice down and devoid of alarm. 'What's wrong?' he demanded.

He was pretty sure she was telling him she was outside. 'You're here?' he asked, already turning and heading for the door, aware on a subliminal level of Billie's interest but too worried about Amber for it to register properly.

'I'm coming now,' he said, as he hung up and pulled the door open.

* * *

Thirty seconds later he was stalking out into the main thoroughfare, spotting Amber looking red-faced and dishevelled near the triage desk, the long fringe of her pixie cut plastered to her forehead in a way that she usually wouldn't be seen dead wearing.

His heart leapt into his mouth. 'Amber?' He strode towards her.

When she flung herself against his chest and dissolved into even more tears, Gareth knew it had to be bad. His and Amber's relationship had been fairly tempestuous since her mother had died and public displays of affection had been strictly forbidden.

He didn't blame her. Amber had been fifteen when Catherine had been diagnosed and had died five months later from breast cancer. Being angry at him was easier than being angry at the entire world. Although she'd been there too.

Patients in the waiting area and members of staff looked on curiously as Amber's loud honking cries continued and didn't seem likely to abate any time soon. He led her into the nearby nurses' handover room, which was essentially a cubicle with three sides of glass. But it had a door he could shut, was relatively soundproof and with various posters stuck on the walls they were obscured somewhat from full view.

'What happened?' he asked, as he shut the door after them. 'Did you break up with Blaine?'

Amber's cries cut off as she glared at him. 'Only three months ago.'

He held up his hands in apology. 'Really?'

'Yes,' she snapped.

Amber had been a good kid but also, in many ways, a typical teenager—everything an overblown drama—and then she'd been a *grieving* teenager, which had put her into a whole different category. It had been like watching a train wreck and trying to be there to pick up the pieces, when she'd let him. Things had been particularly fraught.

And now she was a pissed-off young woman.

And he *still* couldn't tell when her tears were serious or just the I-broke-my-fingernail-and-it's-all-your-fault variety.

Catherine had always known.

Gareth realised suddenly he hadn't thought about Catherine in a while and, with Amber looking at him with those big green eyes the exact shade of her mother's, guilt punched him hard in the chest.

'Okay, so…what *is* the matter?'

Amber sniffled and dragged a ball of crumbled-up paper out of her bag and handed it to him. Gareth took it, hoping it wasn't some 'Dear John' letter that he really *did not* want to read. He unravelled it, the wrinkled page quickly revealing itself to be a lab report.

A sudden spike of fear sliced into his side. He looked at this kind of report every day in his job. But he and Amber had a history with these reports too—not one he ever wanted to repeat.

He ironed it out with his hands as he scanned it.

The top left-hand corner had Amber's personal details. Name. Address, Date of birth. Allergy status. The next line leapt out at him.

BRCA1—positive.

Gareth's breath caught in his throat. His heart thumped so hard his ribs hurt. His vision tunnelled, narrowed down to the stark brevity of that line.

She had tested positive for a faulty gene that dramatically increased her risk of developing breast cancer. The disease that had killed her mother.

Crap!

'I didn't think you wanted the test,' he said, looking at a red-eyed Amber as his brain scrambled to absorb the shocking news.

She shrugged in that belligerent way he was used to but it somehow lost its effectiveness when she looked so devastated. 'I changed my mind.'

Gareth sat down on the nearest chair. 'I thought we were going to talk about it together before you decided.'

'I…couldn't,' she said. 'And anyway it was…spur of the moment.'

Gareth looked down at the page again. 'I didn't want you to go through this by yourself, Amber.'

'I didn't…I had counselling. The cancer centre wouldn't let me do it without.'

He shook his head at the things she must have been going through these last few weeks. He rang or texted most days but Amber was busy at uni, living the college life. Occasionally she rang or texted back. Sometimes happy, sometimes not. Sometimes because she needed money or a place to crash for the night.

And he got that. But this…he would have thought she'd want him around for this.

'I could have been there for you.'

Gareth had had to stop himself five years ago from demanding she take the test there and then. Catherine's death had been devastating and the thought that Amber might have inherited the gene had been too much to bear. He hadn't been able to reach in and rip the cancer out of Catherine, but he could protect Amber from her mother's fate.

They could be forewarned. Forearmed.

But the oncologists and Amber's psychologist had counselled against it at such a young age. And he'd *known* they were right. Logically, he'd known that. She hadn't needed that extra burden at that point, not when she had probably been years away from making any concrete decisions over a potentially positive result.

But his fear hadn't been logical.

Amber may not have been his daughter by blood but he'd

been with Catherine since Amber had been a cute five-year-old with two missing front teeth and he loved her as fiercely as if she were his own.

She shook her head. 'I didn't want to…worry you.'

He gave her his best don't-kid-me look. 'You think I don't worry about you, Amber?'

Her eyes filled with tears then, so like her mother's, and his heart broke for the grief Amber had endured in such a short life.

'What am I going to do, Gareth? I have a forty to eighty per cent chance of developing breast cancer. Do I get a double mastectomy? Do I line up to have my uterus removed and never be able to have a baby?' She looked at him with those big green eyes swimming in tears. 'What man's going to want me with no boobs, Gareth?'

She started to cry again and Gareth stood, reaching for her and sweeping her into his arms. 'Shh,' he said, hugging her close just like when she'd been a kid and fallen off her bike, skinning her knee and denting her pride.

Back in the days when there hadn't been five years of angst and grief and blame between them.

'Hey,' he said, as he stroked her hair, letting her cry, raising his voice above the wrenching noise of it. 'Firstly, you and I are going back to the clinic together so we can have a nice long talk about options.'

He made a mental note to make the first available appointment. 'Secondly, these aren't decisions you're going to need to make for a long time, sweetheart. This just means we have to be more vigilant. And I'm going to be there for you every step of the way, okay?'

'Okay,' she said, and cried harder.

'Thirdly…' This was the hardest one. He didn't relish having to talk to Amber about sexuality and desire. She'd generally thought any topics like that were private and female and not up for discussion with her stepfather.

But if she'd been a patient asking these questions, searching for answers, he wouldn't have hesitated to reassure her.

Gareth prised her gently off his chest and looked down into her red swollen eyes. 'Do you think your mother losing a breast made me love her any less? Made her any less desirable to me as a woman?'

He half expected her to rebel. To screw up her face and say, 'Eww, gross, Gareth,' which had been pretty much her catchphrase from thirteen onwards. But she didn't, she just shook her head at him. 'But you already had a relationship with Mum. You had to love her regardless of her...boob situation.'

Gareth smiled at Amber's typical reluctance to use correct anatomical words. 'I loved your mother from the first moment I met her. And it had nothing to do with her *boobs*.'

'It's still not the same,' Amber dismissed.

Gareth squeezed her arms. 'Any man who can't see past your physical self to the amazing woman you are inside isn't worth your time, Amber. Life's short, sweetie, you don't need me to tell you that. Too short to waste on men who aren't worthy.'

Amber smiled up at him through her tears. She slid her hand onto his cheek and patted his stubble like she used to when she was little and had been endlessly fascinated by its scratchiness. She'd never known her father and Gareth's stubble had been intriguing. She dropped her hand.

'I don't think they make men like you any more.'

Gareth smiled down at Amber, feeling closer to her than he had in a long time. 'Yes, they do, sweetie,' he said. 'And I still have my service revolver for the others.'

She smiled again then pulled away, turning her back to him as she looked absently through the patches of glass to the hustle and bustle of the department.

'Do you think I'm vain for worrying about my boobs?' she asked eventually. 'About someone wanting me when so many women are dead? When Mum is dead?'

Gareth slid his hand onto her shoulder and gave it a squeeze. 'Of course not, Amba-San.' Her old nickname slipped out. She normally chided him for using it these days but not today. 'You can't think about something like this and not think about how it affects you in every way. But you are getting ahead of yourself sweetheart. Way ahead.'

Amber turned and nodded and Gareth's hand slipped away. 'I'm sorry. I guess the results freaked me out a little. They tried to talk to me at the clinic about them but I just ran.'

'It's okay, we'll go back there together in the next couple of days, okay?'

Amber nodded. 'Just promise me you'll find me the best plastic surgeon in the country to give me new boobs if or when this whole thing becomes a reality.'

Gareth smiled, encouraged by her *if*. 'I promise I'll find you the best breast man I can.'

Amber screwed up her nose and said, 'Eww, gross, Gareth,' but she was smiling and she walked easily into his arms, accepting his hug.

When they pulled apart he slipped his hands either side of her face and cradled it like he used to. 'How about you come over tonight? I don't get off till nine but we can get takeaway and watch one of those dreadful chick flicks you like so much.'

Amber laughed. 'Oh, the sacrifice.' She rubbed her cheek into his big palm for long moments before pulling away. 'It's okay. Carly knows. I'm going out with her tonight and drinking way too much tequila.'

Gareth nodded. The father in him wanted to caution her against drinking to excess but he'd been twenty himself once. And Carly was a very sensible young woman. If she knew the circumstances then Gareth had absolute faith she wouldn't let Amber get too messy. Those two had had each other's backs since they'd been nine.

'Okay,' he said. 'Are you sure you're going to be all right?'

Amber nodded. 'Talking with you helped.'

He smiled. 'You can always talk to me, Amba-San.'

'I know. Sorry I can be such an ingrate sometimes. It just still...gets me sometimes and I just don't know what to do with it. It makes me so...angry, you know?'

'Yeah,' Gareth said. He knew *exactly* how she felt. 'I know.'

There was a brief knock on the door and it opened. 'Gareth,' the triage nurse said, peeking her head around the door, 'assault victim, multiple injuries, blunt chest trauma, in a bad way. Ten minutes out.'

He looked at Amber. 'Sorry.'

She smiled and gave him a quick hug. 'It's fine. I'm already late and Carly will be waiting for me.'

'I'll call you tomorrow,' he said.

'Okay.'

'I love you, Amber,' he said.

She gave his stubble a pat again. 'Love you too,' she said, as she departed the room.

Gareth's gaze followed her, his heart beating a steady determined tattoo. Cancer couldn't take her too.

Billie almost collided with Amber as she hurried out of the handover room. 'Sorry,' Billie called after the young woman, who continued on but not before Billie had noticed the tear-streaked face.

Billie glanced up to find a grim-looking Gareth standing in the open doorway, tracking the woman's progress. Clearly something had transpired between them. Was it another nurse she hadn't met yet? Or another colleague? Or a patient's relative?

Whatever it was, it was obviously intense.

Her stomach twisted hard.

CHAPTER EIGHT

'YOU READY FOR THIS?'

Billie looked up from staring down at her gloves, the ambulance siren loud as it screeched to a halt metres from them. It echoed around the concrete and steel bay, reverberating against her chest, drumming through her veins.

She stiffened at Gareth's propriety. 'Yes.'

He still looked all kinds of grim. Was that him mentally preparing for what they were about to see or was it to do with the mysterious woman? A hot knot of emotion lodged in her chest and Billie realised she felt jealous. Which was utterly insane. She had no claim over him to justify jealousy. And it was hardly an appropriate time to feel the hot claw in her gut.

An assault victim was fighting for his life in the back of an ambulance, for crying out loud.

But it was there. It just *was*.

And his *concern* for her rankled. It was courteous and kind and thoughtful. And she hated it.

She didn't need his pity, his propriety or his patience.

Well…she didn't *want* them anyway. She didn't want him looking at her as some cot case to coddle and hand-hold and treat with kid gloves.

She didn't want him to look at her as a chore.

Not when she saw him in an entirely different light.

A paramedic opened the back door of the ambulance. 'It's going to be messy,' Gareth warned.

Billie's irritation ramped up another notch despite the strong stir of nausea in her gut. 'I know,' she snapped.

Did he really think she *didn't* know?

And then it was action stations as the paramedics hauled the gurney out of the back and pushed it quickly towards them, the intensive care paramedic reeling off a handover as they all accompanied the briskly moving trolley.

'Corey Wilson, twenty-two-year-old male, found in an alley in the city with multiple injuries, presumed assault. Unresponsive, bradycardic, hypotensive. Pupils unequal but reactive to light. Intubated on the scene, a litre of Hartmann's given, wide-bore IV access both arms.'

They entered the resus bay and Billie's hands shook as she helped get the beaten and bloodied young man across to the hospital trolley. An endotracheal tube protruded from his mouth and a hard collar protected his neck during the process.

Within a trice the ambulance gurney was gone and Billie was staring into Corey's grotesquely bruised face. Dried blood was smeared everywhere, his eyes swollen and ringed in black and purple. Her stomach turned over.

His shirt, split up the middle by a pair of paramedic shears, hung down his side, revealing more blood and bruising on his chest as ECG dots were slapped in place.

Denise Haig, the emergency consultant, who hadn't yet gone home for the day, barked orders at everyone. 'Let's get him assessed and to CT,' she said.

The oxygen saturations on the monitor were decreased and Denise looked at Billie and said, 'Listen to his chest.'

Billie fought against the urge to turn away, fought the pounding in her own chest, concentrated on her breathing, staring at Corey's chest rather than his face as she shoved her stethoscope in her ears and listened. She felt

Gareth's eyes on her but refused to look at him as she quickly assessed both lung fields.

She was part of this team and she would work with them to save Corey, no matter how affected she was by his battered body.

'Chest sounds decreased on the right, almost absent,' Billie reported. 'Lot of crepitus.'

Which was hardly surprising. Corey looked like he'd taken a real beating to the chest, broken ribs were a given. The oxygen saturations fell further and Corey's heart rate, which had been worryingly slow, suddenly shot up.

'Check his JVP,' Denise said.

Billie was on autopilot now, the adrenaline in her system keeping her going, elevating her to a higher place, allowing her to do her work yet stay removed from the horror of it.

The hard collar obscured his neck veins from her view and she had to peer through the side window to assess it. His jugular bulged ominously. 'Pressure elevated,' Billie said. She flicked her gaze to his windpipe, which appeared, from what she could see, to be skewed to one side. 'Trachea's deviated.'

Denise nodded. 'Tension pneumo. Put in a chest tube, stat,' she ordered.

Billie's hands shook as someone thrust a pair of sterile gloves at her. No time for a proper surgical scrub. This was *emergency* medicine with a capital E. The build-up of air in Corey's chest from a fractured rib puncturing his lung was affecting his venous return and he needed urgent chest decompression.

She looked up as she shoved her right hand into the right glove. *Gareth.* He nodded and smiled at her. 'Good to go?'

Concern radiated from his eyes and Billie was determined to dispel it immediately. She nodded back. 'You got the pack?'

He dragged a small mobile trolley over with all she would

need already laid out. He reached over and squirted some liquid antibiotic on Corey's chest and briskly cleaned a section of skin mid-axilla with some gauze. When it was reasonably clear of dried blood he doused the area again with the brown antiseptic agent.

'Your turn,' he said.

Billie moved closer, reaching for the scalpel. In a normal clinical setting she'd be gowned and masked, she'd inject local, the patient would be draped. But Corey didn't have that time, this was down and dirty. This was life and death.

She was conscious of the screaming of alarms around her and the battering of her pulse through her head as she quickly located the right spot. This wasn't her first chest tube, although it was her first tension pneumo.

Billie made a small incision. Blood welled from the cut and she forced her shaking knees to lock.

'Forceps,' she said, concentrating hard on keeping her voice steady as she handed the scalpel back to Gareth.

He passed her the forceps and she bluntly dissected down to the pleura, puncturing it with the tip of the forceps. She inserted her finger into the hole and swept away a soft clot she could feel there, her stomach revolting at the action.

'Tube,' she said, not looking at Gareth, not looking at anything other than her finger in someone's chest and concentrating on not throwing up. He handed it to her and she placed the tip into the hole, using the forceps to feed it in, advancing it until all the drainage holes lining the tip were inside the chest cavity.

The whole procedure was accomplished in less than a minute and her hands shook as she stripped the gloves off.

The oxygen sats improved almost immediately and Corey's heart rate decreased.

'Well done,' Gareth murmured, just loud enough amidst the chaos for only the two of them to hear. He handed her a pair of regular gloves and connected a drain bottle to the end of the tube.

Their celebration of her competency was short-lived, however, as suddenly a torrent of blood flowed out the tube, draining quickly into the collection device. Before Billie's eyes it filled to halfway and she swallowed back a retch as more rushed in, forming a thick red sludge.

'Haemo-pneumo,' Gareth said.

Denise nodded. 'Not surprising. Push two units of O-neg.'

'Pupils are blown.'

'Right,' Denise said to Gareth. 'Get on to Cat Scan. Tell them we're coming around. Where the hell is Neuro?' she asked no one in particular.

They were snapping the side rails in place when the monitor alarmed again. The heart rate, which had started to slow down again after the chest tube insertion, suddenly flicked into a dangerous tachy-arrythmia. Denise felt through the side windows in the collar. 'We've lost his pulse.'

The rails came down again as Denise issued another rapid-fire set of orders, rattling off some drug doses.

Billie couldn't stop looking at the drainage from the chest, the bottle was three-quarters full now. She couldn't block out the screaming of the alarms. Corey's life was literally draining away.

Just like Jessica's had that night.

He was twenty two and dying. It was too cruel. She wanted to throw up, faint *and* burst into tears.

'Billie!'

Denise's shrill command broke through her inertia. Billie looked at her. 'I said start chest compressions.'

Billie nodded. She faltered as she placed her gloved hands on Corey's chest, looking down at the dried blood streaking his ribs and belly. 'I'll do it,' Gareth said, stepping forward.

'No!' Gareth's interference suddenly snapped Billie out of it. She didn't care how much she wanted to stop and throw

up right now. She needed to prove she could do this. To Denise. *To Gareth*. To her long-dead sister.

And most especially to herself.

She had to know she could get past her physical reaction to the gore and rawness of emergency medicine. She
had to know that she could pigeonhole the human tragedy
that threatened to overwhelm and cripple her and do what
needed to be done.

They worked on Corey for forty-five minutes. Billie sought
and found her earlier state of removal as she pounded on
his chest. Going through the motions, following directions
but all the time placing her mental side, her emotional self,
elsewhere. Buried somewhere at the back of her brain.

Not thinking about Corey or his age or what his last moments must have been like or that he was dying surrounded
by strangers. Not thinking about the drainage bottle being
changed. Or the repeated unsuccessful zaps to the chest. Removing herself from the arrival of his mates and the shout-
ing and loud angry sobs as they were told he was critical
and they had to wait.

Just doing her job.

Her arms ached. Her muscles screamed at her. Gareth
offered to take over but she declined. Several others offered
as well but she refused.

And even when Denise called time of death and everyone stopped and stepped away, it took a moment or two for
Billie to realise, continuing the compressions until Gareth
touched her arm and said, 'You can stop now, Billie.'

She'd been so focused on the action, on breathing with
each one, on the way her gloved fingers looked against
Corey's sternum, she'd zoned out everyone else.

Billie looked around at the defeated faces, the downcast
eyes and stepped back herself.

Denise stripped off her gloves. 'Thanks, everyone,' she said.

* * *

Half an hour later Denise approached Gareth. 'I need you in on the chat with the relatives,' she said.

Gareth nodded. They'd been waiting for Corey's parents to arrive. His mates were still in the waiting room, subdued now as they waited for news about their friend, but as it was against hospital policy to provide information to people who weren't relatives, they hadn't yet been told of Corey's passing.

'You going to do it now?' he asked.

'No.' She shook her head. 'Billie's going to do it. But I'll be there. And so will you.'

Gareth glanced over at Billie, who was writing up Corey's notes. He'd sat in on one too many of these not to know how harrowing they were—he wouldn't wish them on his worst enemy. He certainly wouldn't wish it on a woman he'd come perilously close to bedding a handful of days ago.

'Come on, Denise,' he murmured, 'do you really think she's up to it? Don't you think she's been through enough trauma today?'

Demise nodded briskly. 'I know. But if she wants to do this job, then talking to relatives is all part and parcel of it. Better to get the first one over and done with.'

He quirked an eyebrow at her. He'd worked with Denise for five years. She was good. Fair. Shrewd. And a little old school. 'Tough love?'

'Got to sort the wheat from the chaff.'

'You don't have to do it tonight. She should have knocked off thirty minutes ago.'

Denise shrugged. 'Billie's a good doctor but she's not cut out for this. I know it and I suspect you know it too. It's better that she figures that out early than waste years of her life specialising in a field that doesn't suit her talents because she watched too many ER dramas on TV.'

Gareth shot her a look full of recrimination. 'Steady on.'

'Oh, come on, Gareth, don't tell me you haven't seen them year after year, lining up to work here because it's been glamorised on television.'

Sure, he had, but those residents rarely lasted the distance. 'I think her reasons are a little deeper than that.'

'Okay. Maybe you're right. Maybe it's because she felt a calling or because Mummy and Daddy hot-shot surgeons want her to do it. Whatever the reason is behind her wanting to screw up her life, it's still a bad idea.'

Gareth had to admit that Denise made very valid points but he believed there were some things that people just had to work out for themselves. And that Billie's reasons for setting her sights on emergency medicine *were* a lot more complicated than watching too much television medical drama.

'I think she'll figure it out,' he said.

'This should help.'

'She's due off,' he reiterated.

'She can do this then go home,' Denise said briskly, her mind clearly made up. 'You coming or do you want me to grab one of the other nurses who were in there?'

Gareth sighed. No way could he abandon Billie to Denise's tough love. He put down his pen. 'I'm coming.'

CHAPTER NINE

BILLIE LOOKED DOWN at the notes. Her hands were still trembling and there was a persistent numbness inside but writing the notes helped.

And when she got home—which *could not* be soon enough—there was a bottle of wine in the fridge that would also help.

But for now it was pen on paper.

And she took comfort in that. Writing notes she *could* do. She could be clinical and detached in notes. She could look back at the situation and couch it in neat medical terms. The words formed a mental barrier between the chronology of the event and the *emotion* of the event. They allowed her to report the frantic last moments of Corey Wilson's life in a simple, detached way that she only hoped stayed with her when she got home tonight.

'Billie.'

Billie looked up from the chart as Denise approached, with Gareth hovering behind. They looked very serious and a prickle shot up her spine as she wondered what kind of hell they had in store for her now.

'Corey's parents are here. I know your shift finished half an hour ago but as you were involved in the resus I thought it would be good experience for you to talk to them.'

Billie stilled. Watching Corey Wilson die had been hard enough. Now she had to deliver the dreadful news to his parents too? She'd rather stick herself in the eye with a poker than have to tell these people their twenty-two-year-old son was dead.

She glanced at Gareth, whose face was carefully neutral.

'His parents are going to want to talk to people who were there at the end,' Denise said. 'And it's vital that we provide that for them. That we put aside our emotions and feelings and do whatever we can to make it a little bit easier for them.'

Denise stopped for a moment, as if she was allowing some time for that message to sink in.

'One of the most important things you'll ever do as a doctor is tell someone that their loved one has died,' Denise said. 'It's never easy, especially in sudden death, and it doesn't get any easier, no matter what anyone tells you. But it is a skill you need to learn. I'll be there,' she said. 'So will Gareth.'

Billie nodded. She knew Denise was right. That whatever she was feeling was nothing compared to what those two strangers waiting in that room off the triage desk with the mismatched furniture and the bland prints on the wall were feeling.

'Okay,' she murmured huskily, and rose on legs that felt like cement.

Billie sat on her couch two hours later, her hand still trembling as she sipped on her third glass of wine. She'd been home for an hour, and apart from turning on the fire and collecting the wine bottle and a glass she hadn't moved from this position.

Feelings of helplessness hit her in waves and she blinked back tears, rocking slightly as she fanned her face, breathing in and out through pursed lips as if she were running an ante-natal class. And then the words that she'd written in Corey's chart would come back to her and she would calm down again, holding onto every sentence like she had when she'd been in with his parents, repeating what she'd memorised from the notes to cut herself off from the emotion, to stop herself from breaking down in front of them.

But then the echo of Chantelle Wilson's wounded howl would break through the cool clinical words and the waves would buffet her again. It had been chilling. And the way she'd crumpled, folded in on herself...Billie had seen her mother do that when her sister had died and hated that she was the one inflicting the wound on another mother.

Billie had seen a few deaths in her first year but they'd been elderly people or terminal patients. Not like this.

Not this total waste of a human life that had barely begun.

She'd never looked into the eyes of a mother and had to use the D word. Denise had cautioned about using euphemisms for death as they'd walked to the room. People were in a highly emotional state, they needed clarity, she said.

But even so it had dropped like a stone into the atmosphere of that room and then the howl had sucked all the oxygen away.

A loud knock at the door interrupted her pity party and she flinched, dragging her gaze away from the fire. 'Billie, it's Gareth.' Another knock. 'Open up.'

Tears formed in her eyes again and she concentrated on whistling air in and out of her lips. She was barely hanging on here. If she saw him, if he was kind, she'd break down for sure.

'Billie!' Another sharp rap on the door. 'I know you're in there. I swear I'm going to kick this door in if you don't open it.'

Billie believed him. Unfortunately, Mrs Gianna next door was probably already calling the police due to Gareth's insistent knocking.

The last thing she needed was a police car pulling up in her driveway.

She took another fortifying sip of her wine before rising on legs that felt like wet string, desperately reaching for the cool detachment of her notes. She scrubbed a hand over her face to dispel the dampness on her cheeks as she walked to the door.

Billie drew in a steadying breath as she placed her hand on the knob. *You can do this.*

'Hi,' she said, as she opened the door, the cold night air like a perfect balm on her simmering emotions.

Gareth had expected to find a tear-stained wreck. But Billie looked exactly the same as when she'd left the hospital. Same jeans and shirt clinging in all the right places, a little on the pale side, her freckles standing out but a look of stoic resolve embedded on her features.

'Hi,' he said. 'I called by to check on you.'

She nodded. 'I'm fine.'

Except the tiny crack in her husky voice and the way she had to quell the tremble of her bottom lip with her teeth told him differently.

Gareth's heart went out to her. Incidents like this took their emotional toll on everyone involved. They left a little chink in a person's soul. And those chinks could build up if they were ignored.

'Billie…' he said softly. 'His head injuries were too massive. He probably coned. Nobody could have saved his life.'

'I know that,' she said testily.

He inclined his head. 'I know you do.'

He watched as Billie's throat bobbed. 'Don't be nice to me,' she warned. 'I can't deal with that.'

'Okay…' Gareth buried his hands in the pockets of his leather jacket. 'What are you doing?'

'Getting drunk.'

He smiled. 'Very Australian of you.' He earned a ghost of a smile back. 'You know, you could have joined us at Oscar's. A bunch of us went there at the end of the shift.'

Oscar's was the bar across the street from St Luke's. A very profitable business, especially after shifts like these.

She shrugged. 'I didn't feel like company.'

Gareth understood the sentiment but he'd learned through his years in the military that drinking alone after the kind of day she'd had was not good.

What she needed was camaraderie. To be with people who understood the horror of what she'd been through.

'It helps to talk it out with people who know, you know?'

Billie nodded. 'Yeah. But I *really* didn't feel like company.'

And Ashworth-Keyes' did not break down in front of people.

Gareth regarded her for long moments—it looked like *he* was going to be her sounding board tonight. He knew he could sure as hell do with some alcoholic fortification. Between Amber's news and the bloodied trauma of Corey's death, a beer would really hit the spot right now.

And, besides, there was no way he could leave her to drown her sorrows solo.

'Do you have beer?' he asked.

'Yes.'

'Can I join you?'

'If you want.' She shrugged.

Billie turned on her heel and left him to follow her. She was already feeling stronger for the distraction of something else, someone else to think about.

'Take a seat,' she threw over her shoulder, as she passed the lounge room and headed for the kitchen. The house was dark, she hadn't bothered with lights, but she knew the low glow from the fire provided enough radiance for Gareth to see where he was going.

She opened the fridge door and plucked a beer from the back. She didn't know what type it was. Some boutique beer her father favoured and had left in her fridge for the odd time he dropped around. Usually to check how she was going with her studies and whether she was being a good little Ashworth-Keyes. Telling her how proud they were of her, how proud *Jessica* would be of her.

Billie entered the lounge room, noting Gareth had succumbed to the toastiness of the room and slipped out of his jacket. He was wearing a long-sleeved knit shirt like she was, except his had a round neck as opposed to her V. It obscured the fascinating hollow at the base of his throat, the one she'd used to ground herself during her harrowing talk with the Wilsons whenever emotion had threatened to overwhelm her.

She also noticed he'd chosen to sit on the three-seater where she'd been sitting, and not on one of the single chairs.

Billie handed him the beer as she plonked down next to him, leaving a discreet *just two colleagues talking* distance between them. She picked up her glass of wine and turned slightly side on to him. He followed suit so they were facing each other.

She raised her glass towards him. 'To traumatic shifts.'

Gareth smiled. 'To *getting through* traumatic shifts,' he said, tapping his beer bottle against the side of her glass.

They both drank, their gazes turning to the fake flames of the gas fire bathing the room in a cosy glow. For long moments silence filled the space between them.

Billie looked down into the deep red of her Merlot, the flame reflected in the surface. 'I can't do it,' she announced quietly.

Gareth turned his head. 'You were fine, Billie. And you were great with the Wilsons.'

At another time his praise might have filled her with pride but it was little consolation right now. She looked at him. 'Denise knows I can't do it.'

He shrugged. 'So prove her wrong.'

Billie shook her head. 'She thrives on it. *You* thrive on it.'

'And you don't?'

She shook her head. 'It turns my stomach.'

Gareth watched the reflection of the flames glow in her eyes as he asked her the same question he'd asked her before. 'So...why *are* you doing it, Billie?'

Blind Freddie could see that her heart wasn't in it.

'Oh...now,' she said, taking a sip of her wine. 'That's...'

'Long and complicated?' he said, repeating her answer from the last time he'd asked.

She gave a half-smile. 'Yes.'

Gareth held his beer up to the light. The fluid level had barely moved from the top after his two mouthfuls. 'I'm not going anywhere for a while.'

Billie looked into the fire. Where did she even start? She'd spent so much of her life pretending this was what she wanted that it was hard to remember sometimes why it wasn't.

'My sister died when she was sixteen. In a car accident. She was quite the rebel, always in trouble for something. She sneaked out of her window one night and went joy riding with some friends and never came back again.'

Gareth shut his eyes at the news. What an awful time that must have been for Billie. For her family. 'I'm sorry,' he murmured.

'Thank you.'

'What was her name?'

'Jess,' Billie said. 'Jessica.'

'Were you close?'

Billie nodded. 'She was two years older than me but, yeah...we were close. Close enough to confide in me that not only didn't she want to carry on the mighty Ashworth-Keyes tradition of being a surgeon, she didn't want to be a doctor at all. She wanted to be a kindy teacher.'

'And she couldn't tell your parents that?'

Billie snorted. 'Ashworth-Keyes' are *not* kindergarten teachers.'

'Even if it makes them happy?'

She shook her head. 'What on earth has happiness got to do with it? Ashworth-Keyes' are *surgeons*. My parents, my uncles, an assortment of cousins, my grandfather, my great-grandfather. From the cradle our glorious future in a gleaming operating theatre is talked about and planned incessantly. Everything revolves around that. There is no other career path in my family.'

'Oh, I see,' Gareth said, even though he really didn't.

As a father all he cared about was Amber being happy and well adjusted and contributing to society. But he *was* beginning to understand the conditioning that Billie had been subjected to.

'Of course, my father thought he would have sons, like all of his brothers had, to carry on the family tradition, but unfortunately he was saddled with girls. Still, to give him his due, he took it on the chin and settled into indoctrinating us too. He wasn't going to be *the* Ashworth-Keyes to break with tradition just because he had *girls* who might want to do something unpredictable and girly.'

'It sounds like there was a lot of pressure on you.'

Billie nodded. 'Jessica didn't know how to tell them. And she didn't want to be a disappointment to them. So she just kept telling them what they wanted to hear. That she was going to do medicine. That she was going to become a cardiothoracic surgeon just like them.'

'And would she have eventually, do you think, had she lived?'

Billie shrugged. 'I don't know. She was certainly bright enough. Straight As, even with no studying. Not like me, who had to work for my As. But she was very strong-headed. I doubt she would have done anything she didn't want to do. She was just keeping them sweet, I guess, putting off the inevitable confrontation.'

'Sounds like she was trying to tell them something with her rebellion.'

Billie nodded. 'Yes. I think all her reckless behaviour was really just a cry for help. I think it was her way of trying to goad them into disowning her and then she'd be free to do what she wanted.'

'But it didn't work out so well?'

Billie thought about that awful night. The police. Waking to crying at midnight. Her crumpled mother, a lot like Mrs Wilson. Her disbelieving father. 'No. It didn't.'

Gareth waited for a few moments. Took a mouthful of his beer. 'And so you decided to step into her shoes,' he said eventually. 'To be the daughter they thought she was going to be.'

Billie looked at him sharply. 'Yes.'

He nodded. 'Did you even want to be a doctor at all?'

'Of course,' she said derisively. 'I'm an Ashworth-Keyes, aren't I?'

'Billie.'

The reproach in his voice pulled her up. 'Yes,' she said. 'I did. I've always wanted to be one.'

'But not a cardiothoracic surgeon, right?'

Billie shook her head. 'Not a surgeon at all, I'm afraid. Or an ER consultant. I wanted to be a GP.'

CHAPTER TEN

GARETH LOOKED AT HER, surprised. A general practitioner? The complete opposite of an emergency physician. But he knew, instantly, it was the right fit for her.

Billie was an *excellent* doctor. He'd watched her with patients. She liked to take her time with them, which they loved but wasn't always conducive to the ER. And it wasn't laziness, it was thoroughness.

And her bedside manner was one of the best he'd ever witnessed.

She enjoyed the little stuff that the others had no patience for, the attention to detail, and she loved a medical mystery, loved getting to the bottom of what was making a person sick.

He knew without a shadow of doubt that she'd make a brilliant GP. And, God knew, there weren't enough of them.

'What's wrong with being a GP? They're just as vital to the health care system.'

Billie snorted. Her father would have apoplexy at hearing such sacrilege. 'Ashworth-Keyes' aren't—'

'GPs,' Gareth finished off with a grimace. 'And you never told them either?'

She shook her head. 'I was relying on Jessica being the trail blazer. Rocking the boat first, upsetting the apple cart, and then I could sneak in behind, wanting to be a GP. I figured they'd be so grateful I still wanted to be in the medical profession at all that they'd give me a pass. But then my mother…she completely fell apart after Jessica died. She didn't operate for an entire year.'

Billie paused and rubbed her arms, feeling suddenly cold again. 'She was just this…shell, this…husk. She'd just sit for hours and stare at the wall. Apart from looking at my sister's dead body, it was the most frightening thing I've ever seen.'

Gareth slid his hand onto hers. He thought back to how emotionally whammied he'd been when Catherine had died. It had only been his duty to Amber, her emotional distress and neediness that had kept him from spiralling into his own pit of despair. Amber had looked at him sometimes with fear in her eyes, fear that he just might sink into depression and then what would she do?

So he didn't. But there had been days when it had been very hit and miss.

'I'm sure it was,' he murmured.

'Finally, she came out of it. Finally, she came back to her old self, started seeing patients, resumed her surgical schedule, but she never seemed quite as robust again, like she could still break at any second. And somewhere along the way she decided that *I* was going to take Jessica's place. That *I* was going to live the life that Jessica had supposedly wanted because that would be the perfect way to honour my sister. She became obsessed with it and there were so many times when she seemed so fragile I just couldn't tell her the truth so I…went along with it. I couldn't bear the thought of her…going back to that dark place… Pretty pathetic, huh?'

Gareth shook his head. He understood the weight of parental expectations and the things people did to live up to them, and that was without a tonne of grief behind it all.

His father had never quite forgiven him for eschewing a job as his building apprentice to become a nurse. *Real men weren't nurses,* according to him. It was only joining the military that had made it more respectable in his eyes.

And, he guessed, GPs weren't real doctors to Billie's high-flying parents. 'I think we all do things we don't want to in order to keep from disappointing the people we love,' he said.

Billie nodded. It sounded like Gareth had some experience in that department too. 'What did you do?' she asked.

Gareth withdrew his hand and looked away from her as he took a long drag on his beer. When he was done he rolled it back and forth in his hands, watching the firelight catch the gold in the label.

'I became NUM of the ER,' he said eventually.

Billie blinked. He hadn't *wanted* to be NUM? Now, *that* she hadn't been expecting. She'd have thought that would be the pinnacle of his civilian career.

'For who?' she asked his downcast head, as his inspection of the shiny label continued.

Gareth glanced up at Billie. The firelight gilded the warm brown of her eyes and added pink to her cheeks. 'My wife.'

Billie stilled. His *wife?* He was *married?* But…she'd been in the tearoom when a couple of the junior nurses had been swooning over him and had gleaned there that he wasn't married. *And* he didn't wear a ring. Neither did he have a white mark where one had recently been taken off.

So then he must be divorced.

He had to be. Gareth had been nothing but honourable. She couldn't believe that he would have kissed her—no matter what psychological state she'd been in—if he hadn't been free and clear to do so.

She felt ill just thinking about it.

And the way she'd come on to him. His frankness about the…*thing* between them. He wouldn't have allowed that, acknowledged their vibe, if he'd been married.

He wouldn't be here now, surely?

Billie swallowed hard, battling against the invective raring to leap from her throat, and simply asked, 'Why?'

He frowned. 'Why did I do it for her?'

Billie nodded, still fighting the urge to demand he clarify his marital status immediately.

Gareth steeled himself to answer. He didn't talk about Catherine often, especially to colleagues or people he barely knew. But he did know Billie. Probably better than a lot of people he'd worked with for years.

And he knew her even better after the events of today, after their talk tonight.

Besides…there was just something about a fire that encouraged confidences.

'Because she was dying,' he said, capturing Billie's gaze. 'And she was happy and proud and excited for me and because she knew it would be more regular working hours for Amber after she was gone.'

'Amber?'

'Our daughter.'

It all clicked into place then for Billie. He was a widower. He had a daughter. Suddenly she knew Amber was the young woman she'd seen him with at teatime. 'She was there today…Amber…'

'Yes.'

Relief flooded through her. Cool and soothing. 'I'm sorry…about your wife. How long ago?'

'Five years.

'What cancer was it?'

'Breast,' Gareth said. 'From diagnosis to her death was five months.'

Billie shook her head sadly. Cancer was a real bitch. 'How old was she?'

'Catherine,' Gareth said. He wanted Billie to know her name. 'Her name was Catherine and she was forty. We'd been married for ten years.'

'How did Amber take it?'

He shrugged. 'She was fifteen. She blamed me.'

Fifteen. About the same age Billie had been when Jessica had died. Not the same thing as losing your mother but still an utterly devastating experience.

'Why did she blame you?'

'I was on tour in the Middle East when Catherine found the lump. She waited until I came home almost two months later before she did anything about it.'

Billie couldn't contain the gasp that escaped her throat at that particular piece of information. 'Why did she wait that long?'

Gareth felt the old resentment stir. 'For a lot of reasons— none of them very sound. She didn't want to worry me or Amber. She didn't want to cause a fuss and have me brought home over something she was sure was nothing. She didn't really think it was anything because she'd always had lumpy breasts. She didn't want to go through the investigations alone…'

Billie watched as he ticked each one off on a finger. The firelight caressed the spare planes of his face, picking up the grooves on either side of his mouth, the whiskers shadowy there. She almost reached out and traced the fascinating brackets.

'The list goes on,' Gareth continued, and he sounded so grim and bleak Billie had the strangest urge to put her arms around him. 'Not that it would apparently have mattered that much, the cancer was so aggressive. But, in her bad moments, Amber felt betrayed by Catherine. She felt that her mother had put me and my job—*"the stinking army"*, I believe were her exact words—first. That Catherine had loved me more than her own flesh and blood.'

Billie winced. 'That must have been rough.'

He shrugged. 'She was a grieving teenager. She was lashing out. I was just the dad. The stepdad at that.'

'She's not your biological child?'

He took a sip of his beer, shaking his head. 'No. She

was five when Catherine and I met. Cute as a button. Both of them were.'

He grinned suddenly, raising the bottle once more, his lips pressed to the rim, still smiling. And it was so sexy, so masculine her stomach took a little dive. He obviously had wonderful memories.

'You loved her.'

He nodded as he looked directly at her. 'Of course. She filled up my heart.'

Billie was touched by his sincerity. Not some stupid fake Valentine's Day sentiment but something deep and honest. She'd never known love like that.

'I'm sorry,' she said again, topping up her wine and taking a sip, watching him over the rim of her glass.

He shrugged and looked back at his beer but not before she glimpsed a dark shadow eclipsing the blue of his eyes. It spoke of pain and grief and *stuff* that hid in dark recesses, hijacking a person when they least expected it.

How long had the grief consumed him? And was that what had caused the incident that Helen had spoken about on her first day, the one that had seen him demoted?

She knew it was none of her business but sipping on her wine, feeling warm and floaty, she knew she was sufficiently lubed to ask. 'So why aren't you still NUM? I understand there was some kind of…incident that resulted in your demotion?'

Gareth looked up at her sharply. An *incident?* 'Where'd you hear that?'

She shrugged. 'The grapevine.'

Gareth was speechless for a moment then he laughed. It was good to know that some things at St Luke's never changed. Clearly it didn't matter if there was no ammunition for gossip—people would just make it up.

He drained his beer. 'There was no *incident*,' he said, as he placed his empty bottle on the table. 'Amber became independent. She graduated from high school, went off to college, got a car and a part-time job. I stepped down because I didn't need to work regular hours any more.'

Billie frowned. 'You just…stepped down?'

'Yep.'

'But…why? Surely managing an emergency department in a tertiary hospital is a prestigious career opportunity? How do you just walk away from that?'

Gareth could hear the incredulity in her voice. He guessed for someone who had grown up where prestige mattered above everything else, it was a big deal.

'It's easy when you don't care about prestige.'

Billie blinked. She'd had prestige rammed down her throat from a very early age. No matter how many times she'd fantasised about telling her parents where they could stick their aspirations for her, she'd never for a moment imagined that she'd walk away from them. And Jessica's death had made that near on impossible anyway.

She wished she had even an ounce of Gareth's resolve.

'But you must be highly qualified?'

'Sure. I spent a decade in field hospitals, triaging the wounded fresh from battle. I did multiple tours in the Middle East.'

'And you really didn't want to be NUM with all *that* experience?'

He shook his head. 'Nope, I *really* didn't. Being in charge of a civilian unit is not like being in the military. There's too much paperwork and being stuck in an office or going to round after round of meetings.'

Billie nodded. Gareth had obviously been very hands-on during his overseas tours. He exuded vitality and energy and she could just imagine him in head-to-toe khaki under the blades of a chopper with an injured soldier lying on a gurney as the sand whipped up around her.

He certainly strode around St Luke's like a man very

comfortable in his environment. Like there was nothing that could be thrown at him that he hadn't already seen.

Somehow she couldn't quite picture him sitting in a white-walled office at some dreary quality or bed-management meeting.

'I guess St Luke's must be a little tame for you.'

'Nah. I've had more than enough excitement to last a lifetime.'

'But you thrive on it.' She'd said it earlier and it seemed even more so now. 'Why didn't you join up again?'

'I have to be here. For Amber.'

Especially now. Amber needed him to be here more than ever at the moment.

'It was okay being away for long periods of time while Catherine was still alive but I'm *it* now. I'm her only family. I can't abandon her even if she is independent and doesn't need me like she did when she was fifteen. And besides…' he rubbed his fingers along his jaw '…trauma medicine, field medicine…it's tough. Mentally tough. I have enough images in my head to fuel nightmares for the rest of my days. I don't see the point in adding to them.'

Goosebumps broke out on Billie's arms at the rasp of scraped whiskers. Her nipples followed suit. He was looking at her with shadows in his eyes again. Her heart almost stopped in her chest as she thought about the things he must have seen. The danger he'd been in.

'Were you scared?'

Gareth shook his head at Billie's husky question. 'I was never near the action. I was safe.'

She quirked an eyebrow. 'Are you ever truly safe in a war zone?'

He gave her a half-smile. 'We were safe.'

The smile played on his mouth and her gaze dropped to inspect it. Orange glow from the flames licked across his lips and she had the sudden urge to try them out. See if they were cool like the beer or scorching hot like the fire.

Billie had her money on the latter and suddenly felt pretty hot herself. 'Do you want another beer?' she asked, as the silence grew between them.

Gareth roused himself. Two beers around this woman would not be a wise move. He'd been dreaming about her in his bed for days now. The last thing he needed was anything that loosened his inhibitions and ruined his common sense. 'No. I should get going.'

Billie quelled the urge to protest the notion out loud.

She didn't want him to go. And she didn't think he wanted to go either.

He hadn't come in and sat opposite her and spent the whole time lecturing her about getting too involved in her job while drinking tea. He'd sat next to her, drunk a beer, listened to her talk.

And he'd been right. It was better to be around people who understood how you were feeling after a particularly harrowing day at work. People who had been right there, side by side with you.

They were debriefing. Being human.

But she wanted more. And maybe, for tonight—after everything she'd been through today—that was possible?

His palm was flat against his leg and Billie tentatively slid her hand onto his. 'Don't go.'

CHAPTER ELEVEN

GARETH LOOKED DOWN at Billie's hand. It was pale compared to his. There were no rings. No nail polish. No fuss. Just like the rest of her.

His heart thrummed in his chest. Not just at her touch but at what she was offering. He swallowed hard. His interest was already making itself felt inside his underwear.

There were only so many denials in him.

He looked up at her, his speech ready to go on his lips, the words he'd said to her the other morning in the car about being in different places easy to repeat. But she didn't give him the chance. She'd edged closer, pushed her hand higher.

'Gareth,' she murmured.

And any words he'd been about to say died on his lips as she pressed her mouth to his.

He sucked in a breath at her boldness and his senses filled with her. Not banana daiquiri this time. Something much more seductive. Red wine and lip gloss. Every nerve ending in his belly snapped taut as her mouth opened, her tongue touched his bottom lip. She pressed herself closer, her thigh aligning with his, her shoulder brushing his.

'Kiss me,' she whispered, her lips leaving his, travelling along the line of his jaw, nuzzling his earlobe, pulling it into her mouth. A hot flush of goosebumps prickled at his skin and he shut his eyes to their seduction.

'Kiss me,' she repeated, her breath hot in his ear, her

voice a sexy whimper, full and wanton. 'I know I shouldn't want you,' she groaned, her lips heading back to his mouth. 'But I can't stop.'

Her mouth claimed his again and there was nothing light and teasing about it. She opened her mouth and dragged him in, sucking him into the kiss and dumping him in the middle of a thousand carnal delights.

The slim thread of his resistance snapped so loudly Gareth swore it could be heard ricocheting off the walls. He groaned, stabbed his fingers into her hair and yanked her head closer.

'Damn it, Billie.'

And then *he* had the con.

The kiss was his to master and he did, taking control, steering the course, opening his mouth wide and demanding she do the same. Seeking her tongue and finding it, duelling with it. He grabbed her then, sliding his hands around her waist, pulling her towards him, putting his hand on a knee, parting her legs, urging her to straddle him, which she did with complete abandon, rubbing herself against him as their hips aligned perfectly.

Her hands glided to his cheeks as he settled her onto him and from her vantage point above him she returned his kiss. Twisting her head to meet his demands, moaning when his tongue thrust inside her. Would this be how she sounded when his tongue thrust inside her at a point significantly lower than her mouth?

Would she moan? Would she whimper? Would she gasp?

Would she squirm against him like she was now, trying to ramp up the friction between them by rubbing herself back and forth along the length of his erection?

He didn't know. But he wanted to find out.

'Shirt,' she gasped, against his mouth.

Shirt.

A one-word cold shower.

Gareth dug his fingertips into her hips as she reached for the hem of his shirt, battling the demons that told him this was a bad idea, praying they wouldn't win, hoping they would.

He held fast, trapping her between his body and the barrier of his arms. She squirmed in protest, trying to move, to strip him of his shirt. His pants. His sanity.

But he knew if he didn't stop this now, he wouldn't stop at all. Once her hands were on his bare, naked flesh, once his were on hers, he was going to be a goner for sure.

'Billie,' he panted, 'stop.'

Billie shook her head. 'No, no.' She kissed his neck, her hot tongue running up the length of it. 'Please…no.'

Gareth shut his eyes, trying not to think about how good her tongue would feel running up the length of something else.

Her hands reached for his pecs and he covered them with his own, capturing them against his chest and refusing to let them move, to cause any kind of rub or friction.

His libido just wasn't that strong at the moment.

'Billie…' he murmured in her ear, as she collapsed against him in frustration, 'we can't do this.'

Billie couldn't believe what she was hearing. They were so close to getting naked and doing the wild thing. And he wanted it as much as she did, she knew he did.

Why couldn't they do this? Why was he being so damn honourable?

'Why not?' she asked. 'I know you want to.'

Gareth shut his eyes and asked the universe for patience to be forthcoming—ASAP.

'Of course I want to, Billie,' he said, keeping his voice low, turning his head so his lips brushed her hair. He sat with her there for long moments. He needed her to know that this wasn't about what he wanted.

He shifted then, applying pressure to her hips, urging

her to sit back a little. Somehow along the way her pony-tail had loosened from its clasp, her hair falling forward to form a curtain around her face, and he pushed it back so he could see her.

'But you've been drinking,' he said, peering into her face. With her back to the fire it was heavily shadowed. Her eyes were dark, taupe puddles and he couldn't tell what she was thinking. 'So have I. This isn't the kind of decision we should be making now.'

Billie snorted. 'I've had three glasses of wine, Gareth. I'm hardly messy drunk.'

'And as you well know, consent can't be given under the influence of drugs or alcohol.'

She crossed her arms. 'You want me to sign a waiver?'

'Billie...'

Gareth shut his eyes briefly as she moved, swinging her leg off him and sitting back on the couch, taking care to leave a good distance between them. What seemed like an acre of orange glow flickered between them. He raked a hand through his hair.

She was furious.

'I'm sorry. I just don't want you to regret this tomorrow.'

Billie laughed. She couldn't help herself. She was beginning to wonder about his prowess between the sheets. 'Are you that bad, Gareth?' She almost laughed again at the affronted look he shot her.

'I've never had any complaints,' he said stiffly, and Billie had to admire his restraint. Any other man would have bragged. Any other man might have been tempted to make her retract her deliberately bold statement by resuming what they'd started. But she was fast coming to realise that Gareth Stapleton was not like any other man.

Billie rose from the couch and stalked to the fire. She couldn't sit a moment longer. Not next to him anyway. He was driving her mad and she needed to pace.

She stared into the fake orange flames for a few moments, trying to come up with the right words that would give him some insight into her feelings.

'I think I'm the best judge of what I will and won't regret,' she said eventually.

Gareth stared at the dip at the small of her back and the way it arched up so elegantly to the span of her ribs. He admired the straight line of her shoulders.

'You think I like this?' he murmured. 'You think I think that self-denial is some bloody balm for the soul? Because I don't. But not only are you under the influence, you've also been through some heavy emotional stuff tonight. Using sex as some kind of emotional eraser *isn't* the right way to handle it.'

Billie turned to face him, her arms folded. 'Well, *gee whiz*, Gareth, thanks for the lecture, but how about you let me handle my stuff my way and you handle yours your way, okay?'

'I have had some experience with this, you know.'

He looked kind of grim again and Billie wondered what experience he meant. His time in the military? The horror of the things he must have seen there? Or the things he'd seen during five years in a busy city emergency department?

Or was he thinking about his wife?

Had he used sex after his wife's death to *handle* it?

Had he had a bevy of women, mistresses, who had helped him through it or had his transactions been more…random? Had he preferred hook-ups to any further potential emotional entanglements?

'Okay. So what is the right way to handle it?'

Gareth stood. 'Believe it or not, talking about it with someone who knows.' He shoved his hands in his pockets as he moved closer lest he do something really dumb like think *Screw it* and drag her into his arms. 'Which is exactly what we were doing before we went and…'

'Complicated it?' she supplied.

'Okay…sure.' Gareth had been going to say 'ruined it'. Complicated was far less severe.

'Fine,' Billie said. 'But you should know I'm about all talked out now. I'm going to sit here and finish the bottle of wine. You can either stay and watch me or you can leave. But I must warn you if you stay I *will* be outrageously provocative. I'll probably get grabby. I may even take off my clothes. Because…' she pulled her shirt away from her tummy and fanned it back and forth a couple of times '…it's getting kind of hot in here, you know?'

Gareth nodded. He was burning up.

'So…' She gave him a half-smile. 'Probably best you leave now, unharassed and unmolested.'

Gareth smiled back, glad that she was trying to make light of the situation. 'I think plan B sounds like the wisest choice.'

She raised a derisive eyebrow. 'Imagine my surprise.'

He laughed. 'I'll be off now, then.'

Gareth was relieved, as he followed her to the door, that their earlier antipathy seemed to have dissolved and they were back on a more even footing.

'Thanks for coming over,' she said, as she opened the door and stood aside for him to exit.

It was his turn to lift a derisive eyebrow. 'Really?'

Billie laughed. 'Yes. Really. It did help, doing that talking stuff you're so big on.'

'Really?' He grinned.

Billie rolled her eyes. 'Really. Just don't come over again unless you plan on doing an Elvis.'

'An Elvis?'

She grinned. 'A little less conversation, a little more action.'

Gareth chuckled. Billie Ashworth-Keyes was an intriguing woman. She was a strange mix of smart and unsure, vulnerable and strong, funny and sober. He knew, standing on her threshold tonight, a warm orange glow behind her gilding her chestnut hair, soft yellow from the streetlight caressing her face, that sooner or later he and Billie were going to end up in bed.

Just not tonight.

Sure, he'd been telling himself since they'd met that it wasn't going to happen but denial seemed useless now. He could feel the power of their attraction in the stir of his loins and the thrum of his pulse. And he knew, even though it was wisest, he wasn't going to be able to ignore the dictates of his body for ever.

He was, after all, only a man. And he wanted her.

He just needed to remember that they couldn't have anything permanent. That underneath her cool, funny façade Billie was a mess. A ticking time bomb ready to explode, and he'd had enough of bombs—metaphorical and actual—to last a lifetime.

She had a lot of things to work out in her life or she was going to wind up completely miserable, and most of it, unfortunately, she was going to have to figure out by herself.

And he didn't want to be collateral damage while she did.

He stared at her mouth for long moments—it really was utterly kissable—before he dragged his gaze back up to hers.

'When we do finally do it, Billie, and I promise you *we will*, I will Elvis your brains out.'

And while she was standing there, blinking up at him, her mouth forming a delicious little O, he smiled and said, 'Goodnight.'

CHAPTER TWELVE

Two DAYS LATER Gareth sat in a counsellor's office at the cancer clinic with Amber. They were listening to the pros and cons of double mastectomy versus regular intensive screening and hyper-vigilance.

'In short, Amber, we don't recommend such a radical step at such a young age,' Margie, the counsellor, said regarding the mastectomy. 'Certainly not without extensive counselling and taking some time to really think through the implications.'

Margie was a breast cancer survivor herself. She looked to be in her sixties, her hair grey, short and spiky, and Gareth could tell that Amber valued her opinion. It was also clear that Amber was desperate to be told what to do, clutching at all advice as an absolute.

'So you're saying I shouldn't?' Amber asked.

Margie glanced at Gareth before addressing Amber. 'No.' She shook her head. 'I'm saying that you're young, that there is currently no sign of breast cancer on any of your scans or blood tests. I'm saying this is a big decision and that you have time to make it. I'm saying that you should take that time. No decisions have to be made straight away, Amber. You might not have to do anything about it for years yet.'

Amber turned to him, a tonne of indecision in her eyes. 'What do you think?'

'I think Margie's being very sensible. She's urging caution and that you take your time. I think that's wise.'

'So you don't think I should either?'

Gareth leaned forward in his chair and placed his hands on top of Amber's fidgeting ones. 'This isn't up to me, sweetie. Or Margie. All she's saying, all we're both saying is you don't need to feel pressured into making such a huge decision right now.'

'But if I did go ahead, you'd support me, right?'

Amber's huge eyes filled with unshed tears that punched him hard in the gut. She'd looked at him with those eyes the day the oncologist had told them Catherine was terminal. Eyes that said, What the hell are we going to do?

Gareth squeezed her hands, he could not have loved this young woman any more than he did at this moment, standing at this truly horrible crossroads with her. She may not have been his from the beginning but she'd been the centre of his world from the moment she'd grinned at him with her gappy, five-year-old smile and called him Carrot.

'Of course I will, honey,' he said, and when she nodded the tears spilled from her eyes and he pulled her close, tucking her head under his chin like he used to when she was little.

'Amber,' Margie said after a few moments, having given them some time to hold each other. 'There's a really good support group here for women who deal with familial breast cancer. A lot of them are your age, facing the same kind of dilemma and questions that you are. How about I hook you up with them? You can listen to what they have to say, to their stories. It might help.'

Amber broke out of the embrace. 'Okay,' she sniffled. 'That sounds good, right?' she said, turning to look at Gareth.

He nodded. 'It sounds great.'

* * *

They walked out of the building fifteen minutes later with another appointment for a further counselling session, a bunch of pamphlets and the details for the support group Margie had recommended.

'You okay?' Gareth asked.

Amber nodded. 'Yeah. I think so. This will be good, I think,' she said, brandishing the card with the support group details.

'Yes,' he agreed. 'Fabulous that there's a meeting Saturday week too. Not that long to wait. Will you be able to get to it?'

'Yep, I should be able to.'

'You want me to see if I can swap my shift next Saturday and drive you there? I can hang around. We can grab a bite to eat after, if you want.'

She shook her head. 'Nah. I'll be fine.'

'Well, come over for tea Saturday night and tell me about it.'

'Can't,' she said. 'Carly's organised a pub crawl for Del's twenty-first.'

Gareth winced. Carly's stamina could kill an ox. 'Okay. Why don't you come around for breakfast on the Sunday after the meeting, then? Bring Carly if you want to. Sounds like you're going to need the resuscitative qualities only bacon can provide and you know I cook it better than anyone.'

Amber smiled at him and then suddenly her eyes were full of tears again as she stood on tiptoe and hugged him. 'Deal,' she whispered.

That Sunday afternoon Gareth was getting some details from his patient in cubicle three when Billie slid the curtain partially back and stepped inside.

He nodded at her, slipping on his cool, professional mask. They had only seen each other in passing since their impulsive passion the other night. The department had been busy and he was fairly certain she'd been avoiding him.

Which was fine by him.

Thinking about her every night as he drifted off to sleep, having extremely inappropriate erotic dreams about her, was hard enough. It was imperative he didn't let any thoughts of the way she'd rubbed herself against him, the way she'd kissed him the other night enter his head. They were at work and John deserved their full, undivided attention.

'Hi,' he said.

'Hi.'

She was dressed in requisite scrubs, her normal pony-tail—not one hair out of place—falling down her back. She looked like any other doctor here.

Except he wasn't treading water with any of them.

He dragged his gaze away from the gloss on her mouth. 'This is Dr Ashworth-Keyes,' Gareth said to John.

'Call me Billie,' she said, smiling at her patient.

Gareth watched John's mouth drop open. He sympathised with the guy.

'This is twenty-two-year-old John Sutton. John was kicked in the testicles during a basketball match and has what appears to be a large haematoma on his left testicle.' He looked at John. 'Dr Ashworth-Keyes will be assessing your injury.'

John's eyes practically bulged out of his head and he cast Gareth a stricken look. '*She's* going to be looking at my nuts? Don't you have a dude doctor?'

Gareth quelled an inappropriate urge to laugh as he sympathised with John again. He doubted his junk would behave itself if Billie was down there, poking and prodding, either.

'I'm sorry, Billie is it. But don't worry. She's highly qualified. Seen a thousand testicles,' he joked.

'Uh…okay.'

Billie saw John swallow visibly as a dull red glow stained his cheekbones. She cringed inwardly. The guy was already embarrassed and she hadn't even lifted the green surgical towel placed strategically across his lap.

This was going to be bad.

John was going to get an erection and die of complete mortification. She would then, in turn, also want the floor to swallow her whole.

No amount of saying it was a perfectly normal biological reaction was going to make this job any easier.

'Gareth?' A nurse opened the curtain a little and stuck her head in. 'Mrs Berkley's asking for you.'

Gareth sighed. 'Okay,' he said as the nurse disappeared. He looked at Billie. 'I'd better go check on her. Just yell when you're done.'

John's alarmed gaze darted to Gareth before giving Billie an extra stricken look. Billie felt for him. This had to be an embarrassing situation for him. Some guys would relish it, brag about it to their mates come Monday morning, but John didn't look like a bragger. John looked like he was already mentally trying to conjure up the least sexual things in the world.

Cane toads. Dental extraction. Burnt toast.

Billie stepped in front of Gareth, barring his exit, a forced smile on her lips. 'Can I…talk to you outside for a moment?'

Gareth frowned. 'Okay…'

Billie turned to John, her smile feeling utterly fake. 'We'll be right back.'

They stepped outside the curtain and Gareth pulled it closed. The department was busy and people bustled around them. Billie waited for a nurse to pass before she started. 'You can't leave me in there with him,' she said, her voice low. 'You have to stay.'

Gareth blinked. 'What? Why?'

'Because!' Her voice dropped. 'The guy is clearly worried that…' She switched to a whisper, '*Things* are going to happen as soon as I examine him, and I'd rather save him and myself the embarrassment.'

'The guy's got a black and blue testicle,' Gareth whispered in reply. 'I don't think *anything's* going to happening down there any time soon.'

'Maybe. But the point is, *he* thinks it will,' she murmured, still keeping her voice hushed but not whispering any longer.

'And how is me being in there with you going to help?'

'Because you're a *guy*. You can distract him with guy things.'

He quirked his eyebrow. 'Guy things?'

'Yes. You know. Beer and football and…'

Billie wasn't sure what men talked about. The men in her family talked about the latest surgical technique. She didn't think that was what John needed to hear, considering he was probably going to be under a surgeon's knife by night's end.

'…mountain climbing.'

Gareth laughed. Beer and football he could manage. Everest not so much. 'Mountain climbing?'

His low chuckle was equal parts sexy and irritating and Billie glared at him. 'Sporty stuff.'

Gareth shoved his hands on his hips. 'And what would you do if I wasn't here?'

'I'd find another male on staff to accompany me.'

'And what would happen if there were only female staff on?'

'Then, of course, I'd do it myself,' Billie said. 'But you *are* here and I don't have to. Now, can you please help a fellow male out and distract him for me?'

'With all my mountain-climbing stories?'

Billie rolled her eyes. 'With whatever you like.'

'Okay. But only if you help me with Mrs Berkley after.'

She narrowed her eyes. 'What's wrong with Mrs Berkley?'

'She's an eighty-four-year-old PFO with a fractured wrist.'

Billie frowned. 'PFO?'

'Pissed and fell over.'

'I *know* what it means, Gareth,' she said. She may have only have been in the ER for a couple of weeks but she'd picked up the vernacular quickly.

Medicine was full of acronyms. Both official and unofficial. 'But…eighty-four?'

He grinned. 'Yup.'

'Do I want to know what she was doing?'

'I believe it was the Chicken Dance at her great-grandson's wedding.'

Billie whistled. 'Go, Mrs Berkley.'

'Easy for you to say. She's a little high and…' Gareth searched for the right word and smiled as their conversation from the other night came back to him. 'Grabby.'

Billie regarded him for a moment as he plunged her straight back into the middle of that night, their kiss, his erection pressing hard and urgent at the juncture of her thighs.

Crap.

She'd been doing just fine pretending it hadn't happened but suddenly she was there again—the firelight, the confidences, the wine.

'Please, Billie.'

Billie dragged herself out of the sexual morass. Gareth looked more than a little desperate and it was almost comical to see such an experienced nurse worried about a little old lady. 'Since when did the big military guy have problems fending off a sweet old lady with a broken wrist?'

'I don't have a problem,' he said firmly. 'I'd just rather have a female member of staff there while she's not in her right mind. Between the alcohol and the happy juice the ambos gave her, she's not quite herself.'

Billie laughed at the picture Gareth was creating. 'Well, at least she's not feeling anything.'

'Oh, she's not feeling a thing. She's singing sea shanties.'

'She sounds a hoot.' Billie grinned.

'A hoot with wandering hands.'

Billie laughed again. She couldn't blame Mrs Berkley. Gareth was utterly grab-worthy. 'Okay, fine.' She checked her watch. 'John first then the irrepressible Mrs Berkley.'

'Deal,' he said, as he pulled back the curtain and they both trooped back in.

'Right, John,' Billie said, approaching the nervous patient briskly, professionally, reaching for some gloves that were in a dispenser attached to the wall behind the gurney and quickly snapping them on. 'Let's see what you've done to yourself.'

As she pulled up the corner of the green towel she heard Gareth say, 'So, done any mountain climbing, John?' and it took all her willpower not to laugh.

The urge died quickly as the extent of John's bruising was revealed. Gareth was right—it was black and blue. And very, very swollen. She winced.

'He's had some pain relief?' she asked.

Gareth nodded. 'Morphine.'

She looked at John, who was looking anywhere but at her. 'How's the pain?'

'It's better,' he said, the blush darkening on his cheeks as he spoke to a spot just beyond her ear.

'Okay, good, but I'm sorry…I have to have a feel, okay?'

John swallowed. 'Okay.'

Billie carried out the examination as gently as she could, feeling both testicles methodically. Gareth prattled on about Sherpas and carabineers. She flipped the towel back over when she was done and stripped off her gloves.

'Right. We're going to get the surgical doctor on call to come and see you but I think you've got yourself a nasty haematoma down there that'll need to be evacuated.'

John, a nice colour of beetroot now, nodded, looking at his toes. 'The surgical doctor, is it a…woman?'

Billie bit the inside of her cheek. It was heartening if somewhat foolish to meet a guy who was more concerned about the sex of the doctor than the fact his testicle looked like a battered plum.

She patted his foot. 'Dr Yates is very much male.'

John's sigh of relief was audible.

CHAPTER THIRTEEN

'AH, THERE YOU ARE, you gorgeous young man.' The elderly woman lying on the exam table located in the middle of the room had a twinkle in her eyes as she waggled her fingers at Gareth and Billie almost laughed out loud at her greeting. 'I thought you'd skipped out on me.'

'Me? Skip out on you, Mrs Berkley?' Gareth murmured, and Billie blinked at the low, easy, flirty tone to his voice. 'Never.'

'Oh, and you've bought a pretty young woman with you.' Mrs Berkley beamed at Billie. 'Come in, my dear.' She gestured with her good arm. 'My goodness, how *do* you young people get things done around here with so much to distract you?'

He glanced at Billie. Their gazes locked and her breath hitched for a second.

'It's a challenge, Mrs B., I can't deny that,' Gareth said, before switching his attention to the patient, sitting himself down on the stool beside the table and swinging slightly from side to side.

Mrs B. cackled merrily. 'I can imagine. I remember when me and my Ted were going around. Couldn't pass each other without wanting to tear each other's clothes off.'

Billie blinked at the frank admission and Gareth stopped swivelling on the stool as the room filled with a pregnant silence.

'Hah.' The octogenarian cracked up again. 'That shocked the cotton socks off you, didn't it? What, you think you young people invented sex?'

Gareth recovered quite quickly. 'Absolutely not, and I thank you and your generation most earnestly for your pioneering ways.'

Mrs B. grinned from ear to ear. 'You're welcome,' she said, her hand covering Gareth's and giving it a pat. 'I could tell you some stories that would make you blush right to the roots of your hair.'

Billie's mind boggled but Gareth had her measure. 'I don't embarrass easily, Mrs B. We nurses aren't prone to being shocked.'

Billie was pleased Gareth wasn't shocked because she had to admit to feeling just the tiniest bit so. She didn't know if Mrs B. was always this outrageous or if it was the combination of alcohol and drugs but Billie wasn't used to such freeness of expression *in eighty-year-olds*.

But it appeared Mrs Berkley was on a roll. The older woman gave Gareth a secretive smile and tapped the side of her nose three times. 'I still reckon I could teach you a thing or two, young man.'

Gareth, looking completely unconcerned by the flirting, grinned and said, 'I'll bet you could.'

Mrs B. turned her eyes on Billie. 'Isn't he marvellous, dear? I mean, really, do they have those nudie calendars for male nurses…you know, like they do for the firefighters? This young man could be the centrefold.'

Now Billie really was at a loss for words and not just because they'd been uttered by a great-grandmother. The illicit thought of Gareth stripped nude made her lose her train of thought.

She glanced at Gareth, who was looking at her with a quirked eyebrow. 'Yes,' he mused. 'Why don't we do calendars?'

Billie really felt like she'd leapt into an alternate universe. She needed to get them out of this bizarre conversation immediately. Why was Gareth encouraging her? Hadn't he asked her in here to defend his honour?

'Inappropriate perhaps?' she said, smiling sweetly.

Mrs B. nudged Gareth and said in a stage whisper they could probably hear out in the ambulance bay, 'Ooh. She's a bit of a spoilsport, that one.'

Gareth, his gaze still locked with hers, a small smile playing on his lips, nodded. 'Yes, she is.'

Billie almost choked on his statement. She wasn't going to stand by and be defamed when nothing could be further than the truth. 'Don't listen to a word he says, Mrs Berkley. The only spoilsport around here is Gareth.'

She raised an eyebrow back at him. It hadn't been her who had knocked him back. *Twice.* He had the good grace to look away.

'Right,' he said, turning back to his patient. 'Let's get this cast on, shall we? A nice light fibreglass one for you today.'

'Ooh, can I have a purple one?' Mrs Berkley asked. 'My great-granddaughter Kahlia had one last year.' She glanced at Billie. 'It looked very groovy.'

Gareth nodded. They had a selection of colours for paediatric patients so why not? 'Purple it is. Let me get set up.'

She beamed at him and patted his cheek. 'Such a good boy.'

Gareth smiled and extracted himself. He rummaged through the supply cupboard and found some rolls of purple. 'Can I help?' Billie asked, appearing at his elbow.

'Sure. Fill this halfway,' he said, thrusting a stainless-steel basin at her.

'What are you doing?' she whispered under her breath as she took it. 'Why am I here if you keep encouraging her?'

'Because I just spent twenty minutes talking to a very confused guy about hiking boots and grappling hooks.'

She rolled her eyes. 'You didn't have to talk to him about mountain climbing and you know it.'

Gareth grinned at her. 'Now, where would the fun have been in that?' He nodded his head to the right. 'Sink over there.'

A few minutes later they were set up. Gareth had the rolls of plaster soaking in the basin that had been set on a trolley, and he was sitting back on his stool, pulled in close to the table. Billie was sitting on the other side of Mrs Berkley, also on a stool.

He positioned her arm correctly and started to apply the padded underlay. His hair flopped forward as he worked his way up to her elbow and Mrs Berkley reached out her unbroken hand and pushed it back off his forehead.

Gareth looked up at her, startled. 'I miss running my hands through a man's hair,' she said wistfully.

'Okay, Mrs B.,' Billie said, taking the older woman's hand and bringing her arm back down beside her. She intertwined her fingers with the patient's and gave the gnarled old hand a squeeze. 'How about we let Gareth finish his job?'

'Yes, of course, dear,' Mrs Berkley said, and tutted to herself a couple of times. 'I guess I'm probably making a bit of an old fool of myself. I just so rarely get to hang out with younger people these days.'

Billie squeezed her hand again. 'Of course not,' she murmured. 'You're just keeping Gareth on his toes.' She glanced across at him. 'Men need that.'

'Damn straight,' Mrs Berkley hooted, her crinkly face splitting into a hundred different ravines, deep and beautiful.

Once the padding was in situ Gareth plunged his gloved hand into the basin and removed the first roll. 'You sure about purple?' he asked.

Mrs Berkley nodded her head enthusiastically. 'Quite.'

He squeezed the roll out gently, removing the excess water, and started applying the first layer. 'You should ask this young lady out,' Mrs Berkley said, out of the blue.

Billie's alarmed gaze met Gareth's across the top of their patient. Gareth returned his to the job at hand, but not before murmuring, 'You don't say?'

'Oh, yes.' Mrs Berkley nodded. 'You'd look good together. Make *beautiful* babies. Her hair and complexion, your eyes and strapping physique. Perfect.'

'But we work together, Mrs B. You know they say you should never mix business with pleasure.'

Mrs Berkley snorted. 'What a load of old tosh. What do *they* know? They are the cat's mother. And what do cats have to do with it?'

Billie frowned. What indeed? she thought as she tried to follow the muddled ponderings. But somehow in this very strange conversation nothing seemed too bizarre.

'What do you reckon, Billie? You fancy a date?'

Mrs Berkley gave a horrified gasp. 'Young man, that is no way to ask a young lady out. Where are your manners? Now, do it again. Properly this time!'

Billie glanced at Gareth, who was looking suitably chastised, and she bit down on her lip to stop laughing.

'You do know how to ask, don't you?' Mrs Berkley said, clearly not done with her disapproval.

'To be honest,' Gareth said, the smile slipping from his face, 'it's been a while for me.'

A shiver wormed its way up Billie's spine at Gareth's sudden grimness. Been a while since what? He'd gone on a date? It certainly hadn't been a while since he'd kissed a woman—she could attest to that. Or did he mean it had been a while since he'd taken a woman to bed?

Had he slept with anyone since his wife had died?

'You say,' Mrs Berkley said in a voice that was half

imperious, half exasperated, '"Would you do me the honour of accompanying me to dinner?" Or wherever you're going.'

His patient's disgust brought Gareth back from the edge of the familiar darkness that had overwhelmed him for a long time. He laughed.

Mrs B. was so affronted it was hard not to.

'Of course, you're right, Mrs B.' He unwound the last of the first roll then looked across at Billie as he picked up the second. 'Willamina Ashworth-Keyes, will you do me the honour of having a drink with me after work tonight?'

His blue eyes sparkled playfully, the shadows she'd seen there moments ago banished, making it hard for Billie to ascertain if he was serious or just humouring Mrs Berkley. It worked anyway as the octogenarian nodded approvingly.

'Good. Now you…' she looked at Billie '…say, "Why, thank you, I'd be delighted to have a drink with you after work tonight."'

Billie glanced at Gareth, who gave her an encouraging little wink before returning to the cast. So they were just humouring their patient, then…?

Disappointment trickled down her spine.

'Why…thank you, Gareth Stapleton,' she said, forcing an equally light tone to her voice. 'I'd be delighted to have a drink with you after work tonight.'

He chuckled as he worked and Billie's disappointment grew. Mrs Berkley clapped. 'There, see. Perfect. My work here is done.'

'And so,' Gareth announced as he unrolled the last of the roll, smoothing the end down thoroughly, 'is mine. There you go.' He stood. 'All pretty in purple.'

Mrs Berkley looked at Gareth's handiwork. 'I love it,' she said, grinning.

'Another happy customer,' he said, smiling at Mrs Berkley with such genuine affection it took Billie's breath away. Was there nothing the man couldn't do? Pull heart-attack victims out of wrecks, run an emergency room with military efficiency, while calming freaked out residents *and* charm little old ladies.

'Now, let's get you up and outside for a while. You'll need to stick around for an hour or so in case there's swelling, then you can be on your way.'

'Right you are,' Mrs Berkley said, as Gareth ushered her into a wheelchair. 'Hand me my bag, will you, dear?' she asked Billie. 'I'll text my granddaughter to come and get me in an hour.'

Billie handed Mrs Berkley her handbag, still trying to wrap her head around an eighty-four-year-old with a smartphone. Gareth flipped the brake off with his foot. 'Hold tight,' he said.

'It was nice meeting you, Mrs B.,' Billie said, as the wheelchair drew level with her. 'Maybe no more chicken dancing for a while.'

Mrs Berkley smiled at her. 'I'm old, my dear. I'm going to chicken dance while I can.' She patted Billy's hand. 'Gotta make hay before those chickens hatch. Enjoy your date.'

Gareth grinned and winked, pushing the chair past her before Billie had a sensible reply. She watched them go, Mrs Berkley saying, 'I don't suppose you could round me up a cuppa, could you, dear? I'm desperate for one,' as Gareth pushed her down the corridor.

His deep 'Of course I can, anything for you, Mrs B.,' as they disappeared from sight was typical Gareth. From CPR to cups of tea, he was a regular knight in shining armour.

He'd certainly saved her ass more than once.

CHAPTER FOURTEEN

A FEW HOURS LATER, Billie changed out of her scrubs in the female locker room. It had been a long day and her feet were killing her. She needed a hot shower, a glass of wine and her bed. Slipping into her trendy, buckle-laden boots, she threw her Italian leather jacket over her arm, grabbed her bag and headed out.

Gareth was lounging against the opposite wall when she opened the door. He was wearing jeans that looked old and worn and soft as butter, some kind of duffle coat and a smile. The coat was open to reveal a snug-fitting shirt and he looked all warm and rugged and just a little bit wild, like he was about to throw his leg over a motorbike. Billie had to grind her heels into the ground to stop herself from slipping her arms inside his coat and snuggling into the broad expanse of his chest.

'I thought you were never coming out,' he said, as he pushed off the wall and moved closer.

'Sorry,' she said, puzzled. 'Did I miss signing something?'

'Nah.' He indicated that she should walk and they fell into step. 'Mrs B. just rang to make sure that I was collecting you for our date.'

Billie stopped for a moment. 'She did?'

He grinned and nodded, also stopping. 'She did.'

'Wow,' Billie murmured, as they commenced walking

again, conscious of Gareth's arm casually brushing hers. 'I'm surprised she can even remember through all that happy juice.'

'I have a feeling that Mrs B. doesn't miss much at all.'

Billie laughed. 'I think you may be right.'

They got to the end of the corridor and Billie went to turn right for the lifts and the car park.

'Hey, where are you going?' Gareth asked. 'What about our date?'

Billie's breath caught in her throat. He was looking at her with a tease in those blue eyes and something else, something very *frank*. His promise to Elvis her brains out echoed around her head but that had been a few days ago and nothing he'd done since had indicated that the event was likely to happen, much less imminently.

'Oh…I didn't think that was real,' she stalled.

He shrugged. 'It wasn't but…I'm pretty sure Mrs B. has this place bugged and when she rings tomorrow looking for me—and she *assures* me she's going to—I'll be able to put my hand on my heart and tell her I was the epitome of a gentleman.'

Billie didn't think he looked remotely gentlemanly right now. He looked all whiskery and hunky and she could suddenly picture him beneath the rotors of a chopper, accepting a wounded soldier. She certainly didn't want him to act all gentlemanly. She wanted him to push her against the wall in the deserted corridor and kiss her until she didn't have any breath left in her chest.

She wanted a quick, hard military incursion.

Billie blushed and covered her embarrassingly real fantasy with a spot of mocking. 'You? *You're* frightened of a little old lady.'

'*That* little old lady?' Gareth grinned. 'Hell, yeah. What do you say? A quick drink at Oscar's for Mrs B.'s sake?'

Billie knew she should say no. But Gareth was hard to

resist when he was being all charming and he-man. And who was she to disappoint an octogenarian?

'Okay, sure. But I expect you to be on your very best behaviour or I'll tell Mrs Berkley.'

'Yes, ma'am,' he murmured, saluting her, and Billie's pulse just about ratcheted off the scale.

Billie was very pleased as they entered Oscar's that she'd decided to dress nicely that morning. She was wearing her designer jeans and a fluffy-on-the-outside, fleecy-on-the-inside zip-up jumper that pulled nicely across her breasts and showed off a decent hint of cleavage.

She knew that this was just them humouring an old woman but it didn't hurt to be looking her best either.

Gareth held out a chair for her and Billie smiled. 'Very gallant,' she murmured. 'Keep this up and I'll expect you to throw your cloak over a puddle for me.'

Gareth grinned. 'Sorry, I'm fresh out of cloaks. But I will buy you a drink. Wine?'

Billie nodded. 'Red.'

She watched him walk away. He'd removed his jacket and the way his jeans hung to the long, lazy stride of his legs should have been illegal. Billie felt a little flutter in her chest. They weren't even on a real date and Gareth was already doing better than any other man she'd been out with.

She watched him laughing with the guy behind the bar as he picked up their drinks and brought them over. Everything seemed easy with him. From his laid-back chuckle to the looseness of his stride, to the slow spread of his lazy grin.

'Baz recommends the Merlot, apparently,' he said as he placed the glass of ruby liquid in front of her.

Billie smiled. Of course he knew the name of the guy behind the bar—Gareth knew everyone. He sat and raised his glass towards her. 'To Mrs Berkley,' he said, smiling as they clinked their glasses.

Some froth from Gareth's beer clung to his top lip and Billie had to drag her gaze away from it as she groped around for a distraction. 'So…what now?' she asked.

'Well, I guess we should do that getting-to-know-you stuff that dates are for.'

Billie gave a half-laugh. 'You already know about my dead sister, my fragile mother, my pompous father, my inability to deny them anything and my pathological dislike of gore. I know about your wife, your stepdaughter, the way you handle yourself in an emergency and what you've been doing for the last decade or so. What else is there to know?'

Gareth laughed. That was a very good question. 'We have done the big stuff, haven't we?'

He was sure there was more for both of them—hell, they both had a tonne of baggage. But Gareth wasn't in the mood for heavy tonight. Suddenly he wanted to know the little stuff.

'What's your favourite colour?'

Billie blinked. 'My favourite colour?'

'Sure. Let's do the pop-quiz version.'

Okay…that could be fun. 'Um…yellow,' she said. 'What's yours? No…hang on, let me guess…khaki?'

Gareth laughed. 'Ha. Funny girl. Definitely not.' He looked at her hair then back at her. 'Chestnut,' he said, taking a sip of his beer.

Billie's pulse skipped a beat.

He took another swig of his beer, taking care this time to remove any errant foam, for which Billie was exceedingly grateful. 'Favourite food,' he said.

'Jam on toast.'

Gareth threw back his head and laughed. '*That's* your favourite food?'

Billie raised an eyebrow at him. 'You got a problem with that?'

'Nope. Just find it hard to believe that Willamina Ashworth-Keyes eats jam on toast.'

'Well, *she* doesn't. But plain old Billie Keyes loves it!' She took a mouthful of her wine. 'I suppose yours is caviar? No, wait…quiche!'

He grinned at her deliberate goading. 'A steak. Big, thick and juicy.'

'How very tough guy of you.'

Gareth laughed some more. 'You don't like tough guys?'

Billie's gaze wandered to where the hem of his sleeve brushed his biceps. She raised her eyes to his face and warmth flooded her cheeks. She'd had no experience of tough guys whatsoever. The men she'd been with had been cultured and urbane.

'I'm liking them more and more.'

Their gazes locked for long moments then Gareth smiled. 'You're good for my ego.'

Billie pulse fluttered as she dragged herself back from the compelling blueness of his eyes and reminded herself this wasn't a real date. 'Well…we won't tell Mrs B. that.'

Gareth found himself laughing again. It felt good to talk and laugh with a woman—really good. It had been a long time since he felt this *all over* good and he was suddenly overwhelmed by how easy it was.

Billie put him at ease.

When she wasn't tying him in knots.

His smiled faded a little as he contemplated the implications. 'I like you, Willamina Ashworth-Keyes.'

Everything stilled inside Billie as the sudden, serious admission fell from his lips. She didn't know what to say but she knew she felt the same way. 'I like you too, Gareth Stapleton.'

The bar noises faded into the background as they stared at each other, their drinks forgotten in front of them.

'Hey, guys, Gareth and Billie are here.'

The words yanked them out of their little bubble and they turned to see a bunch of emergency nurses heading their way.

'Uh-oh,' Gareth said. 'Date's over.'

Billie nodded. 'Leave this bit out when you speak to Mrs B. tomorrow.'

Gareth smiled. 'Good idea.'

And then they were being swamped with company as half a dozen colleagues descended and Billie gave herself up to the mayhem.

Because it wasn't a real date anyway.

The following Saturday, Gareth watched Billie through a crack in cubicle four's curtain. He was supposed to be doing paperwork so he could finish up and get out of there but his gaze continued to be drawn to her.

She was examining a nasty cellulitic arm from an infected scratch. She said something to her patient, a fifty-two-year-old male, and he laughed. Billie laughed with him and he admired the effortless way she put people at ease.

They responded to her.

And Gareth knew that patients who liked and trusted the doctors they saw were more likely to take their advice.

He liked seeing her at ease. It was her natural habitat and a far cry from the woman she became when confronted with the rawness of a medical emergency. There was something compelling about her. She looked cool and confident. Sure of herself.

And that was very, very sexy.

He'd tried hard not to dwell on their *date* this past week and had failed miserably. It seemed to be the only thing he *had* thought about and he was thinking about it again now as she charmed her patient. The teasing and the banter had been fun and he realised he wanted to see more of her.

Sure, there were a lot of reasons why seeing her outside

work was dumb. They both knew that. But right from the beginning there'd been an inevitability about them, he'd felt it and so had she. Hell, he'd told her that night at her place that something would happen between them sooner or later.

And the time for fighting it was over.

He wanted to see her, touch her, kiss her. He didn't want to keep his distance, push her away again. He wanted her in his bed. For however long it lasted.

And he hadn't felt this way since Catherine.

So forget the rest of it.

Billie glanced up and Gareth realised he'd been caught staring. Their gazes held for a long moment before she turned back and said something to her patient, and Gareth felt as if his chest wall had just been released from a vice.

When she strode towards him a minute later, he was still recovering.

'Shouldn't you have knocked off by now?' she said, as she took the chair beside him at the work station, her voice casual but he could tell she was being deliberately so.

'Yep,' Gareth said. 'Just finishing up some charting.'

'Ah,' she murmured, as she opened the chart in front of her, 'the never-ending paperwork.'

He laughed. 'Yes.' They continued their charting in silence for a moment. Gareth glanced sideways at her, briefly admiring her neat handwriting. They were the only two at the work station for now. 'I think we should go on a proper date,' he said.

She looked up and her ponytail swished to the side. She frowned at him, which emphasised her freckles. 'R-really?'

Gareth nodded. 'Yes.'

Her throat bobbed and his gaze followed the tantalising movement. 'When?'

'Tonight?' Why not. *Seize the day.*

There was a drawn-out silence as she regarded him solemnly. 'There seem to be a lot of reasons why we shouldn't.'

She was looking at him as if she was remembering the last two times she'd tried to reach out to him and he'd rejected her. 'Yes, there are.' He nodded. 'But I don't care any more.'

Gareth took her nervous swallow as a good sign. A nurse swished past the desk and Billie faked interest in the chart until they were alone again.

'Could I take a raincheck?' she asked, lifting her gaze from the chart. 'I'm not off for a couple of hours yet and I'm beat. The thought of having to go home and get dressed up and go out...'

Gareth tried really hard *not* to think about her getting dressed up. For him. 'That's okay. Just come to my place straight from work. I'll cook you dinner and you don't have to get dressed up.'

Also, if he didn't do this now, he was frightened he'd chicken out altogether. That common sense would win out.

'Oh.' Billie looked back at the chart again and Gareth wasn't sure if that was a good thing or a bad thing. Was she weighing up the pros and cons or freaking out?

When she lifted her eyes there was a directness to her gaze that was utterly compelling. 'Thank you. I'd love to.'

Gareth hadn't realised how much had been mentally riding on her acceptance until she'd uttered it and he sagged a little.

'Can I bring something?' she asked, her gaze unwavering. 'Beer, wine, dessert?' She looked around surreptitiously and lowered her voice. 'Condoms?'

Gareth blinked but their gazes still held. She wanted to know the lie of the land—he could understand that. He shook his head. 'I'm good. For *everything*.'

Her mouth quirking up at the side was the only indication that they were talking about something they probably shouldn't have been, considering where they were. And it added to the anticipation of the moment.

'In that case, I look forward to it very much, thank you,' she murmured.

Gareth's mouth quirked up too. 'My pleasure.'

She held his gaze for a little longer. 'I hope so,' she said, then returned her attention to the chart.

CHAPTER FIFTEEN

BILLIE WAS NERVOUS when she pulled up at Gareth's just after eight-thirty. She couldn't quite believe how up front she'd been about her expectations of this night and she cringed a little now, thinking about it.

But she was a grown woman, a fully qualified doctor, for crying out loud—she knew what she wanted and she wasn't ashamed to ask for it. It was past time for them to stop beating around the bush. This wasn't some fake date for the sake of an old lady.

This was the real thing.

And there was something between her and Gareth. She'd felt the pull from the beginning and that hadn't lessened. Every time she looked at him, every time he was near she felt it and she knew he did too.

Okay, she had a lot going on in her life at the moment. She was struggling with decisions in her life she didn't feel she had any control over. But she didn't care about that right now because she did have control over this. Tonight she needed to be with him and that's all she cared about.

And Gareth, thankfully, had agreed.

Billie's breath misted into the air as she climbed the five stairs and put her foot on the wide veranda that continued all the way in both directions, typical of the old Queenslander style of architecture.

She rapped on the door, wishing again she'd thought to

wear something a little more elegant to work this morning instead of a pair of track pants, a turtleneck sweater and her seen-better-days college jumper.

Yes, it had been freezing, as it was now, but she could have at least worn something more along the lines of what she'd worn the day they'd ended up on their fake date.

She wasn't even wearing matching underwear.

Sure, he'd seen her looking worse—in plain baggy scrubs at half past stupid o'clock in the morning, tired and cold and hungry and feeling like death—but he'd also seen her in her best sparkly cocktail dress with full make-up and hair in curls.

Of course, she'd thrown up on him then too so maybe that didn't count...

Billie heard footsteps and she could see his shape coming towards her in the glass side panes of the door. Her pulse sped up. The light flicked on overhead and she quickly pulled her hair out from the constraints of her standard workwear ponytail and fluffed it a little as the door opened.

'Hi,' Gareth murmured, a smile tugging at the corners of his mouth.

He was wearing jeans and a long-sleeved button-up shirt, left undone at the neck, and his hair was damp. He looked so good and clean and warm and laid-back, casual sexy, she couldn't decide if she wanted to snuggle him or jump him.

'Hi,' she said, suddenly realising she was staring.

They didn't say anything or do anything for a few moments. Gareth just looked at her and Billie's stomach twisted in a knot.

'You look good,' he murmured.

Billie laughed then because she knew good was stretching it. 'It's okay. You don't have compliment me,' she said. 'Trust me, I'm a sure thing.'

He shook his head, slid his hand onto her hip and pulled her in close to him, bringing his mouth to within millimetres of hers, hovering it oh-so-close. So close she could feel the warmth of his breath and smell the mint of his toothpaste.

'You look good,' he repeated, his husky voice reaching inside, plucking at the fibres of her belly deep and low.

Then he dropped his mouth to hers and Billie felt the impact to her system like a lightning bolt. She moaned as he opened his mouth over hers and demanded she do the same. And she did. He urged her body closer and she went.

She wrapped her arms around his neck, flattened her breasts against his chest, aligned her pelvis with his and then somehow she was inside and the door was shut and a warm wall was hard behind her and he was hard in front of her and he groaned her name like it was torn from the depth of his soul and she never wanted to let him go.

And when he broke the kiss off she mewed in protest, their breathing harsh in the sudden silence.

'Sorry,' he murmured, pulling away slightly to look at her. 'I promised myself I'd wait but I've been fantasising about doing that for hours.'

Billie shrugged. His lips were wet from her mouth and she wanted them back on hers again. 'Don't stop on my behalf.'

'Oh, no, if I don't stop now I won't stop at all and what would Mrs Berkley think if I invited a young lady to dinner and then she didn't get any?'

Billie laughed. 'I think she'd disapprove. I'd think she'd think you quite ungentlemanly.'

He grinned. 'Me too.' He dropped his hands from her hips and took a reluctant step back. 'Come on, I've even cooked for you.' He held out his hand and she took it. 'I hope you're hungry.'

'*Very*,' she murmured, as he led the way through the house, his completely asexual touch doing funny things to her legs anyway.

He chuckled at her emphasis, leaving her in no doubt

he knew she wasn't talking about food. 'I made a basil and cherry-tomato pasta.'

They entered the kitchen. 'Glass of wine?'

'Yes, please.' If he was determined that they eat first then she was going to need to do something with her hands other than putting them all over him.

'Take a seat,' he said, gesturing to the stools along the far side of the wide central kitchen bench.

'This is a nice place,' she said, looking up at what she figured had to be a twelve-foot ceiling. That, combined with the panelled walls and the wraparound veranda, confirmed its architectural heritage.

'Yes,' Gareth, said as he poured a glass of red wine for her and cracked the lid of a beer for himself. 'It's not mine, I'm just house-sitting, but I believe it's almost one hundred years old. The owners had it moved from a homestead out west.'

'You're house-sitting? For friends?'

Gareth shook his head as he handed over her glass of wine. 'No. It's what I do. I house-sit for people.'

'You don't have a…permanent home?'

'Nope,' Gareth said, as he went and checked the food on the stove. 'I sold our house a couple of years after Catherine died, when Amber headed to uni, so I could put half of it in trust for her.'

'Oh.'

He turned and lounged against the oven. His jeans pulled tight against his thighs as he casually sipped his beer. He looked calm and comfortable in his skin and that cranked the sexy up another notch.

Billie was thankful there was a bench separating them.

'Catherine didn't really have anything of monetary value to leave Amber. Only what we had together, like the house and cars. And I wanted Amber to be able to have a legacy from her mother, something that could help her get a good start in life when she was ready.'

'So you sold your house?'

Gareth shook his head. 'It was our house. And, besides, it felt empty, not like a home any more. Catherine was gone and Amber was at college. Without them to fill it up it was just four walls and a roof.'

He stared into his drink for long moments, suddenly sombre, and Billie was pleased anew for the bench separating them. She wanted to go to him. Go to him, comfort him.

Which would probably embarrass the hell out of him. And herself. But the urge was there nonetheless.

'The house sold much faster than I'd anticipated so I was going to rent until I found something, but at the same time a friend of mine was going away for a few months and asked if I wanted to house-sit and it sort of snowballed from there. I'm with an agency now and I haven't been without a place to stay since. These owners have moved to Switzerland for a year.'

Billie's heart broke a little for Gareth. She loved her house—the one thing she'd accomplished without any help from her parents after she'd refused their monetary assistance.

Because she'd wanted to do it herself but mostly because of the guilt strings that came attached.

She loved how it grounded her. How she walked into it after a shift and it felt familiar and right, it felt like a home. She couldn't imagine walking into her house and it not feeling like a home any more.

She couldn't imagine walking away from it.

'Isn't it strange, having nowhere to call your own? Eating in someone else's kitchen, sitting on someone else's couch, sleeping in someone else's bed'

'Nah. I'm used to moving around from my years in the military. It feels right.'

'So you'll never get your own place again?'

He shook his head. 'I will…one day, I guess. The money's there. I could have done it at any point. But I liked the gypsy lifestyle. I've felt very…cast adrift these last few years, I guess…so this suits me for now.'

Billie sipped her wine. 'And how does Amber feel about that?'

'Amber has her own life. As she should. And she has financial security that she wouldn't have if I was still in the house. And as long as there's a spare bed for her when she needs it, she doesn't care where I live.'

'She sounds like an extraordinary young woman.'

'Yes.' He nodded. 'She is. Considering what she's been through.'

'She sounds like she's lucky to have you.'

Gareth shook his head. 'No. *I'm* lucky to have *her.*'

Billie's throat clogged with emotion. She'd never met a man like Gareth. A man who was unashamedly frank about his feelings, who had his priorities straight. She thought about her own father, who'd never told her how lucky he was to have her. He *had* told her *frequently* how lucky she was to have him, though.

His experience, his influence, his name.

He'd never even cried at Jessica's funeral.

'I hope you tell her that,' Billie murmured.

'Yep, as often as I can.' He smiled at her. 'I'll serve up.'

Gareth took their plates through to the formal dining room and set them down at the large table that seated twelve.

'Wow,' Billie said, looking above her at the imposing chandelier. 'Do you eat in here?'

'Nah, I usually eat in the lounge room in front of the telly; I like to catch up on the news but I figured an Ashworth-Keyes is used to formal dining,' he teased.

Billie grimaced. She *had* grown up with formal dining. In fact, they'd had a chandelier quite similar to this one.

'I vote for the lounge,' she said. 'This Ashworth-Keyes prefers relaxed and casual.'

Gareth's gaze met and held hers for a brief moment. He smiled at her and her breath hitched. 'There is nothing casual about you.'

Billie blushed. She didn't know what he meant by that exactly. Did he mean that she was too serious, too much of a mess? Or did he mean she wasn't going to be casual in his life?

She looked down to hide her confusion, her daggy jumper staring back at her. 'I don't know,' she said, looking back at him. 'I'm not exactly dressed for the opera.'

He grinned as he picked up the plates. 'All the better to undress you.'

Billie's insides quivered as she followed.

Gareth put some music on low and they chatted as they ate. Billie seemed stilted at first—not that he could blame her after his blatant statement of intent in the dining room— but she soon warmed up.

Conversation quickly drifted to his time in the military and they talked long after they'd set their bowls aside. He told her a bit about his postings and she asked him about the things he'd seen that had given him faith in the human race.

The question surprised him. Most people wanted to know the gory details. But he guessed, given Billie's abhorrence of gore, she was positioned to ask an atypical question.

'Was it hard to leave?' she asked.

Gareth shook his head. 'I loved being in the military. Putting on that uniform made me feel proud and worthy. It took me places and gave me opportunities to make a difference I wouldn't have had otherwise, but I was away from home a lot and if someone had told me that I was going to lose Catherine after only ten years together, I would have ditched the military in an instant and spent every one of those years by her side. We thought we'd have decades.'

Billie slid her hand onto his. 'Life's shorter than we think sometimes,' she whispered.

Gareth glanced at her. Moisture shimmered in her eyes. Was she thinking about her sister? 'I'm never making that mistake again,' he said, turning his hand over, her fingers automatically interlocking with his.

'She didn't mind you being away so much?' Billie asked.

'No. She knew how much I loved my job and Catherine was the most self-reliant woman I'd ever met. She'd been a single mother for five years, she could look after herself and she didn't mind being on her own.'

'She sounds great.'

Gareth nodded. 'You would have liked her.' He looked down at their hands. '*She* would have liked you.' The silence grew between them and Gareth glanced up. Billie looked wistful and a little sad. 'Sorry… God…' He shook his head. 'Way to kill a mood…talk incessantly about your dead wife.'

She laughed then. 'No, it's fine. I don't mind. I wish I could talk more about Jess. But she's such a taboo topic at home.'

'It's too painful for your parents still?'

'Yes,' Billie said. 'Mum can't even bear to hear her name uttered. And I think Dad feels this sense of…failure. My father comes from a long line of successful, ground-breaking surgeons; everything the Ashworth-Keyes clan have ever attempted has ended in success. And they like to talk about their successes, celebrate them. They don't talk about their failures. And I think he feels like he failed with Jess most of all.'

'I'm sorry,' Gareth said.

She shrugged. 'It is what it is.'

Gareth put his arm around her and snuggled her into

the crook of his shoulder. Her head fitted under his chin, the silky strands of her hair brushing his skin. Their legs were already stretched out in front of them, their bare feet propped on the coffee table. He inched his foot closer to hers and rubbed it gently against her.

'What *was* she like?' he asked, as he absently dropped a kiss on the top of her head.

Billie didn't answer for a while and he could feel the tension across her shoulders as if the memories had been kept inside for so long it was taking an effort to drag them out and dust them off. But he didn't mind waiting. The music was nice and she was snuggled in close and he knew the benefits of talking about those you'd loved and lost.

He and Amber often talked about Catherine.

'She had this mad laugh,' Billie said after a while. 'Like…really loud…*honking*, my father called it. He always thought Jess did it deliberately to annoy him.'

'And did she?'

'No. Well…maybe she took some pleasure in emphasising it.'

He chuckled. 'What else?'

'She was beautiful. And *fun*. And she loved kids. She wanted a dozen. I think she would have too, you know,' she said, shifting to look up at him, her eyes misting. 'She'd have made a great mother.'

Gareth's heart swelled in his chest. 'It sucks.'

'Yes. It does.'

'It helps to talk, though.'

She nodded. 'Yes. It does. And sometimes…' her gaze zeroed in on his mouth and it tingled so hard it hurt '…it helps not to talk at all.'

Gareth sucked in a breath. He couldn't agree more.

CHAPTER SIXTEEN

BILLIE WHIMPERED WHEN Gareth's mouth took hers in an achingly tender kiss. It was sweet and soft, warm and gentle, exploring the contours of her mouth in unhurried detail.

It broke her and healed her all at once.

When he pulled away, Billie's head was swimming from its intensity. 'No,' she murmured, reaching for him. Needing him to do it again.

'Shh,' he whispered against her mouth, as he dropped another gentle kiss on her lips. 'Not here,' he said, extricating himself and standing, holding his hand out to her. 'I want to lay you out on my bed. I want to look at you.'

Billie's stomach dropped right out as his words washed over her. She slid her hand into his and stood, her legs trembling in anticipation. Gareth smiled at her and led her though the house, down a darkened hallway, until they reached the double doors at the end.

He pushed one open and tugged her in after him.

The low-lit room was beautiful but Billie didn't notice the expensive furnishings or the plush carpet underfoot, she only had eyes for Gareth, who was turning and taking her in his arms again, kissing her mouth and her eyes and her nose. Nuzzling her ear and her neck, his hands stroking down her back, pushing underneath her jumper and her top to find her bare flesh.

'Off,' he muttered in her ear, pushing both pieces of clothing up. 'I want to kiss you all over.'

Billie didn't have to be asked twice as she ducked her head out of the clothing and Gareth flung them on the floor.

His breath hissed out as she stood before him in her bra and track pants. His gaze devoured her and her nipples beaded before his thorough inspection. He traced a finger from the hollow of her throat to the cleavage of her bra.

'I knew you'd be this beautiful,' he whispered, his eyes never leaving her, his fingers stroking lightly along her collarbones. 'I haven't been able to stop thinking about you.'

Billie's eyes fluttered closed under his silky caress.

'I've dreamed about being inside you,' he said, and her eyes opened at his frank admission. He sank on his knees before her and kissed her belly. She sank her hand into his crinkly hair as his tongue dipped into her navel.

'Gareth,' she moaned, her legs threatening to give away.

He grabbed her other hand and placed it on his shoulder and Billie held on for dear life, bunching his shirt in her hands as his tongue traced from one hip to the other.

'Damn...you taste good.' She felt his groan hot against her belly.

Billie whimpered at the want and ache in his voice. Ached for him too. Wanted to touch him, put her mouth to him as he was to her. She grabbed at his shirt, hauled it up, yanking him up with it, whipping it off, her greedy hands going to his chest, feeling the heat, her palms revelling in the rough smatter of hair as he plundered her mouth, squeezing her buttocks, urging her closer.

And then his palms were sliding beneath the waistband of her track pants, sizzling against the bare flesh of her bottom, and she moaned against his mouth as his thumbs hooked into the band sitting on her hips and pulled it down, her underwear going too. He eased them over her hips, his palms pushing them down her legs.

Billie kicked out of them and then she was completely naked, conscious of the erotic scrape of denim against the bare skin of her thighs and the smooth play of his hands as they caressed her buttocks, kneading and stroking, urging her closer to him.

'Bed,' he said, pulling away slightly to walk her closer to the mattress, stopping when the backs of her thighs hit the edge, urging her to sit, to lie back.

She sat. She lay.

She stretched her arms above her head and looked right at him.

'God…Billie…' he said, his breath rough, 'the things I want to do to you.'

Billie smiled, her nipples peaking under his hot gaze. She lifted her leg and hooked it around the back of his thighs. 'Bit hard to do it from all the way up there,' she murmured.

He slid a hand onto her thigh. 'I just want to look at you some more.'

Billie's cheeks warmed as he did exactly that. Pinned to the bed by the raw sexuality in his blue gaze, her neck flushed, her nipples ruched into tight, hard pebbles, her belly tightened.

The tingling at the juncture of her thighs went from buzz to burn.

'Gareth,' she complained, her voice almost a pant. She was going to die from the anticipation if he didn't do something. 'You promised me Elvis.'

His hand tightened on her thigh and he grinned. 'Do you see me talking?'

'You're talking with your eyes.'

He laughed then. 'Damn straight. Do you know what they're saying?'

'No.' She grimaced. 'But I'm guessing you're going to tell me.'

He grinned again. 'They're saying…where do I start first? Do I stroke? Do I kiss? Do I lick?'

Billie bit back a full-blown moan. 'I'm good with any combination.'

'Do I start at your mouth and work down?' he mused, following that path with his eyes. 'Or do I start at your toes and head up? Or do I just zero in on one bit. And, if so, which bit? Your neck?' His gaze dropped to her breasts, 'Your nipples?' It lingered there for long moments and Billie suppressed the urge to arch her back. 'Or do I start a little further south?'

His gaze moved down to the juncture of her thighs and Billie swallowed—hard.

'You're like a smorgasbord,' he murmured, staring at her there. 'And I'm really, really hungry.'

Billie's leg clamped hard around his thigh. 'Damn it, Gareth,' she groaned. 'A little less conversation.'

He chuckled, cranking her frustration up another notch. 'Where do you want me first?'

'Just kiss me,' she half moaned, half begged, reaching for him. 'Kiss me anywhere.'

And then he crawled on the bed over top of her and kissed her. Long and deep and so exquisitely Billie wanted to cry for the beauty of it. It sucked away her breath and twenty-six years of being an Ashworth-Keyes as she linked her arms around his neck and fell headlong into the perfect insanity.

They kissed for an age. Universes were born and died and still he kissed her. Taking his time, savouring her taste and her moans and sighs. Billie let him lead, followed him eagerly as her own hands explored the contours of his neck, his shoulders, his back. Her fingers brushed the denim waistband of his jeans and pushed beneath, finding other contours, better contours to squeeze and knead.

Suddenly, impatient with any barrier between them, her fingers came around to the front, delving between their bodies, nudging open his button and his zip and pushing at the fabric, taking his underwear as well, easing them both down over his hips as he had done to her.

He lifted, shifted to give her access, wriggled and kicked out of the denim, not breaking his lip lock once, and then he was naked, settling between her thighs, taunting her mercilessly with a slow rub, the long, hard length of him easing through all her slick heat.

'God…you feel so good. So wet…' he groaned against her mouth. 'I want to be inside you.'

'*Gareth,*' Billie gasped, at the strained urgency of his words and the slow erotic grind. She dug her nails into his back. 'Yes,' she panted. 'God…please…yes.'

He lifted away from her and Billie was momentarily bereft. 'No,' she protested, grabbing for him.

He came back to her, kissed her. 'It's okay,' he murmured, dropping soothing kisses against her mouth, her nose, her eyelids. 'Just getting a condom.'

And then he was gone again but he was back quickly and sheathing himself and settling between her legs again and she was opening wide to him, lifting her hips, locking her legs around his waist, blatantly inviting him inside.

She gasped at the first thick nudge of him and when he entered her completely, sliding all the way in, she arched her back and cried out.

'Billie,' he panted, burying his face in her neck.

Billie slid her hands onto his buttocks, clenching them hard in her hands, holding him tight, right where he was as he pressed and stretched all the right spots. 'Feels so good,' she muttered.

He chuckled into her neck and it was sweet and sexy all at once, fanning hot breath onto her sensitised skin. Then he planted the flats of his arms on either side of her head and lifted himself up, rearing over her, their chests apart, their hips joined, his eyes looking right down into hers.

'Hold on,' he said. 'It's going to feel better.'

He moved then, flexing his hips, and she gasped again, gripping his back as he pulled out and slid back in, thick and sure. Billie shut her eyes as pleasure shimmied through the nerve fibres in her belly and thighs.

He was right, it felt *so* much better.

'Look at me.'

Billie opened her eyes and saw his blue gaze piercing her. 'I want to watch you come,' he said, pulling out. 'I want you to be...' he eased into her oh-so-slowly '...looking right at me.'

Billie nodded but her eyes closed involuntarily as his hardness stretched every last millimetre of her and everything clenched inside.

'Billie.' They snapped open at the raw command. 'I said...' he pulled out '...open.' He pushed in.

Billie fought the urge to close them again as pleasure pulled at her eyelids. She groaned, gripped his buttocks, as the maddeningly slow pace continued. 'Come on, Gareth, faster.'

'No.' He grimaced, the veins in his neck standing out. 'I'm going to make you come so slowly you're going to feel every...' he eased in '...single...' he eased out '...second.'

He eased all the way in again.

And it was working. A flutter pulsed low in her belly as she gripped the hard length of him.

'You're beautiful,' he murmured, looking down at her, burying his fingers in her hair as he kept up the slow and easy pace. 'I've wanted you since that first night, at the accident. I could hardly take my eyes off you.'

'Oh, yeah?' she panted. 'Was that before or after I tossed my cookies?' He hit a sweet spot and she gasped, anchoring her hands to his shoulders and flexing her hips. 'Oh, God, yes, just there,' she said, all high and breathy.

He obliged, angling himself just right, massaging the

spot back and forth with the same steady thrusts, cranking up the flutter.

'God, Billie,' he groaned, as he thrust and held tight, seating himself deep. 'You make me crazy. I can't believe I kissed you in the tearoom...I so should not have done that.'

'Yes,' she moaned, as she flexed her hips some more, encouraging him to go deeper. 'You should have.' She looked into his eyes. 'I wanted it.' She locked her legs around his waist, lifting her hips again. 'I *needed* it.'

It was satisfying to see his eyes shut, hear the hiss of his breath. 'Damn it, Billie,' he groaned, his eyes flashing open, piercing her with hungry eyes as he clamped a hand to her hip. 'Stop wriggling like that.'

Billie shook her head, circling her hips again, daring him with her gaze. 'You've kept me waiting for weeks, Gareth.' She clenched internal muscles around him. 'Enough already.'

Gareth groaned then dropped his head, kissing her hard, surging inside her as he released her hip, his elbows digging into the bed either side of her head, giving him greater purchase. 'I wanted to go inside with you that morning in the car,' he said, pulling away from her mouth, his own moist from their passion. He rocked into her. 'And that night, at your place...'

Billie could see his biceps flexing in her peripheral vision as he slid in and out. 'You're here now,' she said, lifting her head, nuzzling his lips. 'So do me already.'

And she kissed him, hot and hard, putting every ounce of herself into it. Showing him the extent of her need, the depths of her desperation. Whimpering, 'Please,' against his mouth. Laying herself bare. Making herself vulnerable to him in a way she'd never done with another man. Needing his possession as much as she needed oxygen.

Did he want her to beg? Because she'd do that too.

Billie was breathing hard when she pulled out of the kiss. So was he.

Gareth looked down at her, his gaze roving over her face, her neck, her breasts, his chest heaving. 'Like this?' he asked, pumping his hips a little quicker.

Billie moaned as he hit all the right spots. 'God...yes.' Her head dropped back, her belly tightened.

He sped up some more. 'You want it like this?' he demanded.

Billie whimpered. 'Yes,' she gasped. 'More.'

'Like this?' he panted, his gaze snagging hers as his thrusts steadily picked up tempo, rocking her head, driving her higher and higher.

The flutter turned into a ripple.

She grabbed his buttocks. 'Yes.'

'You want it hard and fast?' he demanded.

Billie moaned, finding his blue gaze utterly compelling. 'God, yes.' Meaty muscles flexed in her hands with each thrust and she held them fast, anchored herself there.

'More?'

'Yes.' Her heart thundered, her breath rasped. The ripple became a contraction. 'Don't stop,' she gasped. 'Don't. Ever. Stop.'

He didn't. He drove into her relentlessly, their bodies meshed as one, their gazes locked. The contractions multiplied, rippling out, her consciousness slowly fraying at the edges. 'Yes, yes,' she sobbed, her eyes widening, as a wave of pleasure washed over her.

'Yes,' he muttered triumphantly, as she tightened around him. 'That's it...yes. Hold on, I've got you.'

And then as more waves broke he slowed it right down. Billie whimpered as he pulsed in and out slowly, rocking her gently, sweetly, wringing every ounce of pleasure out of each contraction, prolonging it to an unbearable intensity.

She shut her eyes. It was too much. It was going to kill

her. She was going to die, die here in his arms, gasping in pleasure. 'Look at me, damn it, Billie,' he demanded.

She looked at him as she slowly came apart.

'Look at what you do to me.'

He groaned then, long and low, his blue gaze heating to flame, his arms trembling, his hips thrusting hard, jerking to a standstill as he cried out.

Billie gripped him hard, his pleasure feeding hers, the honesty in his eyes overwhelming. 'Yes,' she whispered, snaking a hand up into his hair, twisting her fingers hard into his wavy locks, dragging his head down. 'More,' she said against his lips.

'Yes,' he said, kissing her, moving his hips again.

Billie moaned into his mouth as the pulsing continued unabated, her entire body buffeted by waves of intense pleasure. 'Good,' she whispered. 'So good.'

'Yes,' he agreed.

And he kissed her all the way to the end. Until he collapsed on top of her and they were both gasping and sated.

CHAPTER SEVENTEEN

GARETH WOKE A few hours later with Billie spooning him, her hand lightly stroking his hip. His groin was already well and truly awake. He smiled. 'A little lower.'

Billie laughed as his low rumble vibrated along muscle fibres already in a state of excitability. She slid her hand onto his solid thigh and then down onto his erection.

'Lower?'

Gareth grunted, shutting his eyes as she slid her hand up and down. 'No,' he said, shunting in a ragged breath. 'That's just right.'

She played a little longer before sliding her hand up to his shoulder and urging him onto his back. She threw her leg across his body and claimed his lips and then, before she knew it, he was pulling her over on top of him, settling the slick juncture of her thighs against the hot, hard length of him.

She rubbed herself against his delicious thickness, pleasure pouring heat into the cauldron of her pelvis.

'Mmm,' he murmured, stroking her back. 'That feels good.'

Billie sighed, stilling against him, enjoying the feel of his girth, hard and good, pressing into all her softness. She rested her cheek on his pec, the thud of Gareth's heart and the slow, lazy patterns he was stroking over her back lulling her eyes shut.

Gareth shut his eyes too, remembering how nice this part was. Lying with a woman afterwards. Touching her. Snuggling in the glow. Every nerve ending sated and energised at the same time. Feeling lazy and heavy but also light and floaty.

He opened his eyes after a while. Billie's breathing was deep and even and he wondered if she was asleep. 'Thank you,' he said into the dark. 'I've missed this.'

Billie stirred from the trancelike state she'd entered. She lifted her head to look at him. 'Am I your first…I mean, since Catherine…? Has there been anyone else?'

He smiled at her, his hand stroking down the side of her face, tucking a strand of hair behind her ear. 'Why? Was I that rusty?'

Billie laughed as she made two fists on his chest and propped her chin on them. 'If that was you rusty I hope I'm around for when you're well oiled.'

He grinned at her and Billie's heart hitched a little. 'If we keep going this way, that should be by morning.'

She smiled. 'Lucky me.'

Gareth picked up another lock of her hair and sifted it through his fingers. Lying in the dark with her, her body warm and supple, her breasts pressed against his chest, he felt like he could tell her anything.

'I've had a couple of brief liaisons since Catherine died. One was at a conference. A one-night stand thing. The other was a mother from Amber's school, who'd just been through a rough divorce and was after a little revenge sex.'

Billie smiled, despite the spike of jealousy niggling at her chest. 'She chose well.'

He chuckled. 'It was good. Fun. The first time was only a couple of months after Catherine had died. I was…lost, I guess.' He sought her gaze as he rubbed a copper lock between his finger pads. 'I missed her so much. I wanted to stop feeling so awful, to forget for a while. But…I felt even more awful after, like I'd cheated on her. The second time, Laura, was much later. I was more emotionally ready for it. And I…needed it. I needed to feel like a man again, a fully functioning man.'

Billie sobered. She understood what he was telling her. It was only natural for a man who had lost the love of his life to go through the entire gamut of emotional responses to that loss.

But it beggared the question—what was she? Was she just another signpost on his journey through grief?

She absently traced her finger around his nipple, the hairs tickling. 'Is that was this is? Am I helping you feel like a man again?'

Gareth frowned. Her tone was light but her eyes had gone all serious. 'What? No.' He grabbed her hand. He couldn't concentrate when she was touching him like that. 'No,' he reiterated, bringing her fingers to his mouth and kissing them.

He shifted then, taking her with him as he rolled over, rolling her under him, his body half on, half off her, his thigh parting her legs, pinning them to the bed. He propped himself up on an elbow.

He needed her to understand what she meant. What their coming together tonight meant to him.

Gareth pushed his hand into her hair and stroked his thumb along her cheekbone as he looked into her eyes.

'You're the first woman since my wife died that's meant *anything* to me. For the first time in five years this isn't about me or my grief or what I want or need. I'm attracted to you, because of *you*. And I know the way you know things deep down in your gut that this can't possibly last but I really *like* you, Billie.'

'Yes.' She smiled. 'You told me already.'

'No.' This wasn't the same thing as their fake-date thing. 'I *like you* like you.'

Billie's heart squeezed in her chest at his sudden serious-ness. It wasn't the L word that most women her age seemed to long for but it was such an earnest, heartfelt sentiment that Billie drank it up. Gareth had been through so much, lost so much. That he was even capable of feeling anything again was a miracle. And she cherished it.

She smiled at him. 'I *like* you too.'

'It's okay, I don't expect a reciprocal admission. That wasn't why I said it. I just know I feel very deeply for you already. And I wanted you know it too. I wanted you to know that you're not some way for me to prove that I still have all my working bits or that you're some diversion to keep the blackness at bay. You're not *just* my two-yearly roll in the hay.'

He kissed her then, slow and gentle. Kissed her until she moaned and clung and begged him for more.

They finally woke around nine. Slow and easy at first as they drifted up through layers of sleep then hot and heavy as their bodies woke and desire, sweet and heady, surged through their systems.

'I think I could get used to this,' he murmured.

Billie sighed. She could definitely get used to waking up with Gareth. It would be *no* hardship. She snuggled into him. 'Me too.'

Gareth's hands found her breasts and his groin perked up again. He was surprised it was still physically able after last night. He was about to suggest going again when a loud growl emanated from her stomach. Gareth laughed.

'Wow. That's a helluva belly rumble. I'm impressed.'

Billie blushed at her noisy innards. 'Sorry.' She slid her hand over her navel. 'It must be all that physical activity you put me through. I'm starving.'

'Put you through.' He chuckled again. 'Didn't seem like a chore when you were screaming my name all night,' he murmured, nipping at the patch of skin where shoulder met neck. She sucked in a breath and her nipples beaded in his palm. 'I make some mean French toast. Or would you prefer jam on toast?'

Billie smiled as her stomach rumbled again. 'I *love* French toast. Do you have banana?'

'Yes. And bacon. And maple syrup'

'You are a god amongst men.'

He grinned. 'Damn straight.' He kissed her neck then extricated himself, dropping his head down to kiss her hip before leaving the bed. He grabbed his underwear off the floor and climbed into it before turning to look at her. She'd rolled onto her back, not bothering to pull the sheet up. His gaze wandered up and down the length of her and his recipe for French toast slipped away.

Her stomach growled again and he shook his head. 'Why don't you come and keep me company?'

Billie arched an eyebrow. 'Like this?'

He nodded. 'Exactly like that. You could be my muse while I create food for you. Of course, I couldn't promise that you won't end up covered in maple syrup.'

Billie's head filled with a very erotic image of her spread out on the kitchen bench while he licked maple syrup out of her belly button. And other places. Thinking about where she could lick it off him was equally erotic.

She rolled up onto her elbow and she liked the way his gaze wandered to the fall of her breasts. 'Let me take a shower first. Maybe bring it back to bed after?'

Gareth liked the way she thought. He particularly liked the way she thought when she was naked in his bed. 'Good thinking.' His gaze drifted down to where the sheet cut across low on her hips, hiding one of her best bits from his view.

A fine spot for maple syrup if ever there was one.

Billie was pretty sure she knew where his mind was and

her toes curled beneath the sheet. 'You could always, of course, join me?' she suggested, slowly trailing her palm down the middle of her belly, bringing it to a halt where sheet met skin. His gaze snagged on the movement and she smiled as she slid her fingers under the edge slightly. 'You could make sure I get all those *nooks and crannies* clean?'

Gareth dragged in a shaky breath. He wanted to rip that sheet back and dive between her legs. Make her come so loud she'd be sure to think twice about teasing him so blatantly.

For sure he wanted to take her against the tiles of his shower.

He dragged his gaze to her face. 'Do you want to eat at some stage today? Because if I get you in the shower all wet and slippery, there's no way I'm letting you out for a *very long time.*'

Billie smiled as he snatched up his jeans and left without a backward glance.

She sighed. The man really did have a spectacular butt.

CHAPTER EIGHTEEN

GARETH HAD CLIMBED into his jeans and was whistling by the time he hit the kitchen. He shouldn't be. He had a hunch, despite them both admitting to having feelings for each other, that things with Billie weren't going to run smoothly. She was pretty messed up about her life direction and grief had made him wary, more cautious with his heart.

But today he didn't much care about any of that.

He flicked the radio on. Rock music blared out loud and perfect and he bopped his head to the exhilarating beat as he clanged around in the kitchen, barefoot, bare-chested and one hundred per cent lord of all he surveyed.

He felt indomitable. He felt like a freaking king.

He felt like throwing his head back and crying out Tarzan-style as he beat his chest.

Gareth, King of the Jungle!

He smiled at the notion as he cracked the eggs into a bowl. He couldn't remember the last time he'd felt this good. He certainly hadn't felt this deep down happy with either of his last two liaisons.

Sure, Laura had been fun, a brief superficial distraction that he'd enjoyed very much, but she hadn't left him feeling this bone-deep satisfaction.

This feeling that all was right with the world.

Maybe he was getting ahead of himself. Maybe hormones and endorphins were making him delirious.

But nothing could erase his happy this morning.

Billie towelled off and headed back into the bedroom for her clothes. They lay scattered around the floor and her stomach dropped just remembering everything that had happened since she'd shed those suckers last night.

She picked them up, figuring she could get back into her track pants and turtleneck. She didn't want to get back into her undies but she could go without. If she played her cards right they'd be back in bed before too much longer anyway.

She smiled as she plotted how she might drop her commando state into their breakfast conversation. Or was that brunch?

She quickly jammed a foot into the leg of her track pants, her gaze taking in her surroundings properly for the first time as she stuck her other foot in and pulled the track pants up. The dishevelled bed dominated the room. Off one wall was the en suite. Off the other a walk-in wardrobe.

Billie grinned to herself. Oh, the possibilities!

She sauntered over. Maybe she could find something clean of Gareth's to get into instead?

The wardrobe was extensive but most of it was empty except for a small section of hanging clothes and some occupied drawers. She figured the owners must have taken all their clothes with them and what was left was Gareth's.

She riffled through his hanging clothes and found a russet-coloured business shirt that matched her hair perfectly. She inhaled the sunshine and soap-powder smell of it before removing it from the hanger and shoving her arms through the sleeves.

She turned and inspected herself in the full-length mirror. Her hair was still knotted on top of her head and she quickly released it, shaking it out, watching as it fell down around her shoulders.

She stripped off her track pants and she liked what she saw—pink cheeks, glowing skin, sparkling eyes. She didn't look tired as she probably should be, considering how little sleep she'd had. On the contrary, she looked like a woman who had been kept up all night in the best possible way.

She looked thoroughly sated.

On impulse, Billie undid the top two and bottom two buttons, leaving only two in the middle holding the shirt together. An enticing slice of bare breasts and a glimpse of shadow at the juncture of her thighs looked back at her.

She put her hand on her hip and pouted at her reflection. The action drew the hem of the shirt up even higher, revealing a much bigger glimpse of what was below her navel.

Not the effect she was going for.

She turned to his drawers and searched for some underwear, smiling when she found a pair of fluro green boxers. *Perfect*.

She slipped them on. They were on the baggy side but she rolled the waistband low on her hips and it anchored there well enough. She went back to the mirror, giving herself a once-over. A barely recognisable woman stared back at her. With her hair all loose, her mouth all pouty and cleavage to burn, she looked far from a responsible emergency medicine doctor.

She certainly didn't look like an Ashworth-Keyes.

No. She looked like one of those old-fashioned sex kittens from the magazines of the forties and fifties.

Billie smiled. She hoped Gareth *liked* it too.

Gareth was so engrossed in the music, juggling the cooking of the French toast and the bacon and thinking about how good Billie would look all wet and naked in the shower, he didn't hear the key in the lock or the door open.

He was well and truly in his happy place.

So much so he actually startled when Amber appeared in front of him, saying, 'God, that smell's amazing. Remind me to flip out more often, would you?'

He blinked at his daughter uncomprehendingly for a few moments. 'Amber?'

She laughed. 'Correct. Are you okay? You're looking weird.' She stepped forward and kissed him on the cheek, swiping a piece of piping-hot, crispy bacon off the plate.

Gareth couldn't think for a moment. Crap!

Amber.

She'd been to that support group yesterday and he'd forgotten he'd invited her for breakfast this morning!

'Ooh, French toast?' she murmured, oblivious to his turmoil. 'You've outdone yourself. Great timing too. It's as if you knew I was about to walk through the door.'

He smiled as he gathered his scattered wits. He needed to talk and fast. Billie was bound to be showing her face any time soon. 'Yes. About that...'

Billie followed the sound of music and the smell of frying bacon all the way to the kitchen. Her mouth watered and her stomach rumbled louder.

'Hope you've made double,' she announced as she entered the kitchen. 'You wore me out last night, I need sus—'

Billie stopped abruptly when she realised Gareth wasn't alone in the kitchen.

Amber?

'Oh.' She looked from Gareth to a shocked Amber then back to Gareth again. 'I'm sorry. I didn't realise you had... company...'

Billie wished the floor would open up and swallow her in the tense silence that followed. Suddenly her forties sex-kitten look seemed cheap and tawdry. Or at least that must be how it looked to Gareth's daughter.

Amber looked at her father. 'Who the hell is *she*?'

Gareth grimaced at the poison in Amber's words. She was looking at him with eyes full of anger and confusion and he'd give anything to rewind the last couple of minutes.

He and Amber had never talked about what would happen when this day swung around. When he became involved with another woman.

He'd always figured when—*if*—it did, that it would be a gradual thing and Amber would be along for the ride.

He hadn't expected to be sprung fresh out of bed by his twenty-year-old daughter.

He held up both his hands. Amber looked like she was going to bolt and he didn't want her leaving without knowing that this wasn't what she was thinking. 'I'm sorry, Amber. I forgot you were coming over this morning.'

Clearly the wrong thing to say as Amber went from frosty anger to visible hurt. But she recovered quickly, her wounded eyes turning as hard as stone. 'I just bet you did,' she snapped, whirling away.

'Amber…' he said, striding across the room to stop her exit. He grabbed her arm. 'Let me explain.'

'What are you going to tell me?' she demanded, whirling back to face him. 'That this isn't what I think it is? That this…woman isn't wearing the shirt I bought you for Christmas last year and you haven't been *screwing h*er all night long?'

Billie's audible gasp sliced through him. 'Amber, that's enough.' This had obviously come as a shock to her and it certainly wasn't the way he'd have hoped Amber found out about his private life but he wouldn't let her cheapen what had happened between him and Billie either.

Amber glared at him. 'Screw you too,' she said, jerking her arm out of his grasp and storming out of the house.

Fabulous. Beautifully handled.

Not.

He turned back to Billie, his brain churning with a hundred different things to say, none of them particularly adequate in the face of her stillness or pallor. She was standing, apparently frozen to the spot in the middle of the kitchen, every cute freckle dusting the bridge of her nose standing out.

The fact that she looked so incredibly sexy in his shirt was a particular irony. Amber's impromptu arrival had blown any chance of him getting her out of it now.

He raked a hand through his hair. 'Sorry about that.'

His words prodded Billie out of her inertia. She shook her head. 'It's fine.'

'I...forgot.' He rubbed his eyes. 'I forgot I invited her over.'

Billie nodded. She didn't think Gareth had deliberately set this up for some fairy-tale meet-cute. If he had, it had seriously backfired.

'It's fine,' she said again.

'She's just found out that she has the BRCA1 gene,' he said. 'She went to some support group yesterday. We were supposed to be debriefing this morning but—'

But.

Billie didn't need him to fill in the blanks. She was the *but*. It was *her* fault he'd forgotten. S*he'd* distracted him from his parental responsibilities.

'I'm sorry to hear that,' she said, hugging herself as she sucked in a breath around the painful lump in the centre of her chest. It was stupid to feel slighted—this wasn't about her. Amber must be reeling from the dreadful news. 'She must be feeling very vulnerable at the moment.'

If she kept this about Amber, Billie knew she could keep everything in perspective. And it should be about Amber. The twenty-year-old had just been dealt a huge whammy. It was nothing compared to whatever fledgling thing they had going on.

He rubbed the back of his neck. 'It's been a shock.'

Billie nodded. Of course it had. She only had to look at Gareth's face to know how much it was eating him up. 'I'm just…going to go,' she said.

Gareth looked at her in alarm. 'No…Billie…' He joined her in the kitchen in four easy strides, sliding his hands onto her waist.

He knew he'd gaffed with her too. This morning when he'd woken up he'd felt bulletproof. And then Amber had thrown one hell of a spanner in the works.

'I didn't mean to imply that this Amber thing is your fault. *I* messed this up.'

Billie held up her hand. 'It's fine. *I'm* fine. You should go to her. You need to talk to Amber.'

And she needed some time and space. Billie was still struggling to assimilate what had happened. She guessed it was inevitable that reality would intrude into their bubble sooner or later but she'd figured she'd have a little more time. And reality would come in the form of work or her family, not in the form of Gareth's rightfully furious daughter.

The reality of Gareth's life was that he was a forty-year-old father and that had to be the main priority in his life. The reality was that they *both* had other priorities in their life—how could it ever work?

Reality was a bitch like that.

Gareth sighed. He knew she was right. He had to go after Amber but he didn't want to leave it like this with Billie either. 'Can I see you tonight?'

She stepped out of his arms. 'I'm having dinner with my family tonight.'

It was the first time Billie had ever been grateful for one of the tediously long, pompous do's she was subjected to every month.

'I'll see you at work on Monday, though, right?' she added.

Gareth may have been off the market for a long time but he knew a brush-off when he saw it. Although, to be fair to Billie, this had to be a little overwhelming.

Maybe it was good to have some space.

'Sure,' he said.

'Okay… I'll just…' she looked over her shoulder '…grab my stuff, then.'

Gareth watched her go, thoughts churning around his head as he absently dealt with the half-cooked breakfast. She was back in the kitchen in under five minutes, wearing her clothes from last night. The brief goodbye peck on the cheek she gave him was not encouraging.

Neither was the way she didn't look back as she strode out of his house.

CHAPTER NINETEEN

GARETH WAS STANDING on Amber's doorstep an hour later. He'd showered and changed first, knowing from old that giving Amber some time to cool down always boded well.

Carly answered the door. 'You're in the doghouse,' she said in her usual blunt manner.

'Yes.' Gareth grimaced. 'Can I come in?'

'I think her exact words were, "If that rat shows up here, kick his butt to the kerb."'

Gareth ignored the insult, quirking an eyebrow. 'Is that what you're here to do?'

Carly was possibly the most petite female he knew. Sure, she made up for it with her big, ballsy personality but he could have pushed her aside with one finger.

Carly opened the door wider and stepped aside. 'Nope. She needs to talk to you. She just doesn't know it yet.'

He grinned. 'I've always liked you.'

'Got your back, Jack,' Carly quipped, as Gareth entered.

'So…how is she…really?' he asked, after Carly shut the door.

Carly shrugged. 'I think she's on her bed, sticking pins in an effigy of you.'

Gareth chuckled but quickly sobered. 'I messed up, Carly.'

'Yeah.' Carly nodded. 'She said. But you know what I told her?'

'No, what?'

'That any other hottie father who'd been through what you'd been through would probably have blown through a stack of sympathetic chicks by now and it was about time she stopped putting you on some exalted pedestal and realised you're just flesh and blood. And that Catherine wouldn't have wanted you to be alone for ever.'

Even as an eight-year-old, Carly had said stuff that had been designed to shock, so he ignored her *hottie father* reference. But she'd always been a wise little thing. 'Oh.'

'Yeah…I think she's sticking pins in an effigy of me too.'

Gareth chuckled. 'Well, thank you. That can't have been easy.'

Carly shrugged. 'Ya gotta know when to hand out the tissues and when to dish out some tough love. Breast cancer gene gets tissues. Daddy's got a girlfriend after being a widower for five long lonely years not so much.'

Gareth was grateful that Amber had such a good friend in Carly. He knew Catherine's death had devastated Carly too. He glanced down the hall at Amber's door.

'Going in, then. Wish me luck.'

'You won't need it,' Carly said, shaking her head. 'She can never stay mad at you for long.'

Gareth snorted. 'She was angry at me for two years.'

'That's different. Her mother had died. You think anything's worse than that?'

Gareth shook his head. 'Good point.'

Gareth knocked on the door but didn't wait for permission to enter. It was unlocked so he pushed it open.

'Go away,' Amber said, glaring at him from the bed. Her eyes were red-rimmed and puffy-looking but there were no effigies in sight.

'I think we should talk.'

'I don't want to talk to you.'

'Fine… I'll talk and you can listen.'

Amber stared at him mutinously, crossing her arms. 'How about you turn around and don't come back?'

Gareth shook his head, not easily deterred. 'I'm really sorry about earlier. You coming over had slipped my mind and—'

Amber's snort interrupted him. 'I wonder why?'

'Yes,' Gareth sighed. 'Billie being there distracted me.'

'Billie? That's a stupid name.'

Gareth would have laughed at the childish comeback had he not already been walking a delicate line. 'It's actually Willamina. Willamina Ashworth-Keyes. She's one of the new residents at work.'

'You think I should be impressed that you can pull a doctor?' she said scornfully.

'No, of course not…' Gareth sighed, risking sitting on the edge of Amber's bed. 'I just thought you might like to know more about her.'

'Why?' she flared back at him. 'Is she going to be my new mummy?'

Gareth took a breath and searched for the deeper meaning to the scathing question, like the hospital counsellors had urged him to do. 'You're angry because you think I'm replacing Catherine? That I'm forgetting her?'

'No,' Amber denied hotly, but Gareth could see the hurt in her eyes. 'I'm angry because we were supposed to spend the morning together but you *forgot* because you were too busy with your new girlfriend.'

'She's not my girlfriend, Amber. We've just met. It's just new…' He looked down at his hands as he remembered Billie's noncommittal departure. 'I'm not even certain it's going anywhere.'

'But you're in love with her.'

He glanced at Amber sharply. Her puffy eyes looked

deadly serious and they were demanding the truth. 'We *just* met,' he repeated.

Amber shook her head at him, her lip curling. 'How *old* is she?'

'She's twenty-six.'

'Bloody hell, Gareth!'

'Yes.' The thought was depressing. 'That is one of the complications.'

'Didn't stop you sleeping with her, though, did it?'

'Amber,' he warned. 'I'm not going to talk about my sex life with you.'

'Oh…so you have a *sex life* now?' she demanded.

Gareth grimaced. 'Probably not after today, no…'

Amber didn't say anything for a long time, she just looked at him, her gaze roving over his face, searching for what, he didn't know. But slowly the anger drained from her face.

'You do love her.'

Gareth shook his head. He wished he knew how he felt. 'I don't know, Amba-san. I know I like her. I like her a lot. But it's complicated. She's at a different stage in her life to me.'

Another snort but this one was softer, more mocking than angry. 'No kidding.'

He gave a half-laugh, relieved that Amber's anger had dissipated. He could still see shadows in her gaze but she'd had them since she'd been fifteen.

Amber swung her legs over the side of the bed. 'I'm sorry. I didn't mean to flip out the way I did. I guess I'm doing that quite a bit lately,' she said quietly.

He shrugged. 'You're dealing with a lot.'

'I was…shocked. I guess part of me always thought you'd be faithful to Mum for ever. I know that's not fair to you, though. Carly says I need to cut you some slack and that you're just flesh and blood.'

Gareth smiled. He leaned in closer to her and nudged her arm with his. 'I think we should keep Carly.'

'As if we could get rid of her.'

They laughed then and it felt good after the emotionally charged morning. When they stopped Gareth looked down at his daughter. 'I'm always going to love your mum, Amba-san. No matter what my future holds, she'll always be...' he tapped his chest '...here.'

She turned her face to him and tears were swimming in her big eyes, so like her mother's. 'I have this dream every now and then... I can't remember what she looks like. What if I forget what she looks like, Gareth?'

Gareth put his arm around her shoulder and hugged her to his side. 'You won't forget. Her image is engraved on your heart. And, anyway, there are too many pictures of her around.'

'Don't you ever worry you will?'

Gareth shook his head. 'No. She's engraved on my heart too. And even if for some obscure reason I did and every single picture of the thousands we have were destroyed, I'd just need to look at you.'

They sat together for long moments. He kissed her on the head again. 'You okay now?'

Amber nodded, looking up at him. 'I guess we'd better go and let Carly know she's not going to need to bury a body.'

'Comforting to know she would, though,' Gareth said, smiling as he took Amber's hand and they stood together and headed for the door.

At nine-thirty Billie was ready to fake a heart attack to get away early from the family dinner. But dessert was yet to be served and an Ashworth-Keyes did not leave before dessert, coffee, liqueurs and every single grotesque medical story since the last time they had met had been told.

And it *was* only once a month.

In between grilling her about the emergency department at St Luke's, her grandfather, her parents, two uncles and three cousins were discussing a surgical case that had hit the news due to mismanagement. If she heard the words 'faecal peritonitis' one more time she was going to throw up her beef Wellington.

Did they really have to talk about such things while they were *eating*?

Of course, she should be used to it now—she'd grown up with medical chitchat forming the basis of most teatime conversation, but it all seemed so…clinical. Billie had an insane urge to mention Jessica—something they never talked about—just to get a human, non-medical reaction.

She didn't. *Of course.*

That would be very un-Ashworth-Keyes of her.

But her mind kept drifting to where she'd been this time last night, preferring the memory of being naked with Gareth than anything going on at the table. And when it wasn't there, it was reliving the nightmare of Amber's 'Who the hell is *she*?'

Coming face to face with the reality of Gareth's life had been a wake-up call. She hadn't handled it very well. But running away from things was what she did best.

'Billie?'

Billie blinked as her father's harsh voice dragged her out of the events of this morning. All eyes were on her. 'I'm sorry?'

He sighed impatiently. 'What on earth is the matter with you tonight? Why are you so distracted?' he demanded.

The whole table was looking at her, apparently waiting for her response. 'I'm just…tired,' she said lamely, dismissing her father's query with a wave of her hand.

'*Tired!*' her father snorted, as if it was something only lazy people suffered. If only he knew how very little sleep she'd had last night. 'A good doctor pushes through that barrier.'

And then he went off on a tangent about his days of training and how many hours they'd worked and how little time off they'd had, and then her grandfather and uncles joined in and Billie let her mind drift again.

Her phone vibrated in her pocket and she leapt for it as if it was a lifeline and she was drowning. Her father glared at her as she checked the text message. She didn't care. She knew it was bad table manners but so was talking about gruesome surgeries, as far as she was concerned.

Sorry about this morning. Things better with Amber. Thinking of you. Hope you are having a nice dinner with your family. Gareth x

Billie's heart thundered in her chest. She'd been worried about the fallout with Amber all day and had almost texted him a dozen times but had forced herself not to. Gareth needed to focus on his daughter—this mess was not about her. Not really anyway.

She stared at the screen. Her heart fluttered as she read and re-read *'Thinking of you'*. And that little 'x'. What the hell did that mean?

Her fingers shook as she tapped in a quick response.

Am going mad. Rescue me?

Her thumb hovered over the send button. Should she? Shouldn't she?

'Amber.' Her mother's gentle reprimand pulled all Billie's strings.

That was it. She needed to get out of here and the text left the ball in his court. He could send something flippant and noncommittal or he might just help.

She hit send.

Billie nervously placed the phone on the table, ignoring her mother's pursed lips. Would Gareth come to her rescue?

The phone vibrated almost instantly. She picked it up and swiped her thumb across the screen to read the new message.

Getting in car now. I'll be at yours in twenty. Plead a headache.

Billie smiled. She stood abruptly, cutting her father off in midstream as everyone jumped. 'I'm sorry. I have a headache,' she announced. She grabbed her bag from where it was hanging over the back of her chair. 'I'm going home.'

'That was sudden,' her father, who never liked being interrupted, said waspishly as he half stood.

'No, don't get up,' Billie dismissed, waving him back into his chair. She whipped around the table, doling out kisses. 'I'm fine. Just need to lie down in a dark room.'

With a very hot nurse.

'I'll see everyone next month.'

And before anyone could catch their breath she was practically running out of the house, her fingers flying over her phone keyboard.

See you soon.

She hesitated about putting an 'x' there as he had done. After last night it seemed natural but then, after everything this morning, she wasn't sure…

After dithering for a few seconds Billie decided against it, hitting send exactly as it was as she climbed into her car and reversed in a flurry of gravel down the driveway.

CHAPTER TWENTY

FORTY MINUTES LATER Gareth rolled onto his back in the middle of Billie's hallway, half-clothed, and groaned.

'Well…that was intense…'

Billie, her head still spinning, laughed as she slid her head onto his shoulder. 'Only what you deserved for rescuing a damsel in distress.'

Gareth gave a half-laugh. 'Well…you know what they say…you can take the guy out of the military…'

'Mmm,' Billie murmured, inhaling the smell of his skin, revelling in the warmth of his meaty pectoral muscle against her cheek. 'That blew my mind.'

Gareth shut his eyes as her nuzzling streaked hot arrows to his groin. How was that even *possible* so soon? 'A little on the fast side,' he murmured, thinking about their mad dash from the driveway to the door then collapsing to the floor once they'd got inside.

Billie turned her head until her chin was resting on his chest. Her gaze travelled up his whiskery throat to the downward sweep of his eyelashes. 'I don't know,' she murmured. 'I like it that you couldn't wait to have me. It's good for my ego.'

His smile did funny things to her pulse. A pulse that was barely back to its normal rhythm. He opened his eyes and their gazes locked and the humour she saw dancing in all that blueness bubbled in her heart.

'Trust me, your ego is going to be well and truly pandered to tonight.'

Gareth shifted then, displacing her, sat first before vaulting to his feet, adjusting his clothing as he went. He turned to look down at her. Her skirt was rucked right up, her blouse was half-undone and her breasts had been removed from her bra cups. Her cheeks were flushed and her hair lay in disarray around her head.

'Damn, you're sexy,' he muttered, offering her his hand.

Billie grinned as she took it and before she knew it she wasn't just on her feet but was swept up in his arms.

'I'm going to need directions,' he said.

She wound her arms around his neck as a nice buzz settled into her bones. She nuzzled his throat. 'You are the last man who needs *any* direction,' she sighed.

He chuckled and she could feel it reverberate through his windpipe. 'I mean to your room.'

Billie blushed, feeling foolish. 'Oh, yes…straight ahead, third door on the right.'

Gareth made it to her room in ten seconds, throwing her on the bed. He watched as her breasts bounced enticingly. 'I'm going to use your en suite,' he said. 'When I get back I'm going to be naked. You'd better be too.'

She quirked an eyebrow at him. 'Or what?'

Gareth grinned. She looked so sexy barely dressed, her mouth a little swollen from their passion, a flirty little dare sparkling in her eyes. He shoved his hands on his hips and let his eyes rake over her. 'I may have to spank you.'

Billie's breath hitched. She'd never been into that kind of thing but Gareth made it sound enticing. 'Maybe I'll stay dressed.'

He chuckled. 'Up to you.'

But when he strode out of the en suite she'd pulled the covers down and she was lying in the middle of the bed gloriously naked. It was his turn to quirk an eyebrow.

'I think I'm too squeamish for S and M.'

Gareth laughed at her slightly defensive tone. 'It's too much hard work anyway.'

Billie relaxed. 'I agree. Dinner with my parents was hard enough.' And she reached over and flicked out the light.

There was a desperation to Billie this time. In the hallway it had been all about burning off the tsunami of lust that had swamped them when they'd first laid eyes on each other again. This time, it seemed to Gareth, it was as if she was using it to obliterate everything else.

Dinner *must* have been a bust.

She clung to him in the aftermath and Gareth held her tight. Their breathing slowly returned to normal and eventually he said, 'Tell me about dinner.'

Billie stirred as Gareth's words sunk in. 'Nothing to tell.'

He trailed his fingers up and down her arm. 'I feel like we just had exorcism sex and that somehow it was related to dinner, and you won't spill the beans?'

'It's the same as it always is,' Billie dismissed. 'Tales of surgical glory interspersed with grilling me about what I'm doing. And tonight, for a lovely added extra, we got a graphic discussion on faecal peritonitis. *While we ate.*'

Gareth chuckled. He couldn't help himself. He could only imagine how that had gone down with Billie's volatile constitution.

'It's not funny,' Billie grouched. 'Give me a patient with a complex web of medical conditions any day.'

Gareth's fingers stilled on her arm. Surely Billie understood that being a GP came with its own set of gruesome realities?

'You do know that GPs deal with some fairly grotesque stuff too, right? They see their fair share of hideous wounds and unsightly conditions. The GP is usually the first place people seek help and it can be pretty raw there at the coalface. You'll still have to tell your patients they're dying. And they *will* die, Billie. In fact, you'll be the one there for them and their family right at the end.'

Billie rolled on her stomach and propped her chin on his chest. She shot him a reproachful look. 'Do I look naive to you?'

'No. Definitely not after that thing you just did anyway.' He grinned.

Billie whacked him playfully on the arm. 'Of course I know I'll come across stuff that will turn my stomach. That I'll have to look a patient in the eye and tell them they've only got a certain amount of time to live. I know that. And it'll be awful.'

Billie didn't even want to think about how awful some of those moments were going to be.

'But at least I'll *know* that patient. I'll have a relationship, a rapport with them. It won't be a stranger telling them.'

Gareth picked up a strand of her hair and rubbed the tip with the pads of his fingers. 'And you think that'll make it *easier*?'

'For them, yes. And also for me…I think. It'll never be easy, of course, but one of the hardest things to take about Corey's death was the fact that he died in a roomful of strangers. *I* had to tell his parents he'd died. *Me*. Who didn't know them from a bar of soap. It shouldn't happen like that, Gareth.'

Billie searched his face earnestly—he understood, didn't he? 'How many men have you seen die from combat wounds far away from the people who loved them?'

She watched him as he stared at the strand of her hair he had in his fingers. 'Too many,' he murmured.

'Exactly.' Billie continued. 'People should die with loved ones around them, not strangers. Their relatives shouldn't be told such devastating news by someone who doesn't know them. And I get that that's the way it is in emergency depart-

ments and when you're deployed to a war zone. Of course it is. But I don't want to spend the rest of my life imparting bad news to strangers.'

Gareth's gaze cut to Billie as he let the strand of hair drop. 'So don't.'

Billie stared at him. He made it sound so simple. Could she really get out from under twenty-six years of conditioning and manipulation and dare to reach for *her* dream?

'Tell your parents what you want. You're a big girl now. Billie. What's the worst that could happen?'

'A lot of yelling—my father. And tears—my mother. A lot of guilt tripping and subtle threats.'

'Are they going to stop loving you?'

Billie blinked. It had been a lot of years since she'd felt loved by them. She'd felt tolerated and pushed and pressured but love? She was fairly certain her parents were afraid to love too much again.

'They'll stop inviting me to dinner so I guess there'll be an upside,' she joked, her heart not in it.

'But…' he traced her bottom lip with his thumb '…you'll have what you want. You can be what *you* want.'

'You don't understand. I don't do this kind of thing. I'm the good daughter. The peacekeeper. It was hard enough to sell them on emergency medicine. I think my father may well have a heart attack if I tell him I've decided to become a GP. And my mother…'

Billie didn't want to be the one to kill Jessica twice.

'So you're just going to go along with their vision for you? Even if it means you'll be miserable?'

'I won't be miserable,' Billie protested, no idea now why she was defending the thing she didn't want to Gareth. 'I'll just not be one hundred per cent happy. I'll still see a lot of the stuff I like to deal with. A lot of emergency department stuff is GP territory and you know it.'

'Billie.'

She dropped her gaze from his, staring at the strong pulse beating in his throat. She couldn't bear to see the reproach, the disappointment in his eyes. 'You didn't see my mother the night Jess died. She was so gutted. And in those awful months afterwards she looked at me like I was their lifeline.'

Gareth bit back his reply. He wanted to push more. Push her to see she couldn't live someone else's life for them. But he didn't want to be that person. The one who swooped in and tried to fix everything. It could backfire badly and Billie needed to figure it out for herself.

She glanced up at him. 'You think I should tell them to stick it?'

Gareth gave her a half-smile, his fingers sifting through her hair. 'I think…' *I think I have to choose my words very carefully.* 'You have to make the decision that's right for you. And you've got time to do it. You were going to have to do a few years in a hospital anyway before you branched off into GP land, including time in emergency medicine, so none of this is wasted.'

Billie traced her index finger around his mouth, his whiskers tickling. 'Are you always this wise?'

Gareth rubbed his mouth against the pad of her finger. 'I just want you to be happy, Billie. Life's too short to be miserable.'

Billie thought about Corey. And Jess. And Catherine. And Amber staring down a potential death sentence. He was right. It was far too short to be having hypothetical conversations about her career that even she didn't know the answers to when she had a sex god in her bed.

She shifted, crawling on top of him, pushing up into a sitting position, straddling him. 'I know something that makes me happy,' she said, rubbing herself against him.

He sucked in a quick breath clamping his hands on her

hips. 'Coincidentally it makes me pretty damn happy too,' he murmured.

Billie smiled. 'Excellent.'

Gareth had to make a mad dash out of Billie's bed the next morning after sleeping through his alarm and dodging her sleepy advances. 'I'll be quick,' she protested, pulling the sheet back to entice him to stay. 'Like in the hallway.'

Gareth chuckled as he covered her up and kissed her hard on the mouth. It was all right for her, she started at eight, which gave her a whole extra hour to get to St Luke's.

'How about I join you in the shower?' she said from the bed as he headed for the en suite.

'I'm locking the door,' he threw over her shoulder. He'd be late for sure if she was in there with him all wet and slippery and determined.

When Gareth stepped out of the en suite the bed was empty and he could smell coffee and toast. His mouth watered and he followed the intoxicating aromas.

His mouth watered a little more as he entered the kitchen to find Billie standing at the bench in a polar fleece dressing gown, her hair swept up on top of her head, licking jam off her fingers.

'Mmm,' he said, reaching her in three easy strides, slipping his arms around her waist and nuzzling her neck. 'Something smells good.'

'The toast,' she said, picking up a slice and shoving it towards his mouth.

Gareth bit into it. Butter and jam melted against his tongue in some kind of orgasmic mix and he grabbed the slice as she let it go. He stepped back from her, moving to her side, his butt coming to rest against the bench, their hips almost touching.

'Coffee's done,' she said, as the toaster popped and she reached for the freshly cooked slices.

Gareth spied the percolator and headed for it as he downed the last large bite. He pulled two mugs off a nearby stand and filled them both. He knew without asking that she took it black with sugar—the same as him. A sugar bowl sat beside the percolator.

He fixed the coffees and passed hers over. He watched as she took her first sip and gave a happy little sigh. He'd heard that a lot last night and he laughed.

She smiled at him over the rim of the mug and he noticed she had a smear of butter on her top lip. He was just about to lean down and lick it off when a loud knock sounded on the door.

Gareth frowned down at her. 'Do you usually get visitors at six-thirty in the morning?'

Billie shook her head but her eyes held a little twinkle. 'No. I told my other lover to wait until after you'd left.'

He gave her a wry smile as she placed the mug on the bench but he grabbed her and kissed her hard. Pretend lover or not, he wanted her to know who she'd spent the night with.

Billie's head was spinning as she floated to the door, a goofy smile on her face. It was still there when she opened the door seconds later.

Seeing her visitor on the doorstep killed it dead.

'Dad?'

CHAPTER TWENTY-ONE

'HELLO, WILLAMINA.' HER father pecked her on the cheek.

Billie accepted the kiss automatically. 'Oh… Hi. You're here…early…'

'Morning rounds before my theatre list. Like to stay on top of things.'

'Oh…right.'

'Have you got a moment to chat?' he asked, rubbing his hands together vigorously, and Billie noted absently how nippy it was outside.

'Ah…actually…' she said, trying desperately to think of a way to get him to leave. 'I'm running late for work…'

Her father checked his watch and frowned. 'I thought you said you started at eight this morning? Don't worry,' he dismissed in that way of his that wrote off a person's concerns as trivialities. 'This won't take long.'

He indicated that she should let him pass and Billie stepped back out of deference and habit more than anything. 'I feel like you were distracted last night. Pour me a cup of that coffee I can smell and we can talk. You can't afford to be distracted.'

Billie realised suddenly he was charging ahead and she scrambled to get to the kitchen before him but it was too late. By the time she'd followed him in, her father and Gareth were already eyeing each other.

Her father turned to look at her with ice in his eyes. '*This* is your distraction, I take it?'

For the second morning in a row Billie found herself wishing the floor would open up and swallow her. First Gareth's twenty-year-old daughter had sprung them. And now her father.

'Mr Ashworth-Keyes, sir,' Gareth said, coming forward, his hand extended. 'I'm Gareth Stapleton.'

Billie watched her father reluctantly shake Gareth's hand, finally finding her voice. 'Gareth's a…' She glanced at Gareth, who was looking at her with questioning eyes.

How the hell did she explain Gareth to her father, who thought nurses were handmaidens there to serve doctors' needs and fade into the background at all other times? She was too busy fighting the obvious disapproval that there was a man in her apartment distracting her from the hallowed calling of medicine without facing any more judgement.

'We work together in the ER at St Luke's,' she said, suddenly unable to look at the man who'd warmed her bed all night.

Charles crossed his arms across his chest. 'I take it you're some kind of emergency specialist, although…' his brow puckered as he obviously searched his memory banks '…the name's not familiar…'

Gareth glanced at Billie, who had turned pleading eyes on him. Her cheeks were flushed and he knew what she was asking him to do. But he'd been around enough to know that playing it straight was the best policy. If Billie wanted to lie to her father about her own stuff, that was her prerogative. But he wouldn't.

'Actually, sir, I'm a nurse.'

Had Gareth not been in the middle of this awkward conversation he might have found Billie's father's double-take quite comical. But he was.

Charles turned to Billie. 'A nurse? A *male* nurse.'

Gareth almost laughed out loud. The Ashworth-Keyes' and the Stapletons may have been miles apart in socio-economic status but Charles had just sounded exactly like his own father when Gareth had told him what he was going to do.

Billie scrambled to Gareth's side. 'He's ex-military, Dad. He did several tours to Africa and the Middle East.'

Gareth looked down at Billie. He understood what she was trying to do but he didn't need her to talk him up. He was proud of what he did and he was damn good at it. He couldn't care less what the Charles Ashworth-Keyes' of the world thought. He met men like him all the time. But he did care what Billie thought. And that, apparently, was embarrassment.

Maybe he shouldn't have expected anything too much, given their brief liaison, but he'd never thought she found what he did for a living lacking in any way.

And he wasn't sure he could be with someone who did.

'I should go,' Gareth announced picking up his coffee mug and draining it.

Billie's father clearly thought so too, folding his arms and looking down his imperious nose at Gareth.

'Okay,' Billie said nervously. 'I'll see you out.'

'No.' Gareth shook his head. 'You stay. I'll see you at work.' He turned to her father. 'Nice meeting you, sir.'

Billie watched as Gareth strode out of the kitchen and she desperately wanted to call him back. The door shut firmly behind him and she knew she'd blown it.

But…it was complicated with her father.

The morning sure hadn't ended the way she'd thought it would. Clearly they sucked at mornings. They needed to stick to the nights.

That was if Gareth ever spoke to her again.

'*A male* nurse?'

'Would you prefer it if I'd slept with a female nurse?' Billie asked waspishly.

Her father glared at her. 'Don't get sassy with me, young lady.'

Billie gathered her wits and girded her loins. She so did not want to talk about Gareth. Not when there was so much she didn't know herself. She turned away, busying herself with pouring his coffee.

'I take it he's the reason you suddenly developed a head-ache last night?'

Billie doubted her father would understand that she'd walked away from many a family dinner with a splitting headache.

'He's a little old for you, isn't he?'

Billie turned and handed him the mug. 'It's really none of your business.'

He scowled at her. 'I'm the one who paid your exorbi-tant school fees and tutor fees and university and college fees and bought you a car and got you the residency at St Luke's. If you're about to mess it all up then damn right it's my business.'

And here came the guilt trip. 'Gareth has nothing to do with any of that.'

'You can do better than him,' he announced pompously.

Billie gaped at her father. 'Dad…you don't even know him!'

'I know how it's going to look.'

She shook her head wearily, knowing what was about to follow. 'Maybe I don't care how it looks?'

'You will.'

Billie sighed. God help her if her father ever found out Gareth was a single father who drove a twenty-year-old car and didn't even own his own home.

'I keep forgetting what an incredible snob you are.'

Charles gaped at her and even Billie blinked at her

audacity to finally give voice to her criticism. It was the first time she'd ever uttered her innermost thoughts.

'It's them and us, Billie.' He looked down at her the way he looked down on all non-surgeons, like he had some kind of divine right to walk the earth and everyone else deserved his pity. 'It's better for everyone if the status quo is maintained.'

Billie cringed, just listening to his pompous dribble. But she did what Jess had taught her to do when dealing with their father and his *opinions*—take a deep breath and imagine him in the operating theatre dressed only in his underwear and theatre cap.

Billie almost smiled at the thought. 'Plenty of doctors date nurses, Dad, hell, they even marry them, and you know it.'

'Yes, male doctors and female nurses. Not the other way round. If you ever want to be taken seriously as a specialist, you date other specialists. You marry another specialist.'

Suddenly he frowned, his coffee mug halfway to his lips. 'Wait…you're not thinking of marrying this man, are you?'

Oh, good Lord, would this *never* end? 'Dad…I just met Gareth.'

He gave her evasive answer an approving nod—the first time he'd softened since he'd blustered his way into her house and, like Pavlov's dog, she felt herself responding to it. Being the least bright out of her and Jessica, she'd always striven hard for his approval and even more so since she'd announced she wasn't becoming a surgeon.

She really didn't want to ruin the moment by voicing the truth. She had *feelings* for Gareth.

'Good. You don't need this kind of distraction right now. I'll tell you the same thing I tell all my residents, dating and doctoring don't mix. Concentrate on your work until you've settled into your specialty. There's plenty of time for that love nonsense after that.'

Her father put his coffee mug down. 'Right…must dash. I'm pleased we've had this chat.' He patted her on the shoulder. 'You'll see I'm right, Willamina.' He pecked her on the cheek. 'I'll see myself out, you need to get ready for work, don't want to get a reputation for being late. Punctuality is everything.'

And with that he was striding out of the kitchen and disappearing out her front door.

Billie felt too drained from the conversation to move.

Don't want a reputation for being late. Don't want a reputation for dating nurses.

Her father sucked all the joy out of everything.

And now she had to go and face Gareth, *who was angry with her.* And rightly so.

She wished she could blame that one on her father. Only it was all on her. She'd chosen to deny what Gareth did and invalidate it in one fell swoop. Her father may have been the catalyst but she'd made her own bed on that one.

She'd been a coward and had probably ruined everything.

Billie gripped the bench at the thought. She didn't want to ruin it with Gareth.

Please, let me be able to fix it.

Billie hit the ground running as soon as she got to work. She'd glimpsed Gareth briefly and he'd nodded at her politely but that had been the extent of their interaction. She'd fought back disappointment. After the last two nights she'd have expected one of those secret, knowing smiles, a silent communiqué conveying all kinds of sexy messages, like how pleased he was to see her, or how he couldn't wait to get her alone, or he was picturing her naked and screaming his name.

But, then, she only had herself to blame for its absence.

She made a pact with herself to talk to him this morning before their shift was done. To apologise. Although, if he was avoiding her, as she suspected he was, that might be a little difficult.

But she wasn't going to let this fester. No matter what, she *would* talk to Gareth today—even if she had to lock him in the supply cupboard until he heard her out.

With that course of action decided on, the *last* person Billie expected to be talking to entered the staffroom at lunchtime and introduced herself. 'Hi. I'm Amber.'

'Oh…yes… Hi,' Billie said, pausing, a sandwich halfway to her lips. 'If you're looking for Gareth he's up in Outpatients for a few hours.'

'No. It's you I want. Do you think we could go somewhere and talk?' Amber looked around at the three other occupants of the room. 'It won't take long.'

A knot of nervous tension screwed tight in Billie's stomach as she forced a smile to her face. 'Of course. We can use one of the offices.'

Billie located the nearest empty office and walked in, with Amber close behind. It was small, with enough room for a desk, a chair and a narrow exam table against the wall. She shut the door and turned to face Gareth's daughter, her nervousness increasing now they were alone.

'I'd like to apologise for Sunday morning,' Amber said, looking defiant, as if she was daring Billie to contradict her. 'I was rude and out of line.'

Billie blinked. That she hadn't expected. 'It was a shock,' Billie dismissed. 'Don't worry about it.'

'No. Well…yes, it was a shock…but my mother taught me better manners than that.'

Billie tensed at the mention of Catherine. Where was this going? 'Like I said…it's fine.'

Amber eyed her for long moments. 'Gareth told you about my mother?'

Billie nodded. 'Yes. I'm very sorry for your loss.'

Amber grunted. 'Why do people always think those words help somehow?'

Billie blushed at Amber's belligerence. She felt like she was walking on eggshells. 'I'm sorry…you're right. They don't. Nothing helps.'

Amber eyed her sharply. 'You talking from *actual* experience or just doctor experience?'

Billie almost laughed at Amber's prioritising. Her father would have had apoplexy to hear Amber dismissing her doctoring in preference to real life. 'My sister died when I was fourteen. I know that's not the same as a mother but it was the single most devastating thing that's ever happened to me.'

Gareth's daughter didn't say anything for long moments as she regarded Billie. 'How old was she? What happened?'

'She was sixteen. A car accident. Joy riding with friends.'

Amber's shoulders sagged as her defiance and belligerence dissipated. 'I'm sorry.'

Billie nodded. 'Thank you.'

There were more long moments of silence as Amber obviously mentally recalculated. 'I came to say that I'm pretty sure Gareth is in love with you and…that's been a lot to take in…'

Whoa! Billie blinked. That was a different kind of L word. But conviction rang in Amber's voice and shone in her gaze.

Had Gareth *told* his daughter that?

'But it's been five years since my mother died and Carly…that's my friend…reckons any other guy would have found someone else a long time ago…so I'm trying to be grown up about this but…he said that you were both at different stages of your lives and it struck me that he might be more…into you than you are to him so…I just wanted to say, if you hurt him, you'll have me to answer to.'

Billie couldn't quite believe she was being threatened by a twenty-year-old but her admiration for Amber grew tenfold.

'Amber…Gareth's a wonderful man and I don't want to hurt him. But he's right. There are complications.' She thought back to that morning. 'I'm…trying.'

'Well, try harder,' she said. 'Or let him go now, before you break his heart. I don't want to watch that again.'

Amber's words sliced right to Billie's core. Maybe Amber was right. How could she be any kind of equal partner to Gareth when she couldn't even stand up for the things she wanted?

Maybe she should end it. Whatever *it* was.

Her pager beeped, she pulled it off the waistband of her scrubs and looked at the screen.

Incoming trauma.

Bile rose in Billie's throat at the mere thought. 'I'm sorry,' she said. 'I have to go.'

Amber nodded. 'Just think about what I said, okay? After all he'd been through he deserves to be happy. He deserves to be with someone who wants to be with him too.'

Billie nodded. Amber was right. The truth sucked.

CHAPTER TWENTY-TWO

GARETH WAS IN the same cubicle with Billie as they attended to the traumatic amputation of a leg. It was bloody and gory, the male patient having lost a lot of blood—most of it over himself. She did well with holding it together but he was probably the only one in the cubicle who really knew how much it cost her.

How much it had to be turning her stomach.

In fact, when it was done and the patient had been whisked to Theatre, she quickly excused herself. His gaze followed her as she disappeared into the staff restrooms and emerged five minutes later looking very pale and shaky, pressing some paper towels to her mouth.

Gareth would bet his last cent she'd just thrown up.

Their eyes met and she gave him a helpless little shrug.

And his simmering anger cranked up another notch. He'd been furious with her that morning, with the way she'd been uncomfortable about telling her father what he did. But part of him understood she was between a rock and a hard place with her old man.

He understood how fraught those relationships could be. And he understood Billie being reluctant to rock the boat and potentially jeopardise her mother's mental health.

But this...

This...pretence was utter madness. How could she even

182   IT HAPPENED ONE NIGHT SHIFT

contemplate not being true to herself over this? This was the rest of her life.

She was hiding behind a mask that was so thin in places it was slowly cracking. And he couldn't stand by and watch it any longer. It had to stop. He didn't want any part of a woman who had to lie and hide her true self from the people who mattered most. Who was okay with living a lie.

Gareth stepped down from the central work station and stalked towards her. He collected her arm on the way past, spinning her around. 'We need to talk,' he muttered.

Billie should have been annoyed at the firm hold Gareth had on her arm but, frankly, she'd been that close to collapsing it felt good to lean into him. 'Where are we going?'

'In here,' Gareth said, opening the door to one of the back examination rooms that was rarely used. He switched on the light and dragged her inside. 'Sit,' he ordered. She looked like she was about to keel over, for crying out loud.

Billie sat gratefully. 'Before you say anything,' she said, eyeing him as he paced, 'I want to apologise for this morning. My father was rude and insulting and—'

'It's fine,' Gareth dismissed. 'He was taken by surprise, just like Amber was.'

Billie blinked. She hadn't expected him to defend her father. 'Amber's twenty. My father doesn't have that excuse.'

'I don't care about that. Well, I do, but I'm not ashamed of what I am. I was more insulted that *you* felt you had to conceal that than anything your father said. I don't want to be your dirty little secret, Billie, but...that's not what this is about.'

A wave of shame washed over Billie, chasing away the last vestiges of her nausea. She had insulted him. This man who had been nothing but supportive and encouraging.

'You have to tell them you can't be an emergency doctor, Billie. You can't keep going on like this.'

Billie blanched at his suggestion. Her father had just

found out about Gareth. *One bombshell at a time, please!*
She shook her head. 'I don't think that would be very wise.'

'If you don't, you're going to end up here for ever. Throwing up in that loo for ever.'

'I'm fine now,' she dismissed.

Gareth shook his head. 'You're not *fine.*'

'They're not ready to hear it yet.'

Gareth snorted. 'They're never going to be ready, Billie. C'mon…maybe it won't be as bad as you think. Just rip the plaster off, get it over and done with.'

'I've never been a ripper,' she said, shaking her head. 'I'm more an "ease the plaster off bit by bit" girl. And you said it yourself last night. I have to be doing what I'm doing now anyway before I can go down the GP path so why cause a problem before I need to? In a few years I'll face the choice, the *real* choice, and I can upset the applecart then. Why borrow trouble?'

Billie knew it was classic Jess behaviour—tell her parents what they wanted to hear then spring the bad news on them at the last moment. But it had worked for her sister. Jess had gone to her grave with her parents completely unaware of her plans outside medicine.

The perfect daughter, as far as they were concerned.

And now it was she who had to be the perfect daughter.

Gareth shoved his hands on his hips. 'Because I'm worried you *won't* upset the applecart when the moment comes. The longer you put it off the harder it will be, Billie. And why should you *have* to pretend? This is your *family.* You should be able to *be yourself* around your family and expect their support.'

Billie could see the frustration in Gareth's stance, hear it in his voice, but she knew how best to handle her life, not him. 'Look…' She stood, walking over to him, her legs feeling much stronger now. She stopped when he was an arm's length away. 'I appreciate your concern but I've been dealing with my father for a lot of years and I know how to handle him.'

Gareth couldn't believe it. She was really going to suppress what she wanted for a little peace and quiet? 'So you're just going to keep being a…*coward*, like you were this morning when you couldn't even tell your father I was a nurse?'

Heat rushed to Billie's face at his "coward" taunt. 'I prefer to think of it as self-preservation,' she said waspishly.

Gareth raked a hand through his hair. 'Okay, well…that's fine. But I can't do this, Billie.' His hand dropped to his side. 'I don't think we should do this any more.'

Billie frowned, her heart in her mouth. 'This?'

'You and me,' Gareth said. 'I don't want to be around to watch you grow unhappier and unhappier until you self-destruct from the weight of it all.'

Billie's pulse was thundering through her head as the reality of what he was saying sank in. He was ending whatever it was between them before it had even begun.

So much for thinking it was something *she* was going to decide.

She searched his blue gaze for signs of reluctance or disingenuousness. But it was clear and firm.

A flutter of panic swarmed in her stomach. She didn't want it to be over. 'So that's it? Two nights together with the chemistry between us off the charts and you pull the plug?'

Gareth grimaced. He didn't need to be reminded what he was giving up. It hadn't been easy to start this thing with Billie after five years alone and it was frightening how deeply he already felt.

Which was precisely why he needed to get out now.

'All I have as a man is my self-respect, Billie, and I get that by being true to myself. And I want to be with a woman who's also true to herself. I didn't think I'd find another woman I wanted to be with, to share my life with, after Catherine, but then you came along and you made me smile and I felt good and I started to hope…'

His gaze swept over the freckles on the bridge of her nose and the twin glossy pillows of her mouth. He was going to miss that mouth.

'Now you've got to do what you've got to do. That's fine, I can respect that. But I've got to do what's right for me too and that's not being with someone who still lets her parents dictate her life. I think it's best if we get out now before we're in too deep.'

Billie took a step back. He'd been thinking of a future with her? Something small and fragile fluttered in the vicinity of her heart but the grim line of his mouth quashed it. She'd ruined her chances with him by being such a basket case.

'I'll try and roster myself on opposite shifts to you for your remaining time here but it will be inevitable that some shifts will clash. Can I suggest we try and keep things as civil as possible in that eventuality?'

Billie frowned. Did he think she was going to go all me-doctor-you-nurse on him? 'Of…course.'

Gareth hardened his heart to the catch in her voice. He'd seen the collateral damage broken work relationships could inflict and he didn't want either of them to fall prey to that. But he needed to get away from her now before the catch in her voice had him changing his mind and he hauled her into his arms.

'Well…' He stepped to the side. 'I guess I'll see you around, then.'

Billie nodded but didn't bother to turn and face him. The door clicked shut behind her and she groped for the exam bed in front of her, holding onto it for dear life.

That was it. Over before it had truly begun. Her heart ached already.

* * *

It didn't improve at all over the next couple of weeks. They worked a few shifts together but, true to his word, Gareth and Billie passed mostly like ships in the night.

Billie knew it was insane to miss him this much after such a short time together. It wasn't like they had even been *in* a relationship. They'd had two nights together.

That had been it.

But she did miss him.

Lying in bed at night, she craved him. At work, she listened for his voice. She got all fluttery in the chest when he was there and when he walked by she didn't seem to be able to take her eyes off him.

She felt like a teenager mooning over a screen idol.

But she couldn't stop it either and there were times when she swore he found it difficult to drag his eyes off her too.

They may not be together but he was still under her skin. She only hoped the itch wouldn't be permanent.

Another week passed and Billie found herself working a Saturday day shift with Gareth. It was frantically busy so there wasn't any time for idle chit-chat. Not that they indulged in that any more.

Or ever had, for that matter.

As thrilling as it was to work the odd shift with Gareth, the days she did usually ended up being total downers—a case of look, don't touch and the vague feeling that Gareth was judging her for her choices.

She had had one triumph today, though, and she did a little jig as she snapped cubicle eight's curtain back in place, practically running into Gareth as he bowled past.

'Whoa, there,' he said, reaching out his hands to steady her, and Billie was sure they lingered a little longer than necessary.

'You look like you've had a win,' he said, so politely she wanted to scream.

She smiled at him despite his formality. 'I finally diagnosed this obscure skin condition. The patient's been back three times this last week and we finally nailed it. And, best of all, it's totally treatable!'

Gareth sucked in a breath as Billie literally glowed. Her cheeks were pink and her eyes glittered with excitement.

She was so sexy he wanted to kiss her until they both couldn't breathe.

But they had a trauma coming in.

'That's great,' he said, his tone brisk. 'Unfortunately we have a gunshot victim coming in. Head, chest and abdo wounds. GCS nine. ETA seven minutes. Helen wants you in Resus.'

Billie felt everything deflate inside her. *Crap.* Her smile slid right off her face. 'Oh, God, really?'

'Yep. Really.' He paused for a moment and Billie thought he was going to commiserate with her for a second and her pulse fluttered. 'Remember this feeling, Billie. It's not all skin conditions and surgical abdos.'

Gareth felt like an utter bastard as he walked away. But they were in an emergency department, not a dermatology clinic, for crying out loud.

She wanted this? Well, *this* was the reality.

CHAPTER TWENTY-THREE

BILLIE GOT THROUGH the trauma with her usual degree of bluff. It was raw and bloody and the patient died, and the only thing that prevented her from losing her lunch afterwards was the fact she had to sit with the man's wife and tell her.

And all she could hear in her head the whole time was, *Remember this feeling, Billie.*

Remember it? How could she forget it? She *hated* this feeling. But she was trying her best here—surely he could see that?

She knew he didn't owe her anything but at heart Gareth was a compassionate man and she certainly hadn't deserved his condescension.

And she was damn well going to tell him so.

She spied him from the desk, heading out of the department, his backpack slung over his shoulder, and she checked her watch. His shift had finished.

Before she knew what she was doing, she was following him—no time like the present for giving him a piece of her mind.

She caught sight of him as he turned a corner ahead of her and she realised he was heading for the fire escape that led to the rooftop car park. She rounded that corner and stopped abruptly as the sight of Amber and Gareth embracing in the distance greeted her.

Billie fell back, feeling like she was intruding on their privacy. She couldn't hear what they were saying but Amber laughed at something her father had said and was looking at Gareth like he hung the moon. They hugged again then Gareth slipped his arm around Amber's waist and they entered the fire escape together.

She'd never felt that with her own father.

Never had a moment like that where they'd just laughed and loved and revelled in their family connection. Charles Ashworth-Keyes just wasn't the touchy-feely kind.

She was overwhelmed as she stood and stared at the closing fire-escape door. She wanted that.

She wanted to feel loved.

And she wanted to love back.

She wanted kids to hug and kiss and be there for. She wanted a man who was going to be there for her too. And her children.

And she wanted to feel the exhilaration of solving a complex medical puzzle and improving somebody's life. And she *never* wanted the feeling of dread that the piercing tone of a siren elicited.

And if a woman with a skin condition and a dead gunshot victim had taught her anything today, it had taught her where her strengths lay.

If Gareth had taught her anything, it was time she stood up for that. And she was tired of pretending.

She was pretty sure Jessica would have kicked her up the butt a long time ago.

She pulled her mobile out of her pocket and tapped off a quick text as she returned to the work station and the last few hours of her shift.

Four hours later Billie was parked in her car outside her parents' house, waiting. Gareth had texted to say he'd be here but he was late and she was running out of bravado.

Headlights flashed in her rear-view mirror and she breathed a sigh of relief when they pulled in behind her. She got out of the car on shaky legs. The shutting of the door seemed loud in a street full of high walls and immaculately groomed lawns.

'Hi,' she said, as Gareth joined her, and he looked so sexy in his jeans and hoody, like the first time they'd met, she wanted to fling herself at him and beg his forgiveness.

But that wasn't why she was here.

'Hi.' He smiled at her and she felt encouraged. 'What's this about, Billie?'

'I'm telling my parents I'm going to study to be a GP and I needed moral support.'

Gareth regarded her seriously for a few moments. The news made him want to leap in the air but he was aware he'd treated her badly that afternoon. He didn't want her doing it because he'd guilted her into it. If she was going to do something so monumental then she needed to do it for the right reasons.

'Are you sure?'

Billie nodded. 'Yes. I realised today that I'm much better at diagnosing skin conditions than I am at treating gunshot victims. That treating Sally Anders gave me a much bigger rush than treating Danny Wauchope. I don't get the rush that people like you thrive on during a full-on resus. And I think you need that, I think you have to be wired that way to survive in that kind of environment.'

A cold wind blew strands of her loose hair across her face and Billie pushed them back. 'I saw you and Amber together near the fire escape this afternoon and I realised I don't have that kind of relationship with my father and that just seemed…sad. And wrong. Do you want more kids, Gareth?'

Gareth blinked at the unexpected question. 'I'd always thought I'd have more kids…yes.'

Billie nodded. Her future was becoming clearer. 'Can

you please come with me while I break the news to my parents? I've tried so many times in the past and failed. I need someone there who's in my corner. Who will also call me on it if I chicken out.'

Gareth smiled. 'Okay. But I'm pretty sure your father isn't going to be happy to see me.'

Billie looked at the ground. Even the bitumen in this street was perfect. 'I know I'm putting you in an awkward position,' she said, raising her head.

Gareth waved his hand. 'You think I care about that? I just need you to be certain.'

'I have never been surer of anything.'

'Okay, then.' He smiled, holding out his hand. 'Let's do this.'

Waiting for the door to open was nerve-racking and she thanked her lucky stars for the warmth and calm, anchoring assurance of Gareth's hand at her back. Her mother answered the door with a puzzled expression but ushered them in anyway after Billie had performed a quick introduction. It was clear from her mother's wary gaze that her father had already mentioned Gareth.

Once the token politeness of drinks and offering of chairs—which they both declined—had been dispensed with her father came right to the point. 'What's this all about, Willamina?'

'I'm here to tell you that I'm not going to pursue a career in emergency medicine. I want to be a GP.'

The silence in the room was tense and lengthy.

'General practice!'

Her father made wanting to be a GP sound like wanting to be a prostitute but Billie was done with backing down.

'Yes.'

Her father slammed his heavy crystal glass down on the coffee table. 'No.'

'Dad. It doesn't matter what you—'

'I said no!' he snapped, advancing on her. 'This is the most preposterous thing I have ever heard. He…' Charles pointed his finger at Gareth as he came closer '…is dumbing you down.'

'He has a name,' Billie retorted, as Gareth swiftly stepped in front of her, blocking her father's progress.

'I think we need to calm down,' Gareth said.

Charles glowered at him. 'Don't tell me how to talk to my daughter.'

Gareth did not budge. 'You need to step back, sir.'

'I will do *no such thing*!'

Billie was quaking internally at the confrontation. She had expected her father to be upset, but not like this. There was a film of spittle coating his lips and he'd gone a very startling shade of red.

She shifted closer to Gareth, who wasn't giving an inch. He was staring at her father with absolute chilling authority.

'Step. Back. Sir.'

Her father halted at the ruthless determination in Gareth's eyes.

'Your daughter is trying to tell you something important, sir. You need to listen.'

'Don't presume to tell me about my daughter,' Charles snapped. 'You don't know her.'

Billie watched Gareth's jaw clench. 'I know that Billie's a brilliant doctor. I know she can't bear blood and gore yet she's working in an emergency department to please you when all she wants to be is a GP.'

'She's always been squeamish,' her father dismissed. 'But she never wanted it until you came along.'

Billie shook her head, coming out from behind Gareth. 'That's not true, Dad. I've *always* wanted to be a GP. I was just never brave enough to tell you.'

'But, Billie…how can you do this?'

Her mother, who had been silent up till now, grasped Billie by her forearms. 'Do you think Jess would have wanted you to *squander* the opportunities you've been given? She wanted to be a cardiothoracic surgeon and she didn't get the chance. And here you are, alive and well and *spitting* on her memory. First this emergency medicine nonsense and now...*a GP*?'

Billie dragged in a ragged breath at her mother's verbal attack. She was torn between the old habit of shutting her mouth and taking it and the sudden rage inside that demanded her parents know the truth and to hell if it destroyed them.

She'd been silent for far too long.

She wrenched out of her mother's grip. 'Jessica *never* wanted to be a surgeon, cardiothoracic or otherwise,' Billie snapped. 'She wanted to be a kindergarten teacher. But she couldn't tell you that so she...'

Billie didn't realise that tears had sprung to her eyes and were falling down her cheeks until Gareth's arm came around her, and even then she just dashed them away and kept going because she knew if she stopped she wouldn't get this off her chest and after ten years it needed saying.

'...she went out drinking and yahooing and staying out late and she drove in fast cars, hoping that you'd disown her so she could do what *she* wanted.'

Her mother gasped but Billie didn't care about her emotional distress for a moment. It just felt so good to finally get it off her chest.

'You're lying,' her mother said, tears tracking down her face now.

'No.' Billie shook her head. 'I'm not. We talked about everything, Mum. *Everything.*'

Her mother sagged on the couch in a dreadful moment of déjà vu. Her father, to his credit, joined her, putting his arm around his wife's shoulders. Billie wished it didn't have to be this way. But she couldn't sacrifice what she wanted any more in the name of her sister.

And she was pretty sure Jessica—the ultimate free spirit—wouldn't have wanted her to either.

'I'm sorry, Mum…Dad. I didn't want you to find out like this. I didn't want to…upset you. But it's the truth.'

They didn't say anything for long moments. 'So you're just going to throw everything away…all that education and invaluable career advantage?' her father demanded.

'I'm not the kind of doctor you two are,' Billie said, looking down at her confused parents. 'But that doesn't mean my contribution to medicine will be any less important or that you failed. I'm just not interested in the specialty limelight. I'm going to be a damn good GP and that's enough for me. I hope it can eventually be enough for you.'

'And where does *he* fit in?' her father said, nodding his head at Gareth like he was some kind of new species that needed explaining.

'I love him,' Billie said, her heart hammering in her chest as she looked at the man who had turned her whole world upside down.

'He's going to let me be what I need to be, he's going to be the glue that holds me together when I think I can't do it, and one day soon, I hope, he's going to be the father of your grandchildren, who I *will* take time out of work to raise. And you're going to love him too because he's awesome but also because *I* love him and we come as a package from now on.'

Billie held her breath for long moments as Gareth's blue eyes stared back at her. Somewhere deep inside she'd always known she loved him. But him showing up here tonight despite all the stuff she'd put him through had removed her blinkers. All the impossibilities fell by the wayside and they were just a man and a woman who were meant to be together.

'I love you too,' he said, sliding his arm around her.

Billie's heart cracked wide open as she smiled at him. She knew they had a lot to sort out, a lot of *stuff,* and declaring her love for him in front of two people who weren't exactly amenable to the match was a little unorthodox, but it had felt right.

And she'd waited long enough.

Gareth had helped her see so many truths about herself and she didn't want to spend even a second of her life without him in it.

She looked at her parents. 'I want you to meet the man I love,' she said.

Gareth smiled down at Billie, his heart exploding with a wellspring of emotion. In a million years he hadn't expected this outcome.

But in so many ways it was perfect.

He'd been falling in love with her for weeks, not letting himself sink into it completely, not trusting that it could happen twice in his life. But standing here, looking down at her in front of the people who loved her most, he'd never been more certain of anything.

She had shown him it was possible to love again.

He glanced at Billie's parents, who looked like they'd both been struck by lightning. 'Mr and Mrs Ashworth-Keyes, you have my word that I will make Billie happy to the end of her days. I understand that you're more concerned about her career prospects at the moment and hooking up with a man who isn't of the pedigree you'd imagined. But I promise you, I will be her champion, whatever way she wants to jump.'

Billie's heart just about floated right out of her chest. Her parents were clearly still trying to wrap their heads round things but right now she didn't care if they never got it. She'd spent far too long worrying about them and their expectations.

It was time for her.

She glanced at Gareth. 'I love you,' she murmured.

He smiled at her. 'I love you too.'

And right there, in front of her parents, he kissed her. Long and hard. And Billie didn't give a fig what they thought. She wrapped her arms around his neck and kissed him back.

This was her man. Life was short. And she was never letting him go.

* * * * *

TAMED BY HER
ARMY DOC'S TOUCH

BY
LUCY RYDER

MILLS
BOON

Published in Great Britain 2015
by Mills & Boon, an imprint of Harlequin (UK) Limited,
Eton House, 18-24 Paradise Road, Richmond, Surrey, TW9 1SR

© 2015 Bev Riley

ISBN: 978-0-263-24682-7

Harlequin (UK) Limited's policy is to use papers that are natural, renewable and recyclable products and made from wood grown in sustainable forests. The logging and manufacturing processes conform to the legal environmental regulations of the country of origin.

Printed and bound in Spain
by CPI, Barcelona

Dear Reader

It's often said that our families are responsible for the people we become. If that's the case then I must be pretty awesome—because my family is the greatest. We may not always agree, but we never forget that blood far outweighs petty squabbles, and we're there for each other. *Always.*

My hero, Luke, isn't so lucky. He's grown up with emotionally unavailable parents concerned only with their shallow lives rather than being there for their three sons. And, having spent a decade in the military, he's more at ease with actions than emotions. Emotions are messy and they can't be trusted. Give him a crisis any day. He's barely survived his parents' marriages and is determined never to inflict that brand of marital hell on anyone—especially vulnerable kids. In fact he's against marriage and children altogether.

But he does inspire trust in others. He's intelligent, a highly skilled soldier and medic, and he willingly puts himself on the line for others. If that's not hero-worthy I don't know what is.

Lilah has a few 'daddy issues' of her own, having experienced paternal rejection at a vulnerable age. She's bound and determined not to make the same mistakes as her mother. Fiercely independent, she would rather suppress her natural inclinations and go it alone than depend on someone who's not going to be there for the long haul.

Luckily for her, Luke is nothing like her father—or his. He's his own man, capable of making his own mistakes, and it takes history repeating itself—for Lilah, at least— to teach him that love begins with trust. And that, to my mind, is the true gift of family.

Happy reading

Lucy

Dedication

As always, I could not have done this without my
amazing family, who are always there for me—
especially my parents, Peter and Gillian Hucklesby.
Mom and Dad, you're the best!

To my nephew Jason, who took time out of
his busy study schedule to answer my endless
medical questions. Thanks, Jay, you're going to
make an awesome doctor.

And lastly to my daughters, Kate and Ash.
Words cannot express how much I love you.

CHAPTER ONE

IF DR. LILAH MEREDITH had known she'd be going swimming when she'd dressed earlier that evening, she probably would have chosen to wear something that didn't look like it came from some designer lingerie's "wild" collection.

But then again, she'd recently returned from the jungles of South America and had splurged on expensive underwear to celebrate her return to civilization. And if she was in an emotional place where only she got to see the scraps of silks and stretchy lace, then that was okay—she was having a break from men anyway.

But that was before her evening, which had started out normally enough for a bachelorette party, had rapidly descended into disaster. One minute she'd been surrounded by the debris left over from the gift-opening frenzy, a tipsy bride-to-be and a dozen giggling colleagues chanting, "Take it off, take it off!", the next she'd been scrambling through the open window between two ornamental shrubs onto the restaurant's upper deck.

She'd turned away from the embarrassing sight of a buff young guy stripping off his clothes to the bump-and-grind music blaring from the private room's speakers just in time to see a dozen people leap from the party boat into the lake.

Flashing back to her senior year in high school when a group of pot-smoking students had set fire to a boat, Lilah's heart stopped for a couple of beats.

Praying it was just another excuse for youthful high-jinks, she held her breath and waited for them to return to the boat. But the longer she watched the more uneasy she became, especially when it became apparent that someone was clearly in trouble.

With her heart surging into her throat, Lilah lurched to her feet and scrambled over the table to the window, knocking over half a bottle of Chianti and a jug of margaritas. Cutlery, glasses and flowers from the centerpiece went flying. There was a lot of high-pitched shrieking and Lilah had a brief glimpse of shocked expressions and open-mouthed gapes as she dived out the window.

Luke Sullivan folded his arms across his chest, tipped his chair back against the wooden railing and smiled as whoops and whistles of encouragement competed with the stripper music pumping from the system. Greg Turner, the man about to take the walk of insanity down the aisle, grinned goofily as Lindi—or was it Mindi?—ripped off her sparkly skin-tight blouse. She shimmied her balloon-shaped rack in the groom's face while her twin rubbed her awesome curves against him.

It wasn't that Luke had anything against stripper twins or lap dances—heck, he'd participated in enough as a wild student and then again in the army to appreciate the manly tradition. But at thirty-two, you'd think Greg would appreciate something a little less clichéd. Something like… poker night.

Yeah, Luke mused as the girl rolled her hips like a belly dancer. If he ever lost his mind long enough to get hitched— *God forbid*—he'd prefer poker night stag. Now, that was a civilized way to mourn the end of bachelorhood. *If* he were inclined to matrimony, that is, which he most definitely was not! He'd watched his parents' marriages fall apart too many times not to want to put himself or any kid through that kind of hell.

Besides, poker night was a great way for a bunch of guys to kick back, puff on Cuban cigars, guzzle beer and nachos, and talk trash as they bet on a pair of kings. He had a sneaky feeling Greg's wild younger brother had organized the strippers more for himself than the groom.

And while the twins were certainly impressively endowed, Luke thought with a yawn as his gaze slid to the people strolling along the boardwalk below, he preferred his women a little less surgically enhanced. And a lot more natural. Women were not meant to look like they carried alien pods on their chests. They were meant to be soft and curvy. Kind of like the woman dodging through the crowd, barely missing a collision with a couple of teens on skateboards. Her movements were urgent, as if she was either fleeing from someone or racing towards some*thing*.

Instantly alert, he pushed away from the wall and the chair legs hit the deck with a thud. He scanned the crowd for a knife-wielding pursuer but saw nothing suspicious and turned back in time to see her ditch her strappy sandals and hike the slinky dress up a pair of spectacular thighs, before taking off down the pier.

Grinning with masculine appreciation at the flash of long, smooth limbs, Luke rose and headed for the deck railing to get a better view. The woman slowed down enough to shout and wave her arms at the party cruise heading for open water. When no one responded, she shook her head and threw her arms up as if to say, "What now?"

Then, to his growing astonishment, she wriggled out of that short, snug dress—a sight way more erotic than the striptease going on behind him—and headed for the lake at a dead run.

Now, this, he thought as she launched herself off the pier, was way better than watching a couple of barely legal dancers prance around in strips of sparkly fabric. Her body entered the water with scarcely a splash, only to reappear seconds later as people began heading closer to watch the crazy woman take a swim in her underwear.

Just before the gathering crowd blocked his view, Luke saw her strike out, but not for the boat, as he'd expected. Instead, she headed away from it.

Puzzled, he scanned the water, stilling as he caught sight of movement a couple of hundred yards out. The person's flailing arms told him everything he needed to know.

Someone was in trouble.

Without further thought, he vaulted over the balcony and ignored the cries of surprise as he dropped to the board-walk below. Wincing when pain shot through his recently healed thigh, he tucked in his body and rolled to his feet in one smooth move, before sprinting after her.

Barely a minute after the woman had entered the lake; Luke was stripping off his own clothes and taking a run-ning dive off the pier. He knew just how cold the water was and braced for the instant brain freeze.

Despite his training, he tensed as his body hit the water. *Jee-hose-phat.* It was freezing. After fifteen years as far away from the Pacific North West as he could get, the wa-ters of Lake McKenzie still felt colder than the North At-lantic in midwinter.

He surfaced and sucked warm air into his lungs before setting out, his powerful strokes quickly eating up the dis-tance. He was still a good forty yards away when he saw the woman disappear beneath the surface. A girl flailed nearby, alternately sobbing and screaming, "Trent! *Trent!*" as she tried to stay afloat.

She must have spotted Luke because her litany changed to, "Help him, help him! I couldn't hold on." She coughed and wiped her face with a shaking hand. "He…he j-just slipped under and I c-can't find him."

"Stay here," Luke ordered as he swam closer. "And calm down. Panicking won't help." He sucked in a quick breath and followed, his powerful kick immediately taking him several feet below the surface. As he descended, he searched for signs of the boy—and the woman.

Fortunately, light from the huge moon hanging over Lake McKenzie penetrated past the surface, eerily illuminating the cold, silent depths. Luke shuddered before he could help himself. He remembered quite vividly the summer his little brother had almost drowned in the lake and hoped, like that night twenty years ago, everyone walked away having learned a valuable lesson.

Luke looked for bubbles and when he caught sight of a silvery trail rising to the surface, he swam towards it just as a figure rose from the dark depths. It was the woman. She hadn't seen him yet and when he reached out to get her attention she jerked violently and turned.

Her eyes went huge and her mouth opened, as though he'd startled her. A couple of large bubbles escaped and a flash of panic crossed her features. She flailed then began kicking vigorously for the surface.

Realizing she'd swallowed lake water, Luke followed, grabbing her arm and pulling her upwards as he shot past. The moment their heads broke the surface, she slapped at his hands and fought for breath. Feeling a little guilty for scaring her, he grabbed her shoulders and demanded, "Are you trying to kill yourself?"

She made a feeble attempt to pull away but Luke tightened his grip and ignored the furious accusation in her huge eyes. She glared at him between violent coughing spells and he got the impression she'd like to deck him but was too busy hacking up a lung.

Finally she pushed at his shoulders and croaked, "That distinction's yours. Now let go." She shoved him again, and when he reluctantly released her she sucked in a jerky breath and pushed her hair from her face. Realizing she was about to dive, he grabbed her arm and got a foot on his thigh for his trouble.

"Wait, *dammit!*" he ground out, against the zinging pain that made his teeth hurt. "You wait here."

"No time," she snapped. "He's been under too long." And with a final yank she slipped free and he was left watching as her bottom and long legs disappeared beneath the surface.

Cursing stubborn independent women, Luke inhaled deeply and followed her into the cold depths. He'd been about to suggest that he take his turn looking. *Guess not.*

For someone already half-frozen, she moved with surprising speed through the water and he watched with reluctant admiration as long pale legs disappeared into the darkness. Unused to letting someone else act in an emergency, Luke used his big arms and legs to his advantage.

Finally, when his lungs began to burn and the need for air was forcing him to consider surfacing, Luke spotted movement to his left. Turning, he caught sight of a mermaid rising from the darkened depths. In the shifting silvery light her long curvy body and cloud of pale hair floating behind her reminded him of mystical creatures luring mortals to their watery doom.

Only this naiad was struggling sluggishly to save one. Streaking towards her, he wrapped an arm around the boy's chest, hooked his free hand beneath her armpit, and propelled them upwards with a few powerful kicks.

The instant they surfaced, her eyes met his in a long silent stare as she raggedly sucked in air. Before he could interpret her look or wonder at the weird flash of familiarity—or was it *déjà vu*?—she'd moved to support the exhausted girl. Luke was happy to let her go. He would rather take on a village of hostiles than deal with hysterical females.

He adjusted his hold on the boy and ordered, "Try to

keep up," over his shoulder before striking out for the shore a couple of hundred yards away.

They needed to hurry. One glimpse of the kid's face told him Trent had suffered a head injury and was unresponsive. He only hoped the cold had slowed his vitals and they could revive him without permanent brain damage. The kid had been under at least ten minutes. Maybe longer.

He spotted a rubber dinghy speeding towards them and soon hands were reaching down to pull Trent aboard. Luke was relieved to let them. The faster they began CPR and got the kid warmed up, the better.

He helped the coed aboard before placing both hands beneath the woman's scantily clad bottom and shoving her upwards. Finally, he hauled himself over the side just as the twin engines rumbled.

By the time they pulled up to the marina wharf a crowd had gathered. Several men rushed forward to lift their patient off the dinghy and Luke moved to help secure the boat.

The woman, looking cold but spectacular in a slinky leopard-print bra and teeny matching boy shorts, pushed past him and scrambled onto the pier, her low, smooth voice saying, "Stand back, I'm a doctor." She dropped to her knees and put her ear to the boy's chest before gently prising open his eyelids. Luke moved closer, urging the crowd back.

"Give us some room, folks," he said. "Anyone call 911?"

"On their way," someone replied, and shoved his clothing at him.

"Uh, thanks," Luke said absently, his attention already on the expert way the woman was performing CPR. He knelt down and faced her across the boy's prone body.

"Can you do mouth-to-mouth?" she asked, counting the compressions she executed.

"Hell no, lady," he said with a snort, and placed his hands over hers. "I'll do compressions. You breathe."

She slid her hands away and sat back, shoving ropes of

sopping hair off her face. "Fine," she snapped, her expression annoyed. "But keep up a steady rhythm and stop when I tell you."

"Yes, ma'am," he said, his gaze dropping to her wide, lush mouth. "You just give that boy the kiss of life."

Lilah didn't know how long they worked on the unconscious student but she was grateful for the huge guy's assistance. He seemed to know what he was doing, like he'd done it before. She watched him correctly place his big hands and perform the exact number of compressions before pausing so she could inflate the boy's lungs.

The muscles in her arms and legs burned, quivering from the cold as much as from physical exertion. She was clearly out of shape. What made it worse was that the guy didn't even look fazed or out of breath. As though he regularly went swimming in freezing water to save drowning victims.

Maybe he did, she mused, absently noting wide, muscular shoulders, zero body fat and the impressive bulge of biceps as he crouched over her patient. But then again, it might have something to do with all that testosterone pumping off his big, hard body like a nuclear reactor. She could literally feel his heat reaching across the boy's body and wished she could borrow some of it.

He flashed her a concerned look, and Lilah knew what he was thinking. It didn't look good. She felt for a pulse just beneath their patient's jaw and thought she felt a tiny flutter. But when she moved her fingers slightly there was nothing.

She frowned and put her ear at his mouth. "I think I felt something," she murmured, searching for a pulse again.

"Keep breathing," the big guy ordered sharply, without breaking rhythm. "And don't stop until his pulse is steady and strong." Of course Lilah wasn't about to give up. She hadn't spent long minutes submerged in a cold, dark nightmare, thinking she was going to join Trent in a watery grave, to give up now.

They again fell into a grim, silent rhythm until she finally felt the tiniest muscle contraction beneath her hand. She reared back just as Trent's body jerked once, twice and then water began spewing from his lungs in huge spasmodic bursts. Applause and cheering broke the tense silence as she and her companion exchanged a brief glance of shared relief. Trent might not be out of the woods yet, but he was back.

Sucking in a deep breath, Lilah felt her body sag. *Thank God*, she thought as the boy coughed and wheezed. That breathing—ragged and painful as it appeared—was the most beautiful sound in the world…as was the distant wail of sirens.

Pushing back the kid's wet hair to check his head wound, Lilah was unaware she was shaking until a large warm hand encased her trembling fingers. Instant heat and electricity shot up her arm, making her skin buzz. Startled, her gaze flew up and she got caught in eyes as deep and green and calm as the lake waters in summer.

Crinkles appeared at the corners and Lilah's heart gave a slow lazy tumble in her chest that she quickly blamed on the recent crisis.

"You did great," he said in a rough, dark bedroom voice. His darkened gaze dropped briefly to her mouth before lifting once more to lock with hers. His mouth kicked up at one corner. "It was obviously the kiss that did it. He's a lucky guy."

Feeling her face heat, Lilah slid her hand from his and focused attention on examining the boy. "You just didn't want people to know you kissed a guy," she snorted softly and reached for a black T-shirt nearby, pressing it to the bleeding head wound. His deep chuckle vibrated the space between them and made her breath catch in her chest. Or maybe that was just because she was finally coming down off the adrenalin high.

"I can't imagine him liking it any more than I would." He was silent a moment before his large hand reached out to squeeze her shoulder. "Seriously, they're lucky you saw them."

Lilah stilled beneath his disturbing touch and his words. "Someone else would have helped." She looked up briefly as he rose. "You did."

"Couldn't let you have all the fun," he said, and something heavy dropped around her shoulders. Lilah was instantly enveloped in the warm, clean smell of virile man.

Without lifting her head, she snuggled into the garment and checked her patient's pupil reaction. "Do you know where you are?" she asked.

Trent opened his mouth and "Wha-a-at?" emerged on a ragged breath, as though his throat had been scraped raw.

"Stay still a moment," she said, gently soothing him when he made to sit up. "The paramedics are on their way."

He frowned and blinked. "Paramedics?" he rasped, his bewildered gaze clinging to hers, as though he was afraid she would vanish if he blinked.

"Do you know where you are?" she asked, just as someone cried, "Trent?" and the next thing the young coed was dropping down beside him. He turned to blink up at her for a couple of beats and Lilah held her breath. He croaked, "Tiff?" and the girl fell against him, laughing and crying.

Lilah exhaled with noisy relief. If he remembered his girlfriend's name, his head injury wasn't too serious. She heard someone say the paramedics had arrived and rose to give the lovebirds a few moments of privacy. Within minutes Trent was being hooked up to a portable IV and loaded onto a stretcher.

"Is this really necessary?" he demanded weakly, as Lilah rattled off instructions to the ambulance crew.

"Yes," she said, giving his arm a reassuring squeeze. "But it should only be overnight. Depending on that head wound and the results of the CT scan."

"My head hurts." He frowned. "What happened?"

"You don't remember?" the big guy asked, as he appeared beside them.

Trent thought for a minute. "No. The last thing I remember was dancing with Tiff and then…and then people around us were jumping into the lake."

The rest of his answer was drowned out by the arrival of a group of tipsy women noisily pushing through the crowd. Before Lilah could question Trent further she was being enthusiastically hugged by her friends and peppered with demands about what had happened.

"You were with us one minute, the next you were flying out the window," Angie, a colleague from ER, laughed as she squeezed Lilah. "Heck, if we'd known you were planning a public striptease of your own, we'd have been there to cheer you on instead of that sleazy toy boy."

"And thank God you're wearing your good underwear," Jenna Richards, obstetrician and bride-to-be, added. "Imagine if you'd been prancing around in laundry-day undies?"

"Oh, horror," Angie gasped, and everyone laughed, clearly still buzzed from the evening's festivities.

Lilah pushed a hank of wet hair from her forehead and shoved first one arm then the other through the bomber jacket's sleeves. Now that the emergency was over, she was very conscious of the fact that she was practically naked beneath the butter-soft leather.

A cool breeze brushed her bare legs, raising an army of goose bumps and she burrowed deeper into the voluminous folds. She was freezing.

"Let's go," she said, pushing her way through the group, suddenly eager to get somewhere private—and maybe order a couple of brandies. For medicinal purposes, of course.

Sensing no one was following her, Lilah looked over her shoulder and found thirteen pairs of eyes studying her with an array of expressions varying from curiosity to narrow-eyed speculation.

"What?"

"Do you two know each other?" Jenna demanded, craning her neck to look through the crowd of bystanders.

Lilah frowned. "Who? Trent?"

There was general confusion but it was Angie who demanded, "Trent? Who's Trent?"

"The boy I—"

"We're talking about Lucky Luke," Jenna interrupted, gesturing wildly to the people crowding around the big guy whose gaze was locked on Lilah. Her breath caught beneath that intense gaze but she must have looked baffled because Jenna's mouth dropped open to a chorus of gasps.

"You don't know?" She looked shocked.

"Know what?"

"And the lucky girl just happened to see Dr. Hunk of the Decade in his skivvies," another voice drawled. "Did you know his father's a cyber-tech billionaire?"

Lilah followed the direction of the woman's predatory look. "Dr who?"

"Sullivan," Jenna prodded. "You know? The assistant director of medicine Sullivan?"

It was Lilah's turn to look shocked. "But…but…I thought the ADM was a…woman?"

"Honey," Angie said, her face lighting up with a wicked grin, "Harriet Sullivan *is* a woman. You just got an up-close-and-personal view of her *nephew*, Dr. Tall, Dark and Buff, practically in the…well, the buff."

CHAPTER TWO

LUKE CHECKED HIS side mirror, flicked on the indicator and turned his motorbike into the hospital visitors' parking. The sixteen-hundred cc engine rumbled beneath him like a large, hungry predator and responded to the merest flick of his wrist.

He'd been back in Spruce Ridge a few months and still couldn't believe he was here at all. But, then, Spruce Ridge had been the spawning grounds of the Sullivan boys' greatest summer adventures, despite—or maybe in spite of—their parents' widely publicized and bitter divorce.

His aunt and uncle had taken in three bewildered little boys and provided a firm hand and a ton of homemade cookies, along with unconditional love. Looking back, Luke sometimes wondered where he'd be if it hadn't been for summers spent here.

His mouth twisted into a self-deprecating grin as he recalled the wild scrapes he and his brothers had got into, partly in a bid for their parents' attention but mostly because they had been budding delinquents. And punishing his parents had been the main reason he'd joined the army after med school, instead of doing his residency at the hospital his mother pulled strings to get him into.

He'd loved every minute of being in the Rangers—right up until eight months ago when his helicopter had been shot down over enemy territory. The crash had taken the lives of six marines, two rangers, the hostage they'd been sent in to retrieve and Luke's passion for flying.

He and the rest of his team had held off hostiles for fourteen hours before help had finally arrived. Luke didn't remember the rescue. He'd woken up in hospital two days later feeling damn lucky to be alive. He'd also woken up realizing it was just a matter of time before his luck ran out, so he'd signed his release papers and hopped on the first flight home.

Locating an empty parking space near the entrance, he whipped the big motorbike between a faded red truck and a dark blue sedan and brought it to a halt.

Dropping one booted foot to the ground, he killed the engine, released the kickstand and rose to his full six-four height. Shoving up his visor, he stripped off thick leather gloves and turned to survey the parking lot in a move he recognized as a habit left over from a decade in the military. He wasn't concerned about being paranoid—it had saved his ass countless times over the years—but he still had to remind himself that Spruce Ridge wasn't a war zone.

He figured he'd eventually get better at remembering.

Reaching up, he tugged off his helmet and shoved a hand through his hair, ruffling the thick coffee-colored strands. After tucking his gloves in the helmet, he dropped everything into a side storage compartment then headed for the entrance.

People sent him wary glances and Luke smiled and shook his head as they scuttled out of his way. He knew the black leather made him appear the big badass biker, but he'd seen enough accidents involving motorbikes that he wouldn't consider getting on one without wearing all the proper gear.

Reaching for the big zipper tab, he pulled it down and thought about his favorite leather bomber jacket a certain siren had been wearing the last time he'd seen her.

The memory of huge stormy gray eyes framed by a thick

fringe of dark lashes, long ropes of sopping red-gold hair and a lush pink mouth flashed into his head and brought a different smile to his lips. That mouth had breathed life back into a young man's lungs and had featured hotly in Luke's dreams last night.

Stepping through the automatic doors into the air-conditioned foyer, Luke pulled off his aviator shades and slid the earpiece of one arm into the neck of his T-shirt.

He gave a silent chuckle. Okay, so the memory had also included long naked legs and some spectacular curves covered in skimpy leopard-print underwear. He was a guy and hard-wired to recall stuff like that. Besides, in the months he'd been home he hadn't seen anything remotely as impressive or intriguing as the woman who'd stripped in public and dived into a freezing lake to save someone she didn't even know.

That had taken a lot of guts, and Luke was a great admirer of guts.

Entering the nearest elevator, he punched the button for the fifth floor and watched as the doors slid closed. It was his weekend off but he'd decided to check on last night's drowning victim before heading for the marina.

The elevator bell pinged and the doors opened onto a brightly lit corridor. Luke stepped out and the nurse on duty at the ward station looked up as he approached. Her gaze widened and she blinked a few times as her mouth opened and closed. "D-Dr. Sullivan?" she stuttered. "I didn't…I almost didn't recognize you." Then she hurriedly straightened her white and navy top and flipped her hair in a move Luke couldn't fail to recognize. "Can I help you?"

"I heard the drowning survivor was brought up here last night," he said, propping his elbow on the counter and aiming a crooked smile in her direction.

"I…um…drowning survivor?"

"Yeah, Trent something-or-another."

"Oh, him." She gave a husky laugh and slid her gaze all over him like he was a mega-sized chocolate snack and she was contemplating a sugar binge. "We heard all about his dramatic rescue this morning. Everyone's talking about what a hero you are."

"I didn't do anything," he denied, straightening from his slouch. He was used to attracting attention from the opposite sex, but felt like she'd stripped him naked right there beneath the bright fluorescents. He frowned. Sometimes he wondered if the interest had more to do with his father's money or the fact that he'd been discharged from the army with full military honors as well as a Purple Cross. Some women liked that kind of thing. "I wasn't the one who saved his life."

"That's not what I heard." She smiled as though he was being modest, and pointed down the corridor. "Just follow the noise. I'm sure Trent and his friends will be thrilled you stopped by."

"Thanks."

"Oh, by the way, Dr. Sullivan?" she called as he headed down the corridor. "Have you seen the morning papers?"

He paused with a puzzled look over his shoulder. "No, why?"

She winked and fanned herself. "You really should check them out."

He shrugged and said, "Okay," although he had absolutely zero interest in the tabloids. He'd spent enough time as a kid trying to live down his mother's publicized exploits or dodging the paparazzi to care about reading whatever had the nurse looking like she was having a menopausal moment.

Approaching the noisy private room, he slowed his pace and came to an abrupt halt in the doorway. The private room was filled with young studs all vying for the attention of a woman propped beside the window. She was flushed and laughing, looking as young and carefree as a college soph-omore. Luke recognized her instantly. Those long ropes of tousled red-gold curls were hard to miss, as were the soft, full curves beneath the lilac tank top. And the long legs en-cased in snug denim were unmistakably those of the woman who'd absconded with his favorite bomber jacket.

Dr. Lilah Meredith.

Lilah rolled her eyes and laughingly declined her fifth in-vitation for a date. It had been a long time since she'd been around noisy, energetic twenty-year-olds and she couldn't help feeling old—despite their assurances that she was a total "babe" or that she was only a few years older.

Besides, she couldn't remember the last time she'd been on a "real" date, let alone how to behave if she went on one with a couple of babe-crazy students.

Movement near the door distracted her from the disturb-ing image of herself as a lonely cougar—at twenty-nine—and Lilah sucked in a startled breath when she recognized the figure filling the doorway.

The last time she'd seen him he'd been standing head and shoulders above the crowd wearing nothing but low-slung jeans, a scowl and looking like the poster boy for Heroes R Us. The last time she'd seen him she'd thought he was just some hunky hot guy who'd been in the right place at the right time. Instead, he was a colleague—a guy from a world she wanted nothing to do with.

Granted, she'd only been working ER for a short while and had never actually been on rotation with him, but she'd heard enough about Luke Sullivan and seen him from a dis-tance that she should have recognized him. But, then, she'd been too busy to pay attention to more than deep green eyes and big warm hands.

Now the sight of him dressed in black leather and look-ing all big and bad and dangerous reminded her of long muscular legs, mile-wide shoulders and a body made for underwear ads—underwear for real men, that was, and not the pretty boys they usually featured.

There'd been that brief glimpse of him last night in wet black boxer briefs that still gave her heart palpitations when she recalled the way they'd molded to…well, everything.

Pushing away from the window with a breezy "Well, boys, it's been fun," Lilah reached for the shoulder bag she'd dropped on the bedside cabinet.

She slung it over her shoulder to a chorus of "You can't leave now," and pushed her way through the wall of youthful testosterone.

"Since the real hero of the moment has arrived, why don't I leave you to introduce yourselves? Maybe Connor can ask Dr. Sullivan for a date. I hear he's—"

"Already got a date with you, Dr. Meredith," his deep voice interrupted smoothly, sending goose bumps skittering across her flesh. Her eyes widened. *Oh, heck, no*, she thought with a gasp of dismay. *Absolutely no getting all worked up over some rich guy playing a badass biker dude.* Especially not a guy with the kind of look in his eyes that tempted women to sin.

He stepped into the room, abruptly dominating the space and sucking out all the air with a much more potent cocktail of testosterone and pheromones. But, then, he was a full-grown adult male who'd had years to perfect the recipe. *Oh, boy.*

His disturbing green gaze held hers for a couple of moments too long for comfort and his mouth curled—as though he was picturing her in her underwear. *Jerk.*

Lilah's face heated and she nervously licked her lips, which caused his eyes to darken instantly.

"Oh, I'm sure the guys will make much better dates than me," she said, cursing the alarming way her breath hitched and her knees wobbled as she moved towards the door. She paused and bit her lip when he made no move step aside. Her eyes narrowed. He was huge, *darn it*, and surrounded by masculine heat and energy that was way too appealing for comfort.

Couldn't he have waited for her to leave before arriving like a hot avenging angel of doom?

His hooded gaze swept over her face to her mouth before dropping to take in the rest of her body as though she was still wearing nothing but scraps of wet underwear. "I sincerely doubt that, *Doctor*," he drawled, drawing snickers from the group behind her. His mouth curled into a slow grin as sinful as the gaze that rose to hers. "I'll just keep my date with you."

"I wouldn't count on that, Dr. Sullivan," Lilah said smoothly, and was forced to brush past his big body on her way out the door. A chorus of whistles and whoops followed her down the passage and she heard him say, "No offence, Connor."

A burst of laughter nearly drowned out Connor's reply. "None taken, dude," was followed by, "You lucky dog," before she was finally out of earshot.

Face burning, Lilah opted to take the stairs rather than the elevator to the ground floor. She hoped by the time she reached the lobby she could blame her pounding pulse and ragged breathing on jogging down five flights of stairs.

She hit the ground floor and moved across the huge foyer, nodding to a group of ER nurses, who grinned and exchanged knowing looks when they saw her.

Idly wondering what that was all about, she searched through her shoulder bag for her keys, looking up when someone called her name.

Two women who'd been at the bachelorette party the night before, approached. Kim Howard held aloft a folded daily newspaper. "Have you seen the tabloids?" Lilah frowned and shook her head wondering why she should be interested in the tabloids.

"You should take a look, girl," Mandy Morgan advised her. "They're calling you Wild Woman and speculating about which underwear house you're moonlighting for."

Lilah felt her mouth drop open. "Wha-what?"

Kim snapped open the newspaper and flipped it around so Lilah could see the headlines and color picture dominating the front page.

A loud buzzing noise filled Lilah's ears and she thought she might faint. Beneath the headline "Wild Woman to the Rescue" was a picture of her diving off the pier. If she hadn't been so horrified to see herself on the front page—in her underwear—she might have admired the almost perfect execution of the dive. As it was, her cheeks felt numb and her fingertips tingled as though she was about to pass out.

She grabbed the paper. "Oh, my God," she whimpered, too shocked to do anything but gape at the large color pic.

"There's more on page three." Kim bumped her shoulder sympathetically and Lilah turned the page with shaking hands. She gasped when she saw a grainy picture showing her stripping off her dress in full view of an entire waterfront packed with people. There were others too: of her stepping from the boat onto the pier; giving Trent what appeared to be a passionate kiss; and a close-up of her and Luke Sullivan sharing an eye-lock. The caption read *"Wild Woman and Dr. Oh-So-Dishy share a scorching hot look."*

Yikes.

She looked naked. She felt exposed and…and horrified. How could this happen? It was like she was back in high school and someone posted an embarrassing photograph of her on the bulletin board. Only *worse.* Because now everyone in Spruce Ridge could gawk at her in her underwear.

There was a pic of Luke in his wet boxer briefs looking buff and hunky. It was practically X-rated and Lilah could easily imagine thousands of women across the city drooling over him as they enjoyed their morning coffee.

"Where…?" She swallowed the hot lump of mortification that had settled in her throat and tried again. "Where the heck did these come from?" she rasped.

Kim's sideways glance was sympathetic. "Cellphones probably."

"Cellphones?" Lilah turned and gaped at her. "People were filming me with cellphones instead of doing something to help?" She knew she was getting a little hysterical and a lot outraged, but she felt outraged. "Two young people could have died while they whipped out their cellphones and caught it on video?"

Kim shrugged as if to say, *Yeah, go figure* and said, "Yay for teenagers and their technology. They must have made a fortune selling them to the tabloids."

Lilah's eyes dropped to the close-up of her and Luke Sullivan and felt her face go hot. That simmering instant of connection had been caught for all eternity by some pimply faced adolescent. "This is a nightmare." Kim studied the picture and Lilah felt the other woman's sideways look. "What?"

"It looks kind of hot. Like a freeze-frame from a movie where the romantic leads share a sexy moment."

Lilah groaned and covered her face.

"It gets worse," Mandy said, and squeezed Lilah's shoulder in silent support.

"How can anything be worse than this?"

"Easy," Kim said with a snicker. "You've gone viral."

Luke approached the church and took the stone stairs to the open wooden doors. A wedding was the last place he wanted to be. He'd rather be caught in hostile territory without a weapon. But, last night, after he'd helped pour a

wasted Greg into a taxi, he'd made a solemn promise that
he'd be here.

He nodded to the guests gathered at the entrance and
slipped his aviator shades into the inside pocket of his jacket.
He'd had to buy a new suit, but considering the last one he'd
owned was about nineteen years old he'd thought he was
probably due for a new one. Especially if he was contemplating civilian life.

He might hate weddings and all they entailed but even he
knew he couldn't arrive dressed in black leather. Other than
a duffle bag full of army fatigues, jeans and tees, leather
was all he had in his meager wardrobe. And owning one
suit didn't mean he was turning out to be like his mother's
husbands.

Resigning himself to a few hours of excruciating torture, he accepted a program from a pimply-faced usher in
an ill-fitting suit and moved into the church, choosing a
seat near the back. He'd come solo partly because he didn't
know anyone outside of hospital personnel, and partly because women tended to get the kind of ideas at weddings
that he wanted to avoid.

Besides, the only woman he'd been remotely attracted
to since his arrival at SeaTac, just happened to think he
was a card-carrying anarchist who couldn't be trusted. At
least, that's what her expression had said this morning as
she'd sashayed from a ward full of horny twenty-year-olds.

A low murmur of voices approached and a flash of ice-
blue in his peripheral vision caught his attention. It was
only when a tall curvy figure passed and moved further
down the aisle that he realized it was the woman he'd just
been thinking about. And she was being escorted by their
boss, Dr. Peter Webster—smug ER director and all-round
womanizing sleazebag.

Feeling his skull tighten, he watched as Webster indicated aisle seats a few rows down and slid in after her, moving until he was practically in her lap.

Luke narrowed his gaze and watched as Webster leaned close but with a quick head-shake Lilah Meredith shifted until there were a few inches between them. Were they involved or something?

And if he was asking himself what a married man was doing at a wedding without his wife, it was because he'd experienced first hand the devastation that kind of behavior left behind and not because the feeling in his gut felt very much like betrayal.

According to the grapevine, Webster had a habit of targeting young unmarried personnel and Luke wondered why no one had reported him. If there was one thing he hated more than a bully, it was someone using their position to sexually harass subordinates who needed their jobs.

And then he wondered why he cared that Lilah Meredith was involved with anyone. He didn't.

After the service he joined a group of colleagues outside and waited for the newlyweds to leave the church. And while everyone pelted Greg and Jenna with rose petals Luke stood with his jacket slung over his shoulder and his free hand shoved into his pocket. When Lilah finally appeared, Webster's proprietary hand was on the curve of her hip as he ushered her solicitously down the steps.

Solicitous, my eye, Luke snorted silently, and barely resisted the urge to head over and deck the smug bastard. He knew exactly what the man was thinking and it wasn't good manners—especially not with Dr. Meredith dressed in that blue dress and short stylish black jacket. All she needed was a wide-brimmed black hat and she'd look like a sexy gaucho.

Besides, it was none of his business how, and with whom, Lilah Meredith spent her free time. For all he knew, she was enjoying all the attention she was getting from a "respected" professional who could do a lot for her career.

Besides, when he'd been a student it had been common knowledge that a lot of girls dated med students, hoping to snag themselves a doctor. He hadn't thought Lilah Meredith was like that, but what the hell did he know?

Lilah drove through the huge iron gates and down the tree-lined road that led to the exclusive Greendale Hotel. Grimacing at the thought of how out of place her grandmother's old sedan would look amongst all the luxury vehicles, she headed for the portico entrance. She didn't know why she cared. It was way better than arriving in a low-slung sports car with a man who was not only her boss but reminded her of why her recent relief work in South America had gone so horribly wrong.

Peter Webster, with his charming smile, wandering hands and practiced seduction technique, was cut from the same cloth as her ex-boss, Dr. Brent Cunningham the Third—the person responsible for the Amazonian Disaster, as Lilah had come to think of that chapter in her life.

Like Brent, Peter suffered from a God complex and tended to think he was entitled to more than professional courtesy from his subordinates. As if Lilah should feel honored by his attention. She didn't, and had experienced first hand what happened when men like him felt rejected and humiliated by someone like her. Careers suffered and lives were ruined.

Lilah told herself to remember that the next time she felt like kneeing the man in the nuts or punching that perfect nose. If there was one thing she hated, it was influential men taking advantage of vulnerable young women.

Lilah was neither that young nor vulnerable, unless you counted on the fact that she really needed this job. Besides, every time she looked in a mirror she was reminded that her own mother had fallen for a man just like Peter. Handsome, charming, married and wealthy. Rowan Franklin had swept her off her feet with promises of a bright and rosy future together. Only the future hadn't turned out so rosy for Grace Meredith. She'd found herself alone, pregnant and out of a job.

Frankly, no matter how handsome or charming the man, Lilah had absolutely no intention of making the same mistake—even at the promise of career advancement.

Following the stream of cars to the hotel's front entrance, she waited until a young uniformed valet approached her door before grabbing her clutch purse and sliding from behind the wheel.

She murmured her thanks and sent him a smile that made his ears turn red, before heading into the neo-classic lobby. A hundred feet overhead, late afternoon sunlight streamed in through the huge glass cupola and lit up the opulent marbled lobby like the sun god illuminating the temple of Zeus. Lilah had to blink a few times to dispel the image, especially when it highlighted a pair of broad shoulders, a wide tapering back and long muscular legs she recognized almost immediately—a figure that looked oddly out of place in the opulent surroundings when he should have looked right at home. Like a dangerous predator pretending to be housetrained.

She shivered at the image and decided it was the coiled readiness and lazily alert gaze that took in everything around him.

As though sensing her scrutiny, Luke Sullivan turned his head and an errant ray of sunshine fell across his face. It illuminated a slashing cheekbone, hard jaw and a surprisingly sculpted mouth, leaving the rest of his face in deep shadow.

She watched his unsmiling mouth for a couple of beats and shivered again—this time for an altogether different reason. *Dammit*. The man just had to look at her and she was reacting like a high-school sophomore with her first crush.

Reminding herself that he was from a world so far removed from hers that he might as well be from another galaxy, Lilah bit her lip and followed other guests to the ballroom. She told herself that she didn't care since he was out of most women's league. But it didn't help.

It also didn't help that even in an elegant suit Luke Sullivan looked as relaxed as a warrior god in Zeus's temple—like a hero from the Golden Age. It didn't take much imagination to picture him swinging a huge bronze broadsword at some hapless mortal enemy or whipping out a handgun and going all Super Spy on hotel guests.

She'd seen him in scrubs and a lab coat, biker leather, formal suit and almost nothing at all, and had yet to decide which look suited him best. He was a man of mystery, and Lilah didn't need anyone to tell her it would take a determined woman to peel away the layers to get to the real man beneath.

Not that he would allow it, she mused. The man had more layers than an onion and, frankly, anyone stupid enough to try deserved the tears that were sure to follow. She wasn't stupid and had long ago come to the conclusion that men weren't worth getting dehydrated for.

Shaking off the disturbing thoughts, Lilah paused at the ballroom entrance to scan the seating plan for her name. Besides, Luke Sullivan wasn't her problem and she would do well to stay as far from him as she could.

Someone come up behind her and she knew by the way her entire back heated and tingled who it was, even before a deep voice said near her ear, "Table eight, near the far left French doors. We're together."

They were?

Lilah turned and found her nose practically touching a crisp white shirt. Startled to find him so close, she took a step back and slid her gaze up past a green-and-gold-patterned tie, strong tanned throat and hard jaw. Her gaze lingered for a couple of seconds on his mouth before lifting to look into deep green eyes surrounded by fringes of long dark lashes.

Her stomach gave an alarming little dip.

"*Oh...uh...*Dr. Sullivan," she said lamely, and cursed the breathless quality of her voice. "It's you."

"Uh-huh." He lifted one eyebrow in a move that made Lilah wish she could look as mocking. "Expecting someone? Webster, maybe?"

"Peter?" Lilah was confused. "Why would I be waiting for him?"

Luke rocked back on his heels and shoved his hands in his pockets. "Peter?" he demanded with a ferocious scowl. "Since when are you on first-name terms with the Emperor of ER?"

"Since it's none of your business," she shot back, angered and confused by his confrontational attitude. The last time she'd seen him he'd been dressed like a bad biker dude. But at least he'd been smiling. Right now, glaring at her as though she'd done something unforgivable, he looked like a sophisticated angel of doom. A very *sexy* angel of doom. *Darn him. And darn those tingles.*

She turned back to pretend interest in the seating plan and tried to ignore the way the hair at the nape of her neck lifted—as though straining towards him—like he was a giant magnet yanking at every atom of iron in her body. Then he leaned closer and the tingles turned into a full-body shiver accompanied by goose bumps and tightening nipples.

Her eyes widened and she sucked in a shocked squeak.

Stop that, she ordered, but her body ignored the warning despite every instinct alerting her to danger. *Holy cow,* his blatant masculinity called to something deep and primal and feminine within her—something that had chosen now, of all times, to awaken and unfurl deep in her belly. She held her breath and kept her body as still as she could. Maybe he'd think she was a statue and go away.

Please go away.

"Why did you tell everyone I saved the kid, wild thing?" he murmured softly in her ear, and the breath she'd sucked in escaped in a soundless whoosh. She felt at once dizzy and amazingly clear-headed; something that was not only impossible but alarming.

And she didn't like it. And because she didn't, her spine stiffened and she said, "You did."

"Did not," he denied softly, chuckling when she made an annoyed sound in her throat.

Schooling her features, she turned slowly to face him. "I have no desire to become a celebrity," she informed him coolly. And she had no desire to become some rich playboy's newest toy either.

Luke rocked back on his heels, his hands shoved casually in his pockets. One dark brow arched arrogantly. "And you think I do?"

Lilah shrugged. "You have broad shoulders." She let her gaze drift over his wide, solid chest. "You can handle it," she added, before turning on her four-inch heels and escaping into the ballroom.

CHAPTER THREE

THE INSTANT DINNER ENDED, Lilah escaped to the ladies' room to freshen her make-up and shore up her shaky composure. What the heck had Jenna been thinking to seat her beside Luke Sullivan?

Okay, so she knew what Jenna had been thinking. It was what everyone else had been thinking ever since the tabloids had hit the stands this morning. *Damn that picture.* And damn the rosy cloud of romance Jenna was floating around on. She was madly in love and wanted everyone else to be too.

Little did she know that Luke Sullivan was the last person Lilah would ever consider having a romantic *anything* with. And although he wasn't her boss, he was the boss's nephew. In Lilah's mind it was the same thing. It was a nightmare to go along with all the other nightmares she'd had recently. Like South America but with a guy she couldn't ignore no matter how much she tried. A guy who refused to *let* her ignore him.

The harder she tried the more perverse pleasure he seemed to take in sabotaging her. Like brushing against her when she talked to the man on her left or *accidentally* bumping her arm and spilling her champagne down her cleavage.

And he smelled delicious. Like warm, virile man and cool, earthy forest. Every breath she took filled her senses with his wonderfully warm woodsy smell until she was dizzy with the notion of finding out exactly where it originated. With her mouth.

Or maybe that was just the champagne.

Whatever it was, she became excruciatingly aware of his every move, and soon found herself holding her breath, waiting for his next. And, boy, he made plenty. Playing with the stem of his wine glass, invading her space while he kept her champagne glass filled, or removing his jacket and tie, rolling up his shirtsleeves to expose the corded strength of his forearms and his big boney wrists. Accidentally brushing his knuckles against her thigh.

And breathing. Especially breathing.

It all combined to make her as twitchy as a preschooler in Sunday Mass, and if she'd gulped down more champagne than usual, it was his fault. As was the headache blooming behind her eyes.

Exhaling with relief at finally being able to breathe without inhaling his potent masculinity, Lilah joined a host of other women at the mirrors. While listening to the gossip flowing around her, she spent a few minutes wrestling with her hair, even though she knew it was a lost cause. Taming the long curls had always been a challenge.

Finally, when she could no longer avoid the inevitable, she shoved everything back into her clutch bag and left the bathroom, praying Luke Sullivan had ridden off into the sunset on his big black hog. Maybe then she could start enjoying the evening.

Following the sounds of the band, she exchanged a few greetings with other guests on their way back to the ballroom and paused in the doorway as Jenna and Greg took to the floor for the newlyweds' dance.

It was a beautiful moment and she couldn't help feeling a little envious of the way Greg looked at his new bride. The couple practically glowed with happiness, reminding Lilah she hadn't had anything resembling a date in over two years.

The dance ended to hoots and cheers as the couple shared a heated embrace. Without pausing, the band segued into another song and the little pinch of envy became a sharp ache of emptiness as Jenna's father stepped onto the dance floor. He tapped Greg's shoulder then swept his daughter into his arms with a look of such pride and love that Lilah felt tears prick the backs of her eyes.

This was a moment she would never experience for herself. And though she tried to shove them back into hiding, all the old feelings of resentment and abandonment she hadn't felt since adolescence came rushing back.

Right there in the midst of celebration she was sucked back to her mother's death and the letter telling Lilah about her father.

It had taken her almost a year to get past the grief and anger following the plane crash that had killed her mother to summon the courage to open it. Sometimes Lilah wished she never had—wished she didn't know about her mother's summer internship at a prestigious Seattle law firm or her wild romance with the married son of the firm's founding partner. Life would have been so much simpler.

When twenty-two-year-old Grace Meredith had revealed she was pregnant, Rowan Franklin had been furious. He'd accused her of trying to ruin his life and his career, and then he'd offered her money.

Her mother hadn't exactly said it had been for a termination, but Lilah wasn't stupid. She could read between the lines. Even at sixteen she'd known her father had paid Grace to have an abortion then kicked her to the curb like an unwanted pet.

She clearly remembered hopping on an intercity bus with plans to confront him. Lilah snorted silently. She didn't know what she'd expected, but to a girl who'd dreamed of the day she would meet him, Rowan Franklin III had been handsome and dazzling as a movie star. She recalled being struck dumb in his presence as a chaotic mix of anger and desperate hope filled her.

Unfortunately, he'd been no happier to see her then than he'd been the day her mother had dropped the baby bombshell. He'd checked his watch and listened impatiently while she'd introduced herself and explained about her mother's death. When she'd finished, he'd walked to his desk, pulled out his checkbook, and without once looking in her direction he'd coldly asked how much it would take for her to go away.

She'd been devastated. With one stroke of his ten-thousand-dollar gold pen he'd destroyed a young girl's fragile dreams as easily as he'd signed his name.

So she'd reacted badly.

Lilah huffed out a silent laugh. Okay, badly was an understatement. She'd flung scathing insults in his smug, handsome face and when he'd looked her in the eye and denied being her father, she'd snatched some fancy glass paperweight along with several family photographs from his desk and hurled them at the wall of glass cabinets behind him. The destruction had been as satisfying as it had been horrifying. Even to this day she couldn't believe what she'd done.

White-faced with fury, he'd stalked over, grabbed her arm in a bruising grip and dragged her to the door. Then he'd slapped the check in her hand and warned that if she ever contacted him or tried to blackmail him again, he would have her arrested.

She'd walked into that lavishly appointed corner office a nervous, eager child with dreams of finding a father who'd been searching for his daughter and had left with her heart and pride in tatters. She'd also left determined never to let anyone close enough to hurt her again.

That meeting had cured her of any "daddy" issues she might have had. And just in case she forgot, she'd kept that uncashed check of twenty-five thousand dollars as a reminder that she had to rely on herself and that some men made promises they never intended to keep.

Lost in the past, she didn't notice someone come up behind her until a deep voice drawled, "Don't tell me you buy into all this sappy stuff, wild thing?"

Startled, Lilah sucked in a sharp breath and rounded on him. "Will you stop sneaking up on me?" she snapped, slapping a shaking hand over her pounding heart. "And stop calling me that." Besides, she didn't want to be anything like her mother.

Luke shoved his hands in his pockets and hiked a dark brow up his forehead as though she was acting crazy. Lilah felt a little crazy. *He* made her crazy, dammit.

"Lady, you're either in hearts-and-roses land or you need another glass of champagne." He snagged one from a passing waiter and shoved it at her. "Here, maybe this will help."

Lilah stepped back and looked at the glass like it might bite her. Frankly, the last thing she needed was another glass of champagne. Muttering something, she swung away to watch as other couples began drifting onto the dance floor. Maybe if she ignored him long enough he'd get the hint and go away.

But, of course, he didn't. That would be asking too much, Lilah thought furiously. Instead, he chuckled deep in his chest and leaned closer, the heat of his big body sending awareness shivering into every strand of DNA.

His deep voice held more than a hint of amusement when he asked, "Did you just say the only way champagne will help is if I drown in it, Dr. Meredith?"

Lilah fought the embarrassment heating her cheeks and inhaled slowly to give herself time to get a grip. But that only gave her a head full of his amazing scent. Besides, she hadn't meant for him to hear that. Had she?

She finally ground out, "Of course not," through clenched teeth and tried to edge away, but the darned man had practically herded her into a corner. She couldn't escape without drawing attention to herself, and after the past twenty four hours, attention was the last thing she wanted. "I would never be so rude."

He gave another chuckle as though he didn't believe her, and lifted his hand to play with the soft curls at her nape before drawing a light fingertip down her spine to the zipper tab. His touch, so deliberately casual, sent goose bumps fleeing across her flesh, and to Lilah's absolute horror, could be felt all the way to her tingling toes. Her belly clenched, her nipples tightened, and this time she didn't even have the benefit of her little jacket to hide her visceral response.

She hitched her shoulder to dislodge his touch and tried to move away but the man obviously had a hard head if he could ignore such obvious go-away signals. Instead, he dropped his hand to her hip and pulled her back against his chest.

She gasped and tried to jerk away but his fingers tightened. Heat instantly spread up to her nape and down to the backs of her knees—and, heck, everywhere in between. "What are you *doing*?" she demanded in a low voice, and tried to turn, but his palm slid across her jittering belly and pressed her against his front.

Lilah froze at the unexpected intimacy of his embrace. "You haven't answered my question," Luke reminded her against her ear, his thumb idly brushing warmed silk. His deep voice vibrated against her back like the rumble of distant thunder—or maybe a huge satisfied cat after eating a fat pigeon.

She sucked in a shivery breath and tried not to feel like a frightened pigeon. It was humiliating enough to discover how threatened she felt, especially when his touch heated up all the lonely places in her body that hadn't seen action in way too long.

"About what?" she rasped, her throat as dry as the Mojave Desert.

"About buying into all…this romantic garbage," he murmured, using his free hand to indicate the white-and-gold-decorated ballroom. Lilah tilted her head and looked up over her shoulder into his shadowed face.

"You don't?"

Amusement lit up his green eyes and lurked at the corners of his mouth. He snorted. "You're kidding, right?" And when she continued to stare at him he shrugged a heavily muscled shoulder. "I'm a guy. We're allergic to weddings." Her eyebrow rose up her forehead and he chuckled. "Okay, *I'm* allergic to weddings."

"Then why come?"

"I heard the food's great." He must have noticed her expression because he laughed and said, "I promised Greg I would."

When he laughed, golden flecks lit the green depths of his eyes. Like sunlight shining through water. "And you keep your promises?" she asked to distract herself from the feel of his hard body against hers and what it did to her.

Something indecipherable came and went in his expression and the golden lights winked out. "Don't you?"

"I asked first," Lilah countered, and instantly wondered at the shift in the energy around them. His eyes turned somber as they slid over her face before moving to the ballroom. She didn't know why but she got the odd impression he wasn't seeing the opulent room with its flickering candles and laughing guests. As though he'd withdrawn somewhere she couldn't follow—somewhere a lot less cheerful than a hotel ballroom in uptown Spruce Ridge.

His jaw flexed and she felt like she was intruding on a private moment filled with pain and bleak memories. "Some promises are impossible to keep," he murmured, and dropped his hand. Lilah shivered at the abrupt loss of heat and cursed herself for caring.

Something must have happened to put that haunted look on his face, she thought, fighting the urge to turn and wrap her arms around him. Luke Sullivan didn't need her concern. He was big and hard and capable. And dangerous. Very dangerous, she reminded herself. At least to her peace of mind. So when a young resident appeared beside them and asked her to dance, she accepted, suddenly eager to escape Luke Sullivan's disturbing presence.

She didn't know why she sent him a silent look over her shoulder. She certainly didn't need his permission. But when he shrugged and said, "I don't dance," before turning and disappearing from the ballroom, she couldn't help feeling rebuffed.

Fortunately the resident made it impossible to brood and before long Lilah was laughing at his bad jokes as he twirled her around the dance floor. Finally, after a dozen dances with as many new partners, she laughingly cried uncle and escaped out the French doors into the warm night.

A few people were scattered around the torch-dotted terrace and Lilah wandered over to the low stone balustrade. She looked out into a night as dark and lush as black velvet—a night perfect for romance and moonlit trysts. Frangipani and night-blooming camellia scented the balmy air while solar-powered lights led a rambling path through the extensive gardens to a pool, glowing like blue magic in the darkness. To her right the well-manicured lawns rolled towards the lake, slumbering like a sea of ink beneath a fat yellow moon.

The scene might have come right out of a movie if memories of the previous night hadn't flooded her mind. She shivered and rubbed her arms just as someone came up beside her. A jacket dropped around her shoulders in an echo of her thoughts but even before a smooth voice solicitously murmured, "You're cold," in her ear, she knew it wasn't the man she'd been thinking about.

Lilah bit back a grimace and looked up into Peter's handsome face. Just when she'd decided he'd lost interest, here she was cornered on the terrace in the dark. By her boss. *What joy.*

And from the look in his eyes she'd have to think of something fast if she wanted to escape with her job and her integrity intact. Something like an aneurysm or appendicitis. Or maybe mad cow disease. People tended to get a little paranoid when the words "mad" and "cow" weren't being used to describe a crazy woman at a Bloomingdale shoe sale. But then she reminded herself that he was a doctor and would know he'd have to eat her brains before contracting it. She couldn't see that happening in the next five seconds.

Dammit. She was trapped—by good manners and his hands on her shoulders.

"Finally," he murmured, like she'd been waiting all night to be alone with him. *Yeah, right.* In the moonlight his golden hair gleamed almost as brightly as his smile. Like an angel—or some equally perfect celestial being. And if she were any other woman she might have been charmed. But she wasn't. She had too much history with men like him to ever forget that he was married—and used vulnerable women.

"It's been torture, sitting alone," he said deeply, rubbing her arms, and for the second time that night Lilah felt herself pulled back against a man's warm chest. But whereas Luke's chest had felt wide and warm and oddly comforting, Peter's just felt…vaguely threatening.

"Miss me?"

And that was Lilah's cue to escape. She faked a shiver and seized the excuse to pull away. "I'm cold, maybe I should go in." His hands prevented her attempts to slide his jacket off her shoulders. They also kept her swathed in a cloud of expensive cologne and the cool calculation of a practiced seduction. Lilah shivered, this time it was genuine. She had an awful feeling the man had no intention of letting her go without a struggle.

Closing her eyes, she drew in a steadying breath and pushed memories of another man and another seduction attempt from her head. *Damn.* She really needed this job but Peter was making it increasingly difficult for her to remain polite when what she wanted to do was turn and knee him in the nuts and bolts.

Turning abruptly, she backed up against the balustrade and fought the urge to vault over it.

"Dr Webster," she said, deciding to confront him and risk being fired. "You're…um…my boss and…and married."

He hummed in his throat and stepped closer, dropping his hands onto the stone behind her, caging her with his arms and body. She had to press her hands against his chest and lean back to keep a few inches between them.

"My wife doesn't care," he explained with a smile, as though her protests amused him. *God, as though her protests aroused him.* "She does her thing and doesn't interfere with mine." He leaned forward to kiss her mouth but she turned her head at the last moment and his lips glanced off her cheekbone. "It suits us both."

"Well, it doesn't suit me," she said briskly, and grabbed his wandering hand before it could reach her breast.

He sighed and shifted back a little. "Don't tell me you're one of those women?" He sounded a bit annoyed, as though she was playing hard to get when she should be flattered by his attention. Lilah felt her jaw drop open.

"Excuse me?"

He must have heard something in her voice because he sighed and straightened. "All I'm saying is you've been sending out signals all night." *What?* "I'm not the only man to pick up on them, Lilah."

"Signals?"

His mouth slid into a charming, coaxing smile. "I am, however, the only man with enough balls to follow through."

Lilah stared at him as though he was speaking an alien dialect. Besides, the last subject she wanted to talk about was his...well, *that*. "What are you talking about?"

He sighed impatiently. "You're not making this easy, sweetheart."

Sweetheart? "Easy?"

"You're lucky I saw you slip away." She spluttered and he chuckled. "Let's not waste time," he cajoled gently, framing her face in his hands. "We can go back to your place, or get a room at the hotel if you prefer. Your choice. But you should know..." he paused and smiled meaningfully "...I can do things for your career."

Lilah stared up at him for a couple of beats and wondered if he'd lost his mind or was drunk. But he appeared sober and quite serious. As though she would actually consider taking him up on his less than flattering offer. She didn't know whether to laugh or slug him.

She shook her head and shifted to remove his jacket, but he covered her hands with his and drew the satin lapels together like a straitjacket. Maybe he meant it to be comforting but she just felt claustrophobic.

"All right." He chuckled indulgently. "We'll do this your way. Why don't we go to the bar for a drink? Then..." He waggled his eyebrows and Lilah had to bite her lip to keep from rolling her eyes. She wanted to tell him what he could do with his drink—and anything else he was considering—but then again if she agreed, she could say she had to go to the bathroom and then make a break for it.

"Talk about what?"

"Yeah, Webster," a deep voice drawled from the inky shadows. It was so close that Lilah jolted and gave a little shocked gasp. She'd been so intent on escaping unscathed she hadn't noticed anyone approaching.

Luke materialized out of the dark looking big and dark and sinfully dangerous. "Talk about what?" he drawled, and Lilah wondered if she was the only one to detect the edge to his tone. His hair was rumpled as though he'd run his fingers through the thick strands. "About why you're moving in on my date?"

Looking at him, Lilah couldn't help comparing the two men: one as light as the other was dark. Both were tall and good looking, but where Peter was as smoothly handsome as a *male* model, Luke Sullivan was hot—with the kind of hard, dangerous edginess that made women stick out their chests and reach for lip gloss. He made her heart pound, her stomach clench and her knees wobble.

"Your date?" Webster laughed, as though the idea was ludicrous.

Luke instantly stilled and the air crackled with masculine aggression. "Yeah," he said mildly, his gaze on Lilah as though waiting for her to rat him out. "My date." She wasn't about to argue, even when he wrapped his long fingers around her wrist and slowly drew her towards him, making her feel like a fat juicy bone between two snarling alpha dogs.

Without looking at Webster, he slid the jacket off her shoulders and tossed it in the other man's direction. Smiling into her upturned face, he said, "Sorry I got waylaid, babe," in a voice as deep and intimate as a kiss. "A couple of the guys needed an impartial opinion." He finally looked up. "Thanks for keeping her company, Webster, but I've got this."

"You have?"

"Yeah." He leaned down and kissed Lilah's startled mouth and this time she didn't have time to turn away. But maybe that was a good thing? "The band's playing all those slow dances she promised me."

"Go away, Sullivan," Webster snapped, looking for a moment as though he contemplated wrestling Lilah away from Luke. "This is none of your business."

A dark brow hiked up Luke's forehead. "Not from where I'm standing," he drawled, lacing his long fingers with Lilah's and tugging her closer. She sucked in a sharp breath when the smile he aimed at the ER director turned blade-sharp. "By the way, where's that lovely wife of yours?" He looked out over the moonlit garden. "A shame to waste such a romantic setting."

Peter's gaze dropped to their linked hands and his mouth thinned. Lilah shivered and moved closer to Luke's comforting bulk. He gave her hand a reassuring—or was that a warning?—squeeze.

"Yeah," Peter said quietly, his eyes coolly speculative and not at all happy. "A real shame." And with one last look at Lilah he folded his jacket over his arm and walked off, leaving her alone with Luke.

As soon as he disappeared, Lilah slid her hand from Luke's and wrapped her arms around her middle. The whole incident had left a bad taste in her mouth and she was more than ready to escape the tension.

She moved across the terrace to the open French doors and Luke silently fell into step beside her. Sparing a quick glance across her shoulder, she had to tilt her head right back to see his expression. She should have saved herself the neck spasm. His features were shadowed and he was clearly back to his inscrutable self with his hard jaw and hooded gaze. The sight of a small muscle flexing in his jaw sent a brush of feminine warning drifting up her spine.

She swallowed hard and paused in the doorway to rub her tingling arms. "Where are you going?"

"We're going to dance."

"Dance?"

He spared her a hooded glance. "Yeah, dance. You know. I take you in my arms and we sway to music."

"I thought you couldn't dance."

Luke's mouth curled into a mocking smile. "I said I *don't* dance, not that I can't."

"There's a difference?"

"Sure." He snagged her hand and tightened his grip when she tried to snatch it back. "Why don't I show you?"

Lilah got the impression his suggestion was more along the lines of a command and suddenly she'd had enough.

"I don't want to dance," she announced stubbornly, digging her heels into the floor and trying to prise his fingers apart without causing a scene.

He simply ignored her puny efforts and growled, "That's too bad, wild thing," as he steered her towards the dance floor, where he yanked her against his chest and snaked his arms around her. They felt like bands of iron. "Besides, you don't want to make a liar out of me, do you?"

Lilah held her body stiffly and stared over his shoulder in stony silence. Perhaps if she ignored him he'd get bored and find someone else to torture.

After a short while he murmured, "I suggest you make it look good," in her ear.

Lilah tensed and sent him a brief glare out the corner of her eye. "Make what look good?" Despite her determination to remain unaffected, her body kept straining towards him, as though he was the sun and she a flower that had just survived a long cold winter.

Her resolve wavered and he must have sensed her indecision because his hold gentled and he shifted until her every soft curve was molded against hard masculine flesh.

"Webster is watching," he murmured against her ear. "No, don't look," he warned softly, when she began turning her head. "Unless you want him to come over here. Because if that's the case—"

"It's not," she said quickly, lifting her face to his. Her gaze drifted up his strong throat and shadowed jaw, past his sensual mouth to look deeply into his smoldering eyes. Lilah cursed the volatile effect he seemed to have on her senses—which were sending conflicting messages to escape *and* jump him.

Deciding to punish him for the way he made her body react—and for his arrogance—she allowed her hands to drift up his hard chest and over his heavily muscled shoulders. Then she thrust her fingers into the thick hair at the back of his head, her nails lightly scraping his skull.

His body shuddered—or maybe that was her—and with a rough sound in the back of his throat he dropped a hard kiss on her mouth. Unable to stop herself, she let out a soft moan and her eyes drifted closed. Her mouth softened beneath his and the rough sound in his throat became a growl of possession.

Right there on the dance floor of the Cherry Blossom ballroom, Luke Sullivan sucked out her mind along with her breath. The instant before her mind slid away completely Lilah reminded herself that it wasn't real. That the heat and hardness of him, the hungry feeding kiss that felt far too real, was all for one man's benefit.

And it wasn't the man currently kissing her like he wanted to consume her very soul.

CHAPTER FOUR

IF LILAH'S INTENTION had been to get her life on track and keep a low profile when she'd returned to Spruce Ridge, she'd failed miserably. Not only had she managed to get herself on the front page of every local tabloid, the whole incident was also online—and, according to some colleagues, had already had a quarter-million hits.

And if that wasn't bad enough, she'd been hit on by her married boss, and a motorbike-riding dark angel with trouble tattooed on his sexy butt had practically sucked out her brains in the middle of a ballroom.

She was living every good girl's worst nightmare—and Lilah had made every effort as a child to be good so her mother hadn't had to worry.

And where the heck had that got her? She'd been fired from relief work in a developing country for challenging sexual harassment, photographed in public in her underwear, and caught on camera locking lips with a sexy biker dressed in an expensive suit at a society wedding.

The irony was not lost on Lilah. She'd spent her late teens and all of her adult life avoiding rich guys who thought women like her were easy pickings. Now she was being hounded by two of them while being accosted by the press and greeted everywhere she went as "Wild Woman."

She'd even tried hinting that Luke was a war hero to get the tabloids off her back but they kept coming back despite her refusal to cooperate. She sighed. Or maybe because of her refusal to cooperate. She didn't want the notoriety and the last thing she needed was for some reporter to start poking around in her life. There were things she didn't want people to know about her. Things more private than her preference in designer underwear.

Let Sullivan take the heat. Rumor had it he'd been a bad-ass in the army. Frankly, she could believe it. He was surrounded by the kind of dangerous aura of a man who'd lived on the edge and liked it there. Besides, with his thick hide and military training, shouldn't he be fireproof?

Lilah might have wanted to forget the whole incident but newspapers were clearly at a loss for real news if they'd resorted to hounding her for a story that simply wasn't there. In addition, County Gen's director was ecstatic with all the free publicity the hospital was getting, and wanted to milk it. And if that wasn't bad enough, Trent's parents arrived from Europe the following week and Lilah received an invitation to dinner at an exclusive downtown hotel.

Fortunately she was on night shift and could send her apologies. She could understand their gratitude but she wanted to avoid any more attention.

Thinking she'd dodged that particular bullet, she arrived for work one evening to be informed that Dr. Webster wanted to see her.

Heart pounding in her throat, brow wrinkled with foreboding, Lilah made her way to his office and wondered if she was about to be fired—again. *Dammit*, just when she was starting to make friends and settle into the house her grandmother had left her.

Peter's assistant looked up as Lilah entered.

"Good evening, Dr. Meredith," Mercia Grant said coolly, slipping her purse strap over her shoulder and moving out from behind her desk. "You can go right in, he's waiting for you."

Lilah frowned. The last thing she wanted was to be alone with Webster—especially in his office during a shift change. No one was likely to notice if he decided to make good on his promise the night he'd cornered her on a shadowed terrace. Luke Sullivan had saved her then but she knew she couldn't count on that happening again.

Lilah said good-night and moved across the floor to the boss's inner sanctum with a jittery belly. She heard his voice and paused a moment before knocking. He barked out an order for her to enter and looked up when she pushed open the door. He was scowling at someone on the other end of the phone but when he saw Lilah his impatient expression vanished so fast she wondered if she'd imagined it.

He sent her a smile intended to flatter, as though the incident at Jenna's wedding had never happened. Gesturing for her to enter, he abruptly ended his call and rose to come around the large desk towards her—all congenial host—as though she'd simply dropped in for a social visit. *Really weird.*

"Take a seat, Lilah. Can I get you anything?" He'd recently showered and shaved and the scent of his expensive aftershave hung in the air. Confused and a little freaked out, she remained standing and shoved her hands into her lab-coat pockets.

"No, thank you," she said a little warily. "I have to report for duty in a few minutes and it looks like you're on your way to dinner."

"It can wait." He dismissed her objections, leaving her wondering if he meant her shift or his dinner. Sitting on the edge of his desk, he crossed his ankles and eyed her with an odd smile that sent a tremor of unease through her. As though he knew something she didn't. "How are you, Lilah?"

Unease abruptly became confusion and she frowned. What the heck was he playing at? "I'm fine, thank you, Dr.

Webster. The night administrator said you wanted to see me." *Might as well hurry things along so she could leave.*

He gave a low laugh and folded his arms over his chest. "I do. And I thought we'd agreed that you'd call me Peter?"

"You're my boss," she replied warily. *And you're a married jerk.* "Besides, we're at work."

He laughed again and straightened. "We are indeed." He headed for the coatrack near the window. "It seems that you have managed to impress quite a few important people," he announced cryptically, and Lilah didn't know if that was a good or bad thing.

"I'm not following you."

He retrieved his jacket and thrust his arms into the sleeves. "I understand the parents of the boy you saved invited you to dinner." It wasn't a question.

"I declined," she said, as he shrugged into the designer garment and paused before a large mirror to adjust his tie and fiddle with his already perfect hair. His gaze found hers in the mirror and she held it coolly and professionally. If he wanted to fire her, he would have to do it without all the schmoozing and creepy charm.

"Yes, well," he drawled, clearly amused by her attitude. "It seems our board of directors has decided to accept on your behalf."

What? "I'm on night rotation," she reminded him, relieved to have a legitimate excuse—and, *wow*, relieved that she wasn't being dismissed. Besides, Luke Sullivan had most likely also been invited and the last thing she wanted was to see him. Not after that very public lip-lock in the middle of the ballroom dance floor that had scrambled her brains. Not after he'd fried her nerve endings and sent her body into a meltdown she was still trying to recover from. All for nothing if the man she'd hoped to deceive was behaving as though that kiss had never happened.

Webster interrupted her thoughts. "I've ordered your

schedule changed so you can have Friday night off," he said dismissively, turning to face her. And when she opened her mouth to argue, he added, "Orders from above. The Carringtons are insisting, and since they would like to thank the hospital by making a huge donation, the board of directors is also insisting."

Lilah frowned and firmed her jaw. She didn't like being outmaneuvered but didn't want to offend the big bosses either. On the bright side, at least she wasn't being fired.

Peter moved closer and before she realized his intention he'd lifted a hand to play with stray tendrils that had escaped her messy up-do.

"Why not think of it as part of the job?" he murmured soothingly, grazing her jaw with his fingers when she narrowed her gaze and stepped away. "Instead of dealing with the usual Friday night ER carnage, you'll have an excuse to wear something sexy and get to dine out in style. I know how much you women love that." Lilah's eyes widened. "Besides," he continued patronizingly, "I'll be there too. Maybe we can even make a night of it. A weekend perhaps?"

Lilah sucked in a shocked breath. *Was this guy for real?* "It appears that I have little choice in the matter, then," she murmured, with what she hoped was a regretful smile. "About dinner," she hastened to add, when she saw his smug satisfaction. "But I believe I already told you that I don't date married men."

His eyes twinkled. "Who said anything about dating?"

Lilah felt her mouth drop open. *Did women really take this guy seriously?* "I'm seeing someone else," she lied through gritted teeth.

He scoffed. "Sullivan?"

Lilah scarcely blinked as she again lied. "Yes." She was going to hell for all the fabrications popping out of her mouth. But considering it was for a good cause, she thought maybe God would understand.

"You're a beautiful, intelligent woman," he said, and Lilah fought the urge to roll her eyes. "You can do so much better than a washed-up ex-soldier with no ambition beyond his motorbike, the open road and wind in his hair."

She clenched her teeth to refrain from pointing out that he could hardly have wind in his hair if he was wearing a helmet. Instead, she shrugged and said, "He's single." Besides, Luke Sullivan didn't look washed up. He looked—okay never mind how he looked—but at least he wasn't using his position to get women out of their clothes.

He'd manage that effortlessly just by breathing.

Peter slid his hands into his pants pockets, looking all expensive and as shiny as a *male* model. She couldn't imagine him stripping to his tighty-whities and diving into a lake to save someone.

And why was she defending Luke to this creep, anyway?

"Is that what he told you?" He smirked. "Face it, what do you really know about him besides the fact that he owns black leather, drives a large noisy motorbike and can swim?"

That he looks better in his underwear than most men look in expensive suits? Okay, not a lot. But, then, she didn't have to. She had no intention of getting any more acquainted with either man.

She lifted her wrist to check her watch and frowned. *Damn.* Now she was late.

"I have to go," she said, turning to leave.

Peter followed her out his office and pulled the door closed behind him. "You know where to find me if you change your mind," he said, sliding his hand up her arm to cup her elbow as he escorted her from the outer office.

Lilah stiffened and sent him a baffled look when what she wanted to do was yank her arm away and yell at him to back the heck off. "I thought I'd been ordered to attend the dinner?"

He squeezed her arm. "You are." His voice deepened along with his seductive smile. "I was talking about the weekend."

She gave a mental eye roll and stepped away. *So not gonna happen, pal.* She aimed a regretful smile in his direction and said firmly, "I won't," before turning on her heel, feeling like she'd just dodged two bullets.

Luke pressed the transponder and waited for the SUV's alarm to engage before turning to head for the hotel's entrance. It was ten past eight and Aunt Harry had already called and texted three times demanding to know where he was.

He hadn't wanted to attend the damn dinner but Harriet had called, issuing a decree, and even though he'd reminded her that he didn't do fancy society dinners, she'd snorted and told him he should have thought about that before stripping to his skivvies in public to play hero.

There was something very wrong with her statement, Luke thought darkly. Firstly, he wasn't a hero. He just hadn't been able to stand back and let someone—a woman—put her life in danger to save a life. And, secondly, ever since he'd managed to get his half-naked ass in the newspaper, he'd been dodging reporters and fighting off women he didn't know.

Okay, maybe that hadn't been so bad, he thought with a smile, but he hadn't saved the boy's life. That honor went to the curvy redhead heading towards him at a fast clip, searching in one of those little purses that women liked to carry when they went out in the evening. A frown wrinkled the smooth skin of her forehead and her lush mouth looked sulky, as though she was annoyed about something.

He paused with one foot on the stone steps while imagining what she'd do if he pushed her up against the side of the building and took a greedy bite out of that soft sulky mouth—something he'd been thinking about ever since he'd kissed her at the wedding. A kiss he'd said was for Webster's benefit. He'd lied, and wasn't as ashamed to admit it as he should be. He'd wanted to kiss her more than he'd wanted to breathe and had used Webster as an excuse to taste those soft, lush pillows of flesh.

Hell, he'd do it again. In a heartbeat.

His mouth curved appreciatively as his gaze swept from the top of her shining head to the slinky four-inch heels on her slender feet. And instead of baggy scrubs or the lab coat he'd glimpsed her wearing all week, she looked like she'd been giftwrapped in black silk.

His eyes crinkled as he imagined unwrapping her to find out if she was sporting matching tiger-print undies. She liked people to think she was strictly professional, but Luke wasn't fooled. Beneath that calm competent exterior simmered a fiery passion that she kept on a very tight leash—as if she was afraid of what might happen if she let herself go.

Luke felt himself go hard at the thought of what would happen if and when she finally did.

He really wouldn't mind being the focus of all that wild passion. As Lilah had said the night of the wedding, his shoulders were broad—he could certainly take the heat. A smile tugged at the corners of his mouth and his mood rose along with his blood pressure at the sight of her long, shapely runner's legs. And since the evening had taken a turn for the better, he'd have to thank Harry for not taking no for an answer.

"Going somewhere?" he asked when Lilah was a couple of feet away. Her head jerked up and he watched her grey eyes go all wide and startled, like she hadn't expected him. Her lips parted on a silent gasp and Luke couldn't help noticing that they glistened with some kind of slick lip gloss he wouldn't mind eating off. He wondered if she'd taste sweet—like strawberries—or of something spicier…and darker. Suddenly he was ravenous.

She stilled when she saw him and her delicate brows pulled into a frown. "This is your fault," she accused, and his eyebrows rose up his forehead in surprise. Pressing his lips together to prevent a grin from forming, he shoved his hands in his pockets and studied her mutinous expression. She looked mad enough to slug someone. Most probably him, though he hadn't done anything. Yet.

"Oh, yeah?"

Her eyes snapped, turning the soft grey irises stormy. "I keep telling people you saved Trent and you keep telling them I did. And now I have to play nice with the big boys."

He gave her what he hoped was a wounded look and held up his hands, palms outwards. "Hey, don't look at me. I don't want to be here any more than you do."

Her snort told him what she thought of his excuse but when she lifted a hand to adjust a sparkly earring he noticed it was shaking. "Hey." He caught her cold fingers, his study of her face revealing pale flawless skin and smoky eyes dark with distress. She was trembling and trying not to let it show.

"What happened?"

She said "Nothing," and tried to snatch her hand back.

But Luke tightened his grip and repeated, "What happened?"

A host of emotions flashed across her face and she visibly tried to pull herself together by inhaling. If Luke hadn't been so concerned, he might have suffered an instant aneurysm when the tops of her creamy breasts rose above the fitted bodice. Fortunately he'd been trained not to allow distractions to…well, distract him. It's what got a guy killed. *Or led to disaster.*

"Some idiot nearly ran me off the road," she admitted grudgingly, and he forgot all about full creamy breasts and big grey eyes. Okay, maybe not *forgot*, but he was instantly alert and able to focus all his attention on the conversation.

"Where?" he demanded, moving to shield her body with his as his eyes scanned the busy street. "What kind of car was he driving? Did you get the registration? Are you all right?"

Lilah's mouth curved into a reluctant smile and the tightness around her eyes eased a fraction. "Just before Bretton Bridge, a dark sedan, no, it happened too fast, and, yes, I'm fine—just a little shook up."

He rubbed his thumb across the silky skin of her wrist, hoping to soothe her wildly fluttering pulse. When faint color flooded her cheeks, he smiled down at her. "There, that's better. But, seriously, are you sure you don't need a drink first? We can always duck into the bar and hope no one notices that we're missing."

She gave a low husky laugh that he felt all the way to his gut, which tightened almost painfully in reaction. Releasing her hand, he slid his palm to the curve of her waist, the need to touch any part of her overwhelming his good sense.

"I'm fine, really," she said to his chin, as he escorted her into the lobby. "Besides, it's late and everyone will be wondering where we are."

Luke scowled. "By everyone, you mean Webster?" he growled, with something that felt very much like possessiveness tightening his mouth.

She paused to frown over her shoulder and he pointedly ignored the expression on her face that said he was crazy. Hell, he felt a little crazy.

"No, I don't mean him," she snapped irritably. "I'm talking about our bosses, the hospital directors. I don't even know if Webster will be there. And while we're on the subject, I guess you should know I may have hinted that we were…are…um, involved." The last emerged on a breathless rush.

Luke stilled in the process of punching the call button for the fourth time and turned to stare at her. "We as in…?"

Lilah flushed and her gaze skittered away from his. Her tongue emerged to moisten her lips and Luke grinned, his good mood abruptly restored.

Arching his brow, he waved a hand between them. "We? As in you and…me?"

Her flush deepened and she fiddled with her purse. "It's your fault," she snapped. "If you hadn't…um, kissed me on the…um…dance floor, none of this would be necessary."

The doors slid open and Luke ushered her into the elevator, punching the number for the roof restaurant. "And by necessary, you mean what exactly?" he drawled, and when she nibbled nervously on her lip Luke finally understood. The guy was harassing her again. "Why don't you just report him to Personnel?"

Lilah rolled her eyes. "The last person to do that was fired."

"What do you mean, fired?" he demanded in a way that had Lilah staring at him, like he was being deliberately obtuse.

"A lowly nurse accuses a prominent doctor of sexual harassment? Who do you think people are going to believe?" She snorted inelegantly and glared at him as though he was to blame for the inequality as well as the harassment. "Who do people usually believe? The man, that's who, especially when he's rich and powerful."

Luke grunted, silently admitting that she was right, except for one thing. The only thing prominent about Webster was his monumental ego.

Folding his arms across his chest, he propped his shoulder against the elevator wall. "So…how involved are we? Casually or…uh, intimately?"

Lilah's strangled growl made him want to laugh. Schooling his features, he shrugged. "I'm only asking so I know exactly how I'm supposed to act," he explained, sweeping his gaze over her. "You know."

She stared up at him and swallowed hard as the light for the third floor blinked on and then off. "Know what?"

"Well…look at you," he said, waving his hand vaguely in her direction.

Her spine snapped straight. "What's…wrong with me?" she demanded, sounding so offended that Luke's mouth curled despite his attempts to appear indifferent.

"You look too uptight to be involved with me."

Lilah's eyes narrowed. "Too…uptight?"

He tilted his head to the side and scratched his chin as though considering her appearance. "It's the hair." She sputtered for a couple of beats and lifted a hand to her head as if to make sure it was still ruthlessly pulled back into a professional bun.

"What's wrong with my hair?"

He gave an apologetic shrug and lied. "You look like a librarian." She didn't look anything like a librarian. Not with those thunderous grey eyes glaring holes in him, and certainly not with all those curves shrink-wrapped in black silk like a decadent seal-a-meal.

He affected a casual shrug and pursed his lips to keep from laughing at her murderous expression. "If you want Webster to believe we're…what was the word you used?" He arched his brow. "Involved? Then you have to let me make a few modifications."

Her mouth dropped open. "Mo-modifications?"

"Yeah, and we'd better hurry," he said, tugging her closer. "These hi-tech elevators are fast." And before she could demand what the heck he thought he was doing, Luke reached up and plucked the pins holding the mass of hair at the nape of her neck.

"What are you *doing*?" Lilah shrieked, slapping at his hands to keep her French twist from unravelling, but Luke thrust his fingers into her thick hair and with a few deft moves the long curly ropes fell around her shoulders in a glorious cloud of sunset-colored silk.

"*Dammit*, Sullivan," she growled furiously, shoving at his hands. "Now I look like I just crawled out of bed."

Luke's gaze slid over her beautiful face, all flushed with annoyance, and landed on her sulky mouth.

"Not yet you don't," he murmured, and jerked her against him. She squeaked and he took full advantage of her surprise to cover her mouth with his in a kiss that instantly caught fire and shattered his composure. He went from semi to hard in an instant and it was a struggle to keep his hands cupped around her head.

Not that she was trying to escape, Luke thought with fierce satisfaction as the rigid lines of her body softened gradually until she was plastered up against him like a spray tan.

Her breath hitched in her throat and with a rough growl he backed her against the wall and did what he'd thought about earlier. He planted his hands beside her head and fed her hot, demanding kisses as he ate the lip gloss off her mouth. He knew if he touched all that soft, silky flesh he might forget where they were.

He didn't slide into the kiss like he wanted to. There wasn't time. Besides, her mouth softened and clung. *God…* she tasted so good that he was devouring her before he could think that maybe this was a bad idea. A very, very bad idea.

CHAPTER FIVE

THE ELEVATOR RAIL dug into Lilah's back as Luke pressed her into the wall, his body all hot and hard and impatient against hers. She'd had a split second to react before his mouth closed over hers and he was devouring her like he hadn't eaten in a year. She might have put up a token protest if the air around them hadn't instantly turned to steam or if her deprived body hadn't strained towards his—completely without her consent, of course.

And, boy, was she glad his body was plastered all over the front of hers, especially as she couldn't feel her legs and was certain she would slide to the floor without him.

His tongue stroked hers and his mouth created a light suction that almost had her hair catching fire like she'd been plugged into a three-phase transformer. She would have gasped if he hadn't stolen her breath along with her mind.

Dizzy, Lilah curled her hands into his pristine shirt-front and surrendered to the consuming heat of his kiss. She wanted to touch him. She wanted him to touch her—all over—but all he did was touch her with his mouth and feed her wild, hungry kisses while devouring her good sense.

He growled low in his throat as he abandoned her mouth to drag his lips along her jaw. He licked at the delicate skin of her throat and closed his teeth on the tendon joining her neck and shoulder, sending sensation shooting through her body like a hot bolt of lightning.

Lilah shuddered, half expecting her head to explode. Her belly clenched and searing heat rolled over her as everything beneath her sensitive flesh turned liquid.

And then his tongue drew a line of fire down the wide bodice of her dress to where her breasts rose and fell with choppy breaths. She moaned, moving restlessly against him and nearly combusted when the long, thick ridge of his arousal pressed against her. Right where a painful, empty ache blossomed.

"*Stop*," she gasped, and thrust her hands into his hair, unsure whether to hold onto him or push him the heck away. Her nails scraped along his scalp and his big body shuddered against her.

Or was that her?

With a low, savage growl he opened his lips on the exposed upper curve of her breast and drew the soft flesh into the hot, wet cavern of his mouth. Any thought she might have had to push him away vaporized. Her head went light, her body shuddered and for one awful, wonderful moment Lilah thought she might actually faint or…or…

A low, husky whimper escaped and lights exploded behind her eyelids. Someone cleared their throat, followed by muffled chuckles, forcing Lilah to frown and lift oddly heavy lashes at the unwelcome intrusion. And when the haze cleared, her horrified gaze encountered the amused faces of almost a dozen people watching her make a spectacle of herself.

With a squeak of horror Lilah straightened like she'd been shot. Several more flashes blinded her and she shoved frantically at Luke's big shoulders when what she really wanted to do was to bury her flaming face in his chest and pretend she hadn't just been photographed having her… um…chest sucked.

Oh, boy. They'd been caught making out in an elevator like a couple of randy adolescents. By their bosses.

For one scorching instant his hot, sleepy gaze caught and held hers before he drew in a deep breath and then expelled it in a noisy whoosh. Like he'd been floored.

God, she knew the feeling.

Finally Luke turned and aimed a crooked grin at their smiling audience, as though he regularly got caught in elevators kissing women senseless.

He probably did, Lilah thought darkly, ducking behind his bulk to hastily tug her bodice and hem into place. She sucked in a shaky breath and smoothed the messy tangle of curls off her face, praying she didn't look like she'd been dragged through a hedge backwards—or have a man ravish her within an inch of her sanity.

And from the satisfied gleam in Luke's green eyes it was the latter. And exactly what he'd intended.

"Sorry we're late," he drawled, bending to retrieve the purse Lilah couldn't recall dropping. He handed it to her, and with warm fingers wrapped around her arm, ushered her from the elevator as though he knew her knees were wobbly—or maybe suspected that she wanted to bolt. "We were…unaccountably delayed."

Everyone chuckled and Luke took the opportunity to bend close and murmur in her ear, "Now you look like you've just rolled out of bed, wild thing."

All she could do was struggle for control and fume silently that he'd managed, once again, to get them photographed while he was scrambling her brains and vaporizing her bones.

But when she stole a sideways glance at him she remembered that he hadn't been as unaffected as he'd appeared. He'd been big and…hard. Well…everywhere. And for a second he'd looked at her as though he wanted to take one big greedy bite out of her before swallowing her whole.

Whatever his motives, Lilah thought as a fresh wave of embarrassment heated her cheeks, all she had to do to get through the rest of the evening with as much dignity as possible was stay as far away from Dr. Luke Sullivan as she could.

Oh, yes, and hope some other calamity occurred in Spruce Ridge that would draw everyone's attention away from the public spectacle that was her life.

In the week following that embarrassing dinner, heat-wave conditions gripped the entire Pacific North West. Temperatures soared to over a hundred and all ER medics who hadn't succumbed to the stomach virus were put on some crazy rotation hours that made med school and residency seem like a Sunday school picnic.

Lilah couldn't help feeling responsible since she'd prayed for calamity, but she hadn't meant it to be so…well, potentially disastrous, especially when she suddenly found herself working at close quarters with the two men she wanted above all else to avoid. She'd been doing a credible imitation of ignoring Luke but he seemed to take perverse pleasure in cornering her during lulls and scrambling her brains.

When she asked him to stop, he blinked and told her innocently that he was just letting Webster know that she was taken—just like they'd agreed. *Yeah, right*, like he had an innocent bone in his body, Lilah thought darkly. She was not fooled by his sleepy looks, wicked smiles and wickeder kisses—even when they made her forget her own name or why she was supposed to be ignoring him. Besides, she didn't remember any such agreement.

But one thing she did learn about him was that he was an excellent trauma surgeon. He was as steady as a rock and seemed to know instinctively what would work. Lilah guessed it had something to do with years in military ops.

When the heat wave approached the ten-day mark, a state-wide forest-fire warning was announced and County Gen's burn unit was placed on daily alert. Huge areas to the north and south had already been devastated by fires and emergency personnel everywhere were spread pretty thin. Unfortunately, it also meant that in addition to her ER rotation she'd been put on the medevac flight list, even though she'd told the administrator that she got airsick because of inner-ear problems.

She didn't get airsick and her inner ears were fine; she panicked in anything smaller than a commercial jet. Okay, things got freaky then too, but at least they served alcohol on commercial jets. Unfortunately, hospital policy tended to frown on medics hitting the bottle mid-flight.

Then Peter called an emergency meeting to inform them that all medics were required to put in flight hours or face dismissal—which certainly put things into perspective for Lilah. Besides, having someone witness her complete meltdown was preferable to being fired.

But then her rotation finally came and Lilah wondered if being fired wasn't a better option. Especially when she dashed across the roof to the chopper sitting like a giant bug on the helipad, only to find her pilot hunched over, one large hand propped against the metal and breathing like he'd run up sixteen flights of stairs—carrying the chopper.

She gulped as concern—fine, and panic—tightened her chest. "Are you all right?"

He spun round with a snarl, as though he'd been caught doing something illegal and Lilah gasped and stumbled back a couple of steps when she saw who it was—looking like one wrong move from her would trigger a blitz attack.

"L-Luke?" Her voice emerged as a strangled croak. She started forward, pulse skittering with alarm as she took in his ashen pallor, the sheen of moisture covering his face and the wild look in his eyes. "What's wrong? Are you all right?"

"Of course I'm all right," he growled hoarsely. "Why wouldn't I be?" Muttering irritably, he stuck his head into the engine cavity. He fiddled around, huffing, grunting with an occasional curse before finally emerging, sucking the knuckles of one hand. He was all simmering testosterone and impatient masculinity.

Lilah inhaled shakily as he reached up with his free hand to grasp the engine cover before noticing that she was still standing there, gaping at him. He paused and scowled like he'd expected her to have disappeared.

"What are you doing here?"

She gulped and promptly felt herself go pale. *Darn*. She'd forgotten she was supposed to be getting into the metal bug. She licked dry lips and indicated the emergency meds case at her side. "Flight emergency? I'm on call."

"Oh, right," he said with a frown, as though he'd just remembered. And didn't look too happy about it. Yeah, well, that made two of them.

He turned away, but she swore she heard him grinding his teeth as he yanked open the door and pulled himself into the seat. Completely bemused, Lilah watched as he strapped himself into the harness and fiddled with the control panel—as though he had every intention of piloting the chopper.

She went cold and then hot, and her stomach cramped like she'd caught the stomach flu going around.

"Where's the…um…the pilot?" she gulped, wondering why he was behaving so…well, weird came to mind.

"You're looking at him."

What? She felt her head go light and had to steady herself against the chopper's metal frame. "Y-you?" *No way.* She might want to plaster herself up against him but that didn't mean she was going to trust him with her life.

"What?" he demanded, looking like she'd insulted his man code or something. "You have a problem with that?"

"You can…um, fly? A helicopter?"

He growled low in his throat. "Of course I can fly a

helicopter. Why the hell do you think I'm in the damn pilot's seat?" And when she continued to gape at him, he growled impatiently, "Get in, we're burning daylight."

"Where's the, um…other pilot? The *real* one?"

"I *am* a real pilot, woman." He heaved an aggravated sigh. "But if you're referring to Granger, he's puking his guts out somewhere. Damn stomach virus," he ended on a muttered curse, and continued to mutter as Lilah shifted her feet and adjusted the meds case shoulder strap. "You want a pilot? I'm it."

"Actually, I… Is this even legal?" she began, but he was too busy flipping switches to pay attention. The engine started with a whine, and when she made no move to get in—she might even have backed off a little—he actually growled at her.

"In or out, Dr. Meredith?"

Dr. Meredith? Sucking in a shaky breath and with a silent prayer to the guardian angel of people suffering from flight terror, Lilah scrambled through the open door and strapped herself into the copilot's seat.

She really, *really* hoped he knew what he was doing because she would throw herself from the helicopter rather than have to fly this thing herself. She opened her mouth to point out that she didn't know a thing about helicopters but he was back to scowling menacingly at the controls. Out of the corner of her eye she noticed a muscle flexing in his jaw and hoped that didn't mean he was clueless about what they were for.

Tension rolled off him in waves thick enough to choke on and she once again got the impression that he was holding himself together by sheer iron will. Her belly churned a warning.

"Luke? Are you sure you're okay?"

He gave a huge sigh and turned to scowl at her. "Why do you keep asking that?"

"Well," she said sweetly, refusing to be insulted by the sheer masculine annoyance in his tone. "Maybe because you're grinding your teeth into powder and you're sweating like a pig."

He snarled. "Maybe I'm sweating because this model of helicopter doesn't come with air-con," he explained through gritted teeth. "Maybe I'm sweating because it's a damn furnace in here. And in case you didn't notice, you're sweating too."

She gulped as her pulse rate bumped up a couple of notches. *That was from sheer terror.*

"Your hands are shaking," she continued, as though he hadn't interrupted. "You're also hyperventilating and your pupils are dilated. If I didn't know better I'd think you were high on something. Or having a panic attack." *Holy cow, she hadn't thought of that.* "Because if you are, then we have a problem." *Forget problem, it was a catastrophe.*

He snorted his opinion of her diagnosis and flexed his fingers, as though restraining himself from throttling her—or maybe to hide the fine tremor in his hands. Snatching his aviator shades out of his pocket he shoved them on his face, clearly done talking. He put on his headset with suppressed violence and turned his attention to the console, completely ignoring her.

After a few moments he pointed to the second headset and yelled, "Put that on," over the rising noise of the engine. "Or you'll be deaf by the time we head back."

With shaking hands, Lilah snatched up the headset and moistened her dry lips. The rotors sped up along with her pulse until she felt a little light-headed. The instant she adjusted the earpieces she heard him say a bunch of confusing things to the control tower. She didn't much care because the chopper lifted with a sickening lurch and she was too busy gagging on terror. Squeezing her eyes shut, Lilah gripped the armrests—and swallowed a whimper.

She heard heavy, labored breathing and thought maybe she was already losing it. But when she cracked open one eye, a quick sideways glance told her Luke looked as bad as she felt. He was sheet-white, his lips were compressed into a tight line and he was gripping the flight stick with white-knuckled hands as though he was afraid it would bite him.

He was also breathing like he was giving birth to a hippo.

"Luke?" She panicked as they cleared the edge of the building, climbing as they went. She inadvertently looked down and her stomach lurched sickeningly. "What's wrong? Is there something wrong with the engine? The steering joystick thingy?"

"Will you just relax?" he snapped, then shrugged his shoulders as though to shake off something heavy and clingy. Like tension? *Or fear?* "Enjoy the damn scenery or something. There's nothing wrong with the engine or the damn cyclic pitch lever."

"Then why are you cursing, and gripping it like it's about to fly off into space?"

"We're nowhere near space and the CPL's bolted to the floor," he said, tight-lipped, and closed his left hand over some other thingy beside the armrest. The instant he touched it the chopper rose sharply and Lilah sucked in an alarmed breath, her grip tightening until her fingers went numb.

"You know what I mean," she squeaked. "What's wrong? And you'd better tell me because I'm freaking out here. And in case you wondered, I'm terrified of flying commercial. This is…this is really scary. In fact, I'm about to completely lose it."

He really looked at her then, and what he saw must have registered because his features relaxed…marginally. "Hey, chill out. I flew choppers in the army for twelve years. I can do this in my sleep." *She really,* really *hoped he wouldn't have to do that.*

"Then why are you so tense?"

"I'm not tense!" he yelled, then sucked in a sharp breath as though he was struggling to get his temper—or maybe his emotions—under control. "I'm just… It's been a while since I've flown."

He fell silent, clearly expecting her to do the same. But Lilah needed a distraction. She watched him inhale through his nose and exhale out his mouth like he was trying to steady his breathing in much the same way she did when she was trying to get a grip. *Great.* She swallowed a terrified sob. *Just great!* Her damn pilot was more nervous than she was.

After regaining control of her vocal cords, she asked as casually as she could, "So…how long? Since you flew, I mean."

His jaw hardened again and after a couple of beats he replied, "Nine months." Reluctantly. As if the admission had been dragged from him by force.

"Nine months?" Nine months didn't seem that long but, then, what did she know? "What happened nine months ago? And remember the first rule when dealing with a potentially hysterical woman," she warned with false lightness. "You lie and say everything's going to be okay."

His mouth relaxed its rigid lines and he chuckled, but it sounded a little scratchy, as though he was trying to laugh through panic. He must have thought so too because a dull flush rose up his neck. He cleared his throat and checked the instruments, adjusting the chopper's course until they were flying northeast.

Away from the city, Lilah noted with a strangled gasp. Away from civilization, and straight for the mountains. Where huge storm clouds hulked like waiting vultures.

"Well?" she prompted, when he'd been silent for so long that she'd begun to think he didn't intend replying. He sent her a look she couldn't interpret as he was wearing shades, but his taut jaw and uncompromising mouth made Lilah shiver. She could easily imagine him dressed in army fatigues with that badass soldier attitude, flying over hostile territory and dodging ground-to-air missiles.

"I was just wondering what to tell you, that's all."

She didn't think that was all. The big dangerous army guy was as tense as piano wire and probably embarrassed that she would think he was a wimp. *Yeah, right.* Like that was even possible. Not when his blood was probably ninety-nine percent testosterone.

"How about the truth?"

"That's classified."

"Well, how about the PG version, then?" she suggested with a sigh, wondering if all military people were this forthcoming with information. "The version that won't get me killed if I ever get arrested or interrogated by enemy forces."

This time his chuckle was more natural and Lilah felt a flood of relief that left her a little dizzy. Or maybe that was because she'd been holding her breath. She exhaled noisily, feeling absurdly pleased that she'd managed to distract him—and make him smile. Because once he'd relaxed a little she realized he really did look competent handling the controls. Like he knew exactly what he was doing. Which was very good—even if it didn't stop her from freaking out.

"Answer me one question first," he said with a lopsided grin that messed with her breathing and made her pulse rate speed up.

"Sure. What do you want to know?"

"Tiger, leopard or zebra?"

"What?" The abrupt subject change confused her and she turned from her study of the clouds to frown at him. He was grinning at her now, confusing her even more. "What are you talking about?"

"Never mind." He chuckled and turned away. "I can always find out for myself."

Reality dawned and Lilah's eyes widened. While she'd been worried about him—okay, and herself—he'd been imagining her in her underwear?

"Are you talking about my underwear?" she demanded, heat staining her cheekbones when her breasts tightened and her belly gave an interested quiver. "Because we are not discussing that. I'm more interested in why you looked like you were having a stroke when I arrived."

"You're exaggerating." He snorted his opinion of her diagnosis. "I'm just a little dehydrated, that's all," he growled, but his neck darkened as he pretended interest in the controls. "The government doesn't let just anyone fly their aircraft, you know. I'm an excellent pilot with thousands of flight hours." He paused briefly as though choosing his words carefully. "But sometimes equipment failure isn't the only reason choppers crash."

Lilah narrowed her eyes on his carefully blank expression and waited for him to explain. When he didn't, she gasped with dawning horror, "You crashed?" Her belly clenched. "You *crashed*?" She swallowed convulsively when her voice rose a little hysterically. "And now you're scared you're going to crash again." *Oh, God.* This was worse than she'd thought. "*I thought you said you could fly this thing in your sleep?*" she yelled at him, doing a little breathing technique of her own.

"I'm not scared! Jeez," he gritted out irritably.

Lilah could see she'd insulted his manhood again, but she was more interested in the details, so she demanded, "So, why did you crash? Are you all right? Did you suffer any injuries?"

Luke studied her pale face and huge grey eyes. He thought about the long weeks in hospital followed by rehab while waiting for his ribs, leg and hip to heal. Long months during which he relived the crash over and over again, wondering if he could have done things differently. He didn't know and it drove him crazy thinking about it.

"RPGs and I'm fine. But the others…" He paused, thinking about the men who hadn't been so lucky. Good men who'd died protecting the hostage they'd been sent in to retrieve. "Not so much," he said quietly. It haunted him and he felt responsible even though he couldn't have avoided that RPG. But he didn't want to feel responsible for any more deaths. Especially—he looked sideways at the woman staring at him with wide silvery eyes—especially not hers.

There was something about Lilah Meredith that got to him, right in the middle of his chest where it burrowed deep and tightened until he could scarcely breathe. It could just be indigestion, but he suspected it was more. More than her flawless skin and smart mouth. More than her lush curves and the wild rose-colored curls she tried so hard to tame. He suspected it was more than the passion straining to break free of that tight prickly control.

Luke looked into eyes the color of hell smoke and thought that sometimes, when she was unaware of being observed, he caught sight of something soft and fragile and damaged. Something she'd no doubt hotly deny—prickly woman that she was. Something she tried hard to hide behind a smart mouth and a stubborn chin.

Someone had probably done a number on her, Luke decided, fighting the oddest urge find out who it was and hunt them down.

"Hey," he said softly, resisting the urge to touch her—or promise to slay dragons for her. He wasn't a hero, and making promises he couldn't keep was just idiotic. "I'll get you home safely, I promise." Okay, he was officially an idiot. "I'm an excellent pilot." *Finally.* Something he didn't have to lie about.

Lilah's solemn look sent cold shivers up his spine. "What?"

"Some promises," she reminded him quietly, "just can't be kept."

CHAPTER SIX

LILAH LEFT THE tourist center and eyed the late afternoon sky. While she'd been busy saving lives, angry grey clouds had rolled in, covering the sky and most of the surrounding mountains. It was barely six but the turbulent greenish-black cloud cover made it appear much later.

Fortunately the guy they'd been sent to airlift to County Gen had suffered nothing more than an allergic reaction to something he'd come into contact with when he'd left the trail to relieve himself. It hadn't exactly been the life-saving moment she'd expected but he'd responded rapidly to an adrenalin shot, which was probably a good thing considering his opinion of flying outstripped even hers. It also looked like the heat wave was about to end. Spectacularly too, if those clouds were any indication.

A lump of dread settled in her belly at the thought of getting back on the chopper. Her knees had only just stopped wobbling and she'd finally managed to get her pulse and breathing back to normal.

She rounded the building and spotted Luke almost at once. He wasn't alone and both men had their backs to her as they leaned through the open chopper door. One set of wide shoulders drew her gaze as though magnetized and a small shiver edged up her spine.

She would recognize that broad back and those long legs and narrow hips anywhere. It was probably the way he held himself—that irritatingly appealing mix of masculine arrogance and natural athletic grace. As though he knew who he was and didn't care what the rest of the world thought.

She envied him that, she decided as her gaze traced the long length of his tapering back. That supreme confidence in his ability to handle whatever came his way.

In fact, she could almost hate him for it, she thought with a sigh of feminine envy. *And* for the incredibly tight glutes, showcased to perfection in soft worn denim.

Abruptly aware that she was ogling a man's behind and grinning like a crazy person while thinking hot impure thoughts, Lilah tore her eyes from his butt as heat flooded her cheeks.

Yeesh, woman. Get a grip.

Mentally rolling her eyes, she stuck out her bottom lip to blow cool air into her hot face. *Yikes.* She couldn't remember when she'd last had such an intensely…primitive reaction to anyone. Almost as if he was an industrial magnet that had been turned on high and she a hapless paperclip—drawn to him, in spite of the fact that he was the kind of guy someone like her should avoid like a tax audit.

She couldn't actually remember ever feeling anything like it, and it spooked her. So she sucked in a shaky breath and tried to remind herself that she had no intention of getting all worked up over some hotshot ex-soldier—no matter how sexy. She was an adult, for heaven's sake, not an emotionally fragile adolescent easily impressed by a pair of wide shoulders, long legs and pretty green eyes. She sighed. Not to mention big, long-fingered hands…or awesome pecs and abs…or…or those hot, consuming kisses.

Oh, boy.

Embarrassed by her undisciplined thoughts, Lilah willed away the images in her head and the hot flash they gave her. Besides, she really couldn't afford a distraction right now, especially by some rich soldier boy slumming it at a state hospital—no matter how attractive. And, boy, Luke Sullivan was a very attractive distraction; especially bent over a topographical map and frowning while the ranger talked and pointed to something on the map.

Frowning?

Uh-oh. "Is there a problem?" she asked, half dreading the answer. She really didn't want there to be a problem.

Both men turned and Luke opened his mouth to reply but his gaze narrowed as he zeroed in on her face. He straightened abruptly and rapidly scanned the surroundings. "What's wrong?" he demanded. "Is everything okay?"

Lilah gaped at him, momentarily taken aback by the swift change from relaxed to coiled alertness. Like a large predator sensing danger. Or maybe a seasoned soldier anticipating a sneak attack.

"Uh…fine?" she squeaked, looking over her shoulder. Her pulse skittered with alarm and she half expected to see a grizzly lumbering after her. When she saw nothing but a half-empty lot surrounded by forest, she edged closer to the two men, just in case.

"How's the patient?"

"Who?"

His mouth curved and an eyebrow rose up his forehead. "The guy you flew here to save," he reminded her.

"Oh, Mr. Kemp's fine," she murmured absently, turning from her nervous survey of the surroundings to find two large alpha males regarding her with varying degrees of amusement. *What? Oh, right, they were talking about the allergy guy.* "He…um…he just ignored the rule about staying out of thickly wooded areas and developed an allergic reaction." That was the understatement of the year. The guy had swelled up to the size of a blimp and he'd had huge welts all over his body. "Anyway, he responded to the adrenalin shot. He'll make a full recovery."

"You signed him off?"

"I kept an eye on him for a few hours," she explained. "Most of the swelling has gone down. Besides, he refused a trip to hospital." Not that she could blame him. "His wife took him back to their camp site to sleep off the antihistamine I gave him. But don't worry, I got them both to sign the waiver before they completed the paperwork."

Luke studied her silently for a couple of beats. "Then why are you flushed? Are you sick?"

"What?" She patted her cheeks and tried not to look guilty but his gaze sharpened on her as though something had occurred to him.

"Did something happen? Those hikers in the info center were pretty mouthy. Did they give you a hard time?"

Lilah stared at him in fascination. She could easily imagine him going into the restaurant and kicking some serious butt if she said yes. "I think they left." When he continued to study her silently, Lilah's flush deepened and she felt as though he knew she'd been ogling his backside. She licked her lips and her gaze flicked nervously to the ranger watching their exchange with interest. *Oh, God, please don't tell me I'm that transparent. How embarrassing.*

"Hi," he said, "I'm Jeff."

She replied with "Um…hello," as if she was thirteen and had forgotten how to use her voice. She mentally rolled her eyes and prayed something happened so they would stop watching her like they expected her to do something interesting. She shifted restlessly beneath speculative appraisal and wished for divine intervention. Or maybe that grizzly.

"I'm parched," she lied breathlessly, when it was clear they were waiting for her to say something, but her stomach decided to growl loudly at that moment. She pressed a hand to it, hoping they hadn't heard, but when Luke's eyes gleamed with amusement she knew her prayers were just not getting through.

"More like starved," he observed dryly. "Sounds like you need to be fed."

Since that made her sound like a pet, Lilah decided to shift everyone's attention away from her red face and growling stomach. She gestured to the map. "So…what's with the map? Are we flying anywhere else?" *Please, say no*.

After one last probing look Luke reached into a cooler and emerged with a cool drink. He shook his head and relieved her of the steel case, only to replace it with a cold can.

"Too dangerous," he said absently. "The storm's going to hit soon and Jeff just got off the radio with Spruce Ridge. There's a lot of lightning and even if we leave now, we'd be flying straight into it."

"Oh," Lilah said, frowning down at the cold, sweating can in her hand as though she'd never seen one before, when what she was thinking was, *Thank goodness*! She glanced up. "We can't fly around it or something?"

Luke snorted and snatched the can from her hand, flipping the tab before he handed it back. "Look around you, babe," he said with barely concealed impatience. "Which way would you suggest we go?"

Babe? She looked around and wondered if she'd missed something. Like a couple of chalets hidden away somewhere. "But—"

"You really want to fly in that?" Luke demanded, and when Lilah paled and sent him a horrified look he snorted and drawled, "Didn't think so. So what's the problem? Big fancy date?"

She had a feeling he was talking about Peter, and barely resisted the urge to throw the opened can at him.

"Nothing that can't be rescheduled," she lied smoothly, turning away to lift the drink to her mouth, hopefully covering any tell-tale signs of prevarication. The man had eyes like a hawk. She wouldn't be surprised if he had x-ray vision and could see every lie before it formed. *Yikes*. What a notion.

Besides, what woman wanted a hot guy to know that she didn't have a date on a Friday night? That's right. *None*. Not unless she wanted to look like a dateless loser. Which—come to think of it—described her life perfectly.

"Good," he said shortly, turning away to begin folding the map with barely concealed irritation, and Lilah had to physically restrain herself from sticking out her tongue at him. "Jeff says there's a nearby ranger cabin we can use. The present owner is away and won't mind us spending the night."

"Oh," she said, surprised by the offer. "Thank you." *Us?* "That's great." *God help me*. To cover her reaction she lifted the can to her mouth and chugged back a third of the drink.

"It's pretty rustic," Jeff warned, "but at least it's got a bed and a hot shower."

A bed? As in one? Lilah gulped and flicked a glance at Luke, catching him watching her with an unreadable expression. Her heart gave one slow tumble in her chest before setting off like a bat out of hell. *If there's one bed... where is he...?* A smile tugged at one corner of his mouth, as though he knew exactly what she was thinking. And was hugely amused. *The rat*.

Lilah felt her cheeks catch fire and her breath stall in her throat as his gaze turned hot. *H-o-l-y cow!* Her pulse rate rocketed into orbit but she narrowed her eyes in a that's-what-you-think-pal look before turning to Jeff with a smile that was much warmer and brighter than she'd intended. "I'm sure it's wonderful. It has to be better than sleeping in the chopper."

Three hours later, Luke sank onto the bed and wondered if he was losing his mind. He'd turned down going out with the guys for this. This being having the object of his hotter-than-scorching fantasies just across the very narrow hallway. In a very small cabin. All night. Probably naked.

Sighing, he lifted one booted foot to rest on his opposite knee and reached for the laces. Halfway through dinner he'd seriously considered going back to the chopper. Even with the storm battering the area like a prelude to Noah's flood, it had to be safer—and certainly smarter—than spending the night with a woman he couldn't get out of his head. A woman who smiled and flirted with forest rangers like she'd never smiled and flirted with him. A woman who drove him nuts even when she was dressed in wrinkled scrubs.

He scowled and pulled off his boot. It dropped onto the floor with a thud. Maybe that was the problem, he mused. Now that he knew what she hid beneath those shapeless scrubs, all he could think about was getting her out of them.

But she clearly preferred guys in uniform, he told himself. *Which meant she was looking for a hero—just like every other woman.*

And, God knew, he was no hero.

Scrubbing his hands over his face, Luke's jaw tightened when he recalled her catching him hunched over and panicking like a girl. He pulled off his other boot with a snort of disgust. One look at the chopper and he'd gone all woozy, which had been damn embarrassing. The only thing that had saved his ass from a full-blown flashback episode had been the realization that she was more terrified than he was.

Dropping his boot to the floor, he rose to strip off his shirt just as lightning flashed and the air outside exploded. The ground trembled beneath the assault, rain battering the small cabin as though determined to wash everything away.

The next instant an ear-splitting scream abruptly sent the hair on the back of his neck shooting straight up. By the time he'd thought, *Lilah!* he'd vaulted over the bed, yanked open the door and leapt across the hallway.

He slammed open her door and crouched in the doorway,

tensing in anticipation of an attack. Expecting to see her in the clutches of terrorists or at least a family of crazed raccoons, Luke was surprised to find her balanced on top of the bed, clutching a pillow and looking like she'd just seen Jack the Ripper in action.

"What? Where—?" he demanded, momentarily distracted by the sight of her in nothing but a pair of very brief lilac panties and a tight white tank. His eyes widened. *Whoa!*

Her head swung in his direction and with a squeak she launched herself at him, wrapping her arms and legs around him as though she wanted to climb up his body like a capuchin monkey.

Instinctively closing his arms around her, Luke staggered backwards under the full force of her surprise attack. When he collided with the passage wall, he found his arms full of silky, warm woman—his face an inch away from a soft, fragrant cleavage.

Whoa, he thought again as blood rushed to his head and he experienced momentary dizziness. *Fine*, he was light-headed from it rushing south without his permission. He was a red-blooded male, *dammit*. Who hadn't had sex in— well, never mind how long! Besides, it could just as easily be because she had a death grip around his neck.

"*Killitkillitkillit*," she squeaked in terror, tightening her grip with every syllable.

"Wha—?" he croaked, his eyes almost crossing when she wriggled against him and sent his blood pressure shooting through the top of his head.

He tried to loosen her death grip so he could breathe— or get the blood back to his brain before she noticed he was getting aroused.

"Oh, my God!" Lilah squeaked, trembling. "It's a…it's a… It's *huge*."

Luke's eyes widened and his mouth curved in a smirk

of pride. Well, of course it was huge but he didn't like to brag. In fact, he—

"Kill it!" She interrupted his smug musing.

Kill it?

Lilah hid her face against his neck and shuddered, though not in a good way. It should have been his first clue that she wasn't a woman beside herself with lust. In fact, she was whimpering.

What the—?

Deciding he needed to see her expression before his ego suffered irreparable damage Luke grasped her shoulders and eased her back a little.

"What are you babbling about?"

Lilah pressed closer. "S-s-s—" She shuddered, and gulped. "S-snake."

"Snake?" Luke demanded hoarsely, as relief washed away the alarm. He gave a strangled laugh. *Jeez, for one second there he'd thought*— "Why the hell didn't you say so in the first place? I thought you were being attacked by tangos."

"Wha-at?"

"Terrorists," he explained, sliding his hands up her smooth thighs to her bottom, which he squeezed before easing her away. *What the heck are you doing?* an inner voice demanded. *Don't tell me you're going to get all honorable, especially with that firm, silky bounty filling your hands?* But there he was, preparing to be noble. *What an idiot.* He sighed. "So where's this huge snake?"

Lilah pointed behind her towards her room and swallowed. "C-corner, near the window."

"Did it bite you?"

Lilah gave a shudder and for one awful moment Luke thought it had, then she shook her head and he exhaled in a silent whoosh. Pulling free of her stranglehold, he set her down and immediately felt the loss of all that soft feminine warmth. He sighed and wondered if he'd lost his mind. But it was probably for the best. His brain wasn't exactly working well if he could mistake revulsion for…well, never mind what he'd mistaken it for.

He'd clearly lost his mind.

Luke turned away and Lilah wanted to call him back or tell him to be careful, but her vocal cords were frozen. She watched him disappear and reappear almost immediately. His unexpected reappearance made her jump about a foot in the air and utter an embarrassing squeak. Mortified, she slapped a hand over her mouth and blinked at him when he sent her a what-the-heck-is-wrong-with-you-woman? look.

"I'm going to flush it out," he explained, as though to a crazy person, and she noticed for the first time that he was holding out her sneaker. As if he expected her to take it. What the heck was she supposed to do with one sneaker?

"If it escapes out the door, hit it with this."

What? Lilah felt her eyes widen. She gaped at him like he was the crazy person. "Are you insane?" she squeaked. "What if…what if it's a spitting cobra or…or worse?"

Luke shook his head and lifted his free hand to grip the top of the doorframe as though he needed to keep his hands busy. It made every well-defined muscle in his torso ripple and tighten.

Yu…humm! She licked her lips.

For long silent beats he stared at her like she was giving him a headache, which was kind of rude considering she could barely concentrate on anything other than his unfastened low-riding jeans. *Wow. And all that yummy exposed…hard…satiny smooth…flesh.* She was having a hot flush—or coming down with something terminal—just looking at him.

Yeah, a voice snickered in her head. *The terminal hots for Dr. Hot 'n' Sexy.*

Great. Now she was hearing voices too.

Something came at her. She gave another startled squeak and slammed her eyes shut. After a long silence she heard him say, "*Lilah!*" sounding extremely exasperated, and cracked open one eye to find him smirking. *The jerk*.

"Won't you need that?" she asked nervously, making no move to take the sneaker he proffered. Taking it meant she accepted the implied responsibility and there was no way… She snatched it from his hand before he was tempted to use it on her.

With a final hooded look in her direction he disappeared into the room. Almost immediately she heard him moving furniture around and then there was a lot of banging and swearing. It was followed by a short silence during which Lilah held her breath and waited, only to have it escape in a noisy whoosh when he appeared in the doorway, scowling and sucking his right hand.

"Damn thing bit me," he said, sounding outraged, and Lilah stumbled back a step, feeling abruptly woozy.

"Wha—?"

He looked down at his hand, where a row of small puncture wounds welled blood. "Dammit. I was only trying to save the little sh…sucker. And it bit me." He glared at the offending wounds as if he couldn't believe it had happened then lifted his gaze to glare at her like it was her fault. "I haven't been bitten since… Are you going to faint?"

Spots appeared in Lilah's vision until she realized she was on the verge of passing out. She sucked in a shaky breath and when oxygen hit her brain she panicked. "Ohmigod, it bit you? Where's the antivenin kit? Are you going to die? Where's your gun? Where's your hunting knife? Did you kill it?"

Luke's gaze widened. "Are you nuts?" he demanded. "You don't just go around shooting and filleting defenseless wildlife. In case you haven't noticed, we're in a national park."

She stared at him in confusion. *So?* "But…but it's a… snake." She shuddered. "And it bit you. I saw it. That thing's eight foot long and venomous."

"What, this little thing?" he snorted, and brought his left hand from behind his back. And he was holding—Lilah shrieked and lurched backwards—a wriggling black and red snake. And before she knew what she was doing she drew back her hand and threw her sneaker at it—nailing Luke square in the groin.

He made an odd whooshing sound in his throat, doubled over and dropped to his knees. The next thing she knew, the snake—suddenly finding itself free—streaked off down the passage and disappeared into the kitchen.

"Ohmigod, *ohmigod*!" she squeaked, using his hunched-over body as a shield. Clutching his shoulders, she heard herself whimpering, "It got away." Then reality dawned and she shrieked, "*You let it get away!*"

It was hugely embarrassing to be losing it in front of him so she bit her lip then bit his shoulder since it was his fault the darned thing had escaped. Then it dawned on her that it was slithering free in the house. She punched him. "*Why the hell did you let it get away?*"

Luke made a choking sound and his body shook, abruptly reminding Lilah that he'd been bitten. By a snake. She shuddered. *He'd been bitten.* And was going into shock.

Suddenly remembering that she was a doctor and that she'd treated a host of snake bites during her months in South America, Lilah morphed into ER mode.

First she had to make him comfortable. "Luke?" And then…*oh, God*…she'd have to deal with the convulsions. "Luke?" she demanded a little louder, and tugged him towards her. The snake must be highly toxic if he was already going into cardiac arrest.

"*Luke!*"

She finally got a good look at his face and her eyes

widened. She gaped at him for a couple of beats, finally comprehending that while she'd been freaking out that he was going to die he'd been…he'd been… "Laughing?"

She shoved him away from her as though he'd grown fangs and sprouted scales. "You're laughing?" she demanded, and Luke slumped against the wall to grin up at her.

"How can you laugh at…at…?" she stuttered in rising fury, glaring down at him with her hands on her hips. "You…you…." And since she couldn't think of a bad enough name to call him, she sucked in a steadying breath and pointed a shaking finger at him. "*Jerk*!"

"*Ohmigod*," he gasped in a strangled falsetto. "It bit you. Where's your gun? Where's your big soldier knife? Are you gonna die?"

He snorted and tried to control himself but when Lilah narrowed her eyes he howled with laughter. She finally snatched up her sneaker and threw it at him but this time he plucked it out of the air before it could damage anything important.

He paused, snickering rudely. "You're real cute when you get all flustered at the sight of a little snake, Doc. Didn't you just get back from the jungles of South America? The last time I looked they had huge mothers there."

She ignored his reference to South America. Not going there. "Congratulations," she said sarcastically instead, "you just let a poisonous reptile get away. You…you…*dumb-ass*!"

He looked up from inspecting his bleeding hand to grin at her. "What, like a giant spitting cobra?" Lilah glared at him from a distance, not trusting herself to get any closer. She might accidentally kick him.

He snickered. "Relax. It wasn't poisonous."

"How do you know?"

He looked up at her, his brow arched with amused masculine superiority that was damn annoying. "I'm an army ranger. You get to know stuff like snakes."

"It could still poison you."

Luke held out his hand. "Wanna suck it from my body? Save me from an agonizing death?"

"No," she snapped, sending him the kind of look women had perfected when they thought you were a dumb-ass too stupid to live. "I'm going to find a first-aid kit and you're going to find that snake."

Luke frowned up at her with stunned disbelief. "And do what with it?"

Her departing look told him exactly what he could do with it. All she said was, "Kill it, chop it up into sushi bits and eat it, I don't care. *As long as you get rid of it.*"

Luke watched her lilac bottom sway as she stomped down the passage and disappeared into the bathroom. He winced when the door slammed behind her. He didn't know why she was all bent out of shape. It wasn't like she'd been the one bitten—he snorted—by a little ringneck.

Rising to his feet, he called out, "Tastes just like chicken," over his shoulder, as he headed down the passage towards the kitchen. "It's an excellent form of protein."

CHAPTER SEVEN

IT TOOK LUKE about twenty minutes to find, corner and then catch the damn snake—without being bitten. But this time he'd been smart about it. He'd found a mop and a bucket in one of the kitchen cupboards and then hunted it down like a mission operation.

And all the way through the banging and swearing, he kept remembering the way Lilah had looked standing on the bed, eyes huge as dinner plates with those tiny bikini panties exposing her long slender legs and flat belly, and snug tank molded to her naked breasts like cling wrap.

He caught himself grinning like a moron and chuckled when he remembered her throwing her sneaker at him. Good thing she had terrible aim or she'd have put him out of action for a while.

Not that he'd seen any action—that kind, anyway—in a good long while. It was no wonder he was dreaming about huge smoky eyes, soft lips and lush…curves.

He sighed. The woman was making him crazy.

Eyeing the snake at the bottom of the bucket with disgust, Luke slammed the lid on it and went to get his boots. This little sucker was going outside, rain or no rain.

By the time he returned he was freezing and water streamed down his bare chest, arms and soaked jeans, adding to the puddle already collecting around his boots.

He wiped rain off his face and noticed that Lilah had

emerged from the bathroom. She was perched on a stool at the kitchen counter with an array of medical supplies spread out on a clean towel and a water tumbler filled with red wine at her elbow.

He wondered if their host had anything stronger than wine then decided getting drunk probably wasn't a good idea. Alcohol and unrequited lust didn't mix well.

Sweeping his gaze down the elegant line of her spine, he discovered that she'd dressed—which was a damn shame. He kind of liked seeing her in a tight tank and tiny silk panties. She hadn't looked all prim and uptight, not like when she was being cool and professional.

Damn. Now front and center of his brain was an image of her in nothing but her underwear beneath a lab coat. His blood instantly heated, turning the water on his skin to steam. He could almost hear it sizzle as it evaporated.

Toeing off his boots, he said, "Looks like you're waiting for a medical emergency," and reached for his jeans zipper as she turned. "Did something happen?"

Her mouth dropped open and her gaze zeroed in on his hands. After a stunned moment her eyes widened even more. "What...what are you doing?" she squeaked.

Luke paused in the process of unzipping his jeans and glanced up to see if she was serious. "I'm taking off my pants," he drawled, enjoying the wild color flooding her cheeks as her gaze slowly moved up his chest to his face.

"Wha-at?" She blinked, as though coming out of a trance. "But...why? You were bitten on your hand. Oh, God, did it bite y—?"

"My jeans are soaked and I'm dripping all over the floor," he interrupted, and pushed the heavy wet fabric down his thighs. "What are you doing?"

Her fascinated gaze tracked his every move and she swallowed hard before stuttering, "I'm...I'm waiting for you?"

"Me?"

She snagged a large towel and lurched off the stool, looking a little shell-shocked. "Yes, I want to look at you," she announced breathlessly. And then, realizing what she'd just said, turned bright red and buried her face in the towel.

She muttered something that sounded like a curse or maybe a scream and Luke grinned, padding silently towards her. Leaving wet footprints on the floor, he reached out and tugged the towel away from her red face.

"What was that?" he drawled.

Lilah gave a shocked squeak and jumped about a foot in the air when she realized he was inches away instead of across the room. He whipped away the towel, leaving her empty-handed and defenseless. She took one look at him and slapped a hand over her eyes.

"*Ohmigod*, you're…naked."

"Not hardly," he snorted, rubbing his wet hair. "But that can easily be remedied."

Her eyes popped open and skittered around the room as though she didn't quite know where to look. "*No*! I mean I just need to look at your *hand*." Her gaze finally landed on him and she stood indecisively for a moment before firming her mouth.

Luke could literally see her gathering her resolve around her like shield. In the blink of an eye she was suddenly all professional efficiency. Or trying to be, he thought with amusement. She couldn't hide her dismay or the fact that her eyes kept straying over his chest.

"Are you…um, sure that's the only place you were bitten?"

Liking her off balance, he grinned and waggled his eyebrows. "Why? Wanna play doctor and examine me?"

Wild color rose up her neck into her cheeks and he had to suppress an almost violent urge to check where it began—with his mouth. But he didn't think she would appreciate having her scrubs ripped from her body so he could check to see if she was back to wearing a bra and if her breasts blushed along with the rest of her.

She snorted and said sternly, "I don't have to play at being a doctor, you idiot. I am one," but Luke caught sight of the involuntary curving of her mouth. Damn, he liked her smile. It lit her up from the inside and made her eyes sparkle like sunlight off a stormy sea. And he really wanted that soft, wide mouth moving beneath his again. He could practically taste it.

Groaning silently, he wondered wildly what she would do if he yanked her close and devoured her whole. Instead, he found himself chuckling and saying, "Me too. We can take turns being the patient."

Lilah snorted and Luke could see she was trying really hard not to roll her eyes. "In case you've forgotten," she pointed out huskily, "you are the patient." And her voice slid into his veins like a shot of hundred-proof bourbon. It went straight to his head. *And places way south of the border.* So much for not getting drunk.

Feeling a little light-headed, Luke lifted his arm and frowned at his swollen hand like it was an alien appendage. "It's fine."

Before he knew what she was doing, she'd grabbed his hand and growled, "Dammit, it's not fine. This. Is. *Not. Fine.*"

Her touch sent a streak of fire down his spine and he pulled free before he exploded out of his skin. *Jeez*, it felt like his hair was on fire. He felt like it was the first time a woman had put her soft hands on his body and made him harder than a steel spike. He hadn't had this powerful a re-action to a woman's touch since he was sixteen and fool-ing around with Mary Anne Sherman. No, scratch that. Not even then.

"It's just a scratch," he growled, dropping the towel to rub at his chest and—*jeez*—hide the state of his lower body.

Lilah snorted and rolled her eyes, oblivious to his physical discomfort. "Right, that's why your hand is swelling and you're leaking from a few punctures."

Luke gave a snort, glad to shift the focus from his erection to his hand. *It wasn't the only thing swelling.* "I sound like an inflatable tube."

"Luke!"

He sighed and slung the towel around his neck. "Fine, but I need to dry off. You wouldn't want me catching a chill, now, would you?" Her silvery gaze tracked fire over his chest and suddenly the possibility of his catching cold diminished by another hundred thousand degrees. At this rate he would be having febrile convulsions and dying an agonizing death in less than five seconds.

"I thought big bad military guys didn't catch things like chills? I thought they were too tough."

"We are tough but, in case you forgot, I'm standing here in wet underwear."

Lilah's gaze zoomed south and she blushed when she saw that he was indeed standing there in his underwear.

Which was clinging wetly to his skin.

Leaving absolutely nothing to the imagination. Including the fact that he was big. *Oh, hell.* And hard.

She jerked her gaze upwards, her blush deepening. "Oh, um, right," she squeaked, her tongue emerging to moisten her lips in a move that he felt in his groin like a bolt of lightning.

Oh, hell, he thought again. *I'm in deep trouble.*

Lilah gulped and tried not to let her gaze drop further than the awesome pecs at eye level. She squinted at the dog tags around his neck to ground herself when her blood heated to evaporation point and the gas bubbles in her veins made her light-headed.

She swayed closer.

Uttering a tiny mewl of distress, she jerked back. *Damn.*

The man was a marvel of physical perfection. He didn't have an ounce of flab anywhere and he was even more impressively ripped up close. The last time she'd seen him this…unclothed she'd been a little preoccupied. The last time they'd been surrounded by curious onlookers and she would have hated someone catching her on camera ogling him like he was dessert. The eye-lock had been bad enough.

And though she'd secretly pored over all those newspapers, the images had been grainy. Even the videos online couldn't do him justice. All they did was hint at his awesomeness.

Besides, she thought, inhaling on a shuddery breath, how could any image capture the damp silkiness of tanned skin or the heat and testosterone that pumped off him like a nuclear reactor? She gulped. She wanted to reach out and touch. She wanted to slide her palms over the hard contours of his body and feel all that…hardness beneath the tight, satiny skin. She wanted to bury her nose in the soft-looking chest hair spanning the area between his coppery masculine nipples and trace the happy trail all the way to—*gulp*—the damp waistband of his black boxer briefs. Boxer briefs that clung to every inch of his impressive erection.

Oh, boy.

And all she could think of was their last kiss and the way his mouth had felt sucking at her flesh. And how much she wanted him to do it again. *This time all over.*

"Lilah." His voice was a ragged, low rumble in his chest. It had the same effect as if he'd run his rough tongue up her throat to the tender hollow beneath her ear. Prickly heat broke out all over her body and for some reason she was having trouble breathing. The air around her vibrated, heated, and pressed in on her like a living thing.

What the heck was happening here?

"Lilah."

"Hmm?" she murmured, preoccupied with the sheer

willpower it took not to lean forward and swipe her tongue across one hard, pebbly male nipple. She wanted to taste him. It wouldn't take much effort at all. Just stick out her tongue and… She caught herself licking her lips and swallowed a desperate little moan. *Dammit, woman. Get a grip and stop staring at the man like he's a melting ice-cream cone.*

"Stop looking at me like that," he growled softly, echoing her thoughts. Something in his voice had her finally lifting her gaze up his strong tanned throat to his clenched jaw and firm mouth and finally into his eyes. They were glowing hot and green in the dim light.

Lilah gulped at the need burning up the green. It practically vaporized her on the spot and she went abruptly light-headed—like she'd swallowed too much helium.

"Like what?" she whispered in a husky voice she didn't recognize as her own.

Luke swallowed and Lilah saw his Adam's apple bob convulsively. "Like you want to lick me up one side and down the other," he ground out.

Oh, can I? Please? Her heart beat a wild *boom, boom, boom* in her ears and she didn't know what made her do it but she opened her mouth. "You mean like this?" she said in a soft purr as she closed the distance between them and… licked his skin.

Yu-hum.

Luke sucked in a sharp breath and closed his hands over her shoulders. Whether to pull her closer or push her away, she didn't know. And when he did neither, she hid a grin of triumph and whispered, "Or maybe like this?" She sank her teeth into his hard, tight pec before opening her mouth and sucking on his flesh. It was hot and smooth—and tasted of rain and…virile man.

His big body shuddered and goose bumps broke out

across his chest. Before Lilah quite knew how it happened she was in his arms, and his mouth was all over hers.

Raw need pulsed in the air. It was all around her, against her and inside her too, sending her heart rate rocketing into hyperspeed. It heated her blood as though she'd strayed too close to the sun and was beginning to blaze.

She felt like she'd swallowed a star and any second now her flesh would begin to break apart and the blinding heat and light would leak from the cracks. Then she'd radiate like a supernova and explode all over the place.

His groan vibrated against her skin as he moved towards her mouth, his lips leaving a hot trail across her skin. *Holy hell*, she gasped silently.

The instant before his mouth closed over hers she wondered wildly if she'd wake in the morning with scorch marks on her skin.

Then she ceased to think at all because he had one hand on the back of her head holding her still as his mouth closed over hers, quickly shattering every notion she'd ever had about kissing.

This felt like an invasion—like he'd quit toying with her and was bringing out the big guns. And, boy, was his gun big…and hard…and would have been painful if she wasn't already almost half out of her mind with need.

His slick tongue stroked hers and she finally exploded into action. Groaning low in her throat, she opened her mouth wider and sucked his tongue deeper until he moaned too, low and deep—like he was in pain. His free arm snaked around her back to yank her closer and his kiss became hotter, wilder—more passionate.

And suddenly Lilah couldn't keep her hands to herself. She ate at his mouth and streaked her palms over his shoulders, down his arms and then up his broad back. She loved the feeling of his hard muscles shifting beneath the tight, hot skin and dug her nails into his flesh in an almost primitive desire to mark him.

With a savage growl Luke shifted and before Lilah knew what was happening she was being lifted against him. Instinctively wrapping her legs around his waist, she cried out when the long, thick ridge of him pressed right where she needed it most. Right where she was hot and wet and desperately needy.

Arching her back, she wrenched her mouth free and dragged a ragged breath into her lungs before gasping, "Luke...I don't think we should be...doing...this." His teeth scraped against the delicate skin of her throat and she shuddered. "We really shouldn't." But for some reason she couldn't quite remember why.

"Why not?" he rasped, dragging his mouth along her jaw to nip and suck her ear lobe. He shifted and she became aware that they were moving.

"Because...because—" His lips snatched the word from her mouth, effectively silencing her, and just as effectively snatching every thought from her mind.

"No more talking," he murmured between kisses, the feel of his words sending fire streaking from her tingling lips to every part of her body, tightening her breasts and pooling between her thighs. "No more thinking. It's hell. And I'm done with hell. I want heaven." He paused and breathed like he was having trouble getting enough oxygen. His gaze was feverish. "And you're going to give it to me."

Lilah moaned. She was having trouble concentrating on anything but the feel of his body against hers. She'd been living her own kind of hell and wanted heaven too. But there was something she should be doing. She was sure of it. Gripping his hair, she pulled his face away and stuttered, "Wha-what about...your hand?" in one last-ditch effort at rationality, because there was another reason why she shouldn't be doing this. But she couldn't remember what it was. Something about frat boys and her father.

He nipped at her mouth, making her squeak and lose her train of thought. "Later," he growled, and for one awful moment she thought he was talking about kissing her. Then the world abruptly tilted and the next instant Lilah found herself flat on her back.

Blinking in confusion, she tried to focus on her surroundings but Luke slid his hands beneath her shirt and all she could concentrate on was how good they felt. She gave a long low groan of pleasure and shifted against him, pressing all her good parts to his even better parts.

His hands were big and warm and calloused, scraping lightly against her sensitized flesh. They made her shiver like she had a chill when she felt anything but chilled. Even so, when he cupped her aching breasts she shuddered and bit her lip against the whimper that rose in her throat.

It escaped anyway as "Oh, God," as she arched helplessly into his big hands.

Luke chuckled deep in his chest. "No, just me. And I'm very human." *Hoo, boy. She could feel just* how *human he was.* Then he was shoving the material up her torso and murmuring, "Look at you, you're so damn beautiful." Her exposed breasts tightened almost painfully and after a long reverent moment he bent and licked one full curve.

Lilah almost came off the bed but his big body pressed her deeper into the mattress as he fed on her flesh, tormenting her with flicking licks and little nips until she wanted to scream—or burst out of her skin. And when he finally sucked one pebbled tip into his hot, wet mouth Lilah cried out and tensed under the onslaught, clutching at his shoulders like he was the only thing keeping her from flying off into space.

Her hands raced over him as he tortured her with his

mouth and teeth and when he finally released her nipple it was to drag his open mouth down her belly.

Her skin tingled and quivered. "What are you doing?" she rasped, lifting her head to blink at him and follow his teasing progress.

He smiled against her belly and looked up long enough to drawl chidingly, "Are you sure you're a doctor?"

Breathing heavily, Lilah fell backwards and stared unseeingly at the ceiling. "I think…I think I'm about to become a patient," she gasped, wheezing like a geriatric asthmatic.

Luke chuckled and heaved himself upright until he was straddling her on all fours. He grinned down into her stunned face. "Good thing I know CPR. I'm great at the kiss of life."

She thought, *I know*, but what she said was, "I thought that was chest compressions," and his grin turned wicked as he reached out to run his hand over her chest.

"Oh, yeah." He smirked, fondling the plump curves. "I'm great with that too." Sitting back, he slid his hands down her torso to toy with the waistband of her scrubs before yanking them down her thighs. "And I'm excellent with this." And before Lilah could stop him he'd whipped them past her feet and tossed them somewhere into the darkness.

"Oh, man," he breathed, his hot gaze taking in the sight of her lying there in nothing but a pair of tiny silk panties. Lilah fought the urge to cover herself and tried to remember when she'd last been naked in front of a man. She couldn't and attempted to cover herself but he caught her hands.

"No. I want to see you. You have no idea how often I've wanted to strip you to your underwear." His rough whisper rasped against already exposed nerve endings and she realized he liked what he saw. "See if you were wearing another of your Wild African collection."

"Afric—?" Then she remembered him asking her about

tigers and leopards and her breath escaped in a loud *whoosh*. "The helicopter."

His eyes crinkled at the corners. "Yeah, then too. I got hard just thinking about you in leopard-print. But this…?" He paused to toy with the tiny ribbon bow beneath her navel and brush his fingers across her belly until her muscles quivered and heat rushed over her skin. It was like a flash fire settling deep in her belly and creating deep inner ripples of sensation. "This is even better. It makes me want to sit and stare at you all night. And I would," he told her in a rough growl, "if I didn't want to taste what that tiny scrap is hiding."

Lilah swallowed a groan and attempted one last time to think clearly. She was fluttering madly, right where he wanted to…taste? *Yikes*. "But your hand," she began breathlessly. "It's swollen."

Luke chuckled and pressed his erection against her. Lilah's eyes practically rolled back in her head and her world spun crazily off its axis. She thought she heard him say, "Not nearly as swollen as this," but wasn't certain as there was a tornado roaring through her head.

She bit down on his shoulder, needing somehow to keep herself from being swept up into the vortex, or from whimpering with pleasure as her body went liquid with need.

"Too much," she whispered against the ball of his shoulder. "It's too much."

His chuckle rumbled deep in his chest, vibrating against her skin where they touched and setting off tiny explosions of sensation. "Not nearly," he murmured wickedly against her hair. "But soon."

Soon couldn't come soon enough for Lilah, especially when he slipped his hands between her thighs and cupped her over the tiny panties. She wanted him, more than she'd ever wanted anyone, and was beyond ready to give him heaven—as long as he took her there too. Then he slid his hand beneath the elastic band to part her slick flesh and Lilah saw stars.

Her breathing hitched and she was afraid she might hyperventilate. Instead, she moaned and pulled him closer, arching into his touch. The need to feel the weight of him against her, and more than his fingers...*there*...was overwhelming. What she wanted was the hot hard length of him inside her, filling her and banishing the aching, hollow loneliness she hadn't even realized she was carrying around.

"I love knowing I can make you lose control when I touch you like this," Luke murmured, nibbling on her ear as he brushed her tiny feminine bump. "Love knowing that I'm soon going to use my tongue on you. Right where I'm touch—"

"Oh, God, stop...*stop* or I'll..." His barely there touch brushed over her again and Lilah sucked in a shocked breath as a powerful orgasm gripped her. She was scarcely aware of his words, murmured against her throat, as his fingers brushed and stroked her through the sensations roaring through her, threatening to blow her head right off her shoulders.

"Oh, God," she rasped, once she could get her lungs working again. "That was... I never felt... You...*huh*." Her breath ran out with a noisy whoosh and she lay there panting and wondering what had hit her.

Luke's face appeared above her and it took her a second to realize they were both naked and his erection was pressing smooth and hot against her thigh.

Luke snatched the hand she hadn't even realized she was moving down his slick abs to her target. "No."

No?

"I want to touch you." Lilah pouted. "Besides, it's my turn."

"Later," he growled, sounding like he'd run up the side of a mountain with a hundred pounds on his back. Lilah didn't know whether to growl or cry so she sank her nails into his tight butt. Kind of where she wanted to sink her teeth.

His big body shuddered and he grabbed her hands, lifting them above her head. "Touch me, and it's all over."

Lilah's mouth curved into a slow delighted smile even though her wrists were manacled by one hand while he searched through the bedside table with the other. She decided she liked knowing she could push him to the edge and wondered if he was looking for handcuffs.

She'd never thought being handcuffed would hold such appeal. But that didn't mean she was going to lie there quietly while he got a grip on his control. She wanted him losing it—with her.

"What are you looking for?" she purred, moving against him so their groins rubbed and her nipples brushed his chest. Only the friction made her own breath catch in her throat while tiny clenches deep in her belly started all over again.

Holy Moses! That had never happened before. Once was about all she could usually achieve—if she was lucky.

"Condom," he gasped, presenting a small foil packet. Lilah snatched it from him and pushed him back so she could touch him. Her avid gaze locked on his impressive erection and she licked her lips. "Let me," she purred in anticipation, but he retrieved it just as quickly.

"Not on your life. You touch me and we're done."

Lilah huffed out a breath and sank back on her elbows as he ripped open the packet with his teeth. "I'm on a contraceptive," she whispered hoarsely, but after a moment's hesitation he rolled the latex down his thick shaft with shaking hands. Lilah felt her inner muscles clench in anticipation. *Oh, yes! Come to mamma.*

Finally covered, he looked up and the heat in his green eyes had her blood surging through her veins in a way that promptly stole the breath she'd regained after her first climax.

She licked her lips nervously.

"Now," he said with a slow, wicked grin as he came down over her and made a place for himself between her thighs, "let's find heaven together."

CHAPTER EIGHT

LILAH CRADLED LUKE's big hand in hers and gently washed the snake-bite area with warm soapy water. This was something she should have done soon after he'd been bitten and blushed when she recalled why she hadn't.

Frowning at his hand, she probed the red swollen area around the puncture wounds and focused on being a medic. Not an easy task. Not when the heat of his body reminded her of the past couple of hours. Not when every move had her T-shirt—or rather *his* T-shirt—brushing against her tender nipples. Not when she might melt into a little puddle right there on the stool. Or maybe climb onto his lap.

"This looks infected already," she huffed, ducking behind long ropes of tousled curls to escape his too-perceptive gaze. His too-perceptive, *hot* gaze—she corrected with a gulp—currently locked on her face and filled with smoldering heat. She tingled in all the places he'd spent the last couple of hours discovering with his mouth and she didn't have to be a mind reader to know what he was thinking. "Are you sure that snake wasn't poisonous?"

Luke reached out and swept her hair behind her ear as he dipped his head to peer into her face. "Are you blushing?"

"Don't be ridiculous," she said a little breathlessly, dabbing the area dry with an alcohol swab and trying to pretend her face wasn't burning. "It's just a little hot in here."

His chuckle set fire to her nerve endings and further

tightened her nipples. Every time she inhaled, she sucked in the potent mix of pheromones and warm male skin. It was wildly intoxicating. And probably why she felt the need to put her mouth on him all over again.

She sneaked a peek and caught him looking at her breasts.

"Do you need a tetanus shot?" she asked breathlessly to distract him and when his gaze moved slowly up her chest, past her chin and lingered briefly on her mouth before finally lifting to hers, she thought she was having a stroke.

His mouth curled at one corner and he shook his head. "Nope. I'm good." *Oh, wow, he certainly was.* Especially when he—*God, no,* she thought wildly, and forced herself to focus on the antibiotic ointment she was applying to the bite area. *Don't think about that.*

Casting around for something to say, she opened her mouth and, "I'm sorry about…before," popped out before she could stop it.

"Before?"

Lilah licked suddenly dry lips and sneaked another peek. "When I…um…threw my shoe at the snake and…"

"Hit me in the nu—?"

"It was an accident," she interrupted with a spluttered laugh. "I panicked."

Luke smirked. "Good thing you throw like a girl or I'd have been out of action."

"Out of—? Okay, never mind." *Yeesh. Were they really going to discuss that?*

Ducking her head, she hastily covered the wound site with an adhesive bandage before sliding off the stool to prepare a syringe of antibiotics and anti-inflammatory meds. And to move away from the heady scent of his skin. It was making her feel a little drunk. Like she'd been sucking down shooters instead of— He caught her hand and his touch set off deep carnal longing. "I don't need that."

"Yes, you do."

"I already told you—"

"Look," she interrupted testily, and tugged free. "You have no idea where that…that thing had its teeth recently."

"Huh?"

"He lives on the ground, for heaven's sake, and eats dirty little rodents that carry disease. And no matter what you say," she said, shoving the syringe into the vial of antibiotics, "that thing was poisonous."

"How the hell would you know that?" he demanded with his arms folded across his awesome chest. He was scowling at her like she intended doing something illegal instead of administering a tiny little injection. Lilah snickered. Alpha males were so weird about stuff like needles and injections.

"Please," she scoffed with an eye roll. "The area is swollen and inflamed. Besides, even fifth-graders know that bright colors in nature signal danger."

There was a short silence while she searched for an alcohol swab, then Luke reached out and tugged long strands curling over her breast. "Kind of like you," he drawled with a hot smile that made Lilah's nipples tighten and her insides melt.

"Me?" she squeaked, then laughed because she was the least dangerous person she knew. "I'm not dangerous."

"Oh, yes, you are," he drawled softly, deliberately brushing his knuckles across the tip of her breast as he toyed with a ropey curl. "With hair like this you should come with a warning. *Lethal. Keep far away.*"

She gave a tiny smile. She kind of liked being thought of as lethal. "Then why didn't you keep far away?"

Luke snorted and said, "I'm an army ranger," as though that should mean something. Rising to his full height, he gently took the syringe and tossed it onto the counter. "We eat danger for breakfast." His smirk reminded her of where he'd had his mouth earlier. "Among other things."

Lilah gulped and got caught in his smoldering gaze. "You do?"

"Uh-huh." He nudged her backwards until she collided with the refrigerator. "And you are very...*very*...danger-ous." Planting his palms either side of her head, he leaned down until his mouth was barely an inch away from hers. "But that's okay. I'm trained to handle dangerous...explo-sions. And now," he growled with a wicked grin, "I'm going to handle you."

She swallowed convulsively and his hot gaze dropped to watch the movement before he finally closed the small gap to kiss her softly and sweetly on her mouth. She gave a tiny moan and parted her lips. The instant her tongue sneaked out to meet his, the kiss exploded and before Lilah knew what was happening, he'd smoothed his big hands up her thighs to her bottom and lifted her off the floor.

The moment Lilah wrapped her legs around his hips Luke freed himself and thrust into her wet heat, groan-ing when her slick walls clamped down on his shaft. The woman was like a fever in his blood, he thought fiercely, and he couldn't seem to get to the point where he said no more. Maybe he would.

Later.

Much later.

He briefly considered that it might have something to do with the fact that he hadn't had sex in nearly a year, but he had a very bad feeling that it had nothing to do with sex and everything to do with the woman scraping her nails down his back and sinking her teeth into his shoulder.

Sensation bolted down his spine and about buckled his knees, but Luke tightened his grip on her and thrust again. She cried out, wriggling against him, and his eyes rolled back in his head.

"Don't move," he panted, staggering backwards until his butt hit the counter. Turning with her still crushed tightly against him, he caught her mouth with his, driving his tongue into her mouth.

He'd never before experienced these primitive urges thundering through his veins and making him desperate for the feel of a woman's every tiny quiver and shudder. Primitive urges that made him want to take her hard and fast—and then slow and torturous—and never stop. Lust coiled tight and painful in his groin, as if they hadn't spent the last few hours satisfying both their hungers.

He'd wanted her to show him heaven, and, man…she'd taken him places he'd never gone before. But now that he'd tasted her, felt her around him, he wanted it again. And more. Much more.

Wrenching his mouth from hers, he headed for the sturdy wooden table in the dining area and set her down on the edge. She thrust her fingers into his hair and arched against him, yanking his mouth back to hers. He moaned deep in his throat and smoothed his palms up the long length of her thighs to fill his hands with her soft curves. Yanking her closer, he stilled, marveling at the way they fitted together. Tight and wet and…so damn…*hot*.

The sensations were so intense it was almost enough just to be buried deep. But it wasn't, not when he wanted to move more than he wanted his next breath. Not when she was moaning and moving against him too.

His hungry mouth slanted across hers and he fed her hot ravenous kisses that tightened the knot of tension at the base of his spine. Finally when he could no longer remain still, he broke the kiss and rasped, "*Lilah*" in a voice he didn't recognize as his own. With one sweep of his arm he cleared the table of everything and gently shoved her onto her back.

God, she was beautiful—looking all flushed and rumpled and spread out like his favorite meal.

"Lilah," he rasped again, and grasped the backs of her

knees, surging against her until their bodies were locked tight. He did it again. "God," he wheezed, "you make me crazy."

Lilah's husky laugh slid up his spine. "I do?" She smoothed her hand down over her belly to where they were joined and Luke shuddered and surged against her again as though he couldn't get deep enough.

She arched her body and then there were no more thoughts, only heavy breathing and thundering pulses as he pushed her towards release. And when she cried out and clutched at his shoulders as she shuddered and came, he came too, harder than the first or second times. Harder than he'd ever come in his life.

And somewhere in the back of his mind a little alarm bell clanged a warning that he was missing something important. Maybe because he was getting in too deep, that this was too much, too fast. But Luke ignored it. He was too busy fighting for his next breath and basking in the glow of having been to heaven.

The distant sound of banging drew Lilah from a sleep deeper than any she could remember. She briefly considered getting up to see what was going on, but someone had stolen her bones and she couldn't move without immense effort. Sighing dreamily, she snuggled deeper into the bedding and drifted.

The next thing she knew someone was shaking her roughly and murmuring her name in a deep raspy voice. She knew that voice so she hummed and arched languorously beneath the warm touch.

"Lilah," the voice called again, this time a little more firmly, and she frowned irritably. "Wake up. We have an emergency."

Whether from years of conditioning where the word

"emergency" had her reacting, or the quiet intensity in that deep voice, Lilah finally found the energy to roll over and open her eyes.

"What's wrong?" she croaked, blinking in the sudden light spilling from the bedside lamp.

She lifted a hand to shove the hair off her face and found Luke leaning over her with one hand planted on the bed and the other molded to her shoulder.

"Get dressed," he ordered, then straightened abruptly as though he hadn't spent the past several hours intimately exploring her body. Despite his detachment, Lilah shivered in memory of that touch. She greedily wanted more. "There's been an accident."

Accident? Lilah lurched into a sitting position as he turned away and swept her eyes over him, looking for gaping wounds pumping blood. "How did it happen?" she demanded, her heart pounding just as fast at the thought of him being injured. "Where are you hurt?"

His over-the-shoulder look was hooded even as it scorched a path down her throat and across her naked breasts. "I'm fine," he drawled roughly. "But you'd better get a move on, Dr. Meredith, before I forget about medical emergencies and crawl back into that bed with you." Okay, so maybe he wasn't as distant as he appeared. Which was good. Lilah frowned. Wasn't it?

Belatedly realizing she was as naked as a newborn, she flushed and dived for the covers, but Luke had already gone. Besides, it was a little late to be freaking out about being naked in front of Dr. Big and Buff. The man had already seen every inch of her body and had touched all of her with his hands and his mouth. Several times.

Shoving aside the memories of exactly where he'd had his hands and mouth, Lilah threw back the covers and quickly dressed.

Within a minute she was shoving her feet into her sneakers on her way out the room. She found Luke waiting at the open front door, holding the steel meds case and talking in undertones to a park ranger Lilah hadn't seen before.

"How bad is it?" she asked, twisting her hair into a messy topknot and securing it with her fastener. She peered out into the dark. It was still pouring.

"Don't know the details," Luke said, holding out a rain jacket. "But Danny said Jeff's pretty bad. They're bringing him in now."

Lilah took the slicker from him as he herded her out the door. "Jeff?" she asked, looking over her left shoulder and up into the shadowed face of the man who'd not so long ago swept her off her feet and robbed her of her sanity. "The guy who lent us the cabin? What happened?"

"Long story," Luke said abruptly, and pulled the jacket over her head. "Can you run?"

Without replying, Lilah leapt off the veranda and dashed through the mud to the SUV. The ranger was holding open the rear door and when Lilah dived inside he slammed it shut. Within seconds they were on the move, Danny muscling the vehicle round corners and sliding through puddles. Rain pounded the roof and the wipers swished through the deluge as the vehicle skidded and slid over the muddy terrain.

"Where are we going?" Lilah demanded, grabbing hold of the seats in front of her to keep from being tossed around like a shirt in a tumble drier.

"Ranger station," Luke replied. "It's closer to the chopper and has emergency med supplies."

"I've seen the med supplies," Lilah told Luke. "They won't help if the injury is life-threatening."

"Then we improvise." His profile glowed green from the dash lights as he flashed her an odd look over his shoulder. Lilah felt a warning skate up the length of her spine. It raised the hair at the back of her neck and sent goose bumps rolling over her flesh. Pressing a hand to the ball of tension cramping her stomach, she wondered what they would do if Jeff's injury was critical.

She had an awful feeling she knew.

Within minutes they were sliding to a stop near the rangers' center. Another vehicle was already there and someone waited at the top of the stairs with a flashlight.

"What happened to the power?" Lilah asked as she dashed up the stairs.

"Went out about fifteen minutes ago." *Lovely*, she thought dryly. *Just what we need to make things easy.*

"How is he?" she asked, following him as he turned and headed into the dark building.

"He's lost a lot of blood and is struggling to breathe. I left Frank in there with him."

"What happened?" Luke demanded, appearing out of the darkness behind her.

"We went to check on the bridge over the gorge," the park ranger said. "I heard Jeff shout something as he stepped off the road and the next thing he was gone. By the time we reached him he was struggling with a couple of downed trees. I didn't realize he was trying to pull a broken branch out of his chest until it was too late." Lilah sucked in a shocked breath. All she could think of was Jeff as he'd been earlier. Alive. Vital. And smiling.

Luke muttered a choice epithet and Lilah knew what he was thinking. The last thing a victim should do was the first they thought of—remove the object from their bodies. Often, what was impaling them was also keeping them from bleeding out.

And then she hurried into a room lit with dozens of candles and lanterns and saw that someone had cleared the table at the front of the room and placed Jeff on it. Her first thought was that it looked like a sacrificial altar and shivered, hoping it wasn't an omen, but even from the doorway she could hear the dreadful wheeze and rattle as he struggled to breathe.

Hurrying towards him, she was aware of one thing. If they didn't plug that hole, the pressure in Jeff's chest would crush his lungs and he'd go into cardiac arrest even before he could bleed out.

Lilah had seen this kind of injury only once and, like before, as Jeff tried to breathe, the air was leaking into his chest cavity and putting pressure on his heart and lungs.

"Check for tension pneumothorax while I examine his wound," Luke said abruptly, automatically taking charge, and Lilah was glad to let him. She whipped her stethoscope around her neck as he removed the makeshift pressure bandage to cut away Jeff's blood-and-rain-soaked khaki shirt.

Aware of Luke's proximity and his calm assurance, Lilah flattened two fingers and palpated the chest, moving every few inches to repeat the procedure.

"Hyper-resonant on the injured side," she announced, checking Jeff's pulse rate one-handed while inserting the stethoscope earpieces into her ears. She slid the disc over his chest and listened. "Unaffected side fairly normal at this stage," she reported, shifting the stethoscope to the side of his injury. "Absent breath sound on affected side." She looked up briefly. "Tachycardia present and integrity compromised."

"*Damn*," he muttered softly, his eyes catching and holding hers. "Three broken ribs," he reported. "Pleura penetration and I'm not sure but it feels like foreign material in the wound."

He turned to the ranger hovering nearby. "Danny, get me a sharp knife, a water bottle and a roll of cling wrap." His gaze returned to Lilah. "Keep an eye on his vitals. Clean the wound as best you can and seal it with plastic wrap."

"Where are you going?"

"The helo." And before she could ask why, he'd grabbed

the nearest flashlight and was gone, disappearing into the darkness as silently as a shadow.

By the time Danny reappeared carrying a wicked-looking nine-inch filleting knife, Lilah had cleaned the wound and found a roll of surgical tape. Normally she had all the equipment and supplies of a large hospital at her disposal. Normally she had light and all the proper instruments.

She was now working practically blind with kitchen utensils. Fortunately, Luke's solution would stop air from being sucked in through the wound and a thoracostomy would release the trapped air into the water bottle, creating a vacuum of sorts.

Tearing off a section of plastic, she asked the shaky ranger to hold it in place while she cut strips of surgical tape, which she pressed along the edges. Wanting to give the older ranger something to do, she sent him to the restroom for some paper toweling.

While they waited for Luke's return, Lilah rummaged through the meager supplies and tried to calm an agitated patient whose every breath was a struggle. He tried to talk but she squeezed his shoulder, warning him to save his breath.

He reached out. "I—need—to—tell—"

"You need to stay quiet and still," she said firmly, pressing his arm to the table. "It's going to be okay, Jeff. Just relax and let us take care of things."

"But—"

"Here's the p-paper towel," the ranger stuttered as he returned with the entire roll. Lilah's mouth dropped open.

"What did you do, break open the dispenser?"

"I…I thought it would be more s-sterile if I b-brought the whole thing," he stuttered, rubbing a hand over his hair to the back of his neck in embarrassment.

"Oh. Well…um, good thinking," Lilah said, as a huge hulking shadow materialized beside her. She jolted with fright until she realized it was Luke. *Yikes*, the man was like a ninja. Even six feet four and dripping water all over the floor, he moved like he was materializing from another dimension.

It reminded her that he'd been in elite ops and had likely treated a lot of field injuries, most likely a lot worse than this. But then he was dumping supplies out onto the strips of paper toweling she'd laid out and her mind shut out everything but the task ahead.

"I'm going to make an incision just beneath the armpit," he said, tearing open a box of latex gloves. She took two from him and shoved her hands into them before accepting a packaged syringe and needle. "Give him a local around the fifth intercostal."

Lilah quickly stripped off the packaging and pushed the syringe into the vial of anesthetic, recalling the syringe filled with antibiotics and anti-inflammatories she'd administered earlier. After they'd— As though tuned to her emotions, Luke turned from giving the older ranger instruction on how on to fit and operate the manual resuscitator.

"You okay?" he asked near her ear, as she swiped a small area with an alcohol swab. She told herself it was the sound of snapping latex that made her jolt, but couldn't make herself believe it. He'd spent the better part of the night exploring her body and now knew her more intimately than her gynecologist. She didn't know how she felt about that.

"I'm fine," she said coolly. "This should be ready to go in a couple of minutes. What about a ketamine shot? He's a little agitated."

"All right," Luke said absently as he unwound a length of cannula tubing. "Give him thirty ccs."

"Ketamine?" Danny asked, holding Jeff down as Lilah prepped another syringe. "Won't morphine be better?"

"No," she said absently, checking for air bubbles. "It's a pulmonary suppressor. Ketamine will help take the edge off without affecting his breathing even more until we can get him to a hospital." She gestured for Danny to turn Jeff on his side, soothing the ranger when he let out a ragged groan. She finally turned to Luke. "We're going to fly him out, aren't we?"

His brief look was indecipherable but Lilah's heart gave a painful squeeze. After a short pause he gently lifted the arm on Jeff's injured side. "Danny, help Dr. Meredith hold him while I make the incision."

Lilah followed instructions and watched Luke's long fingers probe the fifth intercostal space in the mid-axillary line. Once he was happy with the position, he placed the tip of the filleting knife where his fingers had been and gave a quick, firm push. Blood instantly welled from the incision, which Lilah readily swabbed.

"Widen the incision site and pierce through the pleura if you can," Luke said, reaching for the cannula tubing.

Lilah murmured soothingly while she maneuvered Jeff until she could press her finger into the incision site. She gently rotated her finger to check for any obstacles and her careful pressure was met with only slight resistance. She pushed harder and waited for Luke to position the cannula before sliding her finger out. Within seconds Luke had inserted six inches of tubing, which he'd already attached and sealed to the plastic bottle. It would now be up to Lilah to close the entry site.

After prepping the suture kit, she set about stitching the area around the cannula to minimize leakage. Carefully drawing the filament thread as tightly as she could without tearing the skin, she tied off the thread and snipped it.

Straightening, she held her breath and eyed the bottle. After a couple of beats foamy bubbles began forming in the water. She quietly exhaled.

"Set up Ringer's lactate in the cubital vein while I dress

this," Luke said calmly, nodding to the eighteen-gauge catheter and bag of fluid. "Then we're out of here."

Lilah efficiently set up the drip, her hands quickly performing the task despite the blood draining from her head at the news. "We're really going?" she asked, trying not to freak out at the thought of flying through the mountains in the dark. "What about the storm?"

There was a short tension-filled silence until she looked up and caught Luke staring at her with a hard jaw and steady eyes. "What about it?"

"I…uh," Lilah stuttered, as her heart leapt into her throat. *Oh, help.*

"We can't wait," Luke reminded her quietly, and Lilah felt a little dizzy as she drew in a shaky breath. She swiped her tongue over suddenly dry lips, recalling her embarrassing behavior on the flight in. But embarrassment aside, she could already feel her heart rate increasing and the band of tension around her head tightening.

"Are you going to be okay?" he asked. "I can take Danny if it's a problem." Lilah pressed her lips together and shook her head. There was no way he was leaving her behind. He couldn't fly and tend to a critical patient. That's why pilots flew with medics.

"You're not leaving me behind," she said a little more firmly than she felt, and repacked the supplies as the men transferred Jeff to the stretcher. "Besides, it's my flight call."

"It's bad out there," he warned. "Are you sure you'll be able to handle it?"

Lilah paled as they moved quickly through the building. *Heck, no!* "Can you?"

Luke gave a harsh laugh as they stepped onto the veranda. "Me?" Lilah saw his mouth twist into an ironic smile. "I'm an army ranger, remember."

CHAPTER NINE

WIND WHIPPED LILAH'S wet hair into her face as she scrambled into the chopper. Moments later the stretcher appeared through the doorway and she reached over to help slide and snap it into place.

While Luke strapped himself into the pilot's seat she attached the bag to an overhead hook and tried to ignore the rising whine of the engine. The rotors began to turn and she looked out the window in time to see the rangers duck out of the way and dash back towards the building. The entire aircraft began vibrating and the sound was deafening, setting her teeth on edge, but she forced herself to focus on wrapping the BP cuff around Jeff's arm and not on the rising pitch of the rotors. If she did she might lose it.

The idea that in a couple of minutes they would be flying through the storm sent a shudder of terror right through her. Her mother had died in a light plane crash on a night like this and Lilah tried not to think that she might as well.

Turning on the battery-operated light, she concentrated on maintaining the rhythm of the manual resuscitator with one hand while activating the electronic cuff with the other. She might have managed to fool her hands into thinking they weren't shaking but she jumped about a foot in the air when someone gripped her shoulder. Realizing she was acting like a crazy person, she looked up a little guiltily.

"You okay?" Luke shouted, his gaze unreadable.

Instead of answering, she nodded and dropped her attention to the headset he was holding out. *No way was she admitting that she was close to freaking out.* "Put it on," he yelled over the rotors. "I need constant updates."

Lilah nodded and slipped the headset over her ears with shaking hands. The roar of the engine immediately lessened and his deep voice filled her head.

"Status," he barked as the chopper rose off the ground with a jolt, and Lilah wondered if he was trying to distract her or himself with the abrupt orders. She gave an alarmed whimper when the craft lurched in the buffeting wind and grabbed the webbing behind the seat to keep from being flung around.

"BP one hundred over sixty-five," she reported through chattering teeth.

Luke muttered a curse and a quick look in his direction told her he was clenching his teeth. His face gleamed green and wet in the instrument lights as he battled to keep them from being blown into the tree line. Lilah wondered if it was sweat or rain slicking his skin and decided it was most likely a mixture of both. Heck, she'd broken out in a cold sweat herself the moment she'd known they were flying out.

Blinking to clear her swimming vision, she ordered herself to get a grip. He seemed in control of things but considering the way he'd reacted that afternoon, she wondered if he was really okay to get them back safely without having a flashback, a panic attack or whatever it was he'd had.

To her vast relief he managed to stabilize the chopper and the next second they rose sharply, leaving Lilah's belly behind along with her notion of being in control. She was literally putting her life in the hands of a man who'd crashed his last chopper. If she survived this, she was never leaving terra firma again. Ever.

Praying that some guardian angel was watching over them, Lilah concentrated on Jeff's vitals. She briefly stopped using the resus bag to pull his lip down to check the mucous tissue for cyanosis. She couldn't really see in the dim light and reached for his hand to give the end of his finger a hard pinch. *Dammit*. It was virtually impossible to detect capillary refill either. She would just have to rely on instinct to get him through the worst and pray for the best.

Ignoring Luke's constant mutters and curses as he fought the buffeting wind, Lilah felt herself edge towards the limit of her own control, praying her perception of the endless flight into the mountains earlier had been the result of stress. Hopefully it would be mere minutes before they landed on the hospital roof.

But after what seemed like hours she noticed the water bottle had turned from a light pink to red. She must have said something because Luke's head swung towards her.

"What? What's wrong?" he demanded brusquely, breaking off to curse when he caught sight of the problem.

"I think we just went from a pneumo to a tension haemo and I won't be able to tell where the blood is coming from without opening him up."

"Pulse and BP?" he growled, and even Lilah could hear the tension in his voice.

"About one forty. His BP is dropping," Lilah answered.

"Cyanosis?"

She looked up briefly, but Luke had gone back to concentrating on the instruments. "There's not enough light to see the capillary refill but his lips are pale."

"Okay. Can you check the refrigeration unit?" Lilah abandoned the resus bag for a moment while she reached for the refrigerator. It was filled with trays of medication but no blood.

"It's empty."

Luke cursed. "Set up more Ringer's lactate but watch for haemo-dilution. You don't want his levels dropping below five." Lilah knew what would happen then. There wouldn't be enough oxygen in the diluted blood and his organs would start shutting down.

With shaking hands, she attached another bag and felt for his pulse, detecting arrhythmia in his tachycardia. Her pulse spiked with alarm and she opened her mouth to report it just as light flashed, illuminating the interior like someone had switched on the sun. Almost instantly there was an earsplitting explosion.

The sound engulfed the small aircraft, making it shudder and rattle as it was tossed through the air like a flimsy toy rather than a few thousand pounds of metal. Over the shriek of the engine and the booming echo reverberating through the mountains, Lilah heard herself scream.

"Luke," she yelled, and if he heard her through the headset he gave no indication. Posture tense, the muscles in his shoulders strained, threatening the seams of his shirt. He clearly had better things to do than reassure her they were okay. Lilah hoped that wasn't an omen.

Light flashed again, but this time it was further away and the booming response echoed around them. "Luke," she yelled again, scarcely aware that she was crying until she swiped irritably at the wetness on her cheeks. Her heart was pounding faster than Jeff's and she felt light-headed. "*Dammit*, what's wrong?"

His muttered curse reached her over the terrible noise and out the corner of her eye she saw him wrestle the pitch lever as though it was alive and determined to defy him.

A quick glance at Jeff told her he was in serious trouble. Even in the dim light she could see that his skin was gray and clammy, and blood trickled from one corner of his mouth. The branch must have nicked something more serious than they'd originally thought and he was going into shock.

Then she heard "Uh-oh" through her headset and her stomach cramped violently. She squeaked, "What? What now?" and Luke sent her a quick look over his shoulder that she struggled to interpret.

His eyes were narrowed and intense and a muscle popped along his jaw. "Don't freak out," he ordered, just as the chopper lurched sideways again. "But we have a little problem."

"Problem? *Problem?* Jeff going into shock is a problem. What could be worse?" She gulped back the rising hysteria and felt more tears blur her vision. Dammit, now wasn't the time to lose it.

Or maybe now's the perfect time to lose it.

"The tail rotors are sluggish and the gyroscope is all over the place."

"Wha-at?" *Okay, so that was officially worse.*

There was another blinding flash of blue-white light and she opened her mouth to scream. Searing sulfur scorching her lungs as the chopper slewed sideways, jolting violently. There was a popping sound and she realized with dawning horror that she could literally see each individual rotor blade. The chopper lurched sickeningly and dipped forward.

Lilah gave a squeak of alarm and whipped her head around to gape at him. "Seriously? *Seriously?*"

Luke ignored her, cursing a blue streak. "Hold on," he yelled, hands flying over the control panel as his knees gripped the CPL. "I've got this."

The next few seconds passed in a blur. Lilah watched, eyes locked on his face as he fought the controls, and wondered if they were about to die. It seemed they were, she realized with a gasp of horror as the chopper tilted again and began a slow, lazy spiral towards the ground. Sucking in a terrified breath, she squeezed her eyes closed and braced for impact as a raucous warning alarm filled the interior.

"Oh, God," she whimpered, and fumbled the manual resuscitator, thinking that in a couple of seconds Jeff might not need it.

"Have a little faith, woman," Luke yelled, but his voice

was tight with tension. He was worried and Lilah tried not to imagine how close they were to the ground.

Just when she thought they would slam into the mountain, he launched into a blur of motion. The craft jolted once and then shuddered. *Oh, boy.* It didn't sound good.

"C'mon, c'mon," he urged through gritted teeth, and suddenly there was a high-pitched whine and he whooped, "Gotcha!" as the rotors began to turn with a sluggish *whop, whop.*

Lilah cracked open one eye and imagined the ground rushing up to meet them despite the rotating blades. She gave a terrified squeak just as they lurched upwards, the skids slapping the tops of the trees. *Too close. Way too close.*

Then they were bumping over the canopy and she could finally exhale wondering if her heart would ever return to its normal state.

"I think the lightning fried a couple of circuits," Luke yelled over the continued blare of the warning alarm. "Maybe even struck the tail rotor."

More good news? Lilah gulped. "What…what does that mean?"

"It means we're going to have to land."

"Here?"

Luke steeled himself against the fear and tension he could hear in Lilah's voice and shook his head. In his estimation they were about a mile from the exclusive Greendale Country Club. Yep. There were the lights. He just hoped he could make the golf course without crashing into the lake. The chopper's night vision capability had been fried in that last strike and something was wrong with the terrain awareness warning system. Luke would be flying blind and the damn blaring alarm was getting on his last nerve.

Behind him, Lilah sat frozen with terror and he didn't dare take his eyes off the instruments to reassure her. He'd tried telling her to have a little faith but he suspected she'd stopped listening a while back. He couldn't blame her. This was about as scary as his last mission. At least they didn't have RPGs exploding all around them. Although the lightning had been bad enough and for a minute there he'd thought he was going to have a flashback to rival all flashbacks.

Right now he didn't have time to panic. Which was probably a good thing. He just hoped he didn't lose it until he was alone.

Bellowing instructions to the control tower over the shriek of alarms, he gave them his location and spared a moment to be grateful for his military training and experience. Somewhere along the way he'd stopped hyperventilating and sweating in terror and was now flying on reflex. The black dots obscuring his vision had vanished, leaving him steady and relaxed. Well...as relaxed as he was ever going to be while keeping them from crashing into the rocky cliffs or the icy lake below.

The aircraft abruptly jerked once and then he felt the ailing tail rotors clip the treetops just as they ploughed through the last hundred feet of thick brush.

The instant the chopper made the clearing Luke worked the foot levers, forcing the craft around to keep from spiraling into the ground—or taking out the front of the building.

A muffled "What's wrong now?" was abruptly cut off the moment the right skid clipped the flagpole. Something broke free and the shriek of the rotors sounded like a host of banshees had escaped the depths of hell. Then the chopper jolted and tipped sideways.

Too close, he thought an instant before a rotor plowed into the asphalt. In slow motion they tipped forward and crashed nose first into the ground with a bone-jarring force that slammed his teeth together and sent shock waves through his body. Lilah's cry was abruptly cut off and all Luke could think about was that she hadn't been strapped in.

For a moment he saw stars and, though darkness tugged at him, he fought to remain conscious. He needed to get to her…see if she was okay.

The scream of the straining engines momentarily distracted him and he paused to slam the off lever before the rotors could snap off and became lethal missiles.

For an instant there was absolute silence and then the aircraft toppled backwards in slow motion, finally coming to rest on its side. Outside, rain continued to drum against the metal fuselage and it took him a couple of moments to realize he was seeing water running off the splintered windshield, bleeding light and color into a nightmarish glow.

The utter silence inside the chopper finally nudged him into action.

"Lilah?" He reached for the harness buckle and tugged, then tugged again when it failed to open. Probably because he was hanging at an angle and his weight kept the clasp from opening.

"Lilah!"

Luke felt around with his feet until he could brace himself against the passenger seat and after a couple of yanks the clasp abruptly released.

Freed, he grasped the back of the seat and hauled himself upright to scramble into the rear. In the watery light from the building's security lights he saw a chaos of equipment and supplies. It took a few seconds to locate Lilah pinned against the door by the angle of the disabled chopper. She lay unmoving amidst a scattering of debris and his heart clenched at the sight of something dark and wet staining one side of her face.

Fortunately Jeff was still strapped in and the stretcher remained secured, but a glance in his direction told Luke the man was in serious trouble.

With quick economic movements he cleared the debris away from Lilah and checked for injuries but the only external sign was the steady flow of blood soaking into her hair from the head wound. He leaned closer to examine it while the fingers of his free hand located the sturdy beat of her pulse in the soft flesh just beneath her jaw.

She was alive, he thought on a rush of relief so intense it made him dizzy. After tonight she had a legitimate reason to fear flying and he tried not to feel responsible. But he didn't have time to move her or wait until she regained consciousness. He had to act fast or Jeff would slip away.

Yanking on the defibrillator, he prayed the lightning hadn't fried it since manual chest compressions would cause further damage. Unfortunately, blood in the oral cavity would make his job that much harder. If he had to perform traditional resus, with broken ribs and the intra-thorax drain, who knew what other damage he could cause to an already critical patient. One thing he knew, he had to keep the ranger's heart pumping, no matter what.

Impatiently willing the machine to charge, Luke looked around for the resus bag and spotted it a few feet away. A soft moan sounded and he turned in time to see Lilah's lashes flicker.

"Lilah, open your eyes but don't move," he ordered calmly, as she looked around in a daze.

"What?"

"We landed." Well, in a manner of speaking, he thought with a flash of humor now that her eyes were open and he was sure she wasn't going to die. He retrieved the resus bag and moved back to the stretcher. "Don't move until you've done a full body check." After a couple of seconds he looked her way. "Are you okay?"

"My head hurts."

"Is that all?"

"Nothing's broken, if that's what you mean. But my head *really* hurts."

"I'll check it out later." He sent her a quick look as she

struggled upright, a shaking hand going to her head. "Right now you're lucid and that's the important thing."

"How's Jeff?"

"I'm going to have to defib. Are you up to giving me a hand?"

"I…I think so. Give me a minute."

"He doesn't have a minute. The defibrillator is nearly charged and I need you to hold the bag."

He was conscious of Lilah shuffling closer and resisted the urge to take her in his arms. He knew she was hurting and probably not just her head, but she was being a real trooper. Frankly, the best thing he could do for her was keep her too busy to go into shock. Besides, they had to keep Jeff alive long enough for the ambulance crew to arrive.

He gave her trembling fingers a quick hang-in-there squeeze as he passed over the resus bag. Then, moving quickly, he stripped off the space blanket and positioned the paddles, waiting impatiently for the high-pitched sound to signal the charge.

When it sounded, he said, "Clear." There was a sharp jolt and Jeff's body momentarily arched upwards before flopping back onto the stretcher like a rag doll. "Again." This time the jolt was weaker and Jeff barely responded. Luke moved to reset the machine and noticed the green light abruptly die. He tried it again. Nothing.

He cursed and fiddled with the power switch. "There goes the power," he said, glancing at Lilah. She still looked a little dazed and seemed oblivious to the blood trickling down her face.

She nodded and resumed using the resus bag. "So we do it manually." Her face was ghost white in the stingy light but at least she was responsive and rational, although he suspected she was drawing on sheer willpower.

"See if you can find some atropine. I think I saw some

in the case," he growled, beginning CPR while taking care not to exert too much force on Jeff's ribs.

Lilah located the case, quickly preparing and administering the drug while Luke checked BP.

"Sixty over forty. It's dropping," he said brusquely. "Whatever you do, keep that up. *Dammit, where are they?*"

"Do you think they got the message?"

Luke didn't know so he started praying and just as he was beginning to think the ambulance wasn't coming, he heard the siren wail over the drumming rain and heaved a sigh of relief. Within seconds, flashing lights filled the interior and paramedics were crawling inside, brushing them aside.

Luke told them who he was and shot off rapid-fire instructions as the crew disappeared with the stretcher. When they were gone he turned to find Lilah slumped against the fuselage, her head tilted forward onto her drawn-up knees. The fall of hair hid her face from view. Her arms were wrapped around her shins and even with the rain pinging off the metal he could hear her teeth chattering like a pair of wind-up dentures.

Moving closer he noticed for the first time that she was shivering so hard her whole body shook.

"Lilah."

As though realizing she was under scrutiny, Lilah stilled and Luke could literally feel the tension pumping off her body.

Without looking up, she mumbled something he couldn't hear so he moved to sit beside her and gently bumped her shoulder. "Hey, look on the bright side."

Her voice hitched. "There's a bright side?"

"We made it in one piece."

He'd meant to lighten her mood but when she gave a strangled sob and turned towards him, he opened his arms. She burrowed close and pressed her face into his neck, the move making him aware of the myriad aches he hadn't noticed until now. Now that the adrenalin was fading, he was feeling a bit shaky himself.

He dropped his face into her hair and tightened his grip, sending up a prayer of thanks for their narrow escape.

For long moments they stayed that way until a voice enquired, "You folks need help?" and Luke looked up to see two expectant faces peering through the doorway at them.

"I thought you guys left," he said, pulling Lilah closer as though he thought they might snatch her away. That instinctive move made him pause but then he decided it was probably just reaction from having survived possible death together.

"They didn't know what we would find so they sent two wagons," the paramedic said, gesturing to the crumpled metal and scattered equipment. "You two are damn lucky to be alive."

Luke gave a strangled snort at the understatement and drew in a shaky breath. He didn't need anyone to tell him how close it had been.

"We might as well take you back to County Gen to get checked out," the paramedic continued. "Shock has a way of masking internal injuries."

Lilah couldn't stop shivering. She felt icy to the core even though Luke had wrapped a blanket around her before examining her head wound.

They were in the back of the ambulance as it sped through the night and the scene was so normal—except for her being the patient, of course—that everything that had happened that night seemed like a surreal nightmare. It was creepy and weird.

Luke held up his hand. "How many fingers?"

Lilah squinted against the pain. "Twenty," she murmured, feeling weary beyond belief. Intellectually she knew she was in shock but it didn't help that her skull felt like it wanted to explode. Just moving her head caused excruciating pain to arrow through her skull and her neck felt as if one wrong move would cause it to shatter. Heck, her entire body felt as though it would shatter.

"Yeah, right," Luke growled, ruffling his already tousled hair with his fingers and Lilah had an overwhelming urge to lift a hand and smooth the silky strands. But moving required effort and she just didn't have the energy to do anything more strenuous than breathe.

"I just need a couple of painkillers," she lied. "I'm fine. Really. It's Jeff I'm worried about. And you."

Luke turned to stare at her. "Me? Why me?"

She gave a small smile and managed to lift a hand to his face. His shadowed jaw felt bristly beneath her fingertips and she shivered at the unexpected sensuality of it. It reminded her of the hours he'd spent exploring her naked body—God, had it been just a few hours ago?

"We kind of crashed. I was worried it would bring back bad memories. Of the last time you flew, I mean."

Luke looked momentarily taken aback then his expression turned thoughtful. "Actually...I think it helped me get over myself. In a hair-of-the-dog kinda way."

Lilah studied him closely. "Really?" she asked skeptically. "I got a quick look at the chopper before you closed the ambulance doors. It looked pretty mangled."

Luke drew a gentle finger along the line of her jaw towards her mouth. The expression in his gaze made her pulse leap and her skin tingle. "I'm just glad you're not."

And then he did something that made the backs of her eyes sting and she had to bite her lip to keep from giving in to the tears that had been threatening for what seemed like years. He ran gentle hands over her body as though to reassure himself that she was indeed in one piece and then carefully drew her into his arms.

She went willingly, welcoming his strength and heat.

Welcoming the strong, steady beat of his heart. She wrapped her arms around him and clung.

"Rest now," he murmured into her hair. "I've got you."

CHAPTER TEN

LILAH TURNED THE key again and listened to the ominous click of the engine with growing disbelief. *No, no, no*, she begged silently. *Not now.* It had been a really long week and an even longer shift and she didn't have the energy to face another crisis. *Especially not now, dammit.*

Not when she was feeling fragile and exhausted. Not when she just wanted to go home, climb into bed and pull the covers up over her head so she could hide from the world.

Resisting the urge to drop her forehead onto the steering-wheel and bawl, Lilah gritted her teeth and reached beneath the dash to pop the hood. Besides, weeping never did anyone any good. It clogged the sinuses and made your eyes red and swollen, which was the last thing in attractive. But then again, looking beneath the hood wouldn't do any good either, but at least it felt proactive.

Slowly inhaling, she got out of the car, fiddled around until she found the catch, and lifted the hood. She propped it up and stared into the engine, waiting for divine guidance.

When none came she sighed and went back to lean in through the open door and dig around in her shoulder bag for her cellphone. Only it was as dead as the car. Obviously she'd forgotten to charge it. Again.

Great. Just great. What else could go wrong?

Unbidden, tears pricked her eyes, and her throat ached.

LUCY RYDER   135

It made her wonder what the heck was wrong with her. She wasn't normally this…emotional. She'd handled crises before but now all she wanted to do was curl up in a tight ball and cry like a little kid.

Sniffing, she tossed the phone onto the passenger seat, slammed the door and went back round to peer into the engine. Only thing was, nothing appeared broken—which meant she'd have to go back inside and call for a cab.

But that required too much effort, so she sank back against the car with a sigh of defeat and slid to the ground. With one leg tucked against her butt, she propped her elbow on her knee, shoved her fingers in her hair and squeezed her eyes shut.

God, she was tired. She hadn't had a decent night's sleep since…since…okay, so she didn't want to think about her night with Luke. Or the crash. If she did she might start bawling for real. And she didn't want to think about her earlier run-in with her boss either. He was a jerk and once she started, she probably wouldn't stop until she'd cried about everything that had happened since her mother's death.

She was so wrapped up in her own misery she didn't hear anyone approach until a deep voice said, "Problem?" somewhere overhead. Lilah gave a silent groan. *Why me?* she demanded silently, wishing the earth would open up and swallow her.

She considered pretending to be invisible, but she didn't think Luke would take the hint and go away. He'd been amazingly protective since…since that night and she was worried that she would cling and weep all over him.

It was embarrassing. She'd done enough clinging the night of the crash and wanted to forget the whole thing. Besides, his behavior had most likely been the result of them having survived a harrowing experience together. She would be smart not to read anything into it. That way lay disaster…and heartbreak. At least for her, she reminded herself.

She felt the air change and cracked open one eye to see him crouched at her side. The dim light illuminated half his face, leaving the other in deep shadow. It was frightening how much she liked looking at him.

"What makes you think I have a problem?" she slurred, feeling punch drunk with fatigue. A smile tugged the corner of his mouth not in shadow and he lifted a hand to gently brush a few escapee curls off her face.

"Maybe because you're sitting on the ground beside your car looking kind of pathetic and I feel sorry for you."

Lilah might look pathetic—heck, she felt pathetic—but she didn't need anyone feeling sorry for her. She was doing enough of that herself. She opened her eyes all the way, knocked his hand away and made to stand up, but he gently pushed her back until her butt hit the concrete.

"Stay there while I check your car," he murmured softly, and rose in one effortless move that she might have envied if she wasn't so exhausted.

Of course he knew about cars. He was the kind of man who knew everything and was probably good at it too. *Yep. Even taking a girl to heaven.* The only thing he was really bad at was commitment. He'd told her a little about his childhood the night of the storm, including his determination to never repeat his parents' mistakes. Heck, she could empathize. She was into avoiding bad history herself.

She must have dozed a little because the next thing she knew he was crouching at her side again and running his thumb across her jaw. She blinked up into his face, momentarily confused.

"Wha—?"

"Come on, Sleeping Beauty," he said, closing his hands around her upper arms. "I'm taking you home." When he rose to his feet he drew her up with him and Lilah swayed dizzily for a moment before stepping away from his warm strength.

The urge to cling was still way too strong.

"It's okay," she said, when what she really wanted was to lay her head on his chest and listen to the strong beat of his heart. "I'll call a cab."

"It's almost midnight." His voice was rife with exasperation as he folded his arms across his wide chest and looked at her like she was being irrational. Heck irrational was becoming her middle name. "It could take a while."

"I'm fine, really," she said, turning away to peer at the engine. "So what's wrong with her?"

"Her?" His amused voice was so close that her body heated from neck to thigh as he looked over her shoulder. Shivering, Lilah rubbed at the goose bumps dotting her arms and looked up into his shadowed face. Her breath caught.

God, he was hotter than high noon in Bogota. And just as dangerous.

Which was so not good, *dammit,* she thought when her nerve endings tingled and something hot settled low and deep in her belly. *Dumb, dumb, dumb.*

She turned away to glare into the damn engine.

"Do you know what's wrong?"

"You're exhausted."

"Not me, the car."

"The battery is dead and the starter's fried."

Yeah, she'd kind of figured that. "So I take it I won't be driving home tonight?"

"Yes, you will," Luke said, nudging her aside so he could close the hood. "With me." Without waiting for her permission, he retrieved her keys, dead cellphone, light jacket and shoulder bag and locked the car. "Come on, you look like you need about twelve hours' sleep."

Lilah snatched her belongings from him and stomped away, unaccountably annoyed because he was telling her—subtly—that she looked like crap.

He caught up with her easily and with a firm hand curled

around her upper arm steered her away from the hospital entrance towards a big black bike parked at the end of the row. *Figured he would ride a sexy badass bike.*

Infuriated with his high-handed manhandling—and her own rioting emotions—Lilah yanked at her arm, muttering irritably about arrogant, cocky alpha males.

"What was that?" he asked, and something in his voice made her turn to catch him fighting a smile. She barely resisted the urge to punch his amazing mouth.

"I said you have no idea what I need," she muttered. Actually, neither did she, which might explain her moodiness. And then his eyes turned hot and she sucked in a sharp breath and stumbled back a couple steps.

Holy mother of— No! She didn't need *that*, she assured herself, and hastily backed up again. She needed to be alone. She needed… Luke yanked her against him and before she could demand to know what he was doing he'd caught her mouth in a kiss tainted with wild anger and desperate need.

At first Lilah was too stunned to do anything except withstand the heated assault but after a couple beats her bones began to melt. She fought the sensations but her body took over, swaying closer, and her palms slid up his hard chest despite her determination to keep them stiffly at her sides. By degrees, her mouth softened until it clung to the sculpted lines of his. *God, he tasted good. Like furious masculine need and…dark sin.*

Against her mouth he growled, "Dammit," in between bites and a light suction that made her senses swim. "I didn't want to do this…don't want this."

His words took a couple of seconds to register and when they did Lilah shoved back, feeling unaccountably wounded. She gave him the sharp edge of her shoulder and out the corner of her eye she caught sight of a muscle twitching in his hard jaw as though he was barely holding himself in check.

Good. At least she wasn't the only one struggling with control issues.

Turning to glare daggers at him, Lilah deliberately wiped the back of her hand across her mouth as though to erase the feel and taste of him. *Right, as if.*

Stung by his words as much as his manner, she demanded, "Why are you here, then?"

Luke sighed, planted his big hands on his hips and narrowed his eyes as though she made his head hurt. Considering the unexpected blow to her heart, that made them even.

"Someone has to look out for you."

"Don't be ridiculous," she snapped, and swung away to hide the raw hurt in her eyes. "I can take care of myself." She'd been taking care of herself a long time and was tired of doing everything alone.

She lifted a hand to rub at the ache in her chest.

"Sure you can," he growled, interrupting her pity party. "That's why I find you sitting on the floor of a parking garage at midnight with your car and cell batteries dead. That's why I… Are you crying?"

"Don't flatter yourself." She wasn't, she assured herself, swiping at the scalding tears with her arm. She was just so… so…mad. Mad at him. Mad at herself. Mad at the world. She sniffed and her eyes swam again. *Dammit.*

"C'm'ere," Luke growled, yanking her against him in a move that was more irritable than caring. But when she stiffened and tried to shove him away, he tightened his arms and dropped his chin on her head. The effort of keeping everything together until she was alone was too much and with a strangled sob Lilah buried her face against him as hot tears finally erupted, instantly soaking the soft, warm fabric of his shirt.

She didn't know how long he stood in the dim parking garage simply holding her as she cried about stuff that didn't even make any sense.

Finally, when the storm of weeping passed, she discovered she'd burrowed as close as she could to his warm strength and was gripping his T-shirt with both hands—as though to keep him from escaping. But his big arms had trapped her close as though he didn't intend letting her go any time soon.

She was fine with that. *Really.* She kind of liked the feel of him against her. She liked the sound of his heart thudding beneath her ear and the warm smell of man making her senses swim. It was comforting and kind of…relaxing.

But she'd be fine in a minute.

"Bad day?" His voice rumbled in her ear and sent warm little vibrations zinging through her body. She burrowed even closer and nodded.

"Wanna talk about it?" His big warm hand smoothed a path of comfort from the back of her head down the length of her spine and up again. Lilah quickly shook her head. She really didn't. She wanted to continue standing there wrapped in his arms, feeling warm and safe. She wanted to pretend this was real and not just some hot guy feeling sorry for her because she was a mess.

After a moment Luke loosened his hold and gently put a few inches between them. Cool air rushed over Lilah and she shivered at the abrupt withdrawal of his heat. Ducking her head, she sucked in air, totally embarrassed by her emotional outburst.

She wasn't normally this needy.

"Let's get you home," he growled, sliding his hand down her back to her waist, urging her in the direction of his motorbike. His voice had been deep and rough with suppressed emotion but when Lilah sneaked a peek his face was impassive.

"When last did you eat something?" he asked, opening a side compartment on the bike to remove a spare helmet. Lilah couldn't remember but shook her head before drying her wet cheek on her shoulder. Her stomach revolted at the thought of food.

"I'm not hungry." She took the helmet from him and watched as he pulled on a huge leather jacket. It reminded her of the one she still had in her hallway closet.

"You ever been on one of these?" he asked, zipping up the front with long, tanned fingers. Lilah shook her head, too absorbed—and maybe a little intimidated—by the bad-ass picture he made dressed in black leather, biker boots and well-worn jeans. She shivered—and not just because she was cold.

Pausing, Luke stared at her like she'd just admitted to something indecent. "You're kidding, right?"

She didn't know why she flushed. Guys in black leather had never appealed to her before. Especially not guys radiating sex appeal and testosterone from a hundred paces.

His mouth curled into a wicked smile and his eyes twinkled. "I'd have thought a girl like you would be used to being on the back of some hog with a bad boy."

Lilah narrowed her gaze and stood with one knee bent and her fists on her hips. "A girl like me?"

Luke laughed and fisted the front of her T to yank her against him before dropping a hard, hot kiss on her sulky mouth. "Don't get all bent out of shape, Wild Woman," he grinned, taking the helmet from her nerveless fingers. "I only meant girls who look like you always have a long line of bad boys lined up to take them for a wild ride around town."

Lilah stared at him open-mouthed, knowing he was suggesting something a lot more X-rated than a mere ride around town. "You're kidding, right?"

"Nope. In fact…" he tugged an escaped curl "…I can just picture you flipping all these wild curls over your shoulder and fluttering those hell-smoke eyes at some poor dumb sap. I bet you were beautiful and offhand, leaving a trail of broken hearts."

Lilah snorted at the ridiculous picture he painted. "I was plain and way too serious," she informed him. "Guys don't go for plain, nerdy redheads."

Luke shook his head as though she was deluding herself. "Don't kid yourself. There's nothing plain about you. You're a study in rose, gold and cream and you hide all that simmering passion behind those smoky eyes and neat outfits. It's a wonder you don't combust with all that suppressed emotion."

He shoved the helmet down over her head and all Lilah could think was, *Simmering passion? Me?*

She flipped up the visor to scowl at him. "My mother warned me about boys like you," she said primly, snatching her jacket from him and growling when he laughed because he was as far from a boy as he could get and still carry similar DNA.

"Your mother's a smart woman." He pulled on his own helmet and swung his long leg over the bike to settle on the padded seat. Kicking up the bike stand, he shoved up his visor and the grin he aimed her way was as wicked as his gaze. "But don't worry, wild thing. You're safe with me," he drawled an instant before the bike started with a throaty roar.

No, she wasn't, Lilah thought. *Not really. And certainly not in the way he implied.* But she must be a wild woman because the next thing she knew she was climbing up behind him and placing her hands on his waist. She nearly moaned when his muscles shifted as he turned his head, reminding her of their wild night in a wild storm. His green eyes caught and held hers and Lilah shivered at the heat in them.

"Put your arms around me, wild thing," Luke crooned, his voice all low and rough and wickedly suggestive. "And hold on tight."

For a long heated moment they stared at each other until Lilah could scarcely breathe. She was fighting an over-whelming impulse to escape. Or to hold on as tight as she could. And never let go.

Spooked by her thoughts and the simmering intensity suddenly crackling in the air around them, Lilah flipped the visor closed and gingerly wrapped her arms around his hard body as though he were a live grenade.

For a moment longer Luke's gaze remained on her until he revved the engine and finally turned away to take off towards the exit ramp. By the time the cool mountain air brushed her body she was plastered against his back as though she wanted to be part of him. She could feel every move and muscle twitch from her knees to her shoulders. Every part that was fused to him tingled and melted in the heat pumping off him like a nuclear reactor. It was kind of embarrassing just how much she tingled and melted in places he'd awakened from permafrost just nine days ago.

Embarrassing and exhilarating.

Once they left the city limits and hit the road leading up through the mountains around the lake Luke opened up the engine and Lilah squeezed her eyes closed and pressed closer. Fortunately the roads were quiet as they zipped along the winding road. And each time he shifted, leaning into the curves, she moved and shifted with him.

Sucking in a shaky breath, Lilah wondered if she was imagining the rising heat and excitement. But then laughter rumbled through him and she knew he was doing it delib-erately. Deliberately making her press closer. Deliberately making her tighten her arms and grip his narrow hips and thighs with hers in an attempt to keep from flying off into the darkness.

He was a danger to women everywhere and he knew it. But for some reason she couldn't be mad. Despite the ter-ror of whipping through the night at breakneck speed, she was enjoying the hard powerful feel of him against her and wondered at the bubbles of terrified excitement popping in her veins.

She knew the instant they entered the older, more shabbily genteel suburb of Greenstone Park, where she'd grown up. Luke slowed and geared down to make a couple of turns and Lilah lifted her head to give him directions but he was already turning into her driveway and bringing the bike to a stop.

For an insane moment she didn't want to move, didn't want to let him go. But that was ridiculous. She was fine. She didn't need anyone, especially someone like him. Besides, he most likely had plans of his own and couldn't wait to dump her on her doorstep.

By the time he killed the engine and released the bike stand Lilah had loosened her death grip around his waist. She used his wide shoulders to help with balance as she dismounted, grateful for the hand he shot out when her knees wobbled. She pulled off the helmet and looked up to find his features in deep shadow.

"You could have killed us," she huffed, thrusting the helmet at his belly, but all he did was grin and toss it into a side compartment.

"Please," he snorted, raking a hand through his tousled hair. "I'm an expert."

Lilah snorted her opinion of his delusional statement and rooted around in her shoulder bag for her house keys. "Thanks for the lift," she began, then halted abruptly when she realized he'd gone ahead and was leaning casually against the pillar holding up her porch. He looked big and sinfully dangerous in the dark and she shivered—a good and bad kind of shiver. One that stole her breath, tightened her nipples and clenched the muscles in her thighs. Definitely bad, but it felt so-o-o good.

"What are you doing?" Her voice emerged all breathless and panicky.

"Waiting," he drawled quietly, and the rough, sexy sound
reached out and stroked over her flesh, drawing her towards
him, stealing her will to resist.

"For what?"

His teeth gleamed white in the darkness as he chuckled. "Coffee?"

Lilah gulped and fiddled with the strap of her purse.
"What if I don't have coffee?" she squeaked breathlessly.
"What if I want to be alone?"

He chuckled again, dark and velvet soft, before reaching
out to grab the front of her jacket. He reeled her in slowly
and the glitter in his eyes made her suck in a sharp, excited breath.

She let out a soft "Oomph" as her body thudded against
his.

He leaned down to murmur, "Do you want to be alone?"
in her ear. Hot shivers raced over Lilah's skin, leaving behind a chaos of sensation and goose bumps.

Holy cow, the man was lethal.

She knew she needed to take a step back but the instant
she looked up past his square jaw to his sculpted lips she
couldn't move. Her senses swam and a dangerous lassitude
invaded her limbs. She wanted that mouth on her more than
she wanted sleep.

"No. *Yes*," she gulped, planting her palms against his
chest and attempting to wedge a little space between them so
she could breathe without inhaling the potent mix of testosterone and pheromones that never failed to steal her mind.

"No? Or yes?"

"Um…"

His chuckle was deliciously deep, as though he knew
what he was doing to her. "Why don't I help you make up
your mind, wild thing?" he murmured against her throat,

before sucking the delicate skin into his mouth. Sensation, hot, liquid and exciting, shot into every nerve ending and Lilah abruptly became light-headed.

"I…um…" she stammered on a shaky sigh. "I don't think—"

"Good," he growled, snatching the keys from her grasp as he nipped her ear lobe and slipped his hand beneath her little tank, his warm, rough palm scraping already painfully sensitive nerve endings. "Don't think. Just feel."

He one-handedly inserted the key into the lock and the next thing he was dragging her inside and kicking the door shut. Feeling a little dazed, Lilah swayed and then she was being shoved back against the door as Luke took her mouth with barely controlled violence. As though the tight leash he'd had on his emotions had suddenly snapped.

"I thought you didn't want to do this?" she moaned against his mouth.

"That's the problem," he muttered, nipping at her lips. "I do." Taking advantage of her gasp, his tongue invaded her mouth, the wildly exciting masculine impatience frying all her mental circuits. She could almost hear the snap and sizzle as each IQ point fizzled out beneath the heated onslaught. And when he abandoned her lips to streak a line of fire down her throat and tease a thumb over her tight nipple, Lilah gave a long, low moan and arched into his hands.

She blinked against the light exploding behind her eyelids. "I thought…I thought you wanted coffee," she gasped, fisting his soft, dark hair as his big hands closed over her lace-covered breasts.

Luke bit her neck and then sucked her abused flesh into his hot mouth, making her shudder with excitement. "I don't need coffee," he growled, tightening his grasp and returning to her mouth, where he peppered her lips with teasing nips until she growled in frustration and tried to bite him.

His chuckle was dark as sin.

"What...do...you...need?" Lilah panted, locking her shaky knees at what he clearly had in mind.

Without replying, Luke released her, retreating a couple of feet to stand breathing heavily in the dark. For one awful moment she thought he was backing off. But then he planted a shoulder in her middle and the next thing she was upside down as he jogged up the stairs.

She gave a shocked "*Oomph*" and made a grab for his shirt in an attempt to hold on but encountered smooth, warm skin instead. Momentarily distracted, she let her free hand touch all that yummy hard flesh until a sharp slap on her bottom got her attention.

"Bedroom?" Luke rumbled, and Lilah barely managed to squeak out a reply. The next minute she was flying through the air. She landed with a bounce and a giggle, all the exhaustion and trauma of the past few weeks wiped out by his playful mood.

The air stirred and after a brief pause soft light spilled from the bedside lamp, driving back the darkness. Lilah's breath caught. While most of him was still in darkness, lamplight revealed a portion of Luke's rock-hard abs, his long jeans-clad legs and the impressive bulge behind his zipper. Her pulse lurched drunkenly at the sight. He was hugely aroused, the thick shaft clearly visible beneath the soft, worn denim.

Her breath escaped in a loud whoosh as her avid gaze ate up the vision of masculine perfection standing over her. Then he reached for his zipper and before Lilah had looked her fill he was shoving his jeans and underwear down his legs and reaching for her sneakers. Within seconds he'd stripped her naked and joined her on the bed, his big body enveloping her in delicious heat.

For a couple of beats she blinked up at him, panting like she'd been the one to jog up the stairs carrying a hundred pounds over her shoulder. He was hot and hard against her and Lilah shifted languorously, enjoying the sensation of skin on skin and the anticipation of what was to come. A growl rumbled in his chest and his eyes, sleepy and aroused, burned like green fire.

Lilah's pulse gave a little bump of fear and excitement. The excitement was a no-brainer but the fear was new. Wild, uncontrolled emotions were racing through her, making her hyperaware of every inch of skin-on-skin contact. They were so sharp and painfully intense that a little voice at the back of her mind urged her to run—escape while she still could.

Her body tensed and her heart thundered as she prepared to obey but then—as if he could read her intent—Luke thrust long fingers into her messy curls. Holding her in place, he lowered his head and nipped at her chin.

"I have you trapped, wild thing," he rasped against her flesh. "There's no escape."

"There…there's not?"

He shook his head and dragged his mouth to her ear. "You had your chance."

And Lilah thought, *No, I never stood a chance.* Not against this. Not against the green eyes that were sometimes bright with arousal or laughter, or dark and brooding. And certainly not against the intense pull of his aura on hers.

Then his teeth nipped at her lobe and she gave a full-body shudder, all thoughts of secrets extinguished. Her nipples tightened into aching points and her belly clenched with a deep, aching hunger.

As if he knew what was happening to her, he rasped out, "Now it's mine."

"Y-yours?"

"And I'm ravenous." He opened his mouth over the delicate skin of her throat and sucked it into his mouth, making her moan and shift against him. His fingers tightened against her scalp as though he expected her to bolt. "And I know just where to start."

But the last thing Lilah wanted to do was escape. Not when she ached to touch him. Not when she wanted to experience again the heated rush of anticipation as his mouth moved up to meet hers and his hands greedily claimed her body. She smoothed her palms over his hot, damp skin and arched into his rough touch, her hidden places clenching in wild anticipation. Oh God, yes!

Dragging his mouth over her skin, Luke teased her with barely there kisses until she was breathless and eager for the taste of him. Fisting her hands in his hair, she nipped his lips once, then again.

"Kiss me," she ordered huskily, and with a savage curse he did.

CHAPTER ELEVEN

LILAH STARED INTO the steaming coffee she was stirring and ignored the greasy donut at her elbow along with the discussion going on around her. Her mind was a chaos of panicked thoughts and erotic images of the past month. Ever since Luke had moved in with her, in fact. And she was only vaguely aware of Angie filling Jenna in on all the gossip she'd missed.

Since she'd already heard it all, Lilah had lapsed into her own thoughts. Thoughts that seemed to find their way to the same place, no matter how hard she tried to think of something—anything—else. Thoughts of disasters and history repeating itself.

And, boy, was her current disaster a doozy.

Not that she was ready to share the details with anyone. At least not until she'd stopped hyperventilating and come to terms with it herself. *If she ever did.* But, frankly, she'd never considered *this*—mostly because she'd always been so careful never to make the same mistakes as her mother.

Hey, Mom, look at me now!

Like an idiot, she'd excused her fatigue, emotional vulnerability and lack of appetite on the lingering effects of the crash and long shifts at the hospital. And when Luke had asked if she was okay she'd told him she sometimes reacted to stress with an upset stomach.

Boy, had she been wrong.

Fortunately he'd already left this morning when the scent of the coffee he'd placed beside her bed had sent her scrambling for the bathroom. Once her stomach had stopped heaving she'd rushed out to the nearest pharmacy and bought a few early detection kits. Unfortunately HCG levels didn't lie. Little pink lines didn't lie.

At least, not five sets of them.

She was pregnant. And when she counted back she realized it had been well over two months since her last period, more than a month since the crash and…and almost four weeks since the night her car wouldn't start. Nearly four weeks since that wild mountain ride.

And not once during all that time had they forgotten to use a condom. Except…*yikes*…except for that one time at the ranger's chalet after she'd treated his snake bite. Besides, she was still supposed to be protected by her IUD—which was why she hadn't worried. *Dammit*. Which wouldn't be a problem if the father of her baby wasn't allergic to commitment…or children.

She really didn't want to think about his reaction to her news. It brought back memories she'd rather not deal with.

Besides, Luke wasn't a permanent kind of guy. He'd told her that after ten years in the military he'd only taken the job to ease back into civilian life before deciding what he wanted to do. He'd said nothing about a future with her and when she'd tried to tell him the other night that she understood "this" was a temporary thing, he hadn't disagreed.

Lilah wasn't stupid. She could read between the lines. He didn't need to tell her he had "Temporary: enjoy while you can" stamped on his sexy butt and that all he was looking for was a wild welcome-back-to-civilian-life fling.

She sighed gloomily. *Some fling!*

Besides, he owned a motorbike, for goodness' sake, and everyone knew that guys who owned motorbikes—especially ones that big—weren't the settling-down kind. They

were ready to hit the road when the mood struck. They were
ready to take the next available babe on a terrifyingly exhilarating mountain ride before stripping her naked, toss-
ing her down onto the nearest bed and showing her heaven.
And if the thought of him doing what he'd done to her with
some other woman made Lilah's belly cramp, she blamed
it on the smell of greasy donuts and her fragile stomach.

Frankly, she wasn't ready for more than a fling either,
but things had kind of ambushed her and she no longer
had a choice. Oh, she knew there *were* choices she could
make—if she were so inclined. She wasn't. Wouldn't *ever*
be, in fact. And despite the inherent difficulties, the more
she thought about it, the more she realized how much she
wanted this baby.

She shivered and placed a hand over her belly.

Luke's baby.

Unfortunately, she had to face the fact that he didn't want
children. Or maybe he just didn't want children with *her*?
Lilah sucked in a sharp breath. *Jeez. That* was something
she hadn't considered.

And she would later. Maybe.

Her breath escaped on a whoosh.

Right now her emotions were all over the place and she
was smiling one minute and on the verge of tears the next.
The last thing she wanted to think about was her crappy
past. Clearly, the best thing she could do was concentrate
on her future—a future that would most likely comprise
only her and her child.

Oh, boy.

"I leave for a few weeks and you get yourself into all
sorts of trouble."

What? Lilah jolted, slopping hot coffee over the top of the
disposable cup and scalding her hand. Yelping, she quickly
sucked at the abused flesh before darting her startled gaze
between her friends.

"What?" Had she spoken her thoughts aloud? More importantly, had she said anything revealing? Both Jenna and Angie were staring at her with the kind of look someone gave when you were about to be carted off to the loony ward. *Yeesh.* "Are you talking to me?"

Jenna leaned close and laid a hand on Lilah's arm. "Honey, are you all right?" she asked, sweetly concerned. "That's the fifth time you've sighed in the past two minutes."

"Yeah, and you've been stirring that coffee for at least ten. And what's with all the frowning, head shakes and blowing out air like you're a leaky inner tube? It's disturbing. It's like you're arguing with yourself in your head."

"That's...that's ridiculous," Lilah spluttered, and hurriedly thought up a believable lie. "I'm just worried about Jeff, that's all."

"Jeff? Who's Jeff?" Jenna demanded. "A new boyfriend? I thought Luke—"

"He's a patient," Lilah said quickly, and because she needed something to occupy her hands she picked up the donut and began ripping off pieces. "He's...um... I mean I thought he was doing better but he contracted another infection."

She knew she was babbling but she desperately needed to divert their attention away from the soap opera that was her life. She wasn't ready to discuss her...um, problem, mainly because there wasn't anything to discuss. Not yet, anyway. Besides, a few wild nights did not make a relationship, let alone an affair, even with a little complication eight months or so away.

"But enough about me." She grasped desperately at the first thing that came to mind. "Look at you. You're positively glowing. That must have been some honeymoon."

"It was *the* most fabulous honeymoon ever," Jenna agreed dreamily, and Lilah's breath whooshed out softly at having dodged a bullet. "It was…awesome." Jenna's mouth curved. "And so was he."

"Fine, rub it in," Angie snapped, pointing her half-eaten pastry at her. "Lilah's right. You do look disgustingly glowy."

Jenna waved aside their jealousy. "You have good reason to be envious, girls. But I fail to see what it has that to do with Lilah's sighing."

"It doesn't," Angie snorted. "She's annoyed that you're getting some and she's taking it out on her donut." She turned to Lilah with narrow-eyed speculation that was a little alarming. "Aren't you?"

Lilah froze. Angie was staring at her as though waiting for her to come clean about some deep, dark secret. *Hoo, boy*, she thought hysterically. *She knows. How does she know?* Her face heated beneath the scrutiny.

"I…uh… What was the question again?"

"Huh," Angie huffed, as though Lilah had just confirmed her suspicions. She studied Lilah silently over the top of her disposable cup for a couple of beats before adding almost conversationally, "Now that I think about it, you've been like this for a while."

Jenna perked up, as though sensing juicy gossip. "Like what?" she and Lilah demanded at the same time.

"Distracted, goofy smile, frowning, sighing all the time." Angie ignored Lilah and addressed Jenna. "It's sickening."

Jenna frowned. "It is?"

"Yep. Just like you were with Greg." They both turned to stare at Lilah.

"Omigod," Jenna gasped. "She's in love."

"Wha-a-at?" Lilah practically shrieked, and sat up so fast her coffee went flying all over the mutilated donut. *"No!* Don't be ridiculous," she said with a strained laugh, and grabbed a wad of paper napkins as she swung her gaze

frantically between her two friends. She shook her head forcefully and blustered, "That's just...*ridiculous*."

Wasn't it?

Sure it is, she scoffed silently, mopping up a soggy mess. They'd only known each other a short time and...and he was leaving. Her shoulders sagged. Besides, he was from a prominent family and she'd learnt the hard way that girls like her didn't have happily-ever-afters with guys like him. Falling in love with Luke would be stupid...and...*and, God,* so darn inevitable.

She deflated like an inner tube just as several people entered the cafeteria.

The hair on Lilah's neck rose in warning. She looked up and caught sight of tousled coffee-colored hair—hair she'd had her hands in a little over twelve hours ago—a familiar broad back and...*uh-oh*...her nipples tightened.

She sucked in a startled breath and had to clench her thighs together to stop her body's visceral response from becoming public knowledge. *Holy bejeezers, this is getting out of hand,* she told herself. *And exactly what got you knocked up in the first place.*

A blush crept into her face and she didn't know whether to wrap her arms across her breasts or hide her flat belly—as if to protect the precious new life nestled there.

As though sensing her chaotic thoughts, Luke turned his head and their eyes met, his mouth kicking up at one corner in a wicked half-smile that made her breathless. Okay, he was hot but that didn't mean she was 'in love' with him.

Besides, that would make her an idiot and...and suddenly the room disappeared and it was just the two of them. Lilah felt as though she was suspended in simmering heat waves of sensation. Blood drained from her head and she thought, *Holy cow, it's... Dammit, this is a nightmare.*

He must have suspected something was up because he frowned and without taking his eyes from hers broke away from the group to head in their direction. Through the buzzing noise in her ears she heard Angie say, "Yep, she's got it bad, all right." She turned to Lilah. "So tell me again what happened in the mountains?"

Lilah stared wide-eyed at the blatant intent on Luke's face and gave a strangled sound of distress. There was no way she could pretend she wasn't having an emotional meltdown. Not with everyone watching and listening like she was the new hospital soap opera. She'd either burst into tears or laugh hysterically and blurt out the truth.

And, really, she couldn't face him right now. Not with this HUGE secret she was hiding.

So Lilah did the only rational thing she could think of. Shoving back from the table, she lurched to her feet and with a strangled "Can't talk now," she bolted from the room, conscious of the shocked gazes following her retreat.

Luke watched Lilah blanch then turn rosy as a blush crept up her neck into her cheeks. He might have been concerned by the look of horror on her face if he wasn't instantly distracted by the memory of tracing that delicate tide of color with his lips. Just thinking about it made him a little crazy— as though she was a drug he'd suddenly become addicted to and couldn't be without. And when he remembered the unbelievably sexy sounds she made in the back of her throat, his body went hard and his lips curved in anticipation.

He'd never met a woman who was such a mass of suppressed simmering passion. And when he thought of the way she ignited in his arms, he discovered something about himself that made him a little uncomfortable. A very primitive need to be the only man to see those cool grey eyes turn all smoky an instant before her body caught fire. Because just the thought of her with someone else made him want to hit something.

But those were dangerous thoughts. He'd watched his

parents' marriages implode and had decided a long time ago that he wasn't hard-wired for love and marriage. Besides, the last thing his children needed was the Sullivan brand of marital hell he and his brothers had endured.

Realizing the direction of his thoughts, Luke snorted. Since when was he thinking about marriage and kids? He had no intention of having either. He'd clearly lost his mind and it was all Lilah's fault.

The other night after his heart rate had slowed he'd caught her watching him with solemn grey eyes. And when he'd asked if something was wrong she'd told him she didn't want him to worry about her getting any ideas.

Ideas? What the hell?

Blissfully unaware of his stunned confusion, she'd hurriedly assured him that as far as she was concerned they were just having a temporary fling because she needed to concentrate on getting her life in order. *In order for what?* Besides, he was leaving soon, she'd said, and she was okay with them just messing around until then.

Okay? Messing around? Again, what the hell?

He'd felt a little insulted that so soon after making her eyes roll back in her head she was telling him he was a messy distraction. Instead of being happy—because he sure as hell didn't want anything more than a hot fling—he'd been annoyed because he'd suddenly realized that he wasn't ready to move on. And he certainly wasn't ready for Lilah to move on.

But something was obviously wrong, he thought with a frown, because she was acting weird. Maybe she was having second thoughts about them. Maybe she'd been trying to tell him that she'd met someone else and was letting him down easy.

Easy? Hell. Luke's gut clenched at the thought, and with narrow-eyed determination he headed across the room.

He must have looked a little fierce because Lilah's eyes

widened and she shoved back from the table and scrambled for the exit.

Not about to let her escape, he followed, determined to get to the bottom of her weird behavior.

He found her slumped against the wall beside the elevators, hands over her face and muttering like she was casting a spell—or talking to herself.

He said casually, "Hey, what's up?" and chuckled when she squeaked and lurched upright like he'd zapped her. He wanted to know what the hell she'd been thinking about to put that look of horrified guilt on her face.

"I'd give anything to know what you're thinking right now," he drawled, propping his shoulder against the wall and folding his arms across his chest.

Lilah shook her head, looking adorably flustered—and nervous. Nervous?

"No, you wouldn't," she said, blowing irritably at a tendril of hair. He reached out a hand to tuck the silky strands behind her ear and smiled smugly when his touch made her shiver.

"How do you know I wouldn't?"

She rolled her eyes and scuttled backwards. "Because I'm thinking about how cute babies are even when they're upchucking on you."

"Cute?" he snorted, grinning when he spied some unidentified stains on her scrub top that he assumed was baby upchuck. "There's nothing cute about infant projectile vomiting and even less about it coming out the other end."

Lilah grimaced and shoved him away. "They're not always doing that."

He snorted again. "Right, other times they're screaming loud enough to strip paint off the walls."

Lilah's heart sank. "You really hate kids, don't you?"

Luke ruffled her hair like she was twelve. "Nah. Kids are okay." Her heart lifted hopefully and she managed a smile that faded at his next words. "As long as they're someone else's." He shook his head. "But not for me. I'm not father material."

"How do you know that?" Lilah demanded, and the look on Luke's face sent her spirits plummeting. Dammit, she was getting whiplash with all these wildly swinging emotions.

"I just do," Luke drawled, folding his arms across his chest. "We're products of our upbringing and whether we like it or not history tends to repeat itself." *No kidding*, Lilah thought with a touch of hysteria. "I have absolutely no intention of inflicting my childhood on an innocent kid."

"Who said you would? I mean, you're not your father."

"I know myself," he said with a finality that had tears stinging the backs of her eyes. Reaching out, he brushed a knuckle along her jaw. "Hey, what's up? You seem…I don't know. Sad. Nervous. And you're pale. Is something wrong? Are you still sick?" he asked gently, just as the doors opened to reveal a few department heads with their briefcases.

Peter Webster smiled when he spotted Lilah. Ignoring Luke, he pressed the button to hold the doors open. "You coming, Dr. Meredith?"

Hugely relieved at the offer of escape, she smiled back. "Yes," she said at the same time Luke said, "No," effortlessly preventing her from stepping into the elevator. He even pulled her close in an uncharacteristically possessive move. "We'll take the next one."

When the doors finally closed, Lilah demanded, "What are you doing?" and shoved away from him to retreat a few paces. The only way she could say what needed to be said was to be far away from the temptation to cling and maybe even beg a little. Because this whole disaster had made her realize one important, irrefutable fact. Her feelings for Luke Sullivan were in no way casual. And despite her insistence they were having nothing more than a fling, the joke was clearly on her. What she felt for him was as casual as an outbreak of hemorrhagic fever.

Distressed by the unwelcome realization, she wrapped her arms around herself. "Listen, Luke," she began hoarsely. "I um…I think we need to um…talk."

"Uh-oh," he said, narrowing his eyes on her. "I think I know where this is going?"

Lilah's pulse leapt with alarm. How could he know when she'd just found out this morning?

"You…do?"

"It's okay, Lilah," he sighed, irritably shoving an impatient hand through his hair. "I get it. I got it the first time you brought it up and I totally agree."

Lilah frowned with confusion. Brought what up? What was he talking about? "You do?" she asked again, starting to sound like a parrot.

"Yep. You're not into anything serious with me and you want to keep it light. I get it." He shrugged as if it didn't matter but his jaw was hard and his eyes unreadable. "Besides, I just got out of the military and the last thing…the very last thing I want is more responsibility or a serious relationship."

Lilah swallowed past the hot tears clogging her throat. "It is?"

"Yep," he said again. "The Sullivan boys aren't into relationships and I'm enjoying what we have now. I don't suppose I have to tell you that." He lifted a hand and brushed his thumb over her lips, grinning wickedly when she gasped and backed up a step. His gaze heated at the way she licked her lips. "And I know you're having a great time too," he murmured roughly, clearly thinking about how great a time she'd had last night and then again this morning.

Lilah blushed, tempted to slide into his seductive green gaze and forget everything but the way he made her feel. But she would still be pregnant and he would still be against having children. "I did…I mean I am, but the thing is…" She paused and drew in a shaky breath. "Things, um, change and I—" Suddenly they heard voices and Lilah panicked. "I have to go."

"Not so fast," Luke growled, wrapping his big hand around her arm and guiding her towards the emergency exit. "You're not running away now."

"Wha—? No," she said, but Luke tugged her through the door. "I'm not running." *Much.* "I just can't have this conversation now, that's all."

"What conversation is that?" he demanded, his back to the stairwell door, as though to prevent her escape.

Lilah flushed and nervously smoothed her hair off her face, wondering if she could beat him down the stairs. "Well, that I…um…that I can't afford to mess up. Not again. And especially not now."

"Again?" He sighed. "I told you it wasn't your fault."

Her mouth dropped open. "You did?"

"You're not responsible for other people's actions," he said with gentle insistence. "Your father doesn't deserve you and that moron ex-boss should be arrested. Stop punishing yourself."

"Oh, that."

Luke frowned at her lack of enthusiasm. "What did you think I meant?"

Lilah drew in a shaky breath and blinked back tears. She couldn't do this now. Maybe not ever.

"Nothing. It doesn't matter. I just don't think we should see each other again…I mean, with my career and you…" She petered out at the look on his face.

"And me what?" he demanded, looking a little insulted.

"Well, you're…leaving," she said lamely.

"Yes, but not right now." Luke shoved his hands on his hips. "What the hell is this about, Lilah? I thought this was what you wanted. A good time with no strings."

She licked her lips nervously and couldn't stop a flood

of tears obscuring her vision. She wrapped her arms around her body and her gaze slid away guiltily as she drew in a shaky breath. "The thing is…" She gulped.

In the loaded silence Luke finished her sentence for her with, "You've met someone else?"

Lilah was too shocked to say anything other than, "*Wha-at*?"

"That's it, isn't it?" he growled, and then next instant he pushed her against the stairwell wall, and pinning her hands above her head, pressed his body against hers. "So who is it? Webster?" Lilah lifted her head to stare into his furious green eyes. The automatic denial that rose to her lips died.

Misinterpreting her silence, Luke snarled and pushed closer.

"Fine, then."

"What are you doing?" she squeaked breathlessly, and froze when she felt his hardness against her belly. He was angry and aroused; a combination that made her pulse leap and her blood heat.

"Let's call this a farewell kiss, then, shall we?" he ground out furiously, and lowered his head, crushing her mouth with his and stifling Lilah's gasp.

The kiss instantly spiraled out of control and she was helpless against the onslaught. For several seconds she tried to block out the feelings he aroused in her, but she'd never been successful at ignoring him or the way he made her feel. With a ragged moan she slid her hands up his chest and melted against him.

As though her surrender was the sign he'd been waiting for, Luke abruptly released her wrists and shoved away from her.

"Webster? Seriously?" he panted, looking savagely pleased when she sagged against the wall and stared at him through passion-dazed eyes. "He'll toss you aside faster than a used movie ticket. Is that what you want?"

And when she continued to stare at him he cursed and turned away, ripping open the stairwell door before flinging one last parting shot over his shoulder. "*Fine*. Just… stay out of trouble," he grated hoarsely, before disappearing.

Lilah gaped at the closing door, vaguely conscious that she was breathing heavily and that her body felt boneless. It was all she could do to remain propped against the wall. After a couple of beats she lifted a shaky hand to her bruised lips and thought, *Holy bejeezers. What the heck just happened?*

And why did it make her feel as though her heart was being ripped from her chest? And why was she shivering, hugging herself and crying about the emptiness left behind?

Shoving her fist in her bruised mouth to stifle the sobs, Lilah heard the echo of his final snarled words. *Stay out of trouble?* A hysterical laugh caught in her throat. Oh, boy. That was rich, considering she'd landed herself in a huge heap of it.

And he thought she'd met someone else. Could *be* with anyone else after being with him. Dammit, didn't he know he was like a level-five tornado, sucking up everything in his path? Her bones, her breath…her mind. And she'd need all three if she was going to do this alone because one thing was certain: the Meredith women were idiots when it came to men.

Sighing, Lilah banged her head against the wall as though the move would shake loose the memory of his eyes blazing with wounded anger. Although that was probably just his pride, she thought, because he'd never once hinted that he felt anything for her other than lust.

And she couldn't stay knowing it would fizzle out just as quickly as it had exploded. She couldn't do that to him or her…their child.

Finally Lilah pushed away from the wall. And feeling

more alone than she'd ever felt in her life, she headed down the stairs on heavy, shaky legs.

She really was on her own.

CHAPTER TWELVE

LUKE IGNORED THE people scurrying out of his way and headed for the ER like a man on a mission. At four o'clock this morning he'd gone jogging to clear his head and unclench his gut from the ball of tension that had taken up permanent residence there since he'd left Lilah slumped against the wall in the stairwell, tears swimming in her silvery eyes.

God, the memory of her devastated expression made him feel like a class-A bastard. And after replaying their conversation a million times in his head, he realized that he'd allowed his screwed-up childhood to blind him to the truth. A truth he'd ignored simply because the jumble of confusing emotions Lilah roused in him scared the hell out of him.

He'd looked into her eyes and felt his chest tighten with something he'd never felt before. He'd wanted to crush her close and never let go. He'd wanted to fight all her demons and protect her when he'd never felt the urge before. He'd also wanted to run. Far and fast.

And then she'd sprouted all that garbage about needing to focus on her career and he'd jumped to stupid conclusions, kissing her like he wanted to swallow her whole—before storming away like a rejected adolescent. And later, when he'd seen her with Webster, he'd gone a little crazy because, despite everything, the damn woman had burrowed beneath his skin and wormed her way into his heart.

And now that he was ready to listen, she wouldn't talk.

In fact, she'd gone AWOL and no one knew where she was. Or they weren't talking. Especially not to him. But, *dammit*, he missed her. Missed her smile and the way she made him feel—even when he didn't want to acknowledge it—like he'd finally come home.

And he'd honestly thought she was starting to feel the same way. Until she'd blindsided him with the "I don't think we should see each other" speech. But now, recalling the look of misery on her face, he had to wonder if something else wasn't wrong. Like someone harassing her—threatening to have her fired if she didn't play their sick game. Someone like Webster.

Luke growled low in his throat and vowed retribution if he found out the guy was up to his old tricks with her. As an army ranger he knew a hundred ways to get a man to spill his guts. And he'd use every one of them on the slimeball and enjoy it.

Pausing before the ER doors, Luke pulled out his phone and checked in case Lilah had returned his calls. She hadn't. And he was really starting to worry. Especially since no one knew where she was other than she'd taken a couple of sick days.

He'd tried calling her last night but she hadn't answered and eventually his calls had gone straight to voicemail. So he'd gone to her house but it had been in darkness and she hadn't answered when he'd pounded on the door. If her neighbor hadn't stuck her head out an upstairs window and threatened to call the cops, Luke would have spent the night on her porch—or broken into her house, tied her to the bed and forced the truth from her.

He'd returned home only to head out again at four for a run to clear his head because he hadn't been able to sleep and was clearly a basket case. He was beginning to feel like a stalker. He was beginning to feel that old sense of impending doom. Only this time because he was imagining all kinds of disasters, the worst being that she needed him and he wasn't there.

Thrusting the phone into his pocket, he slammed the doors open with the heel of his hand and ignored the startled looks of people hastily scrambling out of his way as he stomped across the ER waiting room.

He was an army ranger, for God's sake. And considering rangers could find a lone camel in the desert, he could damn well find one annoying woman who thought she could hide from him.

He caught sight of Lilah's friend, Angie Something-or-other, and changed direction, prepared to torture Lilah's whereabouts from her if he had to.

"Where is she?" he growled in lieu of a greeting, and after her initial surprise the woman folded her arms across her chest and looked at him like he was something to be scraped off the bottom of her shoe.

"Why do you care?" she demanded, the hard glint in her narrowed eyes indicating that her mood was as dangerous as his. But Luke didn't have time to feel insulted or explain. He was trying to ignore the growing feeling of urgency.

"Of course I care," he spluttered, straightening to his full height and mirroring her pose. But the woman obviously didn't know a desperate man when she saw one.

"Oh, right," she snapped. "That's why you accused her of sleeping around and dumped her faster than last year's tinned beans when you found out about the baby. Great way to show you care, dumb-ass."

"I didn't accuse her cheating," he said a little defensively. "I was—" He broke off to frown as something she'd said suddenly registered. "Whoa, back up there, sister. Baby? What baby?"

"Nothing. Forget I said anything."

"Oh, no, you don't," he said, grabbing her arm when she made to walk away. "What the hell are you talking about?"

Angie rolled her eyes. "Why do you think she's been so tired and sick lately?"

Luke stared at her, his mind racing. "She told me it was stress."

Angie snorted derisively. "And you call yourself a doctor. She's about eight weeks pregnant, Sullivan." Luke opened his mouth to say that it was impossible because they'd always used a condom, but before he could get anything out Angie moved closer and growled furiously. "And if you say it's not yours, I'll break your nose."

"Wha—?" He paused and shoved shaking fingers through his hair when he remembered the one time they hadn't used protection. *Oh, man*, eight weeks was about right. "Why didn't she tell me?"

"She tried but you kept going on about leaving and being just like your father, blah, blah, blah. Like you haven't got the guts to be your own man." She glared at him as though daring him to deny it. "And because she thinks it's déjà vu all over again. Only this time it's not her father rejecting her but some rich playboy doctor enjoying… His. Latest. Fling." She punctuated each snarled word with a jab of her finger in his chest.

Luke retreated under the attack and stared at Angie as though she'd stuck a knife between his ribs. Hell, she might as well have stabbed him in the heart. "Wha-at? She said that?"

"She thinks she's not good enough for someone like you," Angie snapped.

"That's ridiculous," Luke growled, and shoved a hand through his hair again with mounting frustration. "I never said that. I *would* never say that. Besides, I joined the army to get away from that kind of life and I have no intention of going back to it." He growled. "It's me, not her."

Angie rolled her eyes and growled low in her throat. "That's the oldest line in the book, you jackass."

Luke opened his mouth to object when he realized she was right. He shut it with a snap, his lips twisting into a derisive smile. He was a jackass and he only had to really look at himself to see that he was nothing like his father.

Thinking he found the situation amusing, Angie punched him. "You arrogant jerk, she and the baby are better off without you."

Luke's amusement faded and his gut turned to stone when he recalled the last expression he'd seen on Lilah's face. Did she really think he wouldn't want her…or the baby they'd made together? Did she really think he was just like his father? Or worse. Hers? "How could she not tell me?" he demanded, but he knew. She'd talked about how cute babies were and he'd reacted negatively.

"You're a smart guy," Angie snorted, but her tone indicated otherwise. "Figure it out. But know one thing, you bastard," she said, suddenly fiercely angry. "If anything happens to her or the baby, I'll kill you myself."

Taken aback by her vehemence, Luke felt the blood drain from his head and wondered if he was going crazy. "Happens to her? What do you mean? Where is she?" He was practically yelling by the time he finished and people were staring, but he didn't care. He grabbed Angie's shoulders and shook her. "Tell me," he snarled, and for a moment the woman stared at him as though he was a crazy person. Hell, he felt crazy—and scared.

"She took a flight call."

"Wha-at?" Luke reared back and gaped at her as his mind raced. *Dammit,* he'd pulled strings to get her off the flight list because he'd known she was still having nightmares.

Hell, *he* was still having nightmares…and flashbacks.

She'd all but fallen out of the mangled chopper and promptly tossed her cookies. She'd been injured and had suffered a mild concussion, and he winced when he remembered the extent of her bruising. How could she do that again? Especially as another storm was moving in from the coast. Especially in her condition?

Luke swore viciously and swung away, feeling the need to punch something—anything.

"I told her not to go," Angie gulped, glaring at him as though he was responsible. "But she wouldn't listen and it's your fault."

Shoving both hands in his hair, Luke fought the feeling of helplessness that gripped him and he experienced gut-wrenching fear for perhaps the first time in his life.

"Who the hell ordered it?" he yelled. "I made sure she was taken off the damn—"

"What the *hell* is going on?" an authoritative voice snapped out behind them, and Luke spun around, fiercely glad of a target deserving of his fury. "You're causing a scene," Webster accused impatiently, before Luke could rip him a new one. "Get back to work, Prescott. Sullivan, aren't you supposed to be off rotation? Because if you can't stay away, I suggest you put on some scrubs and take room four. With Dr. Meredith out on flight call we're short-staffed."

Ignoring Webster's question, which was probably rhetorical anyway, Luke demanded, "Who the hell authorized that flight?" His menacing tone froze the other man in his tracks.

Webster blinked. "I did," he admitted, looking a little wary in the face of Luke's hostility. "But she insisted," he added quickly, when Luke's expression turned murderous. "In fact, she said if I didn't let her go she w-would report me for harassment."

Luke narrowed his eyes. "You're lying."

"I'm not," he denied hotly. "I swear. You can even ask my secretary." He gulped, his eyes widening in his suddenly pale face. "She'll confirm it."

Luke's expression turned grim as fear clenched his gut.

"Where did they go and how long have they been gone?" he demanded, his voice tight with fury.

Webster fidgeted nervously before confessing, "Copper Canyon, and they've only been gone a few hours. We lost contact a little while ago but—"

Luke drew back his arm and planted his fist in the smarmy bastard's well-moisturized face. Webster's head snapped back and there was a collective gasp as he staggered and fell. Everyone who'd gathered to watch the scene taking place froze. No one moved to help the head of ER and after a few stunned moments Peter shook his head and blinked up at Luke like he was struggling to focus.

"What the hell was that for?" he gasped, lifting his hand to the blood pouring from his broken nose.

"That's for sending her out with a storm brewing," Luke snarled like an avenging angel. "That's for putting your hands on her, and daring to breathe in her direction." He bent close, seething with fury and fear. "And if you ever go near her again, I'll—"

"Sullivan!"

Luke turned to glare at Greg Turner hurrying towards them, white-faced and urgent.

"Don't try and stop me, Turner," he snarled. "Someone has to teach this piece of—"

"It's Lilah," Greg gulped, barely giving the man on the floor a second glance. "We just got word. The chopper went down in the storm." He gulped and looked as though he was about to cry. "Man, I'm sorry, buddy. It crashed. The chopper crashed in the mountains."

CHAPTER THIRTEEN

THE NEXT FEW hours were possibly the worst Luke had ever endured. For the first time in his life he was afraid—more afraid than he'd been during the fourteen hours he'd held off enemy forces. More afraid than when his helicopter had been shot down by an RPG and he had been trapped with the dead and dying, wondering if he was going to die himself.

Now all he could think about was Lilah out there somewhere, alone and injured, thinking that she was destined to die in a crash, just like her mother. Thinking he didn't care about her…or their baby.

They needed him and he wasn't going to fail them. Not again.

With that thought uppermost, Luke weaseled—okay, threatened—their last known location from the despatcher and tore through the pouring rain to the nearest airfield. If he couldn't find anyone to fly him in this weather, he would take a chopper, fly it into the mountains himself and face the consequences later.

With the rain making a puddle around him, he whipped out his gold credit card and the keys to his bike and shoved them across the counter. "I need the chopper out front."

"What?" The woman behind the counter gaped at him, probably because he looked a little crazy. "But…but…the storm," she stuttered nervously. "It's too dangerous to fly in that."

"It's an emergency," he snapped, and without waiting headed around the counter towards the large board holding a variety of keys. "I'll pay whatever you want. I'll even buy the damn chopper. Just give me the damn keys."

"Sir, you need to sign papers…a waiver? If you wait a moment I'll call the owner."

"Call the police," Luke informed her curtly. "Call the damn National Guard. I need that chopper now. Which keys?"

"Sir—"

"It's a matter of life and death," Luke interrupted impatiently. "Do you want to be responsible for someone's death?"

The woman paled beneath his challenging stare, her eyes going huge. "I…uh…I'm not sure…"

"I didn't think so. Look, the woman I…I…" Luke paused and felt the earth shift beneath his feet as the truth dawned. He slapped the side of his head and thought, *Of course!* Of course he loved her. He loved her smile, the way she gasped his name when she came; he loved her laugh and the way she got all clumsy when she was flustered.

God, he missed her more than he'd thought possible. And he needed her in his life even though he'd told himself he didn't need anyone. It was the reason he'd reacted so badly when in the past he wouldn't have cared if the woman he was with had found someone else. It was the reason he was frantic to find her, keep her safe.

Keep them both safe.

Dammit. If anything had happened to her… *No.* He shook his head decisively. He couldn't…*wouldn't* lose her. Not now that he'd found her. Not now that he realized he needed her as much if not more than she needed him…because if something happened to her he didn't think he would ever recover from the loss.

But he needed to get a grip, and fast. She needed him

thinking clearly, not panicking like a rookie. And he wasn't going to fail her. Not if he could help it. Not like everyone else in her life.

"The woman I…love is out there somewhere," he said, feeling a little shell-shocked by his discovery and the realization that she was in serious trouble. "She's a doctor on a flight emergency when her chopper went down."

"It's really too dangerous out there," she was saying gently, as though placating an escapee from the psych ward, but Luke barely heard her through the pounding in his head.

Dammit, he was wasting time. "I'm sorry but I'm taking that chopper with or without your permission. I need—"

"Fine," the woman interrupted, and turned to snag a set of keys from the board, which she tossed at him. "Here. Go." She waved him away, calling out, "You'd better bring it back in one piece or I'm calling the police," as he ran into the rain.

Lilah drifted in and out of consciousness, vaguely aware that despite being icy cold and wet, fire engulfed her entire right side. She'd tried moving away from the pain but every time she did it intensified.

Her head felt like someone had split it open with a baseball bat and with every breath nausea swam around in her stomach, threatening a major revolt.

At some point she heard an annoying buzzing sound that roused her but when she strained to listen for it, all she heard was the rain. Oh, and someone groaning. She was pretty sure it wasn't her.

She also thought she heard Luke calling her but when she tried to focus her head hurt so much she wept. Exhausted by her efforts, she let herself be drawn back into the beckoning darkness, only to jolt awake when something brushed her cheek.

Thinking it was a wild animal, Lilah cried out and tried

to shift away, but the move sent pain roaring through her like a firestorm while somewhere close she heard a voice calling.

"Lilah." It must be an angel, she decided, because the sound filled her with a sense of peace, drawing her upwards toward the light.

"Lilah, open your eyes, babe. I've got you."

She opened her mouth to tell the angel that she didn't think she should go with him because then her baby would be alone.

Luke would also be alone and she knew instinctively that he needed her. She wished he was there.

His name emerged on a ragged sigh. "Luke."

"I'm here, sweetheart. I'm here. Why don't you open your eyes and see for yourself? No, don't close them," he murmured soothingly, when she blinked and her eyelids involuntarily drifted shut, despite her best efforts to keep them open.

"That's it, darlin'...just a little more." Lilah blinked his face into focus. "There's my beautiful wild woman." Gentle fingers smoothed her hair off her face. "Tell me where it hurts."

Lilah struggled to focus on the words but they kept getting louder then softer and she couldn't see out of her right eye no matter how many times she blinked.

"It hurts," she whispered, her gaze clinging to his fuzzy outline.

"What does?"

"My...my head. Why can't I see?"

"Don't panic, you hit your head and there's a small laceration." His bulk loomed closer and his fingers moved gently through her hair, probing and soothing. She let out a moan when he hit a particularly tender spot and thought he might have kissed her but wasn't sure. Her forehead wrinkled in confusion and she struggled to make sense of what was happening.

"What…what happened?"

"There was a little accident, sweetheart," he murmured, gently smoothing away the stress between her brows. "But you're going to be fine now. I promise."

Lilah tried shifting to relieve the pressure against her side, and ended up breathing through the pain. "Luke…"

"Yeah?"

"I think…I think the chopper crashed," she rasped heavily. "How bad is it? Where's Jerry? I think I heard him moaning." He moved away briefly, returning to brush his knuckles against her cheek when she cried out.

"I'm just going to move this piece of metal," he promised soothingly. "I'm right here."

Lilah sucked in a breath, moaning when something shifted and pain swept through her like a fiery explosion. "Stop. *Stop!*"

"Hey. *Hey.*" Luke gentled her with a large hand on her uninjured shoulder, smoothing a path to her hand and back again. "I've got to get you out of here, babe, and to do that I have to move you. You trust me, don't you?"

Tears blurred her vision and a sudden thought had her gripping him. "The baby," she said fiercely. "Please tell me the baby is okay!" She broke off on a sob, vaguely aware of hot tears streaming down her face to mingle with cold rain.

"Relax, sweetheart," Luke murmured comfortingly, but Lilah wondered at the hoarseness in his voice. She struggled to see his expression, but it was dark and she couldn't seem to focus.

"Luke—?"

"I'm not going to let anything happen to the baby," he promised fiercely, brushing trembling fingers over her lips. Or was she the one shaking? She didn't know. Only that she was cold and his hands were warm. "But I need to move you and I want you to focus on me, on my eyes. Can you do that for me?"

She blinked up at him and sent him a crooked smile. Of course she could. His eyes were a beautiful green, so full of fierce emotion, and she loved looking into them…loved him.

His gaze caught and held hers, intense and serious and… yet…there was something else there as well. Something she couldn't recognize through the haze of pain. Something that filled her with strength and a warm, hopeful glow. But she needed to tell him something…something important.

"Luke…"

"I've got you. If you believe nothing else, babe. Believe that."

With her eyes locked on his Lilah opened her mouth to reassure him and "Don't let me go," emerged on a strangled sob. The last thing she saw was Luke's fervent expression and heard his equally fervent assurance.

"I don't intend to." His fierce murmur faded into the distance, and just before the darkness claimed her she thought he said, "I love you too much to let go ever again."

Lilah became aware of an irritating beeping noise that sounded vaguely familiar and filled her with an urgency she didn't understand. Finally forcing her eyes open, she took in the shadowed room and the familiar sight of hospital equipment.

What the…?

Confused, she lifted a hand to her face and gasped when the move sent sharp pain radiating through her body. Almost instantly a large hand engulfed hers in warm comfort.

"I'm here," a deep comforting voice murmured from the shadows. "Try not to move."

"Where—?"

"You're safe," he said. "Just rest."

Lilah instantly quieted, the firm touch filling her with a strange lassitude and a welcome sense of security.

The voice sounded too emotional to be Luke, she thought woozily, and rasped, "Water," into the silence.

A straw lightly touched her lips and she latched onto it, drinking greedily before the effort exhausted her. She felt her eyelids flutter closed and the hand was back, soothing and gentle as she slid towards sleep.

"Luke."

"I'm here," he crooned. "Everything's going to be just fine." And just before darkness claimed her she thought she heard him say, "I love you, Wild Woman. I'm here. I'll be here when you wake. I promise," and wondered who he was talking to.

The next time Lilah drifted awake it was quiet. The kind of quiet that told her she was alone. Sunlight streamed through the windows and lit up the small room, making it bright and somehow optimistic.

For a few minutes she floated on a cloud of lassitude enjoying the rare opportunity to sleep in. Between one breath and the next memory returned and the warm glow she'd woken with popped.

Her eyes flew open and a quick look around the empty room confirmed her suspicions. She'd survived a chopper crash and was alone in a hospital room. Clearly whatever she'd thought had happened after that had been a dream.

A nice dream…but a dream nonetheless, because in her dream he'd promised to be here. And he wasn't. But, then, she wasn't really surprised since he was probably long go—

"Hey. What's with the gloomy face?"

A storm of conflicting emotions assailed Lilah at the sound of that deep, rough voice. Disbelief, joy, anger, betrayal…and an overwhelming sense of relief. Turning, she caught sight of him in the doorway looking tired and rumpled and just…*wonderful*. Her breath caught at the familiar sight of his amazing green eyes, burning with an expression that made hers fill with tears.

"What's wrong?" he demanded urgently, when she stared silently up at him through swimming eyes. "Are you in pain?"

Lilah bit her lip and shook her head. She wanted to be mad at him but couldn't drum up the energy. Maybe because he looked exhausted and worried…and deliciously rumpled. Maybe because all that emotion was aimed at her.

"You look terrible."

A smile tugged at one corner of his tight mouth and amusement briefly lit his shadowed eyes. "And you look like you got between a chopper and a mountain," he replied, placing his fingers gently against her inner wrist to check her pulse. She didn't know why he bothered as she was hooked up to the machine which was still beeping annoyingly.

"I dreamed a huge eagle rescued me and flew me up into the mountains."

That almost-smile flashed as his eyes studied her intently. "You did, huh?"

"I thought…I thought maybe I was dreaming. I remember the rotors spraying up rocks and branches." She gulped. "I had my eyes squeezed shut, praying really hard, and the next thing—"

"Don't think about it," Luke urged gently, and leaned closer to peer into her eyes. Apparently satisfied by whatever he saw there, he straightened, sliding his hand down to link his fingers with hers and giving them a gentle squeeze.

Lilah gulped at the tender gesture and wondered if she was high on morphine or if he'd lost his mind.

She slid her free hand down to her belly. "The baby—?"

"Is fine," he said, his voice hoarse with an emotion she couldn't quite identify. He swallowed visibly. "You're both fine. Or you will be."

"Promise?"

"You injured your side, but the baby is absolutely okay."

Oh, thank God, she thought with relief, but said instead, "I heard you calling me. It was annoying and woke me up."

His eyes twinkled. "Annoying, huh?"

"I guess it saved me," she admitted grudgingly, and he lifted her hand to his lips, his eyes shimmering over the top of her knuckles as though he was struggling to hold onto his control.

"Why didn't you tell me?" he demanded gently, giving her a little nip and sending delight winging through the pain. "About the baby, I mean."

Lilah's heart clenched and she averted her eyes, tugging her hand free. He might know about the baby but that didn't mean he wanted to be part of their life.

Her own father hadn't.

"I...couldn't," she whispered through a throat tight with tears. "Not when you were so...adamant." She shook her head. "I don't want my child to feel like a mistake."

His eyes flared before he caught at her hand and engulfed it in heat. "Never," she barely heard him say. "Never a mistake, Lilah. How could it be?"

Shock made her speechless. "Wh-at?" she croaked. Okay, almost speechless, but, *damn*...she was getting more confused by the second. Maybe the head injury was more serious than she'd thought.

A dull red rose up his throat and he looked a little abashed. "Not when this baby has someone like you for a mother. They're going to be the luckiest kid alive."

Lilah stared at him for several beats. "What...what about his father?"

"His? What if it's a girl? Because I want a little girl with long sunset-colored curls and big grey eyes."

"What about her father, then?" she whispered, her eyes solemn. "Will he be the luckiest man?"

"Maybe...maybe she doesn't want someone like me to be her father," he admitted quietly, his eyes locked on their hands, as though he couldn't bear for her to see the emotions he was struggling with. "Besides, I broke more than a few traffic laws and stole a chopper so I might get arrested. No little girl deserves a jailbird as a father."

"What?"

He looked up and sent her a crooked smile. "I went a little crazy when I heard you went out on the flight call. *Dammit*, I fixed it so you wouldn't have to go again. Why did you?

Lilah stared at him open-mouthed. "I, uh…"

"And then we heard you crashed and I kind of lost it—*Jeez*." He took a deep breath and his fingers tightened on hers.

"Lost it? Crazy?"

He dropped his forehead onto their joined hands and gave a rough snort before lifting his head to grin. "Everyone is calling me Looney Luke."

"Are you? Crazy, I mean."

"Yep," he said, sending her a stern glance. "And it's your fault."

"Me?" Lilah she was having trouble following the conversation, especially as she was trying to interpret the expression in his eyes at the same time. It made her belly clench, her chest tighten and her head a little dizzy, like she'd swallowed too much helium. But it could also be from concussion. "You're not making any sense."

His mouth twisted into a crooked grin. "I threatened your best friend and punched out your boss."

"Who—Angie?"

"I couldn't find you," he accused. "And you weren't answering your cell. So I acted like a crazy person. It's a miracle they didn't call the cops. Or send Security over to lock me in the psych ward."

A smile bloomed over Lilah's face. "You punched out Webster?"

"It would have been more satisfying if he hadn't gone down like a wimp."

"My hero."

His amusement faded. "No," he said, his expression somber. "I'm no hero, Lilah. I'm just a man." He shook his head and gave a broken laugh. "A man who loves you more than he thought possible. A man who almost lost the best thing that could ever happen to him." He drew in a sharp breath, as though trying to control his emotions. "But I've got you now," he told her fiercely. "Both of you. And I'm going to spend the rest of my life holding on."

"The rest…?"

"But you have to promise never to scare me like that again. In fact, I insist on it."

"You…do?"

"Yep, but I somehow don't think it's going to be a problem."

Lilah frowned at the laughter lighting his green eyes and wondered what he was up to.

"How can you know that?" she demanded, shivering at the way his lips brushed across the top of her knuckles.

"You do realize that you've crashed in two helicopters in the last two months, don't you? Well," he said without waiting for a reply, "no one's willing to bet on those odds and they're signing a petition to have you removed from the roster. They say you're jinxed."

Lilah's eyes widened. "Wha-at?"

Luke snorted. "In fact, since we've both survived two crashes we're both jinxed."

"Jinxed? But that's ridiculous. Do people really believe in that stuff?"

"And since we're jinxed they're saying we deserve each other." His gaze lost its twinkle and turned serious. "That we clearly belong together," he concluded softly, and Lilah sucked in a sharp breath at his fierce expression.

"Together?"

"Uh-huh. They're calling us Looney Luke and Wild

Woman." He chuckled and shook his head. "Like we're some kind of disaster duo comic-book heroes."

"And you, Luke? What do you think?"

His smile became tender and fierce emotion shimmered in his eyes. "Well, I definitely don't deserve you but I think our baby is going to be the luckiest kid alive."

"Because we're the disaster duo?"

"No," he murmured, leaning down to cover her mouth with his. "Because." *Kiss.* "Her mother." *Another kiss.* "Loves her father." *Yet another kiss.* "And her father…" Another kiss, this one lingering for long breathless beats until he broke off to suck in a ragged breath. He stared into her eyes as he struggled with words and some fierce emotions.

"And her father…?" Lilah prompted, just as breathlessly.

"And her father can't live without her mother."

Lilah's breath hitched. "What are you saying, Luke?"

Staring into her eyes, he said quietly, clearly, "I'm saying I love you."

Lilah gasped. That she was shocked by his confession was an understatement and all she could say was, "But you…you don't want a relationship. Or a family."

He grimaced and looked down to where his thumb was caressing the back of her hand. "I know I said that, but I do. As long as it's with you. No, *only* if it's with you."

"What…?" Lilah searched his expression. "What about your plans to leave Washington?"

"Plans change."

"Is this about the baby, Luke?" she asked quietly, tugging at her hand, which he refused to relinquish. "Because if it is—"

"It isn't," he interrupted. "At least, not entirely." He sighed and shoved a hand through his hair. "I love you, Lilah, and when I thought I might never get to see you again or tell you how I feel, I completely lost it. I want—no, I *need*—to be with you."

Lilah gulped and in a small voice said, "Oh."

"Oh?" Luke rose from the chair he'd pulled close to the bed and folded his arms across his wide chest to stare down at her. He was clearly a little steamed. "Is that all you can say? I spill my guts and all you say is 'Oh'?"

"I...I..." Lilah paused and gulped as the words trembled on her lips. Her breath escaped in a whoosh as she prepared to take the plunge. "I...love you too?"

For several beats he stared at her as though she'd admitted to stealing the crown jewels and then his eyes softened to something so warm and tender that tears blurred her vision.

"Finally," he murmured, and sank back into the chair. "I thought I might have to give up my left nut before I got to hear you say those words."

Lilah rolled her eyes. "Your...nuts are safe...for now," she told him with a watery smile. "As long as I get to keep the crazy guy they're attached to."

Luke grinned and turned his head to press a gentle kiss into her palm. "I'm yours, wild thing. Forever. Now it's your turn."

"My turn?" she teased, and when he nipped the fleshy part of her thumb she said on a delicious shiver, "I love you, Luke, as long as you're sure it's me you want and not just the baby."

"I want you," he growled impatiently, and protectively covered the hand placed over her belly. "You." He leaned forward to kiss her. "Although I'm happy about Wild Child Sullivan. Now...could you, Lilah Paige Meredith, marry someone like me? Could you love me forever and—?"

"Yes," she interrupted, her smile serene in the face of his obvious love and acceptance of their little miracle.

His beautifully sculpted mouth curled into a tender smirk. "Yes, what, wild thing?"

Tears filled Lilah's eyes. "Yes," she murmured, lifting her hand to cup his beard-roughened jaw, enjoying the rasp against her fingers. "We'll marry you, Looney Luke Sullivan. And we'll love you forever."

And with a fervently murmured "Thank you, God," the bad-boy army ranger bent and sealed their vow with a kiss.

* * * * *

MILLS & BOON®

MEDICAL ROMANCE™

THE ULTIMATE IN ROMANTIC MEDICAL DRAMA

A sneak peek at next month's titles...

In stores from 6th February 2015:

- **A Date with Her Valentine Doc** – Melanie Milburne
  and **It Happened in Paris...** – Robin Gianna

- **The Sheikh Doctor's Bride** – Meredith Webber
  and **Temptation in Paradise** – Joanna Neil

- **A Baby to Heal Their Hearts** – Kate Hardy
- **The Surgeon's Baby Secret** – Amber McKenzie

Available at WHSmith, Tesco, Asda, Eason, Amazon and Apple

Just can't wait?
Buy our books online a month before they hit the shops!
visit www.millsandboon.co.uk

These books are also available in eBook format!

0115/03